CW00429651

Cor Rotto
A Novel of Catherine Carey

by
Adrienne Dillard

Cor Rotto:
A Novel of
Catherine Carey

ISBN-13: 978-84-937464-7-6

M
MadeGlobal Publishing

For more information on
MadeGlobal Publishing, visit our website:
www.madeglobal.com

A Portrait of a Woman, Probably Catherine Carey, Lady Knollys
Steven van der Meulen, 1562
Photo © Yale Center for British Art

Original cover design by Ronda Lehman,
Lucky Dog Design.
Cover adapted by MadeGlobal Publishing

Part I

A Lady of the Court

English territory in France, Calais:
August - November 1539

The dream was always the same. My feet were filthy. To most children my age this would be expected, something they dealt with every day of their lives as they toiled alongside their parents in the fields, usually too poor to afford proper footwear. But to me it spelled disaster. I knew that soon my grandfather would be home and would be very displeased. Instead of swinging me in the air, plying me with affection as he usually did when he returned from Court, he would stare at my dirt-caked toes and say disdainfully, "You are a Boleyn and you should know your place. No Boleyn will ever live like a beggar child. I have worked hard my whole life to make sure of it." With those scornful words, my heart would be cut in two. I knew I had to find my brother Henry, get back to the house and clean up before our grandfather arrived.

Henry had always been excellent at hiding and I felt as though I had been searching for hours. Quietly I tiptoed through the orchard, making as little sound as possible in the hopes that he would give himself away. Finally I heard a shuffle off to my right. I moved slowly towards the noise and prepared my ambush. I burst through the apple trees into a clearing and saw the scaffold before me. "No!" I shrieked, feet rooted to the ground. I stared on in horror as the sword sliced the head from my aunt's swan-like neck. The executioner raised her severed head into the air by its long chestnut locks. Anne's eyes were wide in shock, her lips still moving, the blood formed a river in the dirt. The last thing I remembered before my world turned black was my own scream.

I smelled my mother before I saw her: lavender and the musk of a restless sleep. Since Anne's death, peace had eluded her and she had begun to surround herself with the calming scent in the vain hope that one night could be nightmare-free. She threw her arms around me and ran her fingers through my hair. She did not even need to ask, the dreams had been coming since I was twelve years old. Three years had passed and each one was as vivid and as dreadful as the last. After planting a kiss on my forehead, she opened the window above my head so that the crash of the sea against the rocks would lull me back to sleep. My last thought before slipping back into that fearful dream-world was of gratitude for the move to Calais.

The bright morning sun streamed in through my window. I burrowed deeper under the covers to escape it. I knew that Matilda, our maid, would soon be in to lay out my clothing and I would join my small family downstairs for breakfast. As if she sensed that I was thinking of her, Matilda appeared in my doorway. "Mistress Catherine, you are going to catch your death sleeping with that window open," she admonished, marching towards the window Mother had opened in the night. I sent a grunt her way from beneath my blanket cocoon.

Suddenly, my world grew bright again as Matilda released the covers from my grasp and threw the counterpane off me. "Matilda," I groaned.

I was out of bed within minutes, standing naked in the middle of the room with my linen night shift crumpled on the floor, the cool air that had settled overnight pricked goose-pimples all over my skin. I prayed that Matilda would choose my clothing quickly so I could be out of my discomfort. The Lord must have been listening to me because moments later Matilda bustled out of my closet, dress in hand. I shot her a confused look, suspicious as to why she had pulled out one of my more formal dresses. Without meeting my eye she said, "Lord Lisle is here. He has news for Master Stafford. I expect he will be joining you while you take your meal."

I softened at her thoughtfulness. I smiled and reached out to brush a strand of hair from her eyes. "Thank you sweet Matilda. You always make sure I look my best."

Lord Lisle was our window to the world back in England. As a cousin to the king, he was well-known by the nobles throughout the realm. He had his eyes and ears on everything that went on at Court thanks to his servant, Master Hussee, who reported back, often, in writing. He took a keen interest in my stepfather, William Stafford.

Stafford initially came to Calais with little more than love for his country, bright hope in his eyes and a drive to work, so Lord Lisle took him under his wing and made him a spearman. Not even his secret marriage to my mother or our resulting exile from Court could turn Lisle away from him. He opened his arms when Stafford returned from London, disgraced, with us in tow. That was a dark time for my mother.

Stafford had never cared for Court. It was a fateful turn of events that he and my mother had even met considering that she was serving her sister, the queen, in London while he was serving across the Channel at the Calais garrison. A trip to France for King Henry and his soon-to-be queen led my mother to Calais and, somehow, she unwittingly found herself in his arms. After the tour she went back to England and, less than a year later, realised that her love was still strong when she spied him across the banqueting hall during Anne's coronation. Soon, my baby sister was growing in her belly and she and Stafford were banished from Court by order of the queen, who was furious that her sister would marry below her station. The child that their love created had not made it more than mere months after its birth, but that only strengthened their bond and it was not long before the cliffs of Dover were far behind us.

Once I was dressed, I grabbed my leather-bound lesson-book and scrambled for the stairs. When I reached the top of the staircase,

I heard murmurs coming from the hall. Whatever Lord Lisle and Stafford were discussing, they did not want an audience. However, their whispers only served to make me more curious. Quiet as a mouse, I slipped down the stairs slowly. By delicately placing one foot in front of the other I managed to carefully avoid the spots that I knew would creak.

"The king wants me, of all people, to attend on the Lady of Cleves?" Stafford snorted in derision. "Well, I guess now that Anne is out of the picture and the woman who so eagerly displaced her is in her grave, the Boleyn connections can finally return to Court."

Piqued by this new information, I leaned further over the railing so that I could see the look of surprise that surely graced my stepfather's face.

"Now William, if your loyalty had truly been in question do you think that the king would have allowed you back at the garrison? He knows where your heart truly lies. And he has always had a soft spot for Mary. Your banishment was more Anne's work than his," Lisle said in a soothing voice.

I heard Stafford's sarcastic reply, "Soft spot for Mary... Every morning I am reminded of that soft spot when my red-headed step-daughter comes to the breakfast table. Thankfully she was born with her mother's sweet disposition and I have come to love her as my own, but it still pains me to be reminded of my wife's time in the king's bedchamber."

Startled by this revelation, I allowed the book I had been carrying to slip from my hands. It tumbled over the railing and fell to the floor below with a dull thud. I struggled to grasp the meaning of his words.

"Catherine?"

I looked down the stairs and into the warm brown eyes of Stafford. I was caught. Instead of looking angry, Stafford appeared concerned. I was certain that he knew I had heard and he was worried about how I would react. I took a deep breath and smiled confidently saying, "Good morning, Stafford. I am so sorry to have disturbed you. Matilda informed me that we have a guest and in my haste I dropped my book." Stafford eyed me quizzically, but accepted my response for the moment and offered his hand to help me the rest of the way down the stairs.

At the bottom he retrieved the book and placed it gingerly in my hands. My eye caught Lord Lisle's and, though he smiled as if he had not noticed the commotion, I noticed a twitch in the corner of his eye and secretly relished his discomfort. "Lord Lisle, so good to see you again," I said as I swept to the floor in a deep curtsey. I showed him far more reverence than was required, but I wanted to put him at ease. I knew the comments were unintended for my ears and I sensed that both of them wished they had been discussing something else.

"Mistress Catherine, always a pleasure. You look more beautiful every time I see you. Please join us," he said gesturing to an empty chair.

Stafford led me over and, moments later, my mother bustled in with trays of food, saving us all from a very awkward conversation. Lord Lisle gave us his commentary on all the events happening across the channel. It seemed that the king had decided to take another wife.

The king's most recent wife, Jane Seymour, had given him the son and heir he craved, but after a tumultuous birth she took ill with a fever and did not live past the first month of her son's life. The king was so stunned by her death that for the first time in his life, after three marriages, he mourned the loss of a wife. The court fell into a period of darkness. In the last few months, however, King Henry recovered from his heartbreak and succumbed to the prodding of his chancellor, Lord Cromwell, to take on another bride - but she was not just any bride.

"She is a Lutheran!" sputtered Lisle. "The king has tired of his battles with the Spanish and French kings and has decided instead to align himself with the Protestant rebels of the Low Countries. He is to marry the sister of the Duke of Cleves."

As Lisle continued to rant about the king's intended, I stared down at my plate, pretending to be interested in a bit of bread. In reality, I was sneaking glances in my mother's direction. Starting at the top of her head I began an inventory of her features. She had strands of grey in her golden brown hair, not a hint of red to be seen. Her skin was a swarthy olive colour, not the pale blush of mine. Her face had a clear complexion, but mine was mass of freckles. I searched my memory for just a small picture of William Carey. Did I share his thin-lipped smile? Was his nose as prominent as mine? Did he hear a song and feel the melody pierce his heart like an arrow, driving in the beauty of the music? Whose blood was coursing through my body? I resolved to corner my mother before the day was over. I needed to know the truth.

After Lisle had gone, I helped my mother clear the table and complete our daily chores. I knew it pained her that she had been reduced to washing her own clothes and scrubbing her own floors, even though she would never admit it. Her father was an earl, her uncle a duke. She had grown accustomed to having a suite of rooms at Court with maids for her every need. Being the queen's sister had had its advantages and my mother had received all the benefits. Well - she did until my father died. The man who, up until hours ago, I had thought was my father. William Carey caught the dreaded sweating sickness and left my mother alone with two children and no money to her name. Her sister, Anne, stepped in immediately and sent Henry off to be educated, but I was left in my mother's care and we learned to lean on each other. After frantic letters to Lord Cromwell, my grandfather's hand was forced to help. I was sent to Hever and she was sent to Court to wait on Anne.

Hever was a lonely place for me. Most of my family was at Court and I was left with a castle full of servants. I had a tutor who made sure I learned my lessons, but mostly I was on my own. It has occurred to me that the reason why I can never find Henry in my dream hide-and-seek game is because he was never with me. Instead, I always found Anne and her bloody head. Why do I always dream of it? I was not even in England when it happened. When Anne was executed, my mother and I were safely across the Channel at Calais.

I had always looked up to Anne. She was beautiful. Chestnut hair, dark flashing eyes, it was obvious that many of the men at Court desired her. Once I had been allowed to visit my mother at Court and found myself in her presence. She paid special attention to me, giving me a small brooch and allowing me to pet her tiny dog, Purkoy. The excitement made me feel as though I were flying, being carried along on her laugh as the wind. I hated the king for her death. I did not like the idea that he could be my father. I thought him a monster. Could his blood be flowing through my veins, making me a monster by inheritance? As the day grew darker, so did my mood.

By evening, I was pacing my room. I started at my bed and worked my way around, ending in front of the window next to it, staring out at the sea. I knew I needed answers, but I needed to ask the questions when my mother was alone and feeling charitable. She did not like to talk about the past because it was far too painful. I shored up my courage and headed for the door.

I padded quietly down the hallway hoping that the element of surprise would lower her guard, but I lost my nerve when I reached her bedchamber. I peered in her doorway. She was sitting in a chair with her back to me. A fire was dancing before her, casting shadows around the room. She was sitting so still and quiet, I thought she was asleep. I exhaled in frustration and decided to ask later. It was so rare to see her so completely relaxed that I could not bring myself to intrude.

"Catherine, is that you?" she called out, looking over her shoulder into the darkness.

"Yes, it is me," I said, skulking into the room. She jumped out of her seat and reached for me. "Please Catherine, sit," she said and gestured to her now empty chair.

I sat down and allowed her to brush the hair from my face. She planted a kiss on my forehead and then dragged a stool across the floor and sat down in front of me. The movement caused the rushes to shift and I was enveloped in the scent of fresh rosemary and juniper, and it comforted me. She reached for my hands and said, "I know what you heard today."

I was stunned for a moment. I had thought I would have to prod, but it seemed she was ready to talk. I swallowed hard and nodded.

Her bright blue eyes looked into mine and she began, "Many years ago when I was first married to William and brought to Court, the king saw me during a masque and decided that he wanted me for his own. He made a deal with my husband and my father and I became his mistress, and even though William benefited from this arrangement, I knew that my relationship with the king hurt him. I tried desperately to avoid falling in love with the king, but he showered me with affection and doted on me as though there were no other women in the world. He was intelligent and kind and I surrendered myself wholly to his charm.

"Eventually, I realised I was with child, but instead of casting me off like I expected, he became more protective. I think he was hoping I would have a boy. When you were born a girl, it was easy for him to believe that you were William's child. I believed it too, because it made me feel less shameful." She paused for a moment to brush a tear from her eye. "But as you grew, you began to look more and more like the king. He could not bear to lose Anne, so he continued to deny your paternity. And I think he was unsure, himself, and refused to brand William a cuckold in his death. So the king helped in ways he could that did not seem suspicious. He and Lord Cromwell made sure that my father took care of us and he welcomed me back to Court, until I defied them all by marrying Stafford, and now he offers you a much sought-after place to serve his new queen."

I was crestfallen at this new revelation. I could not stomach the idea of leaving Calais. It had become my home. I began to protest, but my mother raised a hand to silence me. "It is your duty to serve the new queen. Henry, as your father and your king, commands it. You will not be alone. Stafford and I will be coming back to

England in her train. That is why Lord Lisle was here. He was giving Stafford instructions. Whether we stay in England will depend on how the voyage fares, but if Stafford serves as well as he always has, he may find a position at Court and we will be near."

I covered my face with my hands and mumbled, "Is this some kind of punishment?"

"Catherine!" my mother scolded. "This is your father's way of assuring your well-being. Calais is no place for a young lady, especially one with royal blood. You have also reached an age where it is time to begin negotiations for a husband. We have little to offer a suitable groom, but your place in the queen's rooms will get you far and it is possible the king already has a gentleman in mind. You will look upon this as an opportunity and not as a punishment."

I took a deep breath, nodded and offered my mother a weak smile. She rubbed the back of my shoulder in an effort to soothe and reassure me, but I could tell she was nervous as well. I bade her good night with a kiss on the cheek, and slunk off to my room. I put on my shift and crawled into bed for another fitful night of sleep.

November seemed ever-looming and I was dreading the sea voyage back to England. The trip to Calais had been torture for me. I loved the sea but my stomach could not handle the pitch and turn of the ship. I had spent most of the journey hanging over the railing so I was not looking forward to this return trip and I did everything I could to keep my mind off it.

The house had been in a bustle for weeks, planning for the journey. I was to go over early and meet Lord Lisle's step-daughter, Anne Bassett, in London to help prepare the household for its new queen. The ladies of the garrison had been helping each other prepare for the arrival of Anne of Cleves and for the departure of the families that would be returning to England. We had Lady Honor Lisle over to assist my mother in choosing my wardrobe.

Passing through the hallway, I overheard her bitterly

complaining to my mother about the king's refusal to let her daughter, Katherine, attend upon the queen. "You would think that being married to the king's cousin would assure all of my daughters a place at Court! Why only one? I am going to wear him down, even if I have to bribe him," she laughed ruefully.

"Oh Honor," my mother replied gently. "Be thankful Anne is serving. There are always pretty young ladies being sent the king's way. Each nobleman hoping that his girl will be the next mistress or wife, getting him ever closer to the king's ear. It is the way it has always been and it is the way it will always be. I am sure you remember your time at Court."

Lady Lisle sniggered. "Spoken from the lips of one of those same ladies." Then she added quietly, "You did well though, Mary. Stafford is a wonderful man and your son and daughter have been well-provided for. Things could have turned out far worse."

I could not see my mother's face, but I could feel her pain. I only knew my little sister Anne for a short time before God called her back again and my heart was broken. I could not begin to fathom the hurt I would feel if we had been allowed to build a relationship before she was taken away. To share hurts and dreams, whispered in the dark while the rest of the house was asleep. To share dolls and clothes and compete for a young man's affections. To feel the wonder that Aunt Anne must have felt when she rested her hand on Mother's belly and I kicked her from inside. To share the parts of life that only sisters can, and then have it violently torn from my grasp. I turned on my heel, and ran to my room before the tears began to fall. I could not risk adding to my mother's pain.

Later that afternoon I was lying on my bed, limbs spread out, soaking up the warm sunlight coming through the open window. Just as I began to sink into a peaceful slumber, my door banged open.

"Mistress Catherine," Matilda sang through the doorway. "Your mother would like to see you."

I sat up and breathed in the salt air, shaking the cobwebs out of my brain. I jumped out of bed wondering what new task lay ahead of me and headed to my mother's room.

Mother was sitting on her bed, a trunk at the foot open wide. Lady Lisle was gone and the room was quiet. I looked at Mother and raised an eyebrow. She had a beatific look in her eyes and, for the first time in years, a truly vibrant smile. I had no hint what was coming, but I could feel a tingle run down my spine to see her in such utter happiness. She leapt from the bed and very excitedly said, "Look!" I turned my eyes to the direction her hands were pointing and finally saw what was in the trunk. It was a riot of colour and texture. Crimson velvet, emerald satin and cloth of silver all vied for my attention. As I knelt down to get a closer look, arm stretched into the pile of fabric, I stopped.

"What is all this?" I asked her, reproachfully.

Mother knelt down next to me, taking my hands in hers, and answered, "These are my Court dresses. They are now yours."

"But -" I started. "I thought you left those..." Suddenly, it dawned on me that the whole time we were destitute for money she had been hiding our most valuable assets. I laughed at the irony of it.

"You mean you had these all along?" I asked her incredulously.

"Catherine, I knew you were the king's daughter from the moment of your birth. I knew eventually you would be called to Court. I could never send you in rags and I did not know if that was what we would be wearing when the time came. So I did what I had to do to keep these with me. Stafford knew all along and he agreed with me, so we made do without selling them. And quite a fine life we made, didn't we?" she said a little smugly, colour creeping into her cheeks.

I was amazed at this new giddiness. She seemed almost excited. I gave her a wide grin then whispered, "Let's try them."

Mother had been much older than I when she was at Court, but I was built like my father, tall and sturdy, so they fit me like a glove. I tried them all and relished the feel of the fine fabrics on my skin. Each dress was a new experience for me. It was as though all that my mother had seen and felt when she wore them was soaking though my skin and into my heart. It was when I peered into the mirror and saw my mother staring back at me that I suddenly realised my body was becoming more like a woman and less like a girl. The gowns were all cut low and I flushed at the thought of showing so much skin. I just hoped they were not too far out of style, but even if they were, I realised that I did not care.

Mother stood behind me and nodded her approval. "Perfect," she whispered.

By the time we reached the last gown, Stafford was home and it was time for supper. I heard his footsteps and knew he was coming our way. We looked up in time to see him stop in the doorway. He beamed us a smile and said, "Lovely."

My heart sang with joy.

A month later it was time to board the ship. The frigid salt air burned my eyes, pricking tears that ran down my cheeks. At least that was my excuse when my mother looked at me sternly, warning me not to lose myself in emotion. It was hard enough on her to send off her child, she did not need me causing a commotion, she had confessed to me the night before as she was combing my hair. I rubbed my eyes fiercely and then smoothed my hair back under my hood. When I turned back to the quayside, I was composed and ready to board.

"Hello Catherine!" called an enthusiastic voice.

I turned and saw Eleanor Wells walking towards me. Her cheeks were rosy, and her eyes bright from the biting cold, but she was smiling and waving madly in my direction. She was the daughter of a man in Lisle's retinue. He was not of the peerage, but a member of the gentry. In the past we had little interaction, but I had seen her often at social gatherings and she was always friendly and outgoing. She had an easy charm that appealed to the young men in the garrison and they were often following her around, hanging on her every word. I wondered for a moment why she was at the dock and then I realised she must be sailing back to England as well.

"Eleanor," I said. "Good to see you again. Are you going to be boarding with me?"

She smiled brightly. "I am! My father is sending me to family in London. He hopes that once the queen arrives I will be taken into service. Not as a maid-of-honour of course, those are full," she said rather wistfully. "But I am sure one of the great ladies of the court will be happy to have my assistance."

I removed my hand from my muff and squeezed her icy fingers, giving her a smile. "They would be ever so lucky to have you in their service," I reassured her. Deep down I felt it should be Eleanor in my place. She was everything a maid-of-honour was supposed to be: bonny and charming, flaxen hair, delicate as a rose. I was none of those things. I preferred embroidery and reading to dancing and no one would ever describe me as delicate.

"Ladies, it is time for us to bid you farewell," came my mother's voice, startling me out of my thoughts.

She gave me a hug, holding me for a while in her embrace. I concentrated on her scent, hoping to lodge it in my mind for later recollection when I was feeling lonely or insecure, but all too soon she was sending us on our way. We crossed the rickety gangplank and made our way across the deck of the ship. A young man was waiting to take us down into the hold. His dark hair was matted from the wind and rain, half his face hidden under a beard, but his green eyes sparkled and caught my attention.

"Down here please, ladies," he directed us to our room and took his leave.

I awoke in the darkness, my belly boiling. I did not know if it was morning or night, but I knew I was about to be sick. I crawled out of my bunk and made my way to the deck, gripping my stomach and desperately trying to keep my balance. The ship was pitching in the wind and rain making it impossible for me to walk. The rain soaked my dress and I tripped over my hem, slipping on the deck. I reached the railing in time to vomit my supper into the dark abyss. Just as I straightened, the ship rolled, knocking me to the floor. The last thing I felt before the darkness came was a searing pain in my forehead and my hood being ripped out of my hair.

Someone was calling my name, but I could not make out the voice. My first thought was that I had fallen into the sea, so I kicked for the surface. But instead of the bitter cold water, I kicked hard wood. Startled, I opened my eyes and found myself looking into a pair of green ones that I almost recognised. Then I saw the wind-tangled beard and realised that my rescuer was the young man who had directed us to our cabin.

"My lady, are you all right?" he asked, concerned. He brushed the hair from my face with one hand and cradled my back in the other to keep me off the wet deck. "I saw you come out of your cabin, but I was unsure of what you were doing, so I kept close in case you were in trouble." Then he grinned. "I am glad you leaned over the railing, I would not want to have to clean that mess up."

I groaned. My head was pounding and my throat burned with thirst. I drew my hand across my mouth, wiping away the vomit. "Do you have anything to drink?" I asked him, forgetting my manners.

He broke into a laugh, "Aye my lady, I'm sure I can find you some."

In one swift move he got me to my feet and seated me on a bench. He paused to stare at me for a moment, no doubt taking in my rain-soaked dress and stringy hair, and shook his head. "I shall return," he said with a chuckle.

He came back with a pewter tankard of ale and handed it to me, patiently waiting while I drained it. I wiped my lips again with the back of my hand and a hiccup escaped from my mouth. Both hands flew to my face, mortified. After a moment, I composed myself. "Thank you very much, sir. I think you probably saved my life. Can I ask your name?"

"Richard," was his response.

"Well, Master Richard," I said. "Thank you for your assistance and your courtesy. Please excuse my unbecoming behaviour this evening."

With a broad grin he replied, "It was my pleasure Mistress Carey. We shall be at Dover in just a few hours, so we can only hope they will be uneventful from now on."

My face reddened, but I allowed a small giggle to escape. "I hope so as well."

The skies cleared and the sun began its ascent. Richard wrapped me in a blanket and we rode out the rest of the journey on the bench. He told me of his childhood in York and his love of horses. He hoped to find a place in the king's stables when we arrived in London. I told him of my place in the queen's rooms and of the anxiety I was feeling, but I left out my relationship to the king. As far as Richard knew, I was only the step-daughter of Master Stafford. Soon I began to feel a warmth in my heart that I could not place. I did not know this man before tonight, but I was beginning to feel a connection with him. I knew that I would pray for his success. I truly hoped he would make it to the king's stables. I knew I wanted to see him again.

London, Whitehall:
November – December 1539

We arrived at Whitehall to a raucous celebration. Lively music spilled out of the great hall and most of the windows in the palace were ablaze in torch-light. I eased my way out of the carriage, stiff from the biting cold, and found my footing. A group of pages rushed over to haul the baggage and trunks out of the cart. Carefully, I picked my way through the mud and headed for the warmth of the palace. I had never been to Whitehall so was unsure of my surroundings, but I hoped there would be someone there to guide me to the maids' dormitory. The hall was busy enough, servants hurried by with their arms full, but no one was there to greet me. I stopped for a moment amid the bustle and listened to the music. If I could follow it to the great hall, surely someone could tell me where to go.

I walked down the winding corridors, listening intently. As the music got louder, I knew I was closer to the celebration. I turned the corner and saw an enormous set of doors. They were slightly ajar, so I inched closer to get a peek. The hall was packed, but a space had been cleared to allow for dancing. I had heard that the king loved to watch his courtiers dance. His dancing days were coming to an end, but it did not stop him from vicariously living through the young men and women who graced his Court.

At the centre of attention was a couple dancing the volte. The man was lean and muscular, lifting his lithe companion with ease. Vivacious and lively, she threw her head back in excitement, her golden hair cascading down her back. From a distance it was difficult to tell their age, but the young lady appeared to be near my own. I assumed that she too was to be a maid to the queen. I mentally reminded myself to investigate further.

I took in the rest of the scene. The king was sitting under a cloth of estate in all his finery. A purple velvet doublet trimmed in ermine graced his hefty body. The brilliant jewels on each finger caught the candlelight and glittered. He wore a full beard, still gloriously red. He had aged since I last saw him, but I witnessed not a trace of grey hair. He topped off his look with a wide-brimmed hat trimmed with a jaunty white feather. Unseen, I could take him all in and I stared unabashedly. If only I could read his mind. I watched his eyes follow the young lady in the dance, he smiled at her each time she turned his way. He may have a bride on the way, but he was a lusty king after all, and it would not be long before she was a favourite, if she was not already.

A hand on my shoulder caused me to jump, my heart thudding against my chest. I spun around to see a face I knew well and was very displeased. My late uncle's wife, Jane Rochford, was staring back at me. I expected her to sneer at me, but I received rosy cheeks and the curve of her upturned lips instead.

"Mistress Catherine! I am so happy to have found you. My deepest apologies, I was to meet you at the door but was detained by a chamber-maid. I am relieved that you arrived safely," she said breathlessly.

She appeared genuinely thrilled to see me. My feelings for her were of another sort. I had actually dreaded seeing her. During George and Anne's trials, it was rumoured that Jane had given evidence against them. At least that was what was whispered in the hushed halls at Hever. I overheard two of our servants talking about the shame she had brought on our family. My heart sank when I realised she was to be a guide for me. How would I ever contain my disgust?

Jane left me little time to react. Immediately she was leading me to the maid's dormitory to see that I was settled in and out of my rain-soaked garments. She waited patiently on my bed while the chamber-maid helped me into a dry muslin shift and prepared me for bed. After my long journey I was exhausted, and while it was exciting to see the party in the hall, I was in no condition to join it. The chamber maid scurried off, my wet clothes in hand, leaving Jane and I to stare awkwardly at each other. I waited patiently for her to break the silence.

Jane stood. Clearing her throat she said, "I know what you must think of me and I cannot say that I blame you. Since I found out that you would be coming to Court, I have been going over round and round in my head what I would say to you. It seems only fair that I tell you the truth. We will be together much of our time now and I want you to know what is real and what is false and why I did what I did. Please say that you will give me that chance."

She looked at me with such hopeful eyes that though my stomach was pitching inside, I knew that the only response was my assent, so I nodded.

She began to pace the room, her footsteps kicking up the scent of sage in the newly laid rushes. "It is true that I gave evidence against George and Anne, but it is not what it appears to be." She came to a stop and turned to look me in the eye.

"Cromwell had me in a corner and I was terrified of what he might do. I had to ensure my survival. But I never said that Anne and George had a carnal relationship. I never even alluded to the idea, I swear this to you. I could never come up with that abominable scene, that was all Cromwell and the king's doing. I only repeated that Anne said that the king had not the ability at all times to bed her as his wife and nothing more." She said earnestly. Her face was flushed and her eyes shone with unshed tears.

I was not swayed by her pleading. "You were concerned with your own survival, but not your husband's? Did you not realise that his survival was linked to your own?" I said evenly.

"Please forgive me Catherine, I was afraid," she pleaded.

"We were all afraid," I spat out, slamming my hand down on the bed. I felt anger rising in my throat. "What makes your fear more important than ours?"

She quieted and looked to the floor. After a moment she looked up at me, a tear coursing down her cheek. "A week before I was questioned, I realised that I had missed my courses. I knew then that I was with child, Catherine."

I gasped. I knew they had been waiting for that moment. George had often been found in front of the hearth at Hever gazing at the Ormonde ancestral horn. He had turned it over and over in his hands, rubbing his fingers over the smooth ivory, wrapping the silk ribbon between his fingers. He had longed for a son to pass it on to. It had seemed, though, as if it would never happen.

My breath caught in my throat, "Did George know?"

She gave me a sad smile, "Yes, my dear niece, he did know. He also knew that Cromwell was determined to take his family down no matter who gave evidence of what, and if I did not give him the responses he craved, I would go down with them. He instructed me what to tell Cromwell when my interrogation came. It broke my heart, but I had to do what my husband bade me. I loved George. I would never do anything to hurt him in any way."

I was filled with love for my uncle. He had been fighting to give his child a chance. I pictured his bright smile, the devilish twinkle in his brown eyes as if he were about to tell some marvellous joke. Suddenly, it occurred to me that a small piece of him could exist.

"The baby?" I asked hopefully, and held my breath in anticipation.

Jane began to sob. "The day they executed George, I awoke in the middle of the night bleeding. There was nothing to be done. His child did not want to exist without his father and so he followed him straight to heaven and left me alone here."

With that terrible revelation, my heart broke for Jane and I was filled with rage for the king. Not only did he execute my beloved aunt and uncle, but he caused the death of George's unborn heir. Jane was just as much a victim as Anne and George. All she had was taken from her and, in addition, she had earned a vile, undeserved reputation. I suddenly wanted to be anywhere but here in this treacherous court.

The next day I awoke to a full dormitory. I had fallen into a deep sleep before any of the other maids-of-honour had returned from the festivities and now they occupied the other beds in the room. I rolled over to find myself face-to-face with the pretty young dancer of last night. Her face was tranquil and a small smile played on her lips as though she was in the midst of a wonderful dream. She looked eerily familiar and it dawned on me that she was probably one of my Howard cousins. I knew that I had family at Court besides Jane, but it had been years since I had seen any of them. I reminded myself to ask her later.

I rolled back and swung my legs over the side of the bed. The maid was already quietly stoking the fire. She heard my movement and turned to me for instruction. I smiled and gestured toward my trunk. She rushed over and began pulling out my kirtles and skirts, hanging them in the cupboard. After the trunk was empty, she paused to look at me thoughtfully. She touched her finger to her lips and scurried back to the cupboard, pulling out a tawny kirtle and copper damask skirt that matched my hair perfectly. As quietly as we could, she helped me dress and then we took our leave, leaving the four other girls snoring peacefully in their beds.

We parted ways at the door, she to her duties, I to explore my new surroundings. I made my way through the gallery to the great hall. The palace was drenched in morning sunlight. Beautiful tapestries lined the halls and elegant furniture filled the rooms. I was reminded of my home at Hever, but this was on a much grander scale. Portraits of the king and his family stared down at me. My grandfather, Henry VII, wore a dour expression on his face. How serious he must have been in life. I had been told he was the exact opposite of his son. No wonder the king was filled with an excessive personality. I was sure he had been denied much fun in his childhood.

Eventually I reached the hall. The men were already clumped into groups, talking in hushed tones amongst themselves. Plotting ways to increase their power before breaking their fast, I thought to myself and stifled a laugh. I spied a table laid with apples and bread and hurried over in my hunger. With my bounty in hand, I headed back to our room.

Nan Bassett was already awake by the time I returned. She was sitting in a chair by the fire and leapt up to embrace me as soon as I entered the room.

"I am so glad you made it!" she said brightly. "I was worried about the crossing this time of year, but you seem to be in one piece."

"Yes, it was not a pleasant experience," I laughed. "But I was in good hands."

Immediately her eyebrow went up. "What is his name?" she questioned accusingly.

I just smiled in response and shook my head.

She clapped her hands, "Ladies, let's rise to greet the day!"

The other three girls grumbled, but obliged her, climbing begrudgingly out of bed.

She gestured towards me, "This is Mistress Catherine Carey. She comes to us from Calais." At the mention of her home, she put her hand to her heart.

"Catherine, this is Mistresses Dorothy Bray, Mary Norris and Ursula Stourton. They will be serving the new queen with us. That young lady over there," she said pointing towards my bed, "is Mistress Katherine Howard. I imagine it will be awhile before she manages to rouse herself to join us. She had quite an exhausting evening last night." Dorothy and Mary chittered behind their hands.

Ah, so she was a cousin. I was pleased at the possibility that I could get to know my family better, but also hesitant because of the scorn she was drawing from the other ladies. Maybe she was someone I did not want to be too closely associated with. I would have to be wary.

Nan took a moment to preen in the mirror then spun around and grabbed my hand. "Let me show you everything," she said with a mischievous twinkle in her eye and we headed out into palace.

The coming weeks were filled with preparations for the queen's arrival. New rush mats needed to be woven, tapestries chosen by the king needed to be hung, and the queen's rooms needed to be aired. The maids-of-honour oversaw the servants performing this work and spent mornings doing needlework on a new counterpane for their mistress. During my second week at Court I spied Richard in the gardens and was thrilled he had found his place in the stables after all. He was happy to see me and I managed to convince him that my horsemanship needed work. What else could he do but offer me lessons?

In the afternoons, once my work was completed for the day, I would sneak off to the stables to see him. Sometimes I would catch him in the paddock, combing a mare, singing a lullaby in a quiet voice to calm her, his capable hands checking her carefully for injuries or damage to her hooves. He was so gentle with the animals and it endeared him to me even more.

He would find me a gentle nag and lead me out into the field for a short canter at first, but the more often I rode, the more daring I became and soon I was on a fine palfrey, galloping behind him. I enjoyed our sessions and learned more about Richard and his history every day. He was the son of gentry in York, the youngest with four older sisters who doted upon him. After his mother died, he set out on his own and spent a few years on fishing vessels and trade ships in the channel. Eventually he made his way to the ship that would carry me back to England.

Sir Anthony Browne, the king's newly minted master of the horse saw him working with the horses in our train and asked him to stay on at Court. I was grateful for his intervention because I was falling for Richard more every day. Just seeing him from across the yard was enough to set my stomach aflutter. I did not know if he felt the same, but the look in his eye and his gentle touch when he helped me out of the saddle told me something was there. As a lady, though, I knew I must hold my tongue and, in any case, the queen would be here in a short time and there would be no time for riding lessons.

London, Greenwich:
January 1540

"The queen has landed at Dover!" Nan squealed with delight as she ran into our room. She flopped herself on the bed and heaved a great sigh. "Finally, we shall be able to meet our mistress. I hope she is kind like Queen Jane was. It would be awful if she were as harsh and demanding as the other Queen Anne."

My smile faded. It took a moment for Nan to realise what she had said. Her hand flew to her lips. "Oh Catherine, I am so sorry, I forgot she was ... I did not mean ..."

I raised my hand and stopped her.

"It is fine," I said through gritted teeth. "I realise that my aunt did not always show her best side when she was under pressure, but I could hardly blame her given the situation in which she found herself." Seeing the stricken look on her face I softened. "I am sure she will be a wonderful mistress. I am certain your mother has told Master Hussee all about her stop in Calais in her letters."

At the mention of Lady Lisle's numerous missives to poor John Hussee, Nan and I fell into a fit of laughter. That woman was always writing to demand something from him.

A few weeks after Christmas, we arrived at Greenwich, and the disastrous meeting between the king and his betrothed was the talk of the court. Nan had all of the details and delighted in spreading the gossip. It seemed that the king, in a fit of passion, had taken his men with him and ridden hard to Rochester. He had wanted to strike the Lady of Cleves with, as he said, the 'dart of love'. In his usual fashion, he had burst into her chamber in disguise, hoping that she would fall madly in love upon his arrival. Instead, she had been more interested in the bear baiting taking place outside her window than some outrageously dressed stranger who claimed to serve her husband. Incensed, the king had left her rooms and returned in his regal finery to present her with a gift of sables. She had tried to be gracious once she realised her error, but the damage had already been done. Shortly, after some uncomfortable small talk, Henry had taken to his horse and headed to Gravesend where his barge had been waiting to take him on to Greenwich where the queen was to be formally received.

Nan's face flushed in the telling. I could see her delight in the queen's misfortune and I knew it was not out of cruelty, but jealousy. Rumours had been circulating since Queen Jane's death that Nan would be the king's next consort, but they turned out to be unfounded and Nan had been bitterly disappointed. I don't think she truly loved the king, but she thrived on the attention. Nan would have bloomed like a rose on the throne, but it was not meant to be. She would have to be content with catching the eye of another man at Court, but she was not above taking joy in seeing her replacement's discomfort.

I did not want the Queen's maids-of-honour coming to her giddy on gossip over her troubles so I changed the subject.

"Katherine, what are you wearing to the banquet tonight? I saw the looks that Tom Culpeper was giving you at the last one. It seems you two dance very well together."

Katherine Howard let a small giggle escape and a blush overcame her cheeks. "Whatever do you mean, lady cousin?" she asked her eyes wide.

We all began to laugh. Katherine might seem innocent, but she never hid her emotions. We knew of her affections for the king's groom of the stool, but we were content to let her think us in the dark. Soon, the queen's sad tale was forgotten and we were happily pulling out gowns for Katherine.

The reception for the new queen was a sight to behold. The great ladies of the court and the maids-of-honour waited in the pavilion for the king to make his arrival. Trumpets sounded announcing his arrival as he processed through the park on horseback, dressed in cloth of gold and royal purple. His crown glinted in the bright winter sunlight. John Dudley, Nan's step-brother, was Queen Anne's master of the horse. He stepped forward, dressed in his best, and offered his hand to the queen. She smiled awkwardly and he helped her onto her horse. Dudley led them out to meet the king upon his arrival. The Duchesses of Somerset and Richmond led the way with Marchioness of Dorset, Countess of Rutland and Lady Douglas behind them. The maids-of-honour and other gentlewomen hung back to watch the spectacle.

Once they met in the middle of the park, both the king and queen dismounted. The king doffed his hat and made reverence to the queen and, in return, she knelt low. The king embraced her and they both turned and waved to their court. Back on their horses, they processed to the inner courtyard where they kissed and celebratory artillery was fired. Though I am sure the king was smouldering with anger inside, he never once let on to his people that all was not well. The queen was led to her privy chamber so she could become better acquainted with her ladies. The king withdrew as well, probably eager to berate his councillors for getting him into this untenable situation.

In the queen's chambers I finally had a moment to take her in. I was struck by how sturdy she seemed. I knew that Aunt Anne had been very slight and of middling stature and I had heard that Queen Jane was quite delicate, but this new queen looked as though she could work the land. She was tall and rather stocky, her face ruddy as though she had been out in the fields in the wind and sun. But when she smiled, her face lit up, her doe eyes crinkling at the corners. She seemed nervous and kept her ladies from home near to her. I watched the noble-women of the court pay respects to her. She listened intently as though she were working out the words that they spoke to her and it occurred to me that she knew very little of our language. I knew that the other ladies would take advantage of this and I saw a few begin to cluster and whisper to each other, trying to hide their scorn beneath their hands. I became overwhelmed with pity. I knew that she would not last long in a vain court such as ours.

The formalities done, the English ladies went about their business while the queen sat, hands clasped in her lap, and stared off into space. No-one seemed to know what to do next. Most of us had never served a foreign queen before. After a moment, an idea came to me. I asked one of the pages for a deck of cards. I gathered Lady Rochford, Nan Bassett and Lady Dudley and explained my plan. I thanked the page for the cards and we approached the queen. She smiled at us curiously and I held out the deck. A great smile spread across her face and she clapped her hands together, nodding in excitement. We giggled in relief and spent the day before the fire playing card games with our new mistress.

The day of the wedding fell after Advent so the celebrations would be short-lived, but it was a royal wedding after all. We dressed Queen Anne in a gorgeous cloth-of-gold gown, rubies and sapphires around her throat. Her golden brown hair fell loose down her back, crowned with a coronet of gold and jewels. A garland of rosemary hung around her waist. The ceremony would be private and we would not be there, so I prayed she would be happily received. I had seen the king stomping about the palace earlier in the day and my stomach quaked with fear for her. She smiled serenely and gave a wave as she was led to the king by the Dukes of Suffolk and Norfolk. As he led her out of the room, Charles Brandon, the Duke of Suffolk, gave me a wink and a smile. He been so kind to me since my arrival and I was glad that he would be escorting her. It would be a nice contrast to my Uncle Norfolk's stiff personality.

After the ceremony the rest of the court was invited to the feast. The king and queen dined on the dais under a gold cloth of state, the premier nobles of the court on either side of them. Plate after plate came out of the kitchens, piled high with trout, clams, eel, plover and duck. During Lenten season there would be no red meat, but there was plenty of food from the sea. We ate until our hearts' content, and then made our way to chapel for Evensong. After the service the masques could begin.

The music and ale made me feel as light as a feather. I dropped my inhibitions and my face flushed with my heart light, I danced with every young man that asked, but secretly I wished that Richard could join the celebration. I knew he had nothing to offer my family, but I could not help the attraction I had towards him. Maybe there was some hope. My mother had managed to marry Stafford after all.

I looked around at all the noblemen that graced the court and tried desperately to tamp down my emotions. I caught Katherine's eye. She threw her head back and laughed at something Culpeper whispered to her. I envied her. Culpeper was in her reach, Richard was out of mine. I looked to the king, the man who would decide my fate. I would have to have faith in him. He caught me staring. A broad smile spread across his face and he nodded his head towards me. It was the first time he had acknowledged my presence. In that moment, despite my best efforts, I felt a twinge of love for my father. I was so angry with him for so many reasons, but I began to understand why he was so beloved. It was his charm and charisma. I began to wonder if I would ever figure him out.

London, Westminster:
February - March 1540

On the 4th February, we floated down the frigid Thames on a barge covered in Cleves swans to Westminster. The queen was in her jovial mood. Though she still had not mastered the language, she seemed to be adapting to other aspects of life at the English court. She excelled at cards and often relieved the Duke of Suffolk of his gambling purse during Primero.

We had seen very little of the king since the wedding, but like a good husband he made a point to visit the queen's rooms at least once a week. Knowing the king's reputation with wives who failed to reproduce, I waited anxiously for the chamber-maids to give us the sly look that indicated a maiden's blood on the sheets, but none ever came. By the time we moved on to Hampton Court, where we would celebrate Easter festivities, the queen's ladies had begun to talk.

"Lady Rutland has asked me to approach the queen," Jane Rochford whispered to me as we sat in the window embrasure sewing.

"Is there something you need? I'm sorry I was concentrating on this stitch and missed what you said before," I muttered as I pulled out an errant stitch that had come loose.

Exasperated, she replied, "I do not need anything. You missed nothing. I said Lady Rutland has asked me to approach the queen to ask if she is still a maid. By now there would be some evidence of her pregnancy, but she continues to have her courses on schedule and the king almost never visits her. How does she expect to get a Duke of York?"

I stopped toying with the stitch and eyed her critically. "How long were you married to George before your courses stopped?"

I regretted my words when I saw the hurt on her face. "I'm sorry, Jane, I didn't mean to upset you. But as you know, babies come in the Lord's time and I do not know that it is any of yours or Lady Rutland's business whether the king is intimate with his wife or not. The last time you mentioned the king's inabilities, my aunt and uncle lost their heads. Please do not get involved."

Jane stared down at her lap. "I was just trying to help. Why do I always find myself in the middle of these matters?"

I put down my needle and reached for her hand. "Because, my dear Jane, you have the best of intentions and I know you want to help. But sometimes it is not worth the risk."

"You are right, Catherine. But in this matter I feel I must do as Lady Rutland asks. We all know that the king is not happy in this marriage and it is only a matter of time before he makes a move to get rid of her. And when he does, we will no longer have a place at Court. I cannot bear to be alone at Blickling again. I know my place is here," she implored, her eyes searching mine for approval.

"Jane, you must do what your heart tells you. But I will have no part in it."

I turned to look at the queen. She sat placidly before the fire, her eyes closed, while a musician played a lilting tune on the lute. Her lips curled into a smile. She was calm only because she had no idea of the pressure that was building around her. For her, ignorance was blissful. But like Jane, I too was terrified for her.

Once we arrived at Hampton Court and the weather cleared, I resumed my daily visits with Richard. I loaded a basket with wine, cheese and bread, and we would ride out into the park to see the king's stags. The young ones were in velvet this time of year and I delighted in watching them gingerly pick their way through the brush. Those were the happiest moments of my day. I felt feather-light when Richard wrapped his hands around my waist to lift me from the saddle, and every time his arm brushed mine, my skin erupted in goose bumps.

I lay in bed, tossing and turning in frustration. I could not get Richard out of my mind. Not knowing how he felt was killing me. Katherine grunted beside me. "Stop moving, I am trying to sleep."

I decided to go for a walk. As quietly as I could, I dressed and covered myself in my cloak and crept out of the room, trying not to wake the other maids. The torches were still burning in the hall and I heard whispers in the dark corners. Lover's talk, I thought to myself, and hastened down the corridor. I slipped out of the castle doors and crossed the garden to the stables. I was certain Richard was asleep in his own bed by now, but something compelled me onward.

When I arrived, the light flickering in the open windows from the candles stopped me in my tracks, and for a moment I thought of turning back. Instead, I took a deep breath filled with the scent of fresh hay and strode confidently into the stables as though I belonged there. Once my eyes adjusted to the darkness, I saw him standing by the furnace, his back to me.

"Richard?" I called out tentatively.

He spun around, a look of alarm on his face. "Catherine! What are you doing here?"

I walked towards him, hands outstretched for his. He eyed me warily, obviously confused as to why I had wandered into the empty stables in the middle of the night.

I approached him slowly. "I could not stop thinking of you. I tried desperately to sleep, but all I could think of was the scent of your skin and the sound of your voice. I want to spend all of my days with you. Richard, please put my mind at ease and tell me you feel the same," I said hopefully.

Richard reached out and traced his hand down my cheek. "Of course I feel the same Catherine. I have been out here stacking hay all evening just to keep my mind off you."

Confused, I asked, "Why do you need to keep your mind off me? Do you not realise how happy I am with you? How I want nothing more than to be with you?" I closed my eyes and leaned towards him, wishing with all my heart that he would kiss me.

"Catherine, I cannot do this," he said, pulling his hand away.

My eyes fluttered open. I could already feel the burn behind them, but I willed myself not to cry. "Richard, I know that we should not be together. My mother and William Stafford should never have been together either, but they ran away and did it anyway and they were eventually forgiven. We can do that too. My family would understand," I pleaded.

Richard took my hand and led me over to a bale of hay. The light from the fire in the furnace danced across his face. His eyes looked tired and for the first time I noticed the bags underneath them. He held my hand in his, tracing his finger across the palm of my hand. After a moment of silence, he looked up and said, "I cannot have you because you belong to someone else."

A searing pain spread across my chest and I lost my breath. The wind had been knocked from me. When I finally found my voice I whispered, "What do you mean?"

"Catherine, you are the king's daughter. He has found a husband for you and he is a good man. He will do right by you. He can give you a life that I never could," he said wistfully.

I was taken aback. How could he know I was the king's daughter? Then I remembered the conversation between Lord Lisle and Stafford back in Calais and it dawned on me that the rumours had probably run rampant since I arrived at Court. It was impossible to deny the physical similarities and now that my cousin, the Lady Elizabeth, had been to visit, it was even more evident. She and I looked more alike than her recognised sister, the Lady Mary. My sadness turned to anger, and I leapt from my seat.

"Who? Who has he chosen?" I spat out. I could feel my rage boiling to the surface. I could never choose anything. I would have to suffer the same restraints as Mary and Elizabeth, with none of the benefits of being recognised as a royal bastard. No household, no precedence, no dynastic marriage. I would always be under suspicion and the order of the king.

Richard wrapped his arms around me. Stroking my hair he whispered, "Catherine, please be calm. I know that you are angry, but this is the life you have been given. The king has chosen a fine man for you. Since I have been at Court, I have come to know Francis Knollys. He is kind and generous. He is loyal to the king and, unlike the other men here, he does not connive in dark corners or play sides. He came to the stables today and as I prepared his mount he could not cease talking about you. He told me that the king is waiting for Stafford to come back to Court to tell you. I realised then that we would have to stop our visits."

I knew Stafford had gone to Cottered to help my mother move to Rochford Hall. My great-grandmother had died and she had finally received her inheritance. I had missed her since I left Calais and was looking forward to Stafford's return because he would be bringing her with him. Now I knew why they would be making the journey to Court and I began to dread it.

I leaned forward and kissed his cheek, the rough stubble brushing my lips, soft and swollen from my crying, and then I pulled away from Richard, though everything in my heart begged me not to.

"I have to go," I whispered. "I have been careless. If anyone found me my reputation would be in question."

Richard nodded sadly.

The situation was hopeless. I tried to put on a brave face but I was dying inside. "This may be for the best. My love for you has made me reckless and I can't bear to put you in danger. I must do as my father bids. I wish the best for you Richard, and I will always hold you in my heart."

I turned from him and ran back into the castle without looking back. I knew that if I did not leave, I would lose my resolve and I cared too much for Richard to put him in danger. I slipped quietly back into my bedchamber. Nan was snoring softly across the room, Ursula's arm was hanging off the side of her bed, but my own was empty. Where a sleeping Katherine should have been there was a pile of pillows. It seemed that I was not the only one of the queen's ladies to be slipping out into the night. I put my shift back on and climbed under the quilted counterpane. I tried to fight back the tears but they came anyway and eventually I found release in sleep.

I spent the next few days in a haze. I went about my duties with all the other maids-of-honour, but my heart was not in it. Every evening that we ate in the great hall I scanned the faces, seeing if I could spot the man I was to marry. After three days of this, Nan Bassett elbowed me at the table.

"What is the matter with you?" she whispered, concern written all over her face.

"I will tell you later," I murmured, straightening my posture and forcing a smile. I had to contain my sadness or I would be the subject of more rumours than my paternity.

Later that night, Nan and Katherine cornered me as I readied for bed.

"Catherine, are you all right?" asked Nan, arms crossed, foot tapping. "Why have you been acting so strange?"

"Where were you the other night?" asked Katherine quietly.

I yanked my muslin shift over my head. "I should ask you the same thing!" I shot back.

Nan looked from Katherine to me, her eyebrow raised.

"Oh, you know where she was," Nan laughed. "She was with Culpeper."

Katherine buried her face in a pillow and made a little whimper.

"See," Nan said gesturing towards our bed.

I padded across the floor. Sitting next to Katherine, I put my hand on her shoulder. "Where were you really, Katherine?"

She raised her head, her hair cascading over her eyes. She raised her arm and brushed her golden curls from her face.

"I was with the king."

The silence hung in the air. Suddenly, the focus was off me. Nan pounced on the bed like a panther on its prey.

"What are you doing?" she demanded. "Why were you with the king? What about Queen Anne? We are all going to lose our place!"

Katherine glared at Nan. "We are not going to lose our place. I have asked to have you as my ladies."

Nan and I exchanged a confused look.

"Your ladies?" I asked

Katherine sighed, exasperated by our questions. "Yes! My ladies. When I am queen, you will be my ladies. I have requested it, he has agreed, simple."

Nan sat up straight. "No, not simple. What is going to happen to Queen Anne?"

"The king and the lord secretary are working on that. If Cromwell gets him his divorce, he will make him an earl. I am sure that is incentive enough. She was already pre-contracted to the Duke of Lorraine anyway. At least, that is what the king says." She gestured towards me, "You know how this goes. If the king is unhappy, he finds a new bride."

"What about Master Culpeper?" I asked quietly.

I saw the pain in Katherine's eyes and I sympathised. The king had taken choice from both of us. The burden I had been carrying suddenly lifted when I realised that I would be married to a man that Richard said was kind and compassionate instead of an old, ill-tempered king. Another Katherine would bear the burden of my father now.

"What can I do?" she moaned. "I must do as my king commands me. Uncle Norfolk is pleased beyond words. I could see the greedy look in his eyes when the king informed him of our impending marriage. The king made me come into the room with him to share the happy news when all I wanted to do was hide in shame. I love Queen Anne and I would never want to hurt her, but you know as well as I do that once the king decides he wants something he will do anything in his power to possess it. I cannot fight the inevitable."

I did know that side of the king well. He had possessed both my mother and my aunt, and now he was after my cousin. In a way I found it ironic that he was drawn to Howard women, especially because the first two had caused him so much trouble. Katherine was right. All she could do was bend to his will and hope that she satisfied him.

For the moment, I was off the hook. Katherine's revelations had shaken us all and my misbehaviour was forgotten. We quickly readied for bed and blew out the candles. Ursula, Dorothy and Mary would be back soon and we knew questions would be asked once they saw our emotional state.

A week later, my mother and Stafford arrived at Court. I was out in the garden with Nan choosing posies for the queen when I saw them through the hedge. I picked up my skirts and ran as fast as I could, trying to avoid the puddles of mud. Mother swept me into her arms and for the first time in years I was enveloped in a scent that was not lavender. I stepped back and looked her over. She had become plumper. Her cheeks were rosy and she was smiling.

"No more lavender?" I asked

She gave a light laugh, "No, my dear Catherine. Being back at Rochford Hall has been the best sleeping draught I could have."

I lunged forward and wrapped my arms around her again. I took a deep breath, soaking in her happiness.

"Ladies, if you will..."

I pulled myself away and turned to see Stafford waiting for us, a wide grin on his face.

"You're right," I sighed. "I have to get back to the queen, but I will see you both tonight."

Stafford nodded. "We would like to request your presence at supper in our rooms if the queen will allow it."

I felt a catch in my throat, but I tried not to show it. They must want to share the news of my match tonight.

"Of course, Master Stafford, I will be there."

I made my way back to Nan, who had a bouquet of yellow and white daisies in her hand.

"Your mother is at Court?" She asked incredulously. "I never thought she would come back here. They must have something important to tell you."

I ignored her comment and pretended to be interested in a ladybird that had landed on my hand.

She stood staring after them. After a moment, she took a sharp breath. "Wait! You know, don't you? That is why you were so sullen last week. They have found you a husband haven't they? Why didn't you tell me?"

I put my finger to my lips, "Nan, please keep your voice down. I don't know what is going on, but I am sure they have. That is why I was sent to Court - or requested I suppose - since the king did ask after me. I will tell you after supper."

Nan nodded solemnly and we headed back to the queen's rooms. Lady Rutland and Lady Rochford had already interrogated Queen Anne on her maidenhood and it was obvious that she suspected that something was amiss in the king's behaviour. Instead of her usual calm, she had become suspicious of us all. I knew the flowers would cheer her and I hoped they would improve her mood.

That evening Stafford and my mother carried on about how delighted they were in the king's choice of husband for me. Francis was a Gentleman Pensioner. This meant that he served as one of the king's own body guards. His father, Robert, had died when he was young and his mother, Lettice, was married for the third time. He had been granted the estate of Rotherfield Greys in his home of Oxfordshire and I would be travelling there next month to be married.

My mother would stay here to help me prepare and then travel with us by carriage. I had expected the revelation of this information, but it was still a shock to me to realise that within a month's time I would be someone's wife. I went back to my room hopeful for my future, but in the back of my mind I was terrified. It would not be long before I was a mother. What if I did not know what to do? I knew that we were born to be wives, give birth and raise children, but what if, like Anne, no sons came? I had seen that love could exist in a marriage, but not all men treated their wives as kindly as Stafford. I tried to have faith in the choice that the king had made, but I spent many sleepless nights waiting for my wedding day.

Part II
My Lady Wife

Oxfordshire, Rotherfield Greys: April 1540

The road to Oxfordshire was wet and muddy with the spring rains, making the carriage bounce and shudder the five hours it took to get there from London. By the time we arrived, I was exhausted and nauseated. My mother could tell I was not feeling my best and sent our page on to Greys Court to let my future family know that we would spend the night at the local inn so that I could rest before I met them. I wanted to make a good impression and with the sorry state I was in, that would be impossible.

Mother called for a wooden tub and hot water. Exhausted, I climbed in. The hot water reddened my skin and as I lay back against the stiff boards and closed my eyes, I felt relaxed for the first time in weeks. Mother poured rosewater down my back then rubbed my hair clean with linen rags. I felt like a child again, bathing before the fire at Calais, as if all my troubles were far away. After I dried and put on a new linen shift, she braided rosemary into my hair to perfume it overnight. Though it was still light out, I crawled into bed and slept until morning.

I awoke to the sounds of hoof-beats outside my window. I wondered who it could be. Stafford had been sent on an errand for the king so we did not expect him until the afternoon feasting. It made me sad to think he would not witness my wedding. He had spent more time in my life, guiding and caring for me, than both of my supposed fathers, the king and William Carey, but what could be done? For a moment I panicked, thinking it was Francis coming to take me to the chapel. I buried myself beneath the counterpane as soon as the door flew open.

"Catherine, get up! You have a visitor!" my mother called.

I peeked out from under the blanket.

"Who is it?"

"Why don't you come and see for yourself?" she said with a mischievous grin.

I swung my feet out and, still in my shift, padded into the hall. Stafford and my little brother were leaning casually against the wall.

"Henry!" I shouted and ran towards him, arms outstretched.

"Sister!" he yelped as I squeezed him tightly.

I stepped back and eyed Stafford suspiciously. "I thought you were delivering a message for the king?"

He laughed. "I was, to Sir John Russell. I could not leave without Henry. He begged me to take him."

My brother had been under the care of Sir John since his tutors had gone back to France. I was so pleased to see him after all this time. He had grown since I last saw him. Now he was as tall as Stafford. His shoulders were broad and sturdy. When his face relaxed out of his smile it was as if I was seeing William Carey come back to life.

"Well, I am so glad you both could make it. Now, if you will excuse me, I have a wedding to prepare for."

I swept back into my room leaving Stafford and Henry to chatter in the hallway.

Once I had finally dressed I took a moment to look myself over in the mirror. My bodice was made from dark green velvet and covered with a kirtle in a lighter shade that was trimmed in seed pearls and edged in gold rope. The sleeves were slashed showing the fine white linen underneath. I blushed at the low cut of the bodice as I fingered the jewel at my throat. It was a single emerald pendent, a wedding gift from my mother. It was the first jewel she had received from my father when she became his mistress. A matching hood held back my auburn hair worn loose down my back. I brought a few strands to my face and breathed in the clean scent. My mother's reflection came into view.

"Are you ready, my lady?" she smiled.

The skies had cleared. There was no breeze to disturb the trees and the heat of the sun warmed my back. Stafford helped me into the carriage and we set off for Greys Court. When we arrived we were met at the gate by a young man, tall with sandy blonde hair, astride a dappled mare. He drove our carriage down the lane to the manor and, once there, he hopped down and strode over.

"Welcome to Greys Court, Master Stafford and family. I am Henry, brother to Francis," he said giving a slight bow.

When he straightened, he caught my eye and gave me a broad grin. "And this beautiful lady must be my new sister."

He took my hand and placed a light kiss on my knuckle. I hoped desperately that Francis was as warm as Henry.

"Very pleased to meet you, Master Knollys. I have been eagerly awaiting this day."

Laughing he said, "Are you sure you do not mean anxiously awaiting?"

Both Stafford and my brother chuckled, but Henry Knollys noticed the alarm on my face.

"Oh, my lady, you will soon learn that I am the family fool. They humour me because I am the baby, but I am sure you will find my brother much more serious."

I relaxed, gave him a wink and responded, rather tartly, "I certainly hope not."

He offered his arm to me. "Now, that was the reaction I was hoping for."

Henry took us on a tour of the manor. As a bachelor he resided there and cared for the grounds while Francis was at Court. Sisters Margaret and Joan were already married and settled into their homes and their mother, Lettice, was married to Sir Thomas Tresham and resided at their home in Northamptonshire. It seemed that I would be the lady of the house when I was not at Court serving the queen, and though it intimidated me I was also pleased that I would not have a demanding mother-in-law to contend with.

Once I was in her presence I realised I needn't have worried. Lady Tresham was every bit as warm and welcoming as her son.

My fears had been for naught. So far, it seemed that the king had chosen well for me. But I still had yet to meet the most important member of the Knollys family - my husband.

The time came for us to go to the chapel so I could be wed. I waited outside for the family to go in and be seated. After a few moments I opened the chapel doors and walked slowly down the aisle. Francis was waiting for me at the altar. He was not as tall as his brother and his hair was a darker brown, but his eyes lit up in the same way and a small smile twitched at his lips even though he was attempting to be serious in front of the minister. In a twist of irony we had dressed to match. His doublet was Tudor green and trimmed in gold. My heart thudded in my chest and my hands began to sweat, but my feet were steady as I continued to the altar.

As we repeated our vows, exchanged rings and had our marriage blessed by the minister, Francis never turned his eyes from mine. I could see in them all the love and compassion that Richard had spoken of that night in the stables, and in that instant any thought of Richard evaporated.

We spent the afternoon feasting and dancing. As the sun set, our mothers lit the way to our room with candles and sent us to our marriage bed.

The fire was already lit and the room was bathed in a warm glow. A table in the corner was set with two mugs, a jug of ale and some bread. I began to fumble at my bodice strings, but Francis stopped me with a kiss.

"Here, let me," he whispered huskily in my ear.

His fingers deftly unlaced my gown. As it fell to the floor, he ran his finger down my spine and I felt a chill. Francis felt my shiver. He stepped back, reaching for a blanket and wrapped it around me.

We sat on the bed and stared at each other for a moment. He tucked a tendril of hair behind my ear and let his hand rest on my cheek for a moment.

"I never thought the king would grant my request to marry you," he said sheepishly. "I was in Queen Anne's train when she came from Calais and William Stafford and I became fast friends.

I made a point to seek you out at Court, but I never had the courage to approach you.

"Yet you had the courage to ask the king for my hand?" I teased.

"I had to work up to that, believe me. I saw how kind you were to Queen Anne when she arrived at Greenwich, her ladies laughing at her behind her back. I was disgusted by their behaviour. You were different. You stepped in and made her welcome. When I saw that, I knew I wanted you for my wife. Those women at Court are always so consumed with ambition. They are ever willing to sacrifice the vulnerable for their own amusement and gain."

I leaned my head on his shoulder. "I have seen what can become of ambition. It destroyed my family. The cost is more than I can bear. If I were not the king's daughter I would love nothing more than to run Greys Court and chase after our horde of children and leave the court life to those who desire it," I sighed.

"I considered that when Master Stafford revealed your paternity to me after I asked him for your hand. But I decided that I did not care if we had to spend our life at Court if it meant I got to have you."

He started to kiss me and before my nerves could take over, I surrendered to his touch.

Afterwards I crawled out of bed and knelt, hands clasped to pray. Francis looked over at me sleepily. "Time for prayers?"

I smiled at him and bowed my head, "I made a promise to give my thanks to the Lord for all my blessings before I fell asleep tonight and, as you will learn, I always keep my promises."

London, Durham Palace and Richmond Palace: May – July 1540

We were expected back in London for the May Day festivities so our honeymoon was cut short. The moment we arrived at Durham Palace I noticed an air of nervousness that I could not place. Since I was a married woman, I would no longer room with the rest of the maids-of-honour, but I needed to fetch my belongings to my new rooms with Francis. When I arrived I saw that Katherine Howard's trunk was gone. I quickly gave instruction to the chamber-maid on what to move and then hurried to the queen's rooms to find Nan. She could tell me what was going on.

The queen's rooms were ominously spare for a festival such as the May Day events. The queen sat quietly before the fire reading. Her ladies sat in clusters playing cards or sewing, talking in hushed voices. Lady Rochford noticed me first. She made a beeline towards the door. Before I could say anything she grabbed my elbow and led me out into the hall.

"Catherine, I am so happy to see you again. Congratulations on your wedding," she said embracing me.

"Thank you, it was lovely." Before she could respond I asked, "Where are the rest of the queen's ladies? Katherine Howard's trunk is gone. What has happened?"

Jane looked around to be sure no one could hear us. She moved closer. "The king has sent the queen's ladies back to Cleves. Only the English ladies attend on her now and many of those have been spending more time back at their manors. Lord Cromwell has been made an earl and Katherine Howard has been given her own rooms. Lady Rutland and Lady Edgecombe were questioned by

Lord Wriothesley about the queen's virginity and we have all been in a panic."

"Does the queen understand what is going on?"

"I think she suspects. She was very upset to have her ladies sent home, but for the most part she carries on as if things are normal. Maybe she thinks this is the way things are done at the English court," she said.

I gave her a wry look, "Or maybe she is much smarter than you give her credit for and lets you all think she does not understand."

The squawking of a bird interrupted our conversation.

"That infernal bird," fumed Jane stomping back into the queen's chamber.

I followed her to see what was making the racket. A brightly coloured parrot rocked his cage back and forth in the corner. Jane rushed over and threw a cover on the cage. After a moment the squawking stopped.

I saw by the faces around me that they were shaken. It seemed that recent events had set them all on edge.

The May Day jousts were to be Queen Anne's last public appearance. By mid-June, Katherine Howard had been sent to Lambeth, where the king could visit her without the prying eyes of Court. Quite surprisingly after his elevation, Lord Secretary Cromwell was branded a traitor by the council, had his earldom taken away, and was tossed in the Tower. Queen Anne and her now reduced retinue of ladies were on their way to Richmond for her "health." The king insisted that she was in need of the fresh air, but we all knew the real reason. Queen Anne's reign was coming to an end.

I was given the choice to stay at Court with my husband or to go Richmond with the other maids-of-honour. I struggled with my decision. I wanted to be with Francis every moment I could, but my heart ached for the queen and Nan Bassett. Nan's stepfather, Lord Lisle, had been arrested for treason in May and her mother and younger sisters were under house-arrest. Nan knew nothing of the plot and had no involvement, but at times she had been near hysterical at the turmoil in her family. Her elder sister would be going to Richmond as well, but the Lisles had been like family to me and I wanted to show my support. Francis understood and encouraged me to go.

"I will be waiting here for you when you return, and if we are lucky, the king will let us have a leave to properly celebrate our wedding," he said provocatively as he caressed my naked belly the night before we left Court. I felt an ache of longing, but I had already made up my mind to go.

After two weeks at Richmond, the king's councillors made their much-awaited appearance. At the sight of the Duke of Suffolk, Lords Audley, Winchester, Kingston, Cheyney and Rich filing into her rooms, Queen Anne took fright and fainted, landing in a heap on the floor. We rushed towards her while the councillors looked around uncomfortably. No doubt she had been thinking of the Queen Anne before her, but we pretended as though the heat had made her weak. The mid-summer warmth was stifling, so the councillors appeared to believe our ruse.

The lords made a hasty exit when they realised that they would not complete their mission. We revived the queen and she sent for Ambassador Harst. When he arrived, we all left to the ante-room to give them privacy, but after a while her sobs had grown so loud it was impossible to drown them out. Nan and I exchanged a wary look. Once again my father had caused pain to someone I had grown to love. I did not understand the need for him to put a good woman through this torture. Queen Anne was young enough to be capable of bearing sons, she had the love of the people of England as they willingly demonstrated, calling her name and waving fervently whenever she was in procession, and she brought ready allies against France and Spain. The king was setting her aside only to fulfil his lusts. I knew I should be happy for my cousin, the future queen, but I could not summon the good-will after seeing poor Queen Anne sacrificed.

The councillors returned a few days later for the queen's signature on the annulment papers. She finally marshalled her courage and signed. She placed her ring on the table for them to return to the king. Her fears went unrealised. She was not to lose her head. In fact, she was to be treated rather well. She would be the king's "entirely beloved sister" and third in importance behind the new queen. In addition, she was granted Richmond and Hever. Hever had reverted to the crown after my grandfather's death so I was not surprised that the king was giving it as a gift, but I must admit that I felt some melancholy at the reminder of its loss. I was, however, happy that my home would go to a woman who so deserved it. I hoped Anne would come to love Hever with its beautiful gardens, bountiful orchards and handsome stonework. Maybe she would find it worthy payment for the pain she had received for the grant.

Their mission complete, the councillors made preparations for their departure. The Duke of Suffolk caught my eye and gestured for me to follow him. He led me to the presence chamber. A page saw us enter and scurried out of the room.

In an uncharacteristically serious tone he said, "In a week's time, I need you and Nan Bassett to pack your belongings and make haste to the palace at Outlands. Katherine Howard is awaiting your arrival to prepare her for her wedding."

It was a wedding baptised in blood, for on the same day that Katherine Howard was repeating her vows in her private closet in Surrey, the former lord secretary was placing his head on a block on the Tower green. The death of Cromwell heralded the reign of a new queen.

Oxfordshire, Rotherfield Greys:
October 1540 - April 1541

My time with the court was short-lived. After weeks of Francis and I making up for time spent apart, I woke up one stifling October day and heaved into the piss pot. Only then did I realise that I had missed my courses for two months. In all the excitement and chaos of a royal wedding, I had ceased paying attention to the messages my body was sending me. I waited another month to be sure and spent my time in the queen's rooms sewing a baby blanket. I waited until the time was right and then laid it on Francis's pillow after he had left our rooms for the day. When I came back that night he was waiting for me in front of the fire, a gleeful smile on his face. We made love for the last time that night before the baby was born and it poured down rain from the heavens for the first time since June. I felt as if God were raining blessings upon us.

In November, Queen Katherine, Lady Rochford, and Nan sadly bid me farewell, but Francis was anxious to get me home before the winter storms began. He would return to Court after I was settled. His brother Henry would keep me company until my mother arrived for my lying-in. Excitement welled up in me when I realised that I would be the lady of the house. I warned Francis that he might find Greys Court changed when he returned for the birth of our child. He shook his head and sighed, but he could not hide the delight in his voice when he said, "I would love to see you wield your feminine influence over Henry. He has had the run of the place these last years and I am not sure how welcome your posies and tapestries will be."

I huffed. "He will welcome them and like them."

Francis wrapped his arms around me and whispered into my hair, "Oh how I will miss you."

Henry welcomed me home with open arms. He was amenable to the new tapestries I chose for the hall and my plans for the gardens when spring came, but I was forbidden from touching his rooms. I insisted that new rushes be laid and he agreed, but my influence ended there. Henry was a doting brother-in-law. He made sure I got the best cuts of meat, that the fire never went out and, at night, he would read to me by candlelight. When I would turn irritable from lack of sleep or felt pains from the pregnancy, he would tell me stories of their childhood or jokes to lighten my mood. His impression of the king, hands on his hips and a wide stance stomping through the hall, never failed to raise my spirits.

After Christmas, my mother came to Greys Court to prepare my lying-in, bringing with her my maid from Calais, Matilda. I was thrilled to see her. Forgoing etiquette, I wrapped her in a warm embrace. Seeing her friendly face helped ease my anxieties. For the next three months I retreated to my bed to await the pains of childbirth.

From my bed I listened to the rain pattering against the window. The room was dark and sweltering. A fire burned to heat the chamber and thick tapestries covered the windows to keep out the draft. I was miserable. I wanted nothing more than to stick my face out into the spring rain and feel the drops on my skin and the damp earth in my lungs. But no one would grant my small request.

"We cannot let in the evil airs, my lady," Matilda said as she stoked the fire.

I looked over at my mother; she was sitting in her chair humming a hymn. She nodded in agreement. I sighed and wriggled around trying to get comfortable. My back ached from lying in bed for so long and my mind had grown weary after three months of doing nothing but sleep. I laid my hand on my belly and felt the baby give it a hard kick. I rested my other hand on the mattress beside me and realised it was sopping wet. Before I could say a word I was gripped by a pain unlike any I had ever felt before.

I cried out and in seconds Matilda and my mother had the birthing mattress on the floor. Somewhere in between my yelping and writhing they managed to get me on it. The pain was unbearable. The midwife bustled into the room armed with a wooden spoon. In one swift move, she forced it between my clenched teeth.

"Bite down on that, m'lady," she said brusquely. "It will help with the pains."

I laboured through the night, at turns groaning and crying. I thought my stomach would tear in two. My mother massaged my lower back and caressed my hair in an effort to ease the pain.

"You are doing well," she cooed. "Only a little more now ..."

I held my breath and gave one last push. The sharp sound of a baby's cry pierced the pre-dawn silence.

"You have a son!" my mother shouted. She leaned forward and kissed my forehead. "Oh my beautiful girl, you have a son."

I had son. I had fulfilled my duty to my husband. "He has an heir, he has an heir," I muttered to myself before exhaustion took over and I fell into a deep sleep.

"Catherine, your husband is here to see you. Can you wake up for me please?" A soft voice dragged me out of my slumber. Slowly I opened my eyes. Mother was leaning over me, stroking my hair.

"Francis is here and he is waiting to see you," she said smiling.

I closed my eyes and heaved a contented sigh. Carefully, she eased me into a sitting position to receive my visitor.

The door to my chamber creaked open and he walked slowly out of the shadows. He was even more handsome than I remembered. Light stubble graced his jawline and though his dark eyes look tired they were bright and shining with pride. My mother patted me on the hand and made a quiet exit.

Francis drew a chair near to the bed and before he sat down he bent over and kissed me gingerly. I could taste the rain on his lips and knew he had ridden a long way in the storm to be by my side.

"How are you, my love?" he asked, stroking the back of my hand.

"I am vastly improved now that you are here."

He gave me a coy smile and then the serious look returned to his face. "I had faith that you were in good hands with your mother and Matilda, but I must admit that I was very concerned. All I could think was of Queen Jane and how distraught I would be if I lost you."

I glowed at these words of love. I had always hoped to marry a man who would feel such affection for me and here he was sitting before me.

"Francis, I have many more heirs to give you. I would never forsake you nor leave your side, even in childbirth."

He squeezed my hand. "Where is that boy of mine?"

My mother must have been eavesdropping at the door because as soon as Francis's words were spoken, she bustled in with a bundle in her arms and placed it in mine. I pulled away the blankets and found my angelic son wrapped inside. I could not help but stare at this miniature person we had created. Wisps of tawny hair stood out from his tiny head. His eyes were azure blue like my mother's and his tiny rosebud mouth was pursed looking for my breast. I held his little hand on my finger and instinctively he tightened it into a fist. I was instantly in love. I knew I would do anything in my power to protect him and keep him safe.

Francis climbed into bed with us and we sat together as a family, both of us in awe at the little life before us.

I was the first to break the silence. "We will call him Henry in honour of our beloved brothers. May he have your brother's compassion and kindness and my brother's dedication to learning."

Francis squeezed us both into a hug. Then he said "You do realise the king will think we've given him a namesake?"

I gave him a sly smile and raised my brow. "Well then, we will let him believe that we are obedient courtiers who name their first born for their monarch and the truth will be our little secret."

Baby Henry cooed in agreement.

Francis spent a week with us before he was called back to Court. The night before he left I peppered him with questions about what I had missed and how Katherine was getting along in her new role.

"The Lady Mary hates her," he laughed. "Queen Katherine sent away her favourite ladies because she refused to show her respect in front of the court. Mary was livid and made an excuse to leave and has not been seen since."

"Poor Mary. She has been suffering for so long. The king's marriage to my aunt Anne caused her so much pain and now after two kind and gentle queens, I am sure she believes she suffers at the hand of yet another dreadful Howard woman." As much as I sympathised with Mary, I could not help but laugh. "Do you think I am a dreadful Howard woman?"

Francis stared at me in mock surprise. "Of course not! Now you are a dreadful Knollys woman!"

I shook my head. "I will show you dreadful."

Francis laughed and planted a kiss on my forehead.

Then I turned serious. "Maybe I am blessed after all to be unrecognised as a royal child."

Francis nodded. "The queen has become very haughty and your aunt, Lady Rochford, is the first lady of her bedchamber. They are inseparable and sometimes insufferable. At New Year, Anne of Cleves came to celebrate at Hampton Court and paid much reverence to both the king and queen as if she had not been displaced by the silly woman mere months ago. The king took ill and is just now recovering from a serious fever. We all were petrified of his death with Prince Edward being barely out of the cradle, but he rallied and we were all relieved."

I sighed. "And soon I shall be back among the madness."

Francis leaned over and squeezed my thigh, "No, my lady. Soon you shall be back in my bed while I am among the madness."

I shook my head and kissed his cheek, my lips chafed at the stubble, "You are a shameful man."

"Ah, but I am your shameful man. Is it time for your churching yet?" He teased.

"In good time, husband, in good time."

Leaving my son was as difficult as I had imagined. After three glorious months of morning cuddles and afternoon lullabies, I had been lulled into a sense of deep contentment. Harry, as we had begun to call him, would be in good hands with his uncle and the two nurses we had hired to watch over him, but I was not ready to part with him. Overcome with sadness, I waved goodbye from the carriage and headed back to the glittering Court that awaited me. My only consolation was that Francis would be waiting there for me as well.

The Royal Progress to the North:
June - October 1541

I arrived at Court as preparations were being made for the annual summer progress. The plan had been to leave at the end of May after the king executed yet another threat to his throne.

I was utterly disgusted at the execution of Lady Salisbury. I realised that, as the niece of Edward IV and distant cousin to the king, her sons would always have a possible claim to the throne, and that one of them, Cardinal Pole, was working with the pope against the changes the king was making to the church. But how much of a threat could their elderly mother be? And to be hacked to pieces by an inexperienced executioner was reprehensible. Margaret Pole had loyally served the throne since the reign of the king's father and she deserved a dignified death.

In the previous few months, my father had been at turns kind and jovial one moment, and angry and suspicious the other. We were all treading delicately but hoped that a few months on progress with his new queen would calm his temper. Around the same time as the execution, Katherine came down with illness and the roads were flooded from the recent storms. So much to the king's disdain we left two weeks late. Every day of her illness one of the king's advisers would visit the queen's rooms to ask if we could expect a Duke of York. They were very disappointed when on the fourth day we informed them that her courses had arrived at their expected time.

Francis had been accurate in his description of Katherine. She had become haughty and vain, but I could see sadness too. The king had provided her with every comfort she could want - vast wealth, lands and ladies to serve her in any way she commanded.

Even in her sickness she had insisted upon wearing all of her newly granted jewels. But we could offer her no amount of comfort. The one person she wanted, Thomas Culpeper, was denied her.

Lady Rochford was insufferable. As first lady of the bedchamber she had become the most important of the queen's ladies, and as someone who had spent much time in disgrace, she savoured her new position.

Once the queen had recovered from her illness, the court set out to the North so the king could inspect his lands. At Lincoln, our first stop, I learned what had truly been going on at Court during my absence.

After we were settled in, Lady Rochford cornered me. In her hand she held a cramp ring.

"I need you to deliver this to Culpeper," she whispered conspiratorially.

"I don't understand. Why is the queen giving Culpeper a cramp ring? Is he suffering from some malady? He looked well to me yesterday."

She sighed impatiently. "You are so simple sometimes, Catherine. Never mind why. The queen can give whatever gifts she sees fit to her favourites. I just need you to deliver it."

I shook my head. "Jane, Culpeper should not be the queen's favourite. You, of all people, should know that. The queen would do best to forget that her relationship with Culpeper ever happened. She has married the king and, besides, Culpeper has become dangerous. Francis told me about the incident with the park-keeper. Raping his wife and then murdering him when he came to save her. No, I absolutely will not deliver that to Culpeper and you would be wise to refuse yourself."

I saw the tears welling up in her eyes. She looked around to make sure no one was eavesdropping and whispered, "You must help me Catherine. I am caught in a web and cannot escape."

Sensing her desperation, I looked around for an excuse to leave the room. Seeing the cramp ring gave me an idea. I murmured, "Pretend you have a cramp."

Understanding my ruse, she doubled over and cried out in pain.

"Lady Rochford! What is wrong?" I exclaimed in mock concern, placing my hand on her back.

Katherine looked up from her cards. "What is going on over there?" she called over her shoulder.

"I am so sorry, Your Grace. Lady Rochford just mentioned that her supper did not sit well with her and now she seems to have a stomach pain. I will help her to her rooms and fetch the doctor," I replied.

Katherine, still sitting, turned to face me. A look of suspicion crossed her face, but her eyes softened with concern when she saw Jane hunched over gripping her stomach.

"Please do, Mistress Knollys. Thank you so much for your kindness," she said. I could see the panic begin to rise in her, but she composed herself before anyone else noticed. "We shall enquire on you soon, Lady Rochford."

I wondered why Katherine would panic over Jane's illness. Surely she had plenty of maids to serve her. I guided Jane to her rooms, keeping up the charade all the way down the corridor. When we were safely in her bedchamber, I blocked the door and stared at her expectantly.

She threw herself on the bed. "Catherine, how could I have let this happen?"

"What have you done, Jane?"

"I have made terrible choices. I have become the queen's liaison with Culpeper. At first it was just once, when the king took ill. The Queen panicked and thought he might die. She said she needed someone to protect her if that should happen so she asked me to call Culpeper to her rooms so that she could seek his assistance. I thought I was helping her. She looked so frightened. But then, once the king had healed, the visits continued and the queen begged me not to tell anyone. She said they were in love and as long as the king did not know about it, there could be no harm."

Exasperated, I threw my hands in the air. "Jane! How could you believe that? Your own husband and sister-in-law died for such offences. You should have encouraged the queen to stop. You should have refused her demands."

She gave me a shocked expression. "Catherine, I realise that you were raised very far from Court and you have been gone to Greys for some time, but you know that a command from the queen cannot be refused."

"You cannot refuse her to her face," I spat out. "But you can refuse to put your life in danger. Go to Cranmer, go to Wriothesley. For heaven's sake, go to Suffolk! You could do it discreetly. You should know. You have done it before."

Her face crumpled. "That is not fair, Catherine. Will you never forgive me for Anne and George?"

"No, Jane, it is not fair. It is not fair that Anne and George lost their lives because they were wrongfully accused of doing what Katherine truly is. And instead of going to the king's councillors you aid in her deception."

Jane got up from her bed and came to me. She gripped my hands. "Please, Catherine, do not go to the councillors. If the queen is found out, my life is in danger for helping her. She is your own cousin, would you see her head on a block?" She hung her head. "Can we truly blame her? We all knew she loved Culpeper before the king decided to take her for his own. "

My indignation faltered. She was my family, but for that reason alone she should have known better. The Howards never forgot that the Boleyns had almost brought them down and they reminded us at every opportunity. It was easy to look down at her from the comfort of my marriage to Francis, but I too had been denied my first love. Perhaps if she had truly given the king a chance, she could have been happy and satisfied to be queen. The king certainly adored her and demonstrated it for everyone to see. Instead of accepting her new position, she had acted impetuously and put both her life and Jane's in danger.

"I will not go to the councillors," I said softly. "But I will not be party to this dangerous deception. I will not deliver your cramp ring or any other gifts that the queen wishes to give to Culpeper and I will not help you get them alone. I will not actively seek her fall, but I will not lie when asked about her activities."

Jane nodded. After a moment she said thoughtfully. "You know why she looked so panicked back there?"

I stared at her silently.

"Because I am supposed to help her see Culpeper tonight. They are meeting in her close stool."

Disgusted, I shook my head and left the room.

Francis tried his best to be intimate before bed, but I could not stomach the thought after hearing what the queen was planning with Culpeper.

Frustrated, Francis lay down beside me. "Catherine, you are completely distracted. Have I done something to offend you?"

His worried eyes broke my heart. "Oh Francis, you have never offended me!" I leaned over, kissed him and then lay my head on his chest.

He stroked my hair. "Then please tell me what is wrong. You have never rebuffed me before."

I could not stop the tears from my eyes or the torrent of words that came from my mouth. Before long, the whole sordid affair was out. Francis was angry that Jane had tried to involve me. He wanted me to go to Suffolk, but I begged him not to force me. Finally he agreed. We would not go to the councillors until we were back in London. I knew this was a secret I could not keep for long and I could not bear to put my husband or son in danger. Francis wrapped me in his arms and we slept. His warm muscular body made me feel protected. It would pain me to leave those arms in the morning.

We continued our progress through Pontefract, Stamford and York. We were greeted with crowds and great cheers. It had been such a long time since the king had shown his favour to the

North and after the rebellions in the last five years he was eager
to show his forgiveness. He was also demonstrating his strength
and reminding his people that if they rose up again, they would be
defeated as before. Katherine revelled in the attention and, just as
I suspected, kept up her affair with Culpeper. Along the way she
collected a new secretary. In August, a young man named Frances
Dereham joined our party. He had known Katherine when she was
living at Lambeth, long before she was queen, but I still distrusted
his familiar behaviour towards her.

"Why does Katherine allow this Dereham to speak to her as
though she were a common washer woman?" I asked Nan as we
sat in the garden enjoying the mid-summer sun. The roses were in
full bloom and the heavy perfumed scent enveloped us. That scent
always took me back to the gardens at Hever. I wondered if the
garden had, once again, bloomed into a riot of colour and hoped
that Anne of Cleves was taking full advantage of its beauty.

Nan shook her head. "I cannot fathom. I have heard rumours
that they were friends while Katherine was at the dowager duchess's
home. Maybe we should ask Mistress Bulmer, she lived with her at
Lambeth. Though I suppose I would worry more about the amount
of time she spends with Thomas Culpeper."

Stunned, I gave her a surprised look.

"Oh Catherine," she said. "Don't act so surprised. We have all
noticed the frequency of Master Culpeper's visits and the coy way
in which Katherine speaks to him. We are not blind. She flaunts
it. I believe she thinks that she is safe because the king loves her so
much. Let her believe that and sign her own execution warrant."

"Nan, are you not worried about being sent from Court? Lord
Lisle is still in the Tower and your mother and sisters under house-
arrest. Where will you go?"

She smiled and patted me on the hand. "I have served my third
queen in only my fifth year at Court. As long as we stay above
reproach, there will be yet another queen to serve."

Then she guffawed. "If only the king had married me after
Queen Jane. He would never have found himself in this mess."

"Nan, you would have made an excellent queen," I said. I sincerely meant it.

London, Hampton Court:
November 1541 – February 1542

The queen had been found out without my intervention. Archbishop Cranmer courageously presented the king with the evidence laid against his wife after a service in the chapel. The roar of anger escaping His Majesty could be heard throughout the palace. After a week of being locked up with his councillors, the king made haste down the Thames to Westminster so he would not have to look his queen in the face again. That was his way. No goodbye, no raging, no cold looks. He left Katherine just as he left her cousin that May morning five years ago, with no warning of what was to befall her. He passed me in the corridor on his way to the river and I could see the red rims around his eyes. I felt pity for him. For once he was the victim. I wondered if he believed that this time God truly did punish him because he had spent so much time accusing the Lord of doing just that in his last marriages.

Whatever love the king had for Katherine was gone now and she was treated accordingly. The yeoman guards set up outside her bedchamber and she became a virtual prisoner. The only ladies allowed to serve her were Lady Rochford, Mistress Tylney and Lady Rutland. I suspected that Lady Rutland and Mistress Tylney were there to spy on Jane and Katherine once I learned they had both already testified against her. As we shuffled out of Katherine's rooms, the muffled sounds coming from the bedchamber grew from quiet murmurs to sobs and then wailing. The keening sound of Katherine's cries echoed in my ears long after that night.

I spent much of the next weeks pacing. Katherine had been sent to Syon Abbey to await her trial and Lady Rochford, Culpeper and Dereham had been dragged to the Tower. Dereham had taken Katherine's maidenhead and believed they had been pre-contracted. It must have been quite the shock for him to come back to England and find that the woman he believed to be his wife was now married to the king, and he could not help promoting himself when the chance arose.

The terror on Jane's face as she marched out of the palace with the guards set me on edge. I sobbed when word came from the Tower that she had gone mad. I wanted desperately to visit her but Francis forbade me. As much as I wanted to comfort my aunt, I knew he was right. I was ashamed that after railing about the Howard and Boleyn families' abandonment of Anne for so many years, I was now abandoning Jane. I was just as guilty as they were.

Katherine was finally moved to the Tower after the expected pronunciation of guilt. In December, Dereham and Culpeper were taken to Tyburn to die. At the last moment, Culpeper's sentence was commuted to beheading while Dereham suffered the most, being hanged, drawn and quartered. Their heads rotted on pikes on top of London Bridge.

Christmas at Greenwich Palace was muted. There were no masques or banquets. No festivities of any kind. In February a bill of attainder was passed, Katherine and Jane were to be beheaded. I fought an internal war with myself in the days leading up to their death. The mere thought of watching their execution made me physically ill. Though I hated their actions, I loved them both. My love won out and on the day of their executions I awoke early and dressed in a wool gown of the darkest blue I owned for mourning. I wrapped myself in sables against the chill and followed the throng of people onto Tower Green.

Katherine was first to emerge from the Tower. She was dressed in a simple black gown, her hair tied back under a white coif. I had never seen her so sombre. When she reached the block, she stopped for a moment before kneeling. She closed her eyes and took a deep breath. When she opened them, she gave a small, brave smile. She thanked the king for raising her to high estate and begged forgiveness for her transgressions. The wild, impetuous girl had been tamed.

She knelt and placed her head on the block as if she had practised the motions a dozen times. The crowd was silent. In the past, no queens had ever been executed and now the people of London had seen two go to their deaths in just six years. They did not know how to react and jeering seemed far too cruel. In one move, the executioner raised his axe and sliced her head clean off her slender, alabaster shoulders. The blood spurted out in rivers just as in my dream of Anne. The wounds on my heart from her death ripped open again and I had to turn away. Nan and Ursula ran to the scaffold and shuffled her lifeless body out of the way. I was close enough to see the tears trailing down their sombre faces.

Jane was led out of the Tower next. Her hair was unkempt. She was desperately thin and appeared frail. Her gown was dirty and she gripped handfuls of its fabric in her hands. Head down, she shuffled towards the block. The king had had her declared sane so he could execute her, but anyone would know that the woman standing on the scaffold was not in her right mind.

She looked around wildly, searching for what I do not know. When her eyes landed on me, I gave her a smile and mouthed the words "I love you." She heaved a great sigh of relief as if those words were the only ones she had waited for. The thing Jane longed for the most was love and approval, and that was why she did everything in her power to make people happy. She craved Katherine's affection and for that she was willing to risk her life. Jane knelt and laid her head in the pool of royal blood left by her mistress, then she was gone. Go to your husband, Jane, I thought to myself. Tell him how much I love him. I was deeply saddened by her end, but I felt a ray of hope that she, George and their baby would be reunited.

That night I tossed and turned unable to get the gruesome tableau of death out of my head. Katherine and Jane had committed treasonable acts, but was the king any better? He had caused their misery in one way or another. Once Katherine caught the king's eye, she became the focus of his attention. Katherine had never been in that position before. She had been forgotten for most of her life and was naïve to the expectations required of her. The greatest tragedy was that not one of the great ladies of our house stepped in to teach her. Jane lost everything after Anne's downfall. She was willing to do anything to keep her position and, in the end, it cost her her life.

I woke up nauseated after my fitful sleep. After a few minutes of listening to my heaving, Francis rolled over with a sleepy smile on his face. "Per chance this time, it will be a girl."

Oxfordshire, Rotherfield Greys:
February 1542 - March 1544

With no queen to serve I begged Francis to let me return to my son at Rotherfield Greys. He did not want me to leave, but agreed that with our second child on the way he wanted me away from the tension at Court. The roads were dry so the journey was not long, but it seemed like an eternity to me knowing my son was waiting at the end.

Francis's brother met me at the gate, a grin on his face. When we reached the manor I leapt from the carriage.

"Harry!" I called out. "Where is my boy?"

"Taking his supper, I suppose. He is a strapping young man now," he replied with a laugh.

Wasting no time I ran straight to the nursery. I did not want to frighten him, so I contained my excitement at the door and made a quiet entrance. He was at his nurse's breast. She was gently rocking him, humming a lullaby. The nurse made a motion to stop, but I waved her off. "Let him finish", I mouthed.

I sat in the doorway and lovingly watched them until he was satisfied. The nurse wiped his mouth and stood him up, kneeling over him. Holding his hands with her fingers she helped him toddle over to me. I knelt down to pick him up and was overcome with happiness. I held him close, taking in the scent of milk and skin. He put his pudgy hand to my lips and I kissed his palm. He giggled in response. I brushed my lips against his silky hair. It had darkened to the dark brown of his father's. I breathed in the smell of home. I hoped that the king would refrain from another marriage so I would not have to leave this beautiful baby boy again.

Spring and summer flew by though I tried to relish every moment. I finally got to reap the benefits of the glorious garden I had planned during my last visit. We had sweet grapes, juicy peaches and ripe red berries. The bellflower was in bloom and the roses were beginning to open. Little Harry and I spent the afternoons outside when the weather was fair. He loved to go to the wheelhouse to feed the donkey. My evenings were lonely. Henry tried his best to be good company, but he could never be a substitute for his brother. I missed Francis.

In the middle of August, my mother came to assist me in my confinement. This time, it was more miserable than before. The heat was suffocating. I begged her to put out the fire, but she insisted. Without Matilda, who was ill back at Rochford Hall, Mother was more stubborn than usual and insisted on taking every precaution. My pains were right on time and, blessedly, the labour was much shorter. Francis was right in his prediction. We had a sweet baby girl. Once she had been washed and fed and I was up, my mother brought her in. She was graced with fair skin and almond-shaped eyes. A thick down of dark hair on her perfect head. She favoured the Boleyn side.

"She looks just as George did when he was born," cooed my mother as she held out her finger and the baby instinctively grasped it in her tiny hands.

I laughed. "Well, we cannot name such a beautiful girl George!"

"No, I don't suppose we can now, can we?"

I reached for my mother's hand. "We shall call her Mary for her grandmother."

Mother leaned over and kissed my cheek.

Francis had entered the House of Commons for Horsham that year and was unable to come home for Mary's birth. Once the roads had cleared from the January storms, he made haste to see his family. When he arrived I did not wait for him to settle in. Instead we spent the afternoon making love before the fire. That night a storm kicked up and while the rain pounded against the windows and the wind howled outside, I was wrapped in the safety of Francis's arms.

The king had not yet remarried so Francis reassured me that I could stay at home with the children. I knew it was a difficult decision for him.

"As much as I miss you being at Court with me, I can see your happiness. You have grown lovelier since I saw you last and while I would love our time together, it is much safer for you to be in the country. The nobles are warring and no one knows the king's mind from one day to the next. Today he is burning Catholics, but tomorrow he will be burning reformers." He sighed.

I gazed into his rich hazel eyes. "Which side are you?"

He caressed my face, "I do not know, Catherine. I have grown up in the Catholic church, but their abuses are many and they cannot continue. Every man should have access to the Bible and the king should lead his people in religious matters. Why should he be controlled by a pope who knows nothing of our people? I have not declared myself but, in most matters, I have aligned myself with the Earl of Hertford. But I don't want you to think of this now, Catherine. Concentrate on running our household with Henry and spend your days with our little Harry and Mary. The king has already set his eyes on Lady Latimer and it will not be long before I call you back to Court."

I let his words wash over me. My husband was becoming a Protestant whether he was ready to admit it or not. My Boleyn family was full of reformers so the idea was not entirely foreign to me, but we were still Catholics. We believed in the Holy Sacraments, but we wanted our priests and abbeys to be free of tarnish. I did not know how I felt about reading the Bible and the king being head of the church, but those ideas were not for me to decide. I would follow Francis on whatever path he chose.

When the king finally married Lady Latimer, I was not at Court because after Francis's visit, I was yet again with child. In April, Francis sent word that my stepfather, Stafford, had been sent to Fleet Prison with John and Thomas Clere for eating meat on Good Friday. They were released in May, but I knew it was a sign that Stafford was making his allegiances known. I wanted desperately to ask my mother about it, but she took ill and on 19th July, my mother's soul left this world. I spent the next days in despair. I had no desire but to sleep, so I took to my bed. On the fourth day I opened my eyes to see Francis sitting quietly beside me.

His face was etched with concern. "Catherine, you need to rejoin us. Our children need you and the one in your belly needs you to eat. You have grieved long enough."

He was right and though I was not ready, I forced myself out of bed. I had my mourning gown taken out by our tailor and I wore it for the rest of my pregnancy. My brother inherited Rochford Hall and could not stand to turn out Matilda after all she had done to serve our family, so she came to Greys Court. I was relieved to have her with me for my third confinement. While she could never replace my mother, she was a welcome reminder of her.

My pains came during a November snow-storm and for the first time in three confinements I was grateful for the fire dancing in the hearth. This labour was difficult and not even the midwife's spoon could help ease the pain. I spent hours kneeling on the birthing mattress grunting in pain, willing my baby to come out. When, after a day of labouring, the baby was failing to make its entrance, the midwife decided to check to see if it was breech. As expected, "I feel the feet and no head," was the reply from under my shift.

The midwife reached her arm in as far as she could to turn the baby. It felt as though my insides were being ripped apart. I screamed in pain, but it was only another hour or two once the baby was righted.

"It is a bonny girl!" cried the midwife as she caught my baby in her arms.

I fell back on to the mattress and the world went black.

"Catherine! Catherine!"

I was being shaken awake. I opened my eyes and Matilda came into focus.

"Catherine, Francis is here. We sent for him as soon as the baby came."

I tried to scramble into a sitting position, but my body would not co-operate. Defeated, I stayed on my back.

Matilda smoothed back my hair. "You have lost a lot of blood, so I need you to lie still and be calm. I will bring your husband in."

I watched her backside bustle out of the room. A few minutes later she reappeared with Francis at her heels.

He sat next to the bed and gripped my hand. "How do you fare, my love?"

"Exhausted," I exhaled.

He smiled. "Our daughter is quite the tyrant, screaming her head off, red-faced with wild ginger hair. She is a Tudor if ever I've seen one."

I squeezed his arm. "Shush now! Do not let anyone hear that!"

He laughed, "I named her for my mother. We shall call her Lettice and hope it influences her disposition. Maybe she will inherit her sweet countenance."

"I pray she does, dearest Francis, I pray she does," I murmured, falling back to sleep in my depleted state.

Winter passed and snow melted away, taking with it all my excuses for remaining at Greys Court. I had healed well and all my functions had returned. Lettice was healthy and thriving. Like her grandfather, the king, she was very demanding, but her smile could brighten the room. She was certainly keeping her nurses busy. Harry was full of new words and learning every day. His tutor spoke highly of his precociousness. Mary was my quiet girl. Not yet two, she spent much of her day watching me sew or read. She liked to be near me at all times and as often as she could, would climb into my lap and rest her little head at my breast. I hated to leave them, but I was being summoned back to Court to serve my new queen and it was time I returned to my wifely duties.

London, Westminster and Hampton Court: March to August 1544

In March, I went back to Court. The new queen, Katheryn Parr, was everything Katherine Howard was not. Gracious and humble, she welcomed me into her household. While Katherine Howard would pay no great attention to religious matters, this new queen was well-versed. Her ladies were expected to read the Bible along with their sewing and cards. The king's daughters, Mary and Elizabeth, had been restored to the succession earlier in the year and were now often at Court.

My main duty was to serve the Lady Elizabeth while she was at Court. It was during this time that I got to know the young lady who was called my cousin. Elizabeth enjoyed all the celebrations, music and dancing her father had to offer, but she was a studious young lady in the queen's rooms. She spent much of her time buried in her Bible and translating pieces written by the queen and others into several different languages. Her Latin was impeccable.

One afternoon, with the sun streaming in through the windows, Elizabeth sat hunched over her desk writing furiously on a piece of parchment. Her face was flushed red with exertion, tendrils of fire-red hair slipped out from under her hood.

"My lady, may I ask at what you are labouring so?" I asked as I set a silver platter of sweet comfits down on her desk.

Elizabeth looked up at me, her dark eyes flashing, and for a moment I was reminded of her mother, my Aunt Anne. She sat back and said excitedly, "It is Calvin! His book *Institutes of the Christian Religion*. He has only just written it three years ago and I am translating it into English for my father. Do you think he shall be pleased?"

I looked at her thoughtfully. She was considered a bastard, but she was still a royal, so it would not be in good prudence to disagree with the child of the king. Alternatively, she was a novice at court intrigues and the fact that she was so taken with Calvin was not likely to be something that the king would be pleased with. He detested Lutherans and anyone associated with them. He would not consider John Calvin suitable reading for his daughter.

Looking at Elizabeth's face was like looking beyond the grave. She had her father's nose and red hair, but her eyes and lips were all Anne. Elizabeth and I shared blood and I could not let her suffer for her innocence. Finally, I replied cautiously. "My lady, I think Calvin may be a bit radical for your father's tastes. Is there nothing else you can translate for him?"

Her pink tongue worked at the corner of her mouth while she contemplated this. Eventually, she set down her quill. "I suppose you are right. I had not thought of that in my excitement. Perhaps I should translate my lady the queen's *Prayers and Meditations*. Do you think he would find that better suited?"

I had not read the queen's work, but I knew her religious persuasion. It was likely that her work showed her Protestant tendencies, but I was certain that the king would have read it already and no harm had come to her, so I supposed that a much better alternative.

I gave Elizabeth a calming smile, "I think that would be perfect, my lady. Not only an excellent gift for your father, but I am certain the queen will be touched by your gesture."

Elizabeth grinned, "I do hope you are right."

She picked up the parchment and started to crumple it, but then she thought better of it. She laid it back down on the table and smoothed it with her hand, taking care not to smear the ink. She stared at it thoughtfully, then folded it and tucked it into one of her books.

I was stepping far beyond my place, but I took it upon myself after that day to watch out for Elizabeth. I advised her when it was prudent and listened closely for any words that were spoken against

her. She was a very intelligent young lady and learned the ways of
Court very quickly, but she had spent most of her life under the
care of Lady Bryan far from the court at Hatfield. Being amongst
her father's councillors would be a lesson in discretion and I would
do all that I could to protect her. She may not know it, but she was
my sister and it was my duty.

The king had set up the court at Westminster to plot against
the Scots. King James had been killed at Solway Moss in 1542
and his baby girl, Mary Stuart, was on the throne. My father, the
king, ever keen to take advantage, tried and failed to convince the
Scots to join Mary in marriage to little Prince Edward. In May,
after being rebuffed, he sent the Earl of Hertford and Nan Basset's
brother, now Viscount Lisle, to Edinburgh to attack. "Mark my
words," said Francis, "this is just the beginning."

Almost as soon as Hertford and Lisle were back from Scotland,
the king was already itching to bring France to heel for their aid
to his enemies. He spent the next month fortifying and preparing
an army to set siege to Boulogne. In an act that had not been seen
since his first wife Catherine of Aragon's time, he made the queen
regent in his absence. It seemed he had finally found a trustworthy
queen.

The men departed on 11th July, taking my stepfather and
husband with them. I tried in vain to withhold my sobbing the
night before Francis left, but I was terrified. Not only could I lose
the man I loved so wholeheartedly, but I would be at the mercy of
the king if my husband was killed in battle. He comforted me and
we spent the night wrapped in each other's arms, holding on for
dear life.

In the morning I knelt on the bed behind Francis and embraced
him from behind. I could feel the heat from his naked back through
my shift. I trailed light kisses along his freshly shaved jaw line. "I
will be waiting for your swift return, my love," I whispered in his
ear.

He turned and kissed me full on the mouth pushing me back onto the bed. "I certainly hope so, Mistress Knollys," he murmured into my hair. It was another hour before he attempted to leave again, but this time, he had to go. I bid him good luck and blew him a kiss goodbye. After the door shut behind him, I buried myself under the blanket and cried.

With the king on the battlefield, the queen felt it prudent to call Prince Edward to Court. He and his sisters lodged with us at Hampton Court. The queen took to her task with gusto. She met with the councillors late into the night and insisted they confer with her before making any decisions. The queen's hand was in every detail of the king's campaign, from musters and finances to making sure provisions were sent when needed. She issued royal proclamations and was in contact with Lord Shrewsbury in Wales, keeping apprised of the situation in Scotland.

The king returned in September after his victory in Boulogne to a stable kingdom and a queen much buffeted by self-confidence. Francis returned to find a wife greatly expanding with child. It seemed that with this pregnancy my belly was eager to show off. Shortly after my first missed courses I was having my skirts let out.

"Catherine, my lovely wife," Francis called to me as he entered our rooms. "What a goodly belly you have made for me," he said kneeling down to kiss my protruding stomach.

"Yes, we are quite the fertile pair!" I laughed, giving him my hand to rise up from the floor.

"Of course, just as I get home from campaign, you will be leaving me again," he sighed, a twinkle in his eyes.

"As long as the weather stays fair, I think I would like to stay another month or so."

Francis swept me into his arms and planted a kiss on my lips. "I think I should like that too."

Oxfordshire, Rotherfield Greys:
October 1544 - July 1545

I arrived at Greys Court to find my children crowded into the hall to greet me. Little Harry had grown to my waist and was full of stories about his uncle Henry teaching him to ride the ponies. Mary, almost in her second year, tugged at my skirts. I bent over and picked her up. She buried her face in my neck, thumb in her mouth. Lettice, held in her nurse's arms, shook her little fist and demanded more milk with a shrill cry. I let out a little laugh. "How wonderful to see you all, my little family."

Henry nonchalantly wandered into the hall. He was eating an apple, little more than the core remained, but as he approached, he gave me a small nod. "Welcome home."

I smiled and, with Mary in tow, wrapped him into a hug.

Harry and I spent the autumn months playing in the yellow and brown leaves and as the weather turned colder and the snow began to fall, we moved indoors and spent our days before the fire. Harry played with his wooden toys and I took turns rocking Mary and Lettice. I went into confinement in the first weeks of January. Francis had come home for Christmas celebrations but then headed back to Court to take up his new duties as master of the horse to the prince. He was delighted with his new appointment and I was filled with pride when he told me.

My pains came with the rain squalls in mid-March, and just two weeks before Easter I gave birth to our second son. Francis and I decided to name him William for William Carey and William Stafford. It was our fourth baby in as many years. Our marriage was proving to be a fruitful one.

London, Greenwich:
August 1545 - March 1546

"Welcome back to Court, Mistress Knollys," the queen greeted me on my return to her service. She smiled brightly and gestured to the gathered ladies. "I trust you remember Ladies Herbert, Lane and Denny?"

They all three stepped out and gave me small nods. I smiled my assent.

"Yes, of course, Your Grace. I am pleased to see you all again."

The queen nodded and turned, going back to her books and conversation.

Nan Bassett sidled up beside me, "What was that all about?"

I shook my head, "I don't know. Are those her favourites now?"

"Looks like you are the next to be one."

Nan and I exchanged nervous laughs and hugged. We made our way to the window embrasure to discuss my children and the events I had missed in my confinement.

Later that night I told Francis about the greeting I received from the queen and her ladies. His face reddened.

"That would have been my doing."

I raised my brow and asked, "Any particular reason?"

Francis sat down heavily on the bed next to me and kicked off his boots.

"Those are the queen's favourites and they are secret reformers. Their husbands and I are working together to help the Earl of Hertford's cause. I wanted you to befriend them and learn all you can. The Duchess of Suffolk has been doing much to further the cause as well, even though her husband will never support it. We are on the rise and refuse to let the Bishop of Rome gain foothold in England again."

I sat back against the pillows and out of habit, rested my hand on stomach. I felt it starting to churn. I had returned to a Court in full faction war. How long before this queen came to an end for her meddling in religious affairs?

Nan and I sat in the courtyard. I was mending shirts for Francis and she was quilting a counterpane for her sister, who was still at Richmond serving Anne of Cleves. As we chatted I felt a warm hand on my shoulder. Nan stifled a smile. I turned to see my brother, Henry, standing behind me. I jumped up, dropping Francis's shirt to the ground.

"Henry!" I shouted, wrapping my arms around him.

He awkwardly patted me on the back. "No need to shout, sister."

I stepped back and looked him over. He had grown since I last saw him at my wedding. He was wearing matching burgundy doublet and hose in material finer than I had ever seen him in.

"You have gone formal on me," I chided him, fingering the velvet of his doublet.

He gave a slight nod. "I am a married man now and serve the king with my stepfather and brother-in-law, I need to set a good example."

I grinned. "Is your wife come to Court, Henry? When shall I meet her?

"She is settling in at Rochford Hall, making it our home." Then he looked down at the ground. "It's a fine manor, but I would give it back in a moment if it would bring Mother back."

I reached out and rubbed his arm.

"Oh Henry, please do not feel guilty. We both miss her but she is reunited with our family." I pinched his nose and leaned in to whisper, "And it is a far better place than this foul Court."

Henry allowed a stiff smile, "Don't let your father hear that or you will be following her."

I replied boldly, "Let him try. So when will we expect some nieces and nephews?" I proudly patted my now flat stomach. "Is this new wife as fertile as I am?"

"Soon, sister. It has been wonderful to see you and I hope to spend more time with you now that I am at Court. I must take my leave now, the king will be expecting me."

"Of course." I gave him a slight bow and watched him walk away.

I turned to Nan. "He is so stiff now. He has always been serious, but never this much."

Nan chuckled. "He has grown up now, Catherine. He is handsome too. Too bad he is already married."

"Nan!" I exclaimed. She gave me a devious look. I shook my head, "You are insufferable. Your family had better find you a husband soon."

I had not been at Court for a month when word came that the Duke of Suffolk had passed away. The king was inconsolable. Charles Brandon had been his best friend since before the king had been crowned. I knew it was only a matter of time before the king would follow him. He was becoming corpulent. Gone was the strident young man who could challenge anyone on the tennis courts or in the jousting lists. In his place was a man who had to be carried through the palace on a lift. He was no longer jovial or charming. Everyone came under suspicion. Our 'Golden Prince' was gone.

My stepfather, Stafford, was knighted that autumn for his services in Scotland. I was ecstatic for him. He looked so handsome and knightly at his creation and I wished that Mother had been there to see it.

At New Year, the Lady Elizabeth gave the king a translation of the queen's book *Prayers and Meditations*. Her face looked so hopeful when she presented it to her father as a gift, but I could see his face redden as he flipped through the work. He looked sideways at the queen, but she just smiled serenely, hiding any fear she might have felt. It was becoming increasingly dangerous to have opinions on religion that did not come from His Majesty.

Then in February, a woman named Anne Askew was arrested as a heretic. Francis told me that during her interrogation she named the queen as a Protestant. The king ordered her tortured, but she refused to implicate the queen again. Tensions were high and I was relieved when the month came and went without my courses. I could go back to Greys Court and leave this tangled drama behind.

Oxfordshire, Rotherfield Greys:
April 1546 - January 1547

I had left the court just in time. In July, as the mangled body of Anne Askew was being dragged out to the stake, her body having been racked until she could no longer walk, an arrest warrant was issued for the queen. Queen Katheryn had made the mistake of quarrelling with the king over something in the Bible in front of the leading Catholic at Court, Bishop Gardiner. Gardiner then delighted in whispering poison against the Queen into the king's ear.

Francis told me later: "Fortunately for her, someone dropped the bill of articles against her outside the door to her rooms and she was alerted to the plot. In her fit of terror, the king sent his doctor Mr Wendy and he convinced her to beg the king for his forgiveness. The next day she came into the king's rooms and threw herself on his mercy. Of course, he never truly wanted to act against her so he forgave her right away and to teach Bishop Gardiner and that little toad, Secretary Wriothesley, a lesson, he neglected to tell them of the queen's escape. When they came to arrest her, he slapped Wriothesley full across the face and yelled 'Knave! Fool! Beast!' They could not scurry from his presence fast enough."

Gales of laughter pealed from us both as we pictured the porcine Wriothesley waddling out of the king's sight. His rise under Secretary Cromwell had been much rewarded, but I still thought he was a weasel.

"Francis," I heaved, breathless from my mirth. "I wish I had been there to see it."

He patted my belly. "But I am so glad you were not. The

reformers were all terrified for the queen. Court has been a frightful place and I am relieved to know you are safe in our home."

I put my finger to his lips and then brought them to mine. After a deep kiss, I asked him, "But are you safe, my love?"

His wary eyes stared into mine. "For you, I will do everything I can to keep myself safe."

And, as promised, he continued to stay in the king's good graces and was promoted to Chief Steward and Keeper of the Courts in August.

My pains came in the autumn, and as the leaves turned red and gold, our baby made his debut. Born on the 12th October, the same day as the prince and on the eve of the feast of St Edward the Confessor, it was only natural that he was named Edward. This labour was easy and the babe came with minimal fuss. He was a fair child with light brown hair and wide emerald green eyes. He took to the nurse's breast the quickest of all my children by far.

Court was at Greenwich for Christmas, but I was not ready to go back. Looking back now I am glad I did not go. The king, was closeted at Whitehall deathly ill. While the court was celebrating our Saviour's birth, my father's closest companions were preparing for his death.

Francis brought news of his passing when he finally came home in February.

"We kept his death a secret for three days while Lord Hertford rode to the prince. He took him straight to Enfield and told both Edward and Elizabeth of their father's death. He sent for Mary and now all three wait at Court for Edward's coronation. It is set for the twentieth of this month and your presence is expected."

I nodded. "Of course, husband. Edward is, after all, my half-brother. I would not miss it for anything."

He traced his fingers down my bare arm. My poor Francis looked exhausted. I hoped that he could come home for a while after the coronation, but I knew that it would not be possible. As uncle to the new king, the Earl of Hertford would be closest to the throne and all the reformers would be at Court working to influence Edward. Francis would be needed.

The next day my maid Matilda and I tore my closet apart looking for a suitable gown for a coronation. We settled on pale blue damask with cloth-of-silver woven through. Matilda went to my jewel box and came back with a pair of sapphire and pearl earrings, a gift from the king when I first came to Court. I sat on my bed and held them in my hand, staring as they sparkled in the light. Maybe if I held them in my hand and prayed hard enough, my father would come back. Inwardly I sighed. I knew that was not possible. The king was not coming back.

I had rarely spoken to the man in all my time at Court. I had served three of his wives, danced at his masques, walked through his gardens and in all that time, we had barely exchanged words. Why did I grieve so? After a while, I realised it was because when I saw the king I knew that I belonged. He looked like my father. We had the same nose and squinty eyes. My golden red locks matched his. I had none of the Boleyn traits and I looked nothing like the Careys. I always knew Stafford was not my father so it was no mystery to me why we looked so different. Until I knew where my appearance came from, I had felt like a stranger, as though I did not belong in my own family. Then I came to Court and saw myself mirrored back in the faces of the king and the Lady Elizabeth. It mattered not whether the king recognised me as his, my eyes did not lie.

The king's death was the end of an era. Now we had an untried child on the throne and a bevy of men crowding around to get their piece of the power. Things had been unstable and changing under Henry, but now they were downright frightening. Francis was thrilled, of course, because Edward had been brought up as a reformer. But I had seen enough at Court to know that the situation was never as straightforward as that. My Uncle Norfolk, the leading Catholic at Court may have been locked in the Tower, but there was always another that would rise in his place. The faction wars would continue and they would get even more volatile with a young, malleable boy on the throne.

The door to my room banged open, startling me out of my reverie. In ran my children. Harry, now a tall boy of six, shouted, "Mama, Uncle Henry says I can help him deliver the new pony when it comes!"

"That will be great fun, Harry," I said smoothing back his hair.

Mary crawled onto my lap. She pulled her thumb out of her mouth just long enough to give me a smile.

"Beautiful girl," I said kissing her on the forehead.

Lettice, entering a most rebellious third year, bounded in with her doll in her hand. "Don't be such a baby Mary! *I* don't suck my thumb any more!" she teased as she crawled up on the bed beside me.

I hugged them both. "Girls, we all grow up in our own time. We each have our own strengths and weaknesses and, above all, we do not tease in this house."

The baby nurse brought in Edward, and William toddled in behind her. I moved Mary from my lap and set her next to me, taking Edward in one arm and William in the other. In that moment, I realised that it did not matter if my father was gone, I would always belong in this house, with the family I had created with Francis. I looked to each of my children and saw how different they were. Each one special and wonderful in their own way, and it occurred to me that I did not have to look like my brother or stepfather. They had loved me anyway.

Part III
A New Era

Like our father before him, King Edward spent the week before his coronation in the Tower. Francis and I stayed at Whitehall with the rest of the court. On the afternoon of 19th February, the young king and his retinue left the Tower of London. Francis was in the procession so I went with Nan Bassett to see the festivities. We traipsed through the streets of London, winter frost crunching underneath our feet. Our layers of velvet and damask warmed us against the biting cold, but our faces were left unprotected. Nan pulled her hand out of her sable stole and covered her nose in a feeble attempt to thaw it. A puff of white breath came out of her mouth and we both laughed.

"Poor King Edward is probably in a worse state than us. Did you see how skinny his legs were? No meat on that young man to warm him. Not like us anyway," she giggled, patting her voluptuous bottom.

"Nan, do not talk of the king's skinny legs!" I chided her.

"He cannot hear me."

I shook my head in mock indignation, but I adored her sense of humour. Nan always brought a sense of levity to a serious situation.

The king's gentleman, chaplains and esquires of the body walked at the head of the procession. My husband and stepfather were among them. As they passed, Nan squeezed my arm and I beamed with delight. When the trumpeters sounded, the nobility made their appearance on horseback. The king followed close behind.

We were close enough to get an excellent view of our new king. He was dressed in snow-white velvet embroidered in silver. Lover's knots with pearls trimmed his doublet along with diamonds and rubies. The jewels sparkled in the afternoon sun and shone so brightly it was as if Edward was surrounded in a holy light. Over it all he wore a golden gown and sable cape to keep out the cold. His fine palfrey was covered in crimson satin and decorated with pearls.

The king was flanked by his uncle Edward Seymour and Nan's brother, John Dudley. Both had been promoted to the peerage and were now the Duke of Somerset and the Earl of Warwick, respectively. As the king's closest councillors they would be the premier nobles now. As the procession wound down the street, Nan and I followed behind. This was likely to be the last coronation we would see in our lifetime and we didn't want to miss a moment of it.

Cheapside was richly decorated to welcome the king. It was obvious that more money had been spent on welcoming the king than its inhabitants had spent on food all winter, and the pageants did not disappoint. My favourite was the tribute to Jane Seymour. A phoenix, which had been her device, descended from the heavens to land on a York and Lancaster rose-covered mount. A crowned lion approached with his cub, and two angels from heaven crowned him. Of course Edward the Confessor made an appearance, that was only to be expected as the king had been named for him. Other tableaux greeted our new monarch as he marched towards Westminster. The conduits ran blood-red with wine.

After we took all the cold we could bear, Nan and I hurried back to the palace, eager to warm ourselves before the fire. We sipped spiced mead and watched the fire dance in the hearth.

I took a sip of my warm mead and turned to Nan. "What shall you do now that there is no queen to serve?"

Nan rocked back and forth silently while she considered her response. "I have been called to serve the Princess Mary and will leave for her household after the coronation festivities are over."

I contemplated this. "I suppose that would be an excellent place for you. She still keeps the old ways and I know your family has always kept to them. She will treat you well."

Nan stopped rocking, "What will you do now, Catherine?"

I replied thoughtfully. "Oh, I am certain I will be with child again soon. It is different for me. I have a house full of children waiting for me back at Greys Court. Besides, you know the princess would never request my services," I lowered my voice, "with my husband being a heretic and all."

Nan snorted. "Yes, well, there is that."

"Francis says that should the king die before he has an heir we should all be in fear for what she will do. But I have known Mary since I came to Court. She may be stubborn but I don't think she would cause harm to anyone. All this fuss over religion. Does it truly matter the way that we worship? I shall never understand."

Nan nodded and said sagely, "It has become a game of power."

She was right. I just prayed that my Francis would not be sacrificed in the struggle.

By the time I woke up the next morning, Francis was gone. I knew it would be another long day and the weather was still just as cold, so I bundled into my pale blue gown and found a sable to match. I dug the sapphire earrings out of my jewellery box and kissed them before placing them on my ears. *If you are listening, Father, I hope you see your son ascend your throne today,* I thought to myself.

The king had come by barge down the frigid Thames from Westminster to gather his robes. We watched him, clad in crimson and ermine, process under a canopy carried by the barons of the Cinque Ports to Westminster Abbey. Lords Dudley, Parr and Seymour carried his train. This time the Seymour uncle was the jovial and dashing Thomas. Francis and Stafford followed behind with the other gentleman of the court.

Nan and I took a carriage to Westminster Abbey. I had never seen it decorated so gloriously. The little king walked stiffly to the dais that held his throne. He was so weighed down in his robes and jewels that it was a wonder he made it there at all. He climbed into that imperious chair that had held all the monarchs before him and I wondered if he felt buffeted by their strength around him.

Thomas Cranmer, the Archbishop of Canterbury, began his sermon. He called on Edward to be like Josiah. The biblical King Josiah ascended the throne at the age of eight and set about reforming his church. Cranmer's insinuation was not lost on us. He was asking Edward to continue his father's efforts to break from Rome and free England from its idolatry.

The service dragged on for hours, but eventually Cranmer produced the imperial crown. In a break with tradition, both Cranmer and the lord protector, the Duke of Somerset, placed it on Edward's head. His thin shoulders sank under the weight. The archbishop anointed him and replaced the cumbersome crown with a lighter one that had been created especially for this occasion. Certain members of the nobility handed Edward the sceptre, orb, St Edward's staff and the spurs. Through it all Edward showed a gravity that belied his tender age. This was the moment he had been preparing for his whole short life. The nobility rose and came before him to kiss him, one by one, on his cheek. The young prince had finally come into his inheritance.

After the ceremony, we walked to the great hall to feast. Edward sat high on the dais surrounded by his liege men. It was Lent so, much like the feast after King Henry's marriage to Anne of Cleves, there was no red meat. Platters of trout, crab and oysters made the rounds, along with pheasant, duck and plover. The subtleties were most impressive. I saw palaces made of delicate sugar, and a dragon of St George in the most vivid shades of green and red.

It was a beautiful day in the tiltyards and the perfect weather for a tournament. Francis would not be participating as he was not a knight, but he would be down in the lists preparing the players, so I enjoyed the show with Nan. We climbed the stands that had been set up and found ourselves a comfortable spot.

The peal of trumpets sounded and we all jumped from our

seats at King Edward's entrance. He still appeared quite small, but this time he was not drowning in robes. He wore a doublet of Tudor green trimmed with ermine. The smaller crown from the coronation service sat on his head and sparkled in the late morning sun. He raised his hand and waved to the courtiers. Someone shouted, "God save the King!" and we all responded, "God Save Good King Edward!" The king clapped his hands together in excitement. The Duke of Somerset put his hand on his shoulder and urged him on.

The king made his way to the diminutive throne that had been set up for him and once he was seated we all followed suit. The knights began their parade. Nan's brother came out first, astride a raven black destrier. He tipped his cap towards us as he rode by and stopped for his wife's favour. Next, came the king's other uncle, Thomas Seymour, now Baron Sudeley. Thomas rode a snow-white destrier and, as he came closer to us, he held out his lance to Nan. She giggled shyly and glanced at me.

I sighed. "Well, grant him your favour."

She pulled off a scarf that was tied to her wrist and attached it quickly to Seymour's lance. He gave her a wink and finished his round.

"What was that about?" I asked her.

She flushed. "Lord Sudeley is quite charming. I am sure it was just a mere flirtation."

My eyes followed Seymour as he rode out of the arena. "Yes, I am sure it was."

The afternoon flew by in a rush of lance slivers and flashes of armour. Thomas Seymour won the day and it greatly pleased the king. He was honoured at the banquet that night with a seat next to him on the royal dais. Somerset seemed very annoyed. He spent the evening glaring at his brother and monopolising the conversation with the king.

The dowager queen had moved to her new home at Chelsea so there was no need for me to stay on at Court, but Francis desired my company so I obliged him. The Princess Elizabeth left shortly after the celebrations to go back to her studies at Hatfield. The night before she left I went to visit her rooms to bid her farewell. As I left my bedchamber, I grabbed a small trinket from my jewellery box.

Elizabeth's rooms had been cleaned already. The scent of sage in the fresh rushes greeted me in the doorway. Her back was to me, so I knocked lightly on the door to avoid startling her. She spun around. "Mistress Knollys, you startled me! I wasn't expecting any visitors."

"I came to say goodbye. I will miss seeing you at Court. It has always been a pleasure to serve you during your visits."

"Thank you. I have enjoyed our time together as well." She considered me thoughtfully, "You know I often forget that we are cousins. No one ever talks about my mother."

She plopped down on her bed and sighed. Her legs swung back and forth, just brushing the rushes below her feet. After a few moments of silence, she asked, "Do you miss your children when you are at Court, Mistress Knollys?"

"Please call me Catherine, my lady. Yes, I miss them very much. I wonder how they have grown and what they are learning. I want to tuck them into bed at night and kiss their little cheeks."

She nodded her head. "Yes, I suppose mothers do want to do those things."

I shook my head. "No, not all mothers do, but I do. I feel like my children are a part of me and I miss them as I would miss a part of myself. But not all mothers feel the same way."

She sat in silence, rubbing the toe of her shoe against the heel of the other. Finally she asked, "Mistress - I mean - Catherine, do you suppose my mother would have liked to do those things?" She looked at me hopefully.

I held out my hand, offering it to her. She put her hand in mine. Her fingers were gracefully long and her milky skin was smooth to the touch. They were warm despite the chill in the air.

"Of course I think your mother would have loved to do those things. She loved you very much. I don't know a lot about her, but I do know that. My mother told me how she would visit you at your household at every opportunity. And your wardrobe! She wanted you to have the best pieces and the latest fashions, though you were not old enough to do much more than mess yourself in them." We both chuckled heartily at my remark.

"Catherine, will you tell me what you remember about her?" she asked earnestly.

I searched my memory. "She despised monkeys, I know that. The old queen, Catherine, had a monkey that Anne could not abide, but she did enjoy other animals. She had an adorable puppy named Purkoy that she loved. When she was pregnant with you she craved apples. She loved to dance and, oh, how she loved music. She made such beautiful music on her lute. Your mother was intelligent, well-read and she had the best sense of humour, but she had such a temper."

Elizabeth grinned. "Thank you so much for sharing that with me."

"Of course, my lady." I brushed a tendril of hair from her eyes. "You have her eyes. You look like a Tudor in everything else, but you got your eyes and lips from her."

Those deep brown eyes lit up. "Really?"

"Yes, really."

She stood up from her bed and looked sadly around the room. "I wish we could keep talking, but I have to get ready to go back to Hatfield now. Thank you for all the kindness you have shown me."

I stood up and pulled the trinket out of the small bag I had tied to my girdle. I placed it gently in Elizabeth's hand, closing her fingers around it.

"Keep this with you always. My mother gave it to me and now it is yours." I said.

She looked down and stared at the miniature of her mother, tracing her fingers across the picture.

She looked up at me with tears in her eyes and said, "I will treasure it always."

After serving three queens, I found it rather nice to live at my own pace. Not needing to be in the queen's rooms by a certain hour meant that I could come and go as I pleased. While Francis tended to his duties, I spent my afternoons walking in the gardens at Whitehall, practising my horsemanship in the park, and curling up next to the fire with my embroidery. At night, Francis and I loved made love like newly-weds. I was finally able to give him all my attention.

In March, Lord Chancellor Wriothesley was arrested and forced to resign his post. Francis informed me that it was because he refused to affix the Great Seal to the letters patent naming Somerset lord protector. Lord Rich was appointed in his stead and now Somerset was the most powerful man in England after the king. Francis was pleased that his ally was rising at Court, but he fretted over Somerset's increasing greed and arrogance.

The king and Somerset's men set about destroying the last of the Catholic icons. Royal agents stormed the churches smashing statues of the Virgin Mary and Jesus, breaking out the stained-glass windows depicting Jesus's miracles and making off with the church's goods.

In July the turmoil peaked. After a secret courtship, Thomas Seymour and the dowager queen were married at her home in Chelsea. The king and Somerset were enraged. "How dare she marry? My father is hardly cold in his grave!" I heard the young king shout as I passed by his presence chamber.

I too believed she may have married in haste, but secretly I was pleased for her. It had been obvious to all of us that she had been in love with Seymour for a very long time. Her marriage to my father had been fraught with danger and I hoped she had finally found happiness.

Soon enough, all was forgiven. England was going to war with the Scots and Seymour was a gifted soldier. His skill and experience were desperately needed.

As Francis and I lay side-by-side, I gazed lovingly into his eyes. I cupped his cheek in my palm and kissed him. "Are you ready for another child, my love?" I asked him.

He pulled me closer to him and kissed my shoulder. "My home is blessed. I am so pleased to hear you are with child. It makes the news I had earlier so much easier to take."

I pulled back in alarm. "What news?"

"I am to go with Somerset's army to Scotland. They will not agree to the marriage treaty between our king and Mary Stuart. The king is sending Somerset to bring them to heel. Our army departs next week."

I raised his hand to my lips. "I trust in God to keep you safe and will pray for you and your success on your journey."

Francis raised his eyebrow. "No tears this time?"

I closed my eyes and shook my head.

"I am slightly disappointed," he said, chuckling.

I snuggled into him. "I shall make it up to you upon your return."

Oxfordshire, Rotherfield Greys:
September 1547 - December 1549

The carriage ride back to Greys Court was miserable. We had an early autumn rainstorm only an hour into our journey. Fat, cold droplets of water pounded the wooden plank roof of the carriage and seeped into the cracks on the floor. The roads were filled with ruts and every time the wheels hit one, I bounced against the seat. I had yet to be sick with this child and was relieved to think I would get away this time, but the ride proved me wrong and before long we were stopping at the side of the road until I could control my heaving.

The driver came around the back to check on me. I was bent over spitting out the last of supper from last night.

"My lady, are you sure you can continue in this condition?"

I looked up, wiping my mouth. "Thank you for your concern, but I am desperate to see my children. I will be fine. We can continue in just a moment."

He gave a small nod. "As you wish, my lady."

We arrived at Greys Court a few hours later and after a small ale and some sleep, I felt much better. I awoke to the patter of tiny feet running past my closed door and for a moment lay awake in my bed listening to the giggling of my children. I felt so content to be home again.

I got out of bed and tiptoed quietly across the room. I threw open the door and shouted, "Caught you!"

A little voice squealed with delight. I stepped through the doorway. "Where have my lovely children gone?" I called out.

More giggles and then Lettice's golden red curls bobbed in the doorway down the hall. She peeked out. "Mother!" She broke into a run and slammed head first into my waist. I wrapped my arms around her and lifted her to my hip.

"You are getting entirely too big for me to lift, young lady!"

She wriggled around. "Then put me down!" she cried indignantly.

"As you wish," I said, lowering her to the ground.

She turned to blow me a kiss and then scampered off in search of her brothers and sister.

I slipped my shoes back on, adjusted my hood and made my way downstairs. Two of my children were sitting before the hearth with their tutor. Harry was hunched over his work. His hair was falling into his eyes and I had to restrain myself from brushing it away. Mary sat curled up in the chair, dozing. Her thumb was wedged in her mouth and every time it slipped out she would startle and push it back in. Lettice had not yet returned. She was probably off causing trouble for her nurse. I hung back and watched this domestic scene.

I prayed nightly for my husband's success in Scotland, but I secretly hoped that the Scottish queen would not be sent right away. I had been home only hours and was already dreading my return to Court.

I waited on edge for word from Scotland. Each time a visitor rode up on horseback I anxiously paced by the door waiting for Henry to come in with news, and each time Henry shook his head I went back to fretting. Finally, near the end of the month, Henry came back in with a smile. He held up the wrinkled roll of parchment for all of us to see. "We won! We defeated the Scots! God save King Edward!"

I lunged at Henry and wrapped him in a hug.

"My lady!" he called out, shocked.

Quickly I stepped back; I could feel the heat rising to my face.

"My apologies," I said, mortified. "I was just so relieved for Francis's safety that I did not think."

Henry broke into a laugh, "Oh why not? We are both relieved." He wrapped his arms around me and we both breathed a sigh of relief.

Francis arrived home a week later. He was caked in mud and though he got off his horse easily he was walking with a slight limp. I ran out to greet him. Not caring about the mud, I threw myself into his arms and plied him with kisses.

"Sweet Francis, I am so glad you came home to me. I prayed every night for you."

He squeezed me tighter and I smelled the smoke and dirt seeping from his skin. I pulled him into the house and, while the children attacked him from all sides, I called for a tub to be set before the fire in our room so he could bathe. The children chattered excitedly, shoving each other aside so each could be the centre of his attention. Francis, trying so hard to be gracious and show interest, gave me a weary look.

I clapped my hands together. "All right children. Let's give your father some room to breathe and a chance to get cleaned up. I am certain he will be most happy to spend some time with you all once he has had a bath and a nap. Now, run along and let Uncle Henry know that your father is home."

Francis sighed as the children scattered into the hallway looking for their uncle. "I feel terrible. I have not seen them in so long."

I put my hand on his arm. "No. Don't do that. Rest first. You have been on the battlefield. The children will understand."

We climbed the stairs to our room and for a passing moment I wished I had laid fresh rushes, but we had no warning when he would arrive so the ones out would have to do. The fire was roaring and the heat filled the room. A tub full of boiled water waited for Francis and he smiled in anticipation when he saw it. I helped him untie his doublet and remove his hose, pausing to look him over for wounds. I breathed a sigh of relief when the only mark I saw was a scabbed over cut on his shoulder. I traced the raised line with my finger and then kissed it. I stood behind him with my arms wrapped around his waist, my belly pressed into his back. I laid my cheek on his shoulder and breathed in the scent of his skin.

Francis placed his hands on top of mine and we stood there in an embrace until a movement from my belly startled him.

"She kicked you!" I laughed.

Francis turned to me and grinned. "How do you know it is a she?"

I led him to the bath. "I don't know. It is just a feeling that I have."

He climbed in carefully, favouring his right leg. As he slid into the water, he closed his eyes and gave a groan of pleasure. I set to work scrubbing his back and arms, massaging them as I went along. The muscles had grown tense and firm, his skin browned from the sun.

"Tell me of the battle," I asked after he had finally relaxed.

He kept his eyes closed while he recounted his journey.

"When we got to Scotland, we occupied Fawside Hill. The Earl of Home led a small army of men to our encampment and challenged an equal number of us to fight. Somerset did not want to engage him, but eventually he gave in and allowed Lord Grey to lead our men. We defeated them in the skirmish and pursued them for three miles. That wiped out most of the Earl of Arran's cavalry."

He paused for a moment and then went on as if he were reliving the experience. "Somerset sent a group over to the slopes to monitor the Scots' position. During the night, Arran not only challenged Somerset to a duel but when he was rebuffed he proposed that twenty of our champions fight twenty of his to settle the matter. Somerset refused. In the morning we regrouped with the detachment at the slopes and learned that Arran was advancing towards us. Our ships fired on them from the left and our cavalry attacked on the right. The Scottish pikemen were skilled and inflicted many casualties. Poor Lord Grey was stabbed with a pike in his throat, but we got him to the surgeon in time and he was saved. Unfortunately for the Scots, we had them surrounded on all sides and they began to retreat. Many who were not felled by our weapons drowned in the Esk in their haste to abandon the battlefield."

Francis shook his head at the memory of it. His face crumpled. I laid his head against my breast, the water from his hair soaking my bodice.

"The river ran red with blood. I had seen nothing like it before in my life. Not even in Boulogne. We lost few men, but the Scots lost many and all for their pride. It makes sense for the king to marry their queen. It would unite our kingdoms. But they refuse to give in."

We stared at the fire, watching it dance in the hearth, the silence heavy between us. I ran my fingers through his hair and then kissed him softly on the forehead.

"Your water is getting cold. Let's get you dried off before you catch your sickness."

Francis nodded his assent and stood up, gingerly lifting his foot out of the tub. He stood still as I dried him off. After a moment, he tipped my chin and kissed me deeply. I could feel him growing against my thigh.

I quivered. "Francis, the baby..."

He pulled back. "You're right. I am so sorry. I just missed your touch."

I pulled him back to me. "I want more than anything to lie with you."

"Soon my love. You must keep my little girl safe."

He leaned down and kissed my belly just as the baby decided to kick again.

"See, Maude agrees," he laughed.

"Maude?"

"It just fits. Do not ask why, a father just knows."

I playfully swatted his arm, "I think it is time for that nap."

The afternoon sun bathed the nursery in a warm orange glow. I sat in the rocking chair, Edward wedged in the crook of my arm.

I brushed his silky hair with my hand, coiling a ringlet of his fawn coloured hair around my finger. I leaned forward and breathed in the scent of warm milk and that sweetness that seems to emanate from all babies. I rocked Edward back and forth in time to his rhythmic breathing. He was lost in the land of dreams. He pursed his red rosebud lips and sucked for a moment, as though he was taking nourishment from an imaginary breast. I stared at him in wonder.

The sound of boots disturbed my maternal bliss. I looked up to see Francis and Henry standing in the doorway. I raised my finger to my lips and gave them both a warning look. Francis nodded and led Henry out of the room. Within moments, Edward's nurse was bustling in, untying her bodice as she made her way towards me. She bent over to lift Edward out of my arms and one of her bulbous breasts escaped its moorings. It swung like a pendulum before my face. In one swift movement she lifted Edward and latched him on to her breast. She gave me a small curtsey and sat in the other chair.

I walked into the hall and saw Francis and Henry leaning next to each other against the wall, matching grins on their faces.

I was surprised at the change in Francis's demeanour and relieved that his nap seemed to have restored his good humour. "You two look rather pleased with yourselves. May I ask what was so important that you felt the need to burst into the nursery?"

Francis stood up straight and beckoned Henry and I. "I have news."

We followed him to the hall and Henry and I sat at the great table looking at him expectantly.

Francis looked at me, then at Henry. Finally, with a great flourish, he announced, "I have been knighted."

I leapt out of my chair and threw my arms around him. Henry slapped him on the back.

"That is wonderful news, husband," I said. "Why didn't you tell me before?"

Francis flushed. "I wanted to tell you and Henry together."

Henry grinned. "Well, tell us about it!"

"It was after the battle in Scotland. The lord protector, Duke of Somerset, knighted me in front of the whole company for my bravery. It was one of the proudest moments of my life."

His eyes were shining and I sensed he was trying to contain his emotions.

"Well then, henceforth you shall be *Sir* Francis," teased Henry, falling into an exaggerated bow.

Francis shook his head, but he was still grinning. "All right brother, time to get back to work. Catherine, my love, please see about dinner. I would like to celebrate with a stag tonight."

I kissed him on the cheek and whispered, "I am so proud of you."

Francis stayed at home for another month to ready the property for winter and then headed back to London before the weather turned bad. By the first snow-fall, my belly had outgrown my skirts and we decided that it was best I stay at home until the baby was born. Christmas was quiet as Francis was gone to Court, but we tried to muster as much cheer as possible for New Year. We sent a gold cup to the young king. After the festivities I took to my bed in my confinement. I spent the time enjoying the warmth of the fire, reading and sewing by its light. I found myself exhausted with this pregnancy. No matter how much I slept I was still drowsy, often nodding off with my needle in my hand.

In the middle of March my labour began. This labour was different from any other. The pains were not nearly as strong, but it seemed to go on forever. After two days, the midwife determined that this baby, like Lettice, was breech. She reached in to try to turn the baby while I writhed in pain. After a few tries, she sighed and sat back on her heels.

"I am sorry, my lady, but the cord is wrapped around your baby's neck, I cannot turn it."

My panic threatened to overtake me. "Are you certain? What can we do? Is my baby all right?"

The midwife sounded defeated. "I don't know, my lady. All you can do is push. I need you to bear down and push with all of your might."

The midwife and my maid, Matilda, helped me into a crouched position. I held on to Matilda for stability and pushed as hard as I could. After an hour, I felt the baby's foot emerge. I gritted my teeth and gave another push. My groin was on fire and I was certain I would lose consciousness. One more push and the baby's limp body slithered out. The midwife tried to turn from me when she lifted the baby from between my legs, but I caught a glimpse of her blue face. I snatched my baby from her arms and unravelled the cord from her neck.

"No!" I screamed. "No! You cannot die!" I began slapping the baby's bottom and after a few dreadful moments I heard the sharp intake of breath and then a wail. I groaned and then fell back onto the birthing mattress, cradling the baby against my bare chest to bring warmth to her skin. Only after the child stopped crying did I look to see the sex. Francis had been right, she was a girl.

"Oh Maude," I let out a relieved sigh. "You frightened me."

The last thing I remember is the freckle-spotted milky white face of Meg, our newest wet nurse, coming towards me to take Maude, her curly chestnut hair forming a halo around her head. Her eyes, blue as the sea, were the last thing I saw before I was back in my dream of so long ago.

I was running barefoot in the gardens at Hever. This time I was not looking for Henry, I was just lost. I could not find my way back to the manor because the tall grass was blocking my view. I burst through the hedges and there was Anne and her scaffold.

Instead of running away, I inched closer. A warm, sticky river of blood poured from her neck and ran over my feet, I blanched in disgust. Her lips were moving just as in my previous dreams.

"What are you saying?" I called out. The executioner threw his head back in a terrifying laugh. I strained to see the words on her lips.

Casting aside my fear, I stepped, one foot at a time, delicately through the crimson life that poured out of her. Just before the executioner tossed her head to the ground, I made out the word she was mouthing and my own blood ran cold. She was whispering "Maude."

"My lady."

Someone was shaking me.

"Mistress Catherine," the voice said more urgently.

I struggled out of the cobwebs of sleep. My eyes flew open to see Edward's baby nurse Alice sitting in a chair next to my bed. Her hand was on my shoulder. Seeing the panic on her face, I scrambled to sit up.

I plied her with questions. "Alice, how long have I been asleep? How is Maude?"

Alice took a deep breath before she answered. "My Lady, you have been asleep for nearly a day. We knew how exhausted you were so we let you rest, but we need you now. Maude needs you now."

With terror rising in me, I tried to swing my legs around to get out of bed but it took enormous effort to move them and I fell back, breathing heavily.

Alice stood up and put her hand on my knee, I could feel the weight of it through the thick counterpane. "You have had a very rough birth and we had to bleed you while you were asleep. Please just lie back and I will bring Maude to you."

Breathless from my exertion, I settled back against the headboard. I winced in pain when the bleeding wounds on my back touched its hard surface. Alice scurried from the room. Moments later she re-emerged with a bundle of blankets in her arms. She sat down in the chair and said, with tears in her eyes, "Maude will not feed. Meg has tried to get her to latch on, but she refuses. She will not latch to me either. We have tried everything we know. You will have to feed her, my lady. It is the only way. She will not even cry for her milk. She just lies there whimpering."

She bent over and nestled the bundle of blankets in my arms.

Carefully, I pulled aside the blanket covering my baby's face. It was so pale and translucent I could almost see the tiny thread of veins running through it. Her deep brown eyes were rimmed red and stared off into space. I brushed the soft down on her head and planted a light kiss on her forehead. She whimpered in response. Tears began to stream down my hot cheeks. None of my children had ever been so weak. They were all born with lusty screams and flailing fists. Maude was so delicate and fragile, I worried that one light touch would harm her.

Alice pushed me forward and opened the front of my shift. She instructed me on what to do. I took out my swollen breast and stroked Maude's cheek with my hardened nipple. Maude gave no response. She only lay there in my arms staring out at nothing. After a few failed attempts, Alice moved to the other side of the bed. Hiking up her skirts, she climbed up and scooted on her knees towards us. She pulled the blanket aside revealing two miniature feet. She scraped her nail across the bottom of Maude's left foot. Maude let out a wail and instinctively turned her face towards my breast for comfort. I quickly shoved my nipple in her mouth and she latched on, gulping hungrily.

Alice let out a sigh of relief and a grin broke out on her tired face. "Oh, praise the Lord!"

I lay back and let Maude feed until she was content. It was a strange feeling, breastfeeding. Painful yet pleasurable at the same time. Not an intimate pleasure of course, but a feeling of overwhelming love. I felt a rush of affection for the child in my arms. I held her closer, never wanting to let go.

I continued to feed Maude in the following weeks. Francis was at Court so there would be no coupling between us. I was the only person she would latch on to and her health was far more important to me than the frowns of disgust I would get if the women at Court found out I was eschewing the wet nurse. Unfortunately, even though she was feeding, she was not gaining any weight. All of the milestones my other children passed in their early weeks failed to happen for my little Maude. I felt my time with her was limited so I spent most of my days in the nursery, rocking her in the chair and singing lullabies. Mary would grab her wool blanket and curl up at my feet, humming along with me.

The weather began to change and it seemed like the warmer it got outside, the further Maude slipped away. She stopped crying altogether and no longer even whimpered for her milk. She slept much of the day and even when the nursery was flooded in warm sunlight her tiny body felt chilled to the bone.

The day she left us was a bright, beautiful spring day. I stood at the window cradling her in my arms, basking us in the warmth of the sun, and I swayed back and forth humming. I saw the rose buds in the garden outside. The violets and lilies were in bloom. I wished I could open the window and let their musky sent in, but I did not dare for fear of Maude taking sick. I looked down into her placid face. Her eyes were closed, her long eyelashes brushing her cheeks.

I bent down and nuzzled the soft spot behind her ear. I whispered, "Go if you must, my sweet, but know how much we love you and will think of you always."

I pulled my face back in time to see her eyes open. For the first time, she looked deep into mine. I felt a wave of sadness as I kissed her pale, cool cheeks. As I exhaled, she slipped away quietly. Her body was lifeless in my arms, but I held her close, taking in my last breath of her baby sweetness.

"Meg, will you please open the window?"

Meg gave me a puzzled look, but when I nodded, she complied. I stood in the sunlight and let the scents of the garden surround me as I hugged Maude close and prayed for her soul.

I carried on as best as I could after Maude's death, but the loss of a child was almost too much for me to bear. Francis was tending to matters at Court and unable to come home, so I buried our child alone. I took my meals in my room, ate what little I could stomach, and then went to the chapel to pray. One morning, after a month of grieving, I stood naked before the mirror in my bedchamber and marvelled at the changes my body had gone through in the last eight years. I was no longer the young naïve girl that left Calais. My body now bore the marks of womanhood. My once flat stomach had been replaced by a soft round belly embroidered with the white puckered stretch-marks of all my pregnancies. My breasts were now larger than they had ever been thanks to Maude's feeding and it was a struggle to lace my stomacher in the mornings. Matilda had to brace herself against the tester bed just to pull the strings tightly enough. I sighed and laid my hand on my belly, remembering how it felt when Maude was kicking inside of it. I had been blessed with five healthy children and it was time that I rejoined them.

A bead of sweat slid from behind my ear down my neck on to my bare shoulder where it trickled down into the crease in my bust. I groaned in disgust, but I continued through the garden plucking flowers with Mary and Lettice. The hot August sun burned our backs, but we were intent on harvesting a beautiful bouquet to brighten the hall. Harry played in the dirt while Alice and Meg looked on, their faces flushed from the heat. Matilda was fanning herself with her hand. A plume of dust rose in the distance and the sound of hooves thundered closer.

Harry caught my eye and grinned. "Father!"

He jumped up and took off running towards the gate. I gathered the girls next to me, my hands on the back of their dresses damp with sweat. After a few moments, the sound of hooves quieted and the horse came into view. Francis was on the ground leading the horse towards us. He held the reigns in one hand and Harry's hand in the other. I smiled at the sight of father and son walking together, their steps in synch, a mirror of each other.

After the children had gone to bed, Francis and I sat before the fire in our room and indulged in some wine and cheese.

Francis took a swig of his wine. After he swallowed, he turned to me. "Well," he sighed. "Your little sister has been shamed."

"My little sister?" I asked in confusion.

"The Princess Elizabeth. She has been sent to live with Anthony Denny after her behaviour with the lord protector's brother, Thomas. The dowager queen refuses to see her and the king is in a rage that she has forsaken her good sensibilities to play the harlot to his uncle."

I shook my head and murmured, "That does not sound like Elizabeth. Are you certain?"

Francis nodded and stared into the flames. "They say that the baron would sneak into her room before she had even dressed for the day and chase her around, tearing at her nightgown and spanking her bottom."

I gasped. "What about Queen Katheryn?"

Francis snorted in derision, "Oh yes, she was in on it as well, until she caught them in an embrace in the gallery. I don't know what she was thinking. She had Elizabeth sent from Sudeley and the dowager queen now rests in her confinement awaiting the birth of their child. God willing the birthing will go well or I am certain the baron will set his sights on Elizabeth and the throne."

I sat quietly thinking of the young princess I had left behind after Edward's coronation. I could not imagine Elizabeth taking part in such misbehaviour, but I knew the baron and his reputation so was not surprised that he could act in such a way. It was a shame that for all the women King Henry had taken in marriage after Anne's death, not a single one of them had taught Elizabeth to avoid the plots and intrigues at Court. I feared this was just the beginning. Edward was still young and he had no heirs to follow should something happen to him. As long as Elizabeth was in line for the throne, she would always be a magnet for men and their ambition.

Shortly after Francis went back to Court, we received news that the dowager queen had died of childbed fever after giving birth to a sickly baby girl. As the familiar symptoms of my own pregnancy began to appear one after another, I reflected on the bittersweet nature of motherhood. We surrender our bodies and hearts to the children we bear, risking our very lives to birth them and yet we do it with gladness and little hesitation. Fear over the possibility of our death is insignificant compared to the joy that we feel at the moment of their birth.

I was delivered of a healthy baby girl in the middle of June. When Francis came home to see us I told him that I named her for my grandmother, Elizabeth Boleyn, but truthfully I had named her Elizabeth for the princess. The moment I saw our baby's coppery hair and raven eyes I knew that, like Lettice, she would be a mirror image of the young princess.

Bess, as we came to call her, thrived. Her birth was a joyous celebration after a winter and spring of discord. In February, the baron, Thomas Seymour, was arrested for attempting to kidnap the king. The death of the dowager queen had given him an opportunity to pursue his dynastic ambitions for a new wife and Princess Elizabeth seemed to suit his plan. Fortunately, no evidence was ever found linking Elizabeth to this plot, but her lady of the bedchamber and closest confidante, Kat Ashley, was removed along with her treasurer. These events placed the baron at odds with his brother and the council. When bribing the young king to intercede on the baron's behalf did not work, he attempted to take him by force out of the palace, but was foiled before he could complete his outrageous mission. That council could suffer Thomas Seymour's dangerous behaviour no more. On the king's orders, Somerset threw his brother into the Tower and on 19th March, he was executed.

Summer fared no better as Francis was called back to Court

in mid-July to deal with the rebellion at Norwich. Letters from Francis described the chaos:

"After Wymondham's celebration of St Thomas Becket, which had been outlawed by King Henry at the height of his dispute with the pope, a group of rebels set out to tear down the enclosures that were preventing their animals from grazing on public land. They attacked the enclosures on the property of a wealthy landowner named Kett and, instead of fighting back, he joined the rebels. Gathering recruits as they went, the rebels set up camp outside of Norwich and attacked. The king sent the Marquess of Northampton with an army to put them down, but after being tricked by reports that the rebels wanted to discuss surrender, Northampton was beaten back and the Earl of Warwick, John Dudley, was sent to restore law and punish the rebels. The rebellion eventually was put down, but at great cost to the lord protector. He had underestimated how powerful and determined the rebels truly were and, because of his woeful miscalculation, the council lost their faith in him."

In October, the lord protector was arrested by his own nephew and locked in the Tower.

"Warwick saw his chance and set about convincing an already worried council that the rebellions would not stop until Somerset was removed. Sadly, the king took little convincing as he was already upset that Somerset did not punish his sister, the Princess Mary, for saying Mass in her household and had been, in his opinion, far too lenient on the Catholics." Francis told me sadly when he returned at Christmas.

Somerset had been one of his closest friends and I could see the worry and sorrow etched across his face.

"Wriothesley has taken Somerset's rooms next to the king and at every chance he gets he is whispering in the king's ear, trying to return him to the Catholic church. If he is successful, all of our hard work is undone."

I chided Francis. "Do not even consider for one moment Wriothesley's success. Edward would never return England to the pope. The very suggestion of it is preposterous. Have you ever seen a young man with such disdain for the pope? He cannot even stomach the idea of his own sister holding Mass, which she has done since well before he was born, and must plague her with reprimands though it does not affect him in the least. Wriothesley better take care that he does not find himself in the Tower instead of Somerset."

I saw a smile creep its way onto Francis's face. "You speak wise words, my lady. It is true that our young king could never relinquish his power over the church back to the pope. Warwick and Somerset fighting over it is bad enough. Princess Mary is lucky he is still in his minority or she would rue the day she ever thought to hold Mass in her home."

I sighed. "Well, I know Mary and her conscience. She would never imperil her mortal soul. The king is deluded if he thinks she will ever turn from the old ways. As long as she can get away with it, she will hold Mass and she will encourage her supporters to do the same. And as long as she is next in line to the throne, it is a certainty. She will never lose hope that she can rectify the abandonment of her mother and the church that supported her."

Francis was still for a moment. The intensity with which he chewed his lower lip told me he was deep in thought. Finally, turning to me, he said, "What shall we do if Mary does come to the throne?"

I gave him a puzzled look. "What do you mean?"

"Catherine, I have spent the last decade working with the reformers at Court. It is no secret where my allegiances lie. When Mary comes to the throne, everything I have worked towards will be destroyed and our family could be in danger. We must plan for this outcome."

The very idea that Mary could be a danger to our family stunned me. Mary was staunch in her Catholic beliefs, but I could not begin to imagine her hurting her people. She had always shown me the utmost kindness at Court and she had looked after Elizabeth and

Edward as if she had been their mother. The mere thought that Mary could be dangerous seemed ridiculous.

"Francis," I said. "Isn't this a bit dramatic? Do you honestly believe that Mary would do anything to us? Do you believe that she is capable of that?"

For the first time in our marriage, Francis looked at me with a sternness that stopped the beating of my heart. I had never questioned him on any decision that he made. It was now painfully obvious to me this was not the decision to question.

Francis stood up and knelt before my chair. Resting his hands on my knees, his face softened and he said, "Catherine, you and our children mean the world to me. I would do anything to keep you out of harm's way. I know that you and Mary share blood, and while she does not know that, you still believe she would never hurt us, but I am not willing to take that chance. It is my duty to protect our family and, should Mary come to the throne, it will be in jeopardy. We need to plan for that possibility."

I ran my hand through his hair and caressed his cheek.

"I love you Francis and will do as you bid. I put my trust in you to keep us safe."

Francis smiled and leaned forward, resting his head in my lap. I bent over and kissed the back of his head. After a few moments that way, he stood up, placing one arm behind my back and one below my knees, and carried me to the bed.

Part IV

A Season of Fear

Oxfordshire, Rotherfield Greys:
July – September 1553

I had not realised how serious my husband was when he discussed the possibility of Mary coming to the throne. He had failed to mention one important detail - King Edward was on his deathbed. The first dispatch Francis sent after he arrived back at Court filled me with fear. As Edward coughed up bloody black bile at Greenwich, the Duke of Northumberland and the other councillors had put in motion plans to keep Princess Mary from the throne.

The past three years had been fraught with power struggles, illness and rebellion. Though the king had taken pity on his uncle Somerset and released him from the Tower, the council had refused to give him back his former control. In addition, Somerset had gained a new enemy, his old friend the Earl of Warwick. Warwick had been promoted to Duke of Northumberland and his new-found power created a great deal of enmity between the old friends. Northumberland had even gone so far as to deprive Somerset of his dining table, of all things. Before the first blusters of winter had returned, Somerset was back in the Tower. Linked to yet another uprising, he was found guilty of felony and sentenced to death. In the early morning hours of 22nd January, Somerset's beheading stained the new fallen snow in crimson blood.

Francis deeply mourned the loss of his dear friend. He knew that Somerset had become power-hungry and arrogant in the new reign of the king, but the duke had been his companion since before our marriage. And he had not been the only one distressed by his death. The people of England were livid. Somerset had always been the "good duke" to them. He had sponsored reform to their benefit and spoken out against the wealthy landowners who had enclosed public lands for their use, bringing harm to the poor farmers. His death had been much grieved.

The king managed to live through a bout of smallpox and had headed out on his first progress, but by April he had been taken ill again and had languished at Greenwich ever since.

I felt helpless and trapped in my confinement. The baby would be here in less than a month and I would have to keep to my chamber until my churching. There was nothing I could do but wait for word from Francis.

I was on my third confinement in three years. Two easy labours had brought two thriving sons. Robert was born during an early winter squall in November of 1550 and Richard came on a breezy spring day in May of 1552. I prayed nightly that this labour would come and go as quickly and easily as the last two.

I threw off the counterpane and eased out of the bed. My legs had become stiff with inactivity and I was going mad with worry about Francis at Court. I stood and stretched as much as I could then waddled over to the great oriel window that overlooked the courtyard. I saw a plume of dust and knew that a rider had just been through. Before I could shift my hefty bulk from the window, the door flew open and my son, Harry, burst into the room. He had grown into a young man seemingly overnight. His childlike humour was slowly becoming more serious like his father's. The look on his face as he entered my chamber was so reminiscent of Francis that I had to restrain my smile. The news must have been grave for him to risk entering my bedchamber during my confinement.

"Mother, news from Court," he panted, breathless from barrelling up the staircase.

"What does it say?"

He swallowed hard and blinked his clear blue eyes. "The king is dead."

I had been expecting this after Francis's letters.

"Does it say anything about your father?"

He shook his head.

I bit the inside of my lip hard enough to taste blood, but I was determined not to panic in front of Harry.

"Go to your uncle and give him the note. There is nothing for us to do but wait for your father to return and pray for those at Court."

Harry bowed his head and turned to walk out of the room.

"Wait!" I called out.

He turned back, waiting for my instruction.

"Go to chapel for me please and send prayers for King Edward."

My boy nodded. "As you command, Mother."

I watched the courtyard from the window every day waiting for the tell-tale cloud of dust that a horse had come down our lane, but none ever showed. I tossed and turned at night, never sleeping more than an hour or two at a time. My eyes were dry and gritty from lack of sleep. It was during one of these fitful rests that Francis finally arrived home. I awoke to find him sitting next to my bed anxiously tapping his thumb against his knee, worry etched across his face.

He smiled briefly at me, reaching out to brush a rogue hair from my face, and then the graveness returned.

"Francis?" I croaked. My throat was dry from the heat of the room. "Is it really you?"

"It is really me," he affirmed, bringing my hand to his lips.

I pulled my hand back and struggled to sit up.

"Is the king truly dead? What has happened? Is Mary now the queen?"

Francis nodded soberly. "Yes, the king is now with the angels. I pray that he is resting with his mother and father, though we have failed him."

"How could you have failed him?"

Francis stood up and began pacing in front of the fire.

He was silent for a few moments and then shouted, "His device!" And then repeated in a lower voice: "His great device."

He stopped pacing and stared out the window.

After a heavy silence, he turned to look at me sadly. "And now, poor Jane will die through no fault of her own."

I searched my memories for the Jane he could be referring to, but could only come up with one. Lady Jane Grey. She was the eldest daughter of Lady Frances Grey, whose mother had been Mary Tudor, sister to King Henry. Lady Frances was born of the marriage between Mary and Charles Brandon, Duke of Suffolk. I knew Jane had lived at Sudeley with Princess Elizabeth and the dowager queen for a few years. I had joined Francis at Court back in May when she was married to Guildford Dudley, the moody son of Northumberland. What could she have to die for?

"Tell me what happened," I pleaded.

Francis strode towards me. He bent down and kissed me on the forehead. "Not now, my love. You need your rest. I will tell you more in the morning."

A stabbing pain in my belly ripped me out of my dreams. I awoke soaking wet in sweat and my waters. Matilda leapt off her pallet at my scream and ran to get the midwife. I laboured through the day and as the moon rose to take its place in the sky, our newest child filled the air with his sharp cry.

"Yet another bonny son!" laughed the midwife, laying the babe on my chest.

I smiled sleepily and cradled my boy in my arms. Once the room had been cleaned, the baby nurse, Meg, came to retrieve the baby. As she hustled out of the room, I called out, "Francis! His name is Francis."

I still had received no answers from my husband, but I was too exhausted to care any more. I curled up in my bed and slept soundly for the first time in months.

After a few days of rest, Francis came to see me. He looked

haggard but managed a careworn smile as he settled into the chair next to me. He kissed my hand and said, "You have given me another fine son and even named him for me. I could not ask for more."

I raised myself against the headboard. "If you are so content, Francis, why do you appear so wretched?" I asked worriedly.

He nodded. "Yes, I suppose it is time you know of the events at Court. Why I fear for our safety and the choices I will need to make."

I waited for his words with baited breath.

"Do you remember when we went to Durham House for the marriage of Jane Grey and Guildford Dudley?"

How could I have forgotten it? In one elaborate ceremony, the Duke of Suffolk and the Duke of Northumberland linked their families to two of the most valuable heirs in the kingdom. In addition to Jane and Guildford's nuptials, Jane's sister was wed to the son of the Earl of Pembroke and Guildford's sister to the son of the Earl of Huntingdon. It was a dynastic coup intended to consolidate and strengthen the power of Suffolk and Northumberland. And it had all been done with the king's blessing.

He continued with a deep sigh. "That marriage was created to bolster Jane's claim to the throne. The king and Northumberland intended for her to inherit the crown upon the king's death."

I didn't understand his reasoning, Lady Jane was far down the line of succession. She may have been cousin to the king, but Princess Mary and Princess Elizabeth would both have to die without heirs before she would inherit the crown.

Francis went on. "The device I spoke of? It was the king's will. He called it his device for the succession. I still don't know how much of it was his idea and how much of it was Northumberland's, but in it he named Jane Grey his successor."

I slammed my hand against the mattress in a rage. "He cannot do that!" I shouted.

Francis calmly laid his hand on my shoulder. "He believed he could. His act rendered Mary and Elizabeth bastards again.

He hoped that Jane would have a son before he died to claim the throne, so he tried to name her male heirs as his successors, but as his illness grew he became more panicked about Mary destroying the legacy of his reign and returning to the pope. He amended the will to name Lady Jane..."

"And Northumberland seized the opportunity to make his son, Guildford, king." I finished.

"The duke sent a letter to Hunsdon to trick Mary into coming to Court, telling her only that Edward was ill. Along the way, Mary received word that her brother was already dead. Her suspicions raised, she sent a letter to the council claiming her right to the throne and rode to East Anglia, raising an army as she went."

"And Jane?"

"She had been taken from Chelsea to Syon House. She claimed illness, knowing what lay ahead, but the council would hear nothing of it. The council bowed to Northumberland's will and, bound by the king's device, proclaimed her queen. I was there and saw the whole sorry thing. Jane was a mess, trembling and sobbing, crying out that she was unworthy to wear the crown. The next morning she was dressed in Tudor green and white and taken by barge with Guildford to the Tower to await her coronation. Instead of the cheering and boisterous crowds that had greeted the procession of her predecessor, they were met with stony silence from the banks of the river. The people stared at her as if she were a foreigner."

I gazed down at my hands. They were clasped tightly in my lap, my knuckles turning white.

"Poor Jane," I murmured.

Francis continued. "The council attempted to crown her, but she rebuffed them. Eventually they tricked her by telling her it was only to try it on for size. Once she realised there was no going back, she called Arundel and Pembroke and told them that she refused to name Guildford as king."

"I bet that caused a fine tantrum."

Francis finally gave a small chuckle, "It was a sight to see the duke's son crying at his mother's knee. The next evening a messenger arrived with the letter from Mary. It was read out loud, punctuated by the sobbing of the Duchesses Northumberland and Suffolk. They decided that the other sons of the duke - the Earl of Warwick and Robert Dudley - would be sent to meet Mary, but they never made it. The people were against this coup. After that failure, Suffolk was asked to lead the troops, but Jane was so ill with fear she begged him to stay and Northumberland was sent in his stead. With Northumberland gone, the members of the council wavered and all fell in line behind Mary. She entered Cheapside on the ninth day of Jane's reign and was proclaimed queen by the people."

"And rightfully so," I scoffed.

Francis nodded sadly. "Yes, she is the rightful queen, but shall she be a noble queen or shall we return to the yoke of the Catholic church? For now I have been exiled from Court."

I grasped his arm. "Francis, surely you had no part in this treason?"

A hurt look crossed his face. "Of course not, Catherine. I would never endanger our family in such a way. But I did nothing to stop it and I stood by when the council changed their allegiance to Mary, and because I took no side I have been sent home. But I have been given a mission from Sir William Cecil and Thomas Cranmer."

Sir William was a well-known reformer. Francis had attended a summit held at his home some time ago for the reformers and Catholics to discuss the treatment of the Sacrament.

Thomas Cranmer was King Edward's Archbishop of Canterbury. He had given King Henry his first divorce and had helped instigate the break from the pope. What could they possibly ask my husband to do?

"Go on," I prodded.

Francis hesitated, chewing his lip for a moment, considering his next words. Finally he said: "They have asked me to go to the Low Countries to scout out settlements."

"And who do they suggest will live in these settlements?"

"English Protestants," he said simply.

"Francis! I cannot leave my country, my home."

He gave me a puzzled look. "Catherine, you spent much of your childhood in France."

"In English territory in France," I emphasised. "We cannot just pick up and leave everything behind just because we do not agree with Queen Mary."

Grimly, Francis responded, "We can if our life is in danger. The queen has vowed not to change the religion now, but she has not been shy about her disdain for the reformed 'heretics'. It will not be long before we are burnt at Smithfield. I fear what the future may bring, Catherine. It may not even be necessary, but Cranmer and Cecil have requested this of me and I have agreed. I leave next month and I am taking our son Harry."

His edict silenced me. I trusted that Francis would never put our son in harm's way, but the thought of Harry going on this dangerous journey filled me with terror. My husband had made it clear that no matter how I felt about it, he would not tolerate any dissent from me.

Francis pulled the counterpane back over me, tucking it in tight. Once he was done, he took his leave without any kiss or sign of affection.

I watched Francis and Harry make their preparations for their journey from the oriel window in my bedchamber. I would not be churched for at least another month so, for now, I was still stuck indoors. I could not even sleep with my husband before he set out on his dangerous mission. We had not spoken much since he told me the news. It was not unusual for us to go months at a time without hearing one another's voice, but this was different. Those months he was miles away at Court, not in a room down the hall.

I sat in my room, beneath the open window for air, and read or sewed while I waited patiently for Francis's forgiveness. He had visited only twice since our argument, once to see our son and a second time to tell me that he would be leaving the second week of September and that his brother would be staying at Greys with me. My heart ached at the distance that had grown between us. My warm, thoughtful husband had been replaced by this steely stranger.

Harry was beside himself with excitement. It would be the first time he had travelled farther from Greys than Court. Under the open window I heard the barrage of questions he asked of his father. Where would they sleep? What kind of people were in Germany? What would they see? Francis always responded patiently and managed to direct Harry to another task. As much as I dreaded Harry leaving home, I knew it would be a good experience for him and he would learn much during his journey. I resigned myself to their departure and put my faith in Francis.

A knock at the door startled me from my daydream. I straightened myself and called out "Please come in."

Francis appeared in the doorway, looking sheepish.

I turned to Matilda. "You are excused. I will send for you when I need you."

She nodded and dropped a small curtsey, squeezing out through the door beside Francis.

He walked slowly to my bed and, instead of sitting in the chair as usual, he sat down next to me on the mattress. His hazel eyes fixed on mine.

"I believe I owe my beloved wife an apology," he mumbled.

I cast down my eyes and plucked at a snag in the counterpane. He put his hand on mine, stilling it.

"Will you please look at me?" he pleaded.

I raised my head and looked back at him, my vision watery from the tears in my eyes. I had tried my best to blink them back, but they came unbidden anyway.

I sniffed. "There is no need for you to apologise. You are the head of this household and you will do as you see fit, regardless of what your ignorant wife thinks. That is your right as my husband."

Francis threw his arms around me and held me in a tight embrace.

"Catherine Knollys, I have never in my life believed you to be ignorant. I feel quite the contrary actually. I have always known you to be very intelligent and wise."

I pulled back. "Then why did you treat me so harshly when I disagreed with you?"

Francis sighed. "It is my own behaviour that was ignorant. I will be leaving you for a very long time and wanted to insulate myself. Set myself apart from you so it would not be so painful for us both while I was gone."

I brushed a wayward tear from my cheek. "Francis, you are ridiculous."

He smiled warmly. "I know. See, I told you that you were wise."

I started to shake my head, but he stopped me with both hands, pulling me close into a kiss. I realised just how much I had missed our intimacy. His lips tasted salty from my tears. Deftly, he laid me back on the bed and ran his hand over the curves of my body. I put my hand on his chest and pushed him back.

"Francis, I have not been churched yet. We mustn't do this."

He placed his finger to my lips and shushed me.

"Catherine, our church no longer considers you impure from childbirth. The ceremony is only for thanksgiving, not to purify you. King Edward made it so in the new Prayer Book last year. Have you not read it?"

I laughed. "I guess I should have."

"Yes, my lady, you should have," he chastised me, trailing kisses down my neck.

I gave myself to Francis and we spent the night making love. In the morning I rose early to bid him and our son farewell. I managed to keep the tears at bay while we said our goodbyes. Harry's face was flushed with excitement, his azure eyes shining in pure pleasure. Francis looked less ecstatic, but he stood tall and assured, convinced that he was doing the right thing. Mary, Lettice, William and I stood waving from the courtyard as Francis and Harry rode down the lane and out into the unknown.

London, Whitehall:
30 September – 2 October 1553

Francis and Harry had been gone less than a week before a messenger from Court arrived at Greys. Henry went out to meet him while I waited eagerly in the hall. Now that Francis was no longer serving at Court, who could be sending us letters from London? I paced uneasily before the hearth.

Once I heard Henry's footsteps echo in the entryway, I ran to him.

"What is it?" I asked impatiently.

He lowered his hand and snorted.

"Well?" I was hopping from one foot to another, unable to keep still.

Finally he said incredulously, "The queen has invited you to her coronation."

My hand flew to my mouth and I gave a muffled groan.

Henry laughed. "My thoughts exactly."

I threw my hand out to stop him. "Wait, are you sure that is what the letter says?"

He handed me the letter nonchalantly. "Read it for yourself."

I quickly scanned the letter. Sure enough, it was an invitation to the queen's coronation, addressed to both Francis and I. It dawned on me that, of course, it would be addressed to us both. I was sure the queen had no idea that Francis had headed overseas, for the moment at least. Eventually she would find out, but my husband and son had probably just reached Gravesend.

The coronation would take place in two weeks. I had not considered attending, but this royal invitation required me to go. I also realised that, although Mary never knew and certainly would never recognise that I was her half-sister by blood, it was my duty to support her. I cared not what her religion was or even if England did rejoin the Catholic church. I only cared that my husband was spared punishment for his loyal service to her brother's religion. Attending her coronation to show my support could only help him and keep up appearances. I threw the invitation into the fire and called Matilda in to take my measurements. I would need a new gown.

The day was perfect for a procession. The sun was shining, but a cool breeze was blowing and the sky was fair. I stood among the throng of people halfway between the Tower and Whitehall. The citizens of London chattered excitedly to each other, thrilled to see the daughter of their beloved Catherine of Aragon take the throne. "Long live the queen!" echoed out through the city. While I had been invited to the coronation, I was not invited to participate in the procession, so I watched from the sidelines.

A carriage pulled by six chestnut coursers marched through the city carrying the new queen. She was resplendent in a deep purple gown trimmed in ermine. Precious jewels dripped from her ears and throat. Her hair was worn loose, the auburn waves threaded with strands of the silver-grey that comes with age and misfortune. She was crowned with a circlet of gold encrusted with so many precious gems she had to rest her head on her hands to bear the weight. I wondered if she had made sure to wear every crown jewel from the coffers. She reminded me of a poor man who had inherited a wealth of riches, eager to show that she had been blessed by God with a fortune. Though I looked at her through critical eyes, my heart held gladness for her. As a princess, Mary had been subjected to neglect and abuse I could never imagine inflicting upon a child. Now it was her time to shine and the people of London were thrilled to have her in their presence. She reminded them of the heady, joyous days when the chivalric son of Henry VII and his exotic, beautiful wife were crowned. Surely, they believed, she would be as noble as they.

The knights, bishops, and lords of the court, led by the Privy Council themselves walked behind Queen Mary. It appeared that she had kept many of Edward's councillors in addition to the ones recently appointed. I had never seen so many Privy Councillors in all my times at Court. I could only begin to imagine the infighting that would happen in those chambers. I realised right away that a familiar face was missing. Thomas Cranmer, Archbishop of Canterbury, was nowhere to be seen. In his place strutted Stephen Gardiner, Bishop of Winchester, the loathsome man who had tried to entrap Katheryn Parr. He had been imprisoned in the Tower during Edward's reign. I was sure that the queen had wasted no time in releasing him. He was her strongest link to the old ways of the Catholic church and one of the few bishops to object to her father's divorce. I was certain that while Gardiner replaced Cranmer in the procession, Cranmer was most likely replacing Gardiner behind the Tower walls.

A smaller carriage rumbled along behind the queen's grand one carrying the Princess Elizabeth and Anne of Cleves. I could not help but break into a wide smile when I saw the two of them. Elizabeth looked, as required, regally sombre, but Anne was grinning and waving maniacally to the crowd. I had heard that she had become a bit eccentric in her retirement, but she was beloved by the princesses and all the ladies and gentlemen who served her. I hoped to see both of them in my short stay at Court.

The queen's maids surrounded Elizabeth and Anne's carriage. I strained my eyes to see any I recognised and was pleased when I spotted Nan Bassett. She was on a white mare dressed in her finest emerald hued gown. How good it felt to see my old friends again. Though I had never cared for the intrigues of the Court, I missed the friendships I had made as a result of serving together and I was hit with a pang of jealously that I was missing out.

The conduits were flowing with red wine and, as was customary, the procession was treated to pageants all along the route. The parade halted while the city recorder read out a speech professing loyalty to the queen. The party moved on ahead to Whitehall. I pushed my way through the crowd and followed them to the palace. I had been invited to stay, but since my husband was no longer there, I knew not where I would be lodged. I decided to take my chances and headed out in search of Nan.

The palace was jammed with people. Pages bustled past busy making preparations for tomorrow's celebrations. I weaved through the crowd and followed a group of maids to the great hall. I stood outside the enormous doors and pondered my life since I had first arrived at these very same doors and peeked through them, catching my first glimpse of my father's court, as it came to be after my Aunt Anne's death. I recalled the song that the minstrels were playing and the sound of shoes shuffling across the hardwood floor, the glimmer of jewels in the candlelight and the smell of roasted meat coming from the platters being passed around the long tables. I was lost in time and nearly jumped out of my skin when I felt a warm hand on my arm.

"Catherine! Is it you? I cannot believe my eyes."

I turned to find myself faced with the youthful countenance of Nan Bassett.

"Nan!" I squealed and threw my arms around her. "I am so pleased to see you again."

I stepped back, my eyes sweeping over her.

"You have not aged a day," I sighed.

She laughed, "Well, Mistress Knollys, I have not been in the country birthing an army of children! I imagine the experience is exhausting."

I giggled at her dramatic expression.

"You know something, Nan? It is exhausting. But it is also a joy. My children have far exceeded any expectation I ever had of them in looks, intelligence *and* countenance. In ten children, I have only lost one. I count my blessings each and every day."

Nan smiled. She looked sincerely pleased for me.

"My dear Catherine, I hope that I will be as blessed as you

when the time comes for me to wed. I hope my match will be as perfect as yours."

We hugged again and walked arm-in-arm into the great hall.

Nan was a very gracious hostess. She immediately offered to share her lodgings with me, and that night was like old times. We stayed up late into the night catching up on all the changes in our lives. Nan thrilled me with her stories of the queen's fight for the throne. A small part of me missed the excitement, but I was happy to know I would be returning to my quiet life in the country once the coronation was over.

In the morning, groggy from our lack of sleep, we ambled to the fire to warm up and break our fast. The mulled ale warmed me into a trance and I sat back, mesmerised by the dancing flames. An hour later, Nan's maid came in to help us dress and Nan excused herself to the queen's rooms. She had a job to do and our time together was cut short.

"I will send lots of prayers that the queen finds you a wonderful match soon and that your home will be filled with the sound of tiny feet," I whispered in her ear as we enjoyed one last embrace.

"Thank you," she mouthed, squeezing my hand before she left to ready the queen for her big day.

I walked to Westminster early to try to beat the crowds. The weather was a repeat of the previous day, and by the time the queen came into view on her procession to the abbey, the sun had warmed through my heavy layers.

Mary was riding in an open litter wearing the crimson velvet robes worn by her father and brother before her. The barons of the Cinque Ports carried a brocade canopy over her, shading her from the hot sun. Bishop Gardiner led the way, the ball and sceptre carried by the Earl of Arundel, the orb by the Marquis of Winchester, and the crown by my uncle, the Duke of Norfolk. I was surprised to see that he had been released from the Tower. The queen's father had imprisoned him shortly before his death and it was only because of that death that Norfolk kept his head.

The queen's litter was carried inside the abbey all the way to the coronation chair. The people filed in and crowded the abbey. Once we were all quiet, Gardiner began the ceremony.

"Do you serve now and give your wills and assent to the same consecration, unction and coronation?"

We all responded, "Yea, yea, yea. God save Queen Mary!"

The queen made her coronation oath after receiving the prayers and blessings of the church. While the abbey choir sang, she excused herself and re-emerged from behind a curtain wearing a plum coloured velvet petticoat. Gardiner anointed her with holy oil and she doffed the red robes of state again. The nobles came forth presenting her with the sword, sceptre and orb. She was first crowned with what I recognised as the same crown used during Edward's coronation. Then it was removed and replaced with a new crown I did not recognise. The other nobles crowded around her to pay homage. Then she rose from her throne, climbed back into the litter and was carried in state to Westminster Hall for her banquet.

Overwhelmed by the pageantry of the festivities, I went back to Whitehall to gather my things and retrieve my horse. My servant, Anthony, was waiting to take me back to Greys. I had done my duty and now it was time to go back to my home.

Oxfordshire, Rotherfield Greys:
April 1554 – March 1555

The bleak winter snows had passed, the violets and hyacinths had long been out to play and I had yet to hear word from my beloved husband. Being housebound in the frigid weather made me mad with inactivity and just as the birds fled their winter hiding spots, I too fled the manor.

As I walked past my rose garden in the morning sun, I spotted the nasty weeds that had taken hold over the cold season and I fell on my hands and knees ripping them out of the ground. All of the frustration and fear I had felt over the last months poured out of me as I dug the unwelcome intruders out of my garden. My back ached and my knees throbbed, but when Henry called out to me, I refused to heed his words.

"Catherine, we have a gardener for that."

I ignored him as I carried on with my task and out of the corner of my eye I saw him shake his head and walk away. I worked until I felt the first warm raindrops on the top of my head. I rocked back on my knees and looked to the sky. It was dark and grey, ominous. Raindrops fell in my eyes. I forgot about the dirt on my hands until I rubbed my eyes. My vision blurred and, instinctively, the tears began to fall. The tears I had been holding back since Francis's departure were released in a torrent. I threw down my shovel in frustration and sat in my misery.

Shortly after Francis and Harry's departure, I received a letter from Princess Elizabeth. Word had reached Hatfield of Francis's mission, no doubt from Cecil himself, and Elizabeth had been under the impression that I was leaving with him so she wrote to offer her love and support. It had taken Elizabeth great courage to correspond with those who had dared to defy the queen. The final words she had closed her letter with struck a chord, *Cor Rotto* - heart-broken.

Since reading her missive I had carried those two words branded on my own broken heart. Yes, I had known joy and happiness, but since those dark days over twenty years ago, I had also known profound loss. While I sat in the warm spring rain, I felt a wave of sadness chill me as I counted my losses one by one. The loss of my Aunt Anne had taken a hostage with it, the joy of my innocence. And not only had I lost my mother and fathers (the true and the false one) in death, my stepfather had wasted little time remarrying, fleeing to the continent with no farewell. The man I had loved as my own father and I believed cared for me as well had deserted me in this new and unsettling reign. My beautiful Maude would never grow to enjoy the scent of the very roses I was weeding. She would never feel the warm summer sun on her face or know the love of a young man. Now my husband and our child were travelling in a country unknown to us and I feared their loss as well. I knew I needed to pick myself up off the wet, muddy ground, but it would take every ounce of my courage to swallow my grief and face my children.

I raised my face towards heaven, ready to beg for help, and was startled to see a man in a hooded cape standing over me. Something in his eyes struck me as familiar, but his face was shadowed and I could not make out his identity. I took his outstretched hand and, as I straightened myself, recovered my senses.

"Thank you, my good sir," I sputtered. "Please come in out of the rain."

I ushered him into the front hall. He turned his back to me and I eagerly helped him remove his wet cloak. When he turned to face me, I was struck speechless. It was my Richard.

He had grown plumper since I had seen him last at Whitehall. His beard was still full and it had begun to grey at the edges. His face was more care-worn, but it still glowed with kindness, just as I remembered.

"Richard?" I asked cautiously. "What are you doing here?"

He chuckled lightly. "Well, that is a fine greeting, Lady Knollys! I am pleased to see you as well!"

I sensed a blush creeping up my face. "You are absolutely right, I am sorry to be so apprehensive. You startled me, showing up in the pouring rain with your face covered. We have all been a little on edge lately. Please forgive me."

Richard gave my hand a light squeeze. "I completely understand, my lady. I think everyone in our circle has been a bit nervous these last few months. You are certainly forgiven."

I gripped his hand in mine. "Circle?" I asked in confusion.

He looked hopefully towards the fire in the hearth and said, "Maybe we should sit down."

I called Matilda into the room and she ran to fetch a warm blanket and mulled cider for our unexpected guest.

Richard and I settled into our seats and he spoke of his life since we had parted ways. After the death of King Henry, Richard had maintained his position in the stables under Edward's reign. Serving the most prominent reformers in the country had opened him up to a new outlook on his beliefs and, over time, he joined their ranks. Fearing the new queen's policies, he sought out Sir William and asked him to find a place for him at Hatfield. Soon after he arrived, he fell in love with a serving maid, Susannah, and they were married at Christmas.

"Before I left, she told me she was with child," he glowed with pride.

I was pleased to see such pleasure in Richard's eyes. He was so deserving of a life of happiness, and it seemed as if he had finally found it.

"That is wonderful Richard. I am so happy for you."

"Thank you, my lady. But I didn't come here to talk about me. I am sure you are wondering why I have made this journey all the way from Hatfield."

Officially Richard was working in Princess Elizabeth's stables, but he was truly at Hatfield to assist William Cecil, passing messages between the secret reformers of the country. His wife, Susannah, was a kinswoman to the princess's lady, Kat Ashley. Mistress Ashley had been removed after her part in the Thomas Seymour intrigue.

Richard told me that Hatfield was crawling with the queen's informants. In January, Protestant rebels began a revolt in response to the queen's decision to marry Prince Philip of Spain instead of Edward Courtenay, the Earl of Devon. Their plan was to assassinate the queen and put Princess Elizabeth in her place, betrothing her to the earl. Devon was arrested after the Spanish ambassador alerted Bishop Gardiner to the plot and though the earl revealed the plans under duress, his partner in the plot, Sir Thomas Wyatt of Kent, pushed ahead and all went awry. Since she was the centrepiece to the plot, Princess Elizabeth was, of course, implicated and escorted to the Tower. Lady Jane Grey and Guildford Dudley had found themselves on the scaffold for Jane's father's part in the uprising.

I realised in an instant how secluded I had become out here in the country. I had received no word of these happenings and had no inkling that Elizabeth had been imprisoned. Francis's brother, Henry, must have known. I had seen men come and go in the last few months, but Henry had never shared with me any news he received from Court or otherwise. Once Richard left, I would be sure to corner him and find out why.

Richard reached into his doublet, pulling out a tightly rolled piece of parchment and handed it to me.

"Your husband has been sending reports to Sir William and this time he included a letter for you. I wanted to be sure you received it right away so I set off once we realised to whom it was addressed."

I carefully took the letter from his hand then closed my eyes and clutched it to my heart, feeling the smooth parchment against my skin.

"I am sure you would like to be alone," he said, standing up. "I need to be heading back to Hatfield."

I looked up into his stern face, "Are you sure you will not stay? I worry about you travelling in the rain, and it will be dark soon."

Richard shook his head, "I will be all right, my lady. As much as I would love to stay, I must get back to Susannah. She has been ever fearful since the coronation and I worry about her and the child. I do thank you heartily for your hospitality."

I leaned forward and embraced him in a hug. When I took in his woody scent, I was taken back to a time and place long ago, before I was a mother, before I was a wife, before our thoughts were clouded with fear and apprehension.

Richard was the first to pull away, but he cupped my cheek in his palm and said, "I am pleased to see your happiness as well. As hard as it was to see you get in that carriage the day you left Court to marry, I knew that you were marrying a good man and that he would take care of you in a way I never could. And now, after all these years, I see you, lovelier than ever, with these beautiful children and this comfortable home and I know that I was right to let you go."

I gave him a small smile. "Thank you, Richard. Your words are far too kind. I have been blessed with a marriage I had never believed I would be lucky enough to have. I wish you safe travels and I will be praying for your wife's safe delivery."

He kissed me on the cheek, still warm from the touch of his hand, wrapped up in his cloak and walked out the door.

As soon as the door shut I raced upstairs to read Francis's letter in the privacy of my chamber. I stood before the window and broke open the seal.

My Dearest Catherine,

I hope and pray that this letter finds you well. I am sure you have spent many nights worrying and wondering how we fare and so I write to you to assure you that all is well and we have found ourselves welcomed on the continent with open arms. We left Gravesend with John à Lasco's congregation and made our way to Geneva to meet with the theologian John Calvin. You would be pleased to know that our son impressed Calvin beyond measure and he praised his piety and holy zeal. He has done well on our journey and shown himself to be a young man of virtue and learning. We have raised him well. We left Calvin with his blessing and headed to Lausanne. There we met with Calvin's disciple Pierre Viret, the so-called 'Smile of the Reformation'. He told us of his Reformed Academy, a training school for preachers, and met our proposal with glee. I assured him that our people would be more than happy to patronise his school and support his cause.

As I stare out at the shores of Lac Léman, I think of you and our children often. I appreciate all of the support you have given me in these trying times. And while I am certain of the importance of my mission, I am saddened by our time apart and look forward to holding you in my arms again.

We have arrived today at Strasbourg and will tour the city, moving on to Frankfurt before we return home. It is my hope that by the time this letter reaches you, we will be on our way back to England, successful in our task. I eagerly await your loving embrace.

Forever yours,

Francis

I reread his words, committing them to my memory. As I traced the letters of his signature with the tip of my finger, I imagined all of the sights they must be taking in. I had never seen the snow covered mountains of Geneva or the shores of Lac Léman. At his mention of Germany I thought momentarily, of Anne of Cleves and pondered how she was faring under the new queen. It seemed so strange to me how things could change in such a small amount of time. I found myself on my knees saying a prayer not only for my husband and son, but also for Richard and his family and that all of us would find some safety and constancy in these changing and treacherous times.

Five months later, the season of autumn brought with it the changing colours, cooler winds and the return of my beloved. I was in the pantry taking an inventory of our supplies before the coming freeze when I heard the sound of tiny running feet coming towards me.

"Mother! Mother!" little voices called out.

"Yes my darlings," I whirled around to see Edward, Elizabeth and Robert tugging at my skirt.

Edward stopped tugging and grabbed the shoulders of Elizabeth and Robert pulling them away from me. "It is Father!" he burst out. "Father and Harry are home!"

I knelt down to face them and whispered, "Run!"

They squealed in delight and peeled off in the direction of the hall with me following closely behind. We banged out of the front door, overjoyed to see Francis and Harry standing before us. I nearly jumped into Francis's arms.

"Oh Catherine, my love," he sighed into my ear. "I have waited so long to hold you again."

We parted and he handed the reins of his horse to his brother. I ran to Harry and enveloped him in my arms. He had grown over an inch and was now almost as tall as me. His chin was covered in a light down and his hair had grown into tawny curls hanging over his forehead. My son had grown so much in the time he was gone, I almost could not believe that this was the same child standing before me.

"Hello, Mother," he said very seriously. "I am very pleased to see you again. I had a wonderful time with Father and learned much while I was gone. Thank you for allowing me to go."

I chuckled. "Thank you, my son, for allowing me to believe I had any say in it. Thank you for coming back to me safely. I am certain your brothers and sisters would love to hear about your adventures, why don't you take them inside and tell them all you have seen?"

Harry nodded and, taking Elizabeth and Robert by the hands, he led the children inside.

I could feel the heat coming from Francis as he sidled up behind me. Reaching around from behind me and taking my hands in his he whispered, "Now it is time I take you to bed, Lady Knollys."

He led me inside and up the stairs to our chamber. Once the door was shut behind us, he unlaced my skirts and they fell to the floor. He kicked the skirts out of the way and pulled me to him, lifting me up. I wrapped my legs around his hips and trailed kisses down his neck. He walked over to the bed and sat down with me still wrapped around him. His fingers deftly released the ties of my stomacher and in a moment I was before him in all my naked glory.

Francis sat back and gazed at me, smiling. "The way the sunlight hits your golden red hair makes it look as though you are wearing a halo."

I touched my finger to his nose. "I think you may have been on the road far too long, husband."

He sighed. "Yes, far too long."

He stood and turned to lay me down on the bed and then proceeded to remove his own clothing, coming to lie down once he was finished. The sun began its descent from the sky and Francis and I came together as one for the first time in over a year.

I awoke in the early twilight to a light rap at the door. Francis was snoring softly beside me. I got up and threw my shift over my head and padded across the floor. I opened it slowly so as not to wake Francis. The doorway was empty. I started to step out into the hall, but fortunately, I looked down first. A tray laden with food was sitting on the floor. I laughed quietly to myself. It seems our family had thought better of bothering us after so many months apart.

I carried the tray in, breathing in deep the sharp, smoky smell of the cheese that had been sliced and paired with bread still warm from the ovens, and a couple of sliced apples. I ate a piece of the apple, its crisp tartness made my tongue tingle and my mouth water. I set the tray down before the fire and tore off a bit of bread. The rain was coming down hard and the night was getting darker. As

I chewed my bread, I gazed out of the window, watching the rain splash in fat drops against the glass. Glancing over at the bed, I saw that Francis was still sound asleep, so I cracked open the window as quietly as I could. The rain-soaked air filled my lungs with a fresh clean scent. I could smell the leaves and the dirt and the perfume of the flowers from our garden. As I stood basking in the cool air, I thought of Calais. When I closed my eyes, it was as if the rain splashing my face was the salty sea spray I felt so many times when I lived in the garrison. The lavender, creeping its way in from the south garden, was the scent of my mother coming in to comfort me from my nightmare. I had always taken great comfort from the rain and for an instant I felt my mother beside me letting me know that everything would be all right.

Francis had begun to stir so I closed the window and tiptoed back over to the bed. I sat on the edge of the mattress as he raised himself up to a sitting position against the headboard.

"I smell food," he murmured.

"Of course you do, my love. You always smell food!"

He leaned forward to nuzzle me, but pulled back quickly.

"Catherine, why is your face wet?" he said, wrinkling his nose.

I began wiping furiously at my face with the sleeve of my shift. "Sorry, I had the window open," I muttered.

He reached up and stopped my scrubbing hands.

"Stop that, you are going to irritate your face. I was just a bit startled, that is all. I don't care what is on your face, as long as I may kiss it," he said, planting a kiss on my forehead.

"I was just breathing in the rain and thinking of my mother."

Francis's eyes softened. "I am so sorry, my love."

I looked up at him and shook my head. "You have nothing to be sorry for Francis. You have been so good to me and have given me such beautiful children. I am so happy in our marriage and would not change it for anything."

He took my small hands in his. "Catherine, you do not need to hide your hurt from me. I know how much you have lost since you came over from Calais. You claim happiness, but deep down you must be so ..." he trailed off as if he did not know how to finish.

After a moment of silence I said, "*Cor Rotto.*"

"*Cor Rotto?*"

"It is Latin for broken-hearted. Princess Elizabeth signed her letter with it and I have been turning the words over and over in my head. Yes, sometimes I do feel broken-hearted, but then you come home to me and I feel your love filling in those cracks and making me whole again."

Francis leaned forward and wrapped his arms around me. After a long embrace he pulled back and took my hands in his again. He regarded me very seriously and I knew instinctively that he had something to tell me and he did not want to. I let him simmer and work up the courage on his own. Finally, he heaved a great sigh.

"Catherine, I have some very sad news for you. After Richard delivered your message from me, he went home to Hatfield as he said he would, but by the time he arrived, he was delirious with fever. He lasted a few days, but they were unable to break the fever and he died." He paused to allow me to absorb his words. "I know it has been months since it happened, but I wanted to be the one to tell you. I know you two shared love for each other and that you would take it hard. I wanted to be with you when you found out."

My eyes began to fill with tears. My first love was gone and though I had always assumed I would never see him again, now it was a certainty. I thought of his new wife, Susannah, and the pain she must be feeling. Suddenly, the last part of Francis's revelation hit me and I looked up, startled, into his eyes. I had believed all this time that Francis was unaware of my past feelings for Richard. I could feel the panic rising in my throat.

Seeing the alarm in my face, Francis squeezed my hands reassuringly.

"Catherine, it is all right." He soothed. "I have always known of your feelings for Richard. I was at Court for a very long time before we were married and I saw the way you looked at him during your riding lessons and how you sought him out whenever you were in the gardens at the palace. And I know he felt the same. Before I asked for your hand, I assured him that you would always be beloved and that I would give you the kind of life you deserved to have. I am sure it killed him inside, but he gave me his blessing and I am eternally grateful. Please do not try to hide your feelings from me, I could never be angry at you for mourning the loss of someone you loved so dearly."

Francis's words opened the dam that had been holding back the tears. I threw myself into his arms and as I laid there sobbing, he stroked my hair and planted kisses on my skin. Once I had exhausted myself I began to doze off curled against his warm body.

I reached up and put my arm on Francis's chest and whispered, "I love you."

The next morning, I sent a page to Hatfield with a few sovereigns and a parcel of baby clothes and quilts for Richard's wife. By my calculation, the baby had already come or was well on its way and I knew that she would be in need without her husband. I wished that I had known sooner so I could have gone myself, but there was no way that Francis would let me leave now that he was home. Winter would be coming soon and there were dangers on the road.

Francis fell back into his routine, helping his brother care for the animals and land during the day and then spending his evenings reading and writing by candlelight. He had plenty of correspondence to attend to now that he was back from the continent and I suspected many of those letters were plans for their next move now that Queen Mary had proclaimed us reconciled with Rome. Francis had sounded so indignant when he told me 30th November was to be named The Feast of Reconciliation. I had to hide my smile behind my hand.

Harry was now old enough to be sent to school. We packed up his belongings and after Christmas and New Year celebrations, he and Francis set off to Magdalen College. Though I was sad to watch him go, I silently rejoiced that Magdalen was in Oxford and while Harry would be living there, it was not far from his home.

During their absence, a piece of good news finally came from the Court, in the form of a letter from my beloved Nan. She had finally found her love. Nan and Walter Hungerford had married in the queen's chapel at Richmond and Walter had recently been knighted. I rejoiced at the revelation that she was pregnant with their first child.

Francis returned home in a huff. While at Magdalen, he received word that the queen had reinstated the acts for burning heretics.

"Probably because she feels so secure with the child of that Spanish scoundrel growing in her womb," he shouted, fist in the air, as he paced his study.

We had all been worried once news made its way to us that the queen was with child, but now you could cut the tension with a knife. Once the act had been passed, six Protestants were tried in quick succession.

It was during this turmoil that I told Francis that the queen was not the only one with child. His spirits were lifted for a few days, but then the dark mood returned as he planned and plotted to keep our family safe.

Francis's urgency reached a fever pitch when, on 4th February, John Rogers was burned at the stake in Smithfield. He and Henry were closeted in his study, as they were so often now, discussing the matter. I stood quietly outside the door eavesdropping, but I needn't have bothered. I could hear Henry shouting about doves flying overhead at Smithfield and the burnings of Laurence Saunders at Coventry, Rowland Taylor at Hadleigh, and John Hooper at Gloucester in the days following that first burning. For the first time since my half-sister took the throne, I was terrified.

Travelling to the Low Countries:
February – May 1557

I looked back in sadness and wondered where the Princess Mary I had known had gone. She had been replaced with a ruthless queen I didn't quite recognise. Mary had not always been this way. Though she often carried a dour face and judgment upon everyone, before my half-sister ascended the throne she had treated every soul she met with kindness. Yes, she had been as stubborn as a mule, but she had also been the young lady who had practically raised poor, motherless Elizabeth. In addition, she had gone out of her way to pay the highest respects to Lady Anne of Cleves, even though Anne hailed from the reformed Low Countries and, I am sure, was considered tainted according to Mary's Catholic sensibilities. Whatever animosity Mary had held towards her enemies, she had always kept it to herself, and chose instead to show grace and temperance.

I blamed our father for this change in her. His arrogance and pride had overshadowed the love and affection he held for his eldest daughter and he had treated her no better than if she were mud he had scraped off his shoe. Mary was proof that neglect and harsh treatment could have lasting effects.

Francis had known that the horror I would witness on that wet October morning was coming, but I had refused to believe that my half-sister could condone such a thing. Burning people at the stake for disagreeing with her! If I had not seen it with my own eyes I would still never believe it of her. Queen Katheryn Parr was a reformer and yet when Mary served her at Court, they laughed and danced together. They happily worked together on their sewing and read by firelight in the queen's rooms. I am certain Mary would never have thought of ordering Katheryn's execution. I made up my mind that even though Francis had chosen the path of fear, I would choose to believe in the goodness I knew in Mary until I witnessed otherwise.

As I bumped along in the coach on the rutted road to Dover, I thought about that dreadful day.

I was awakened at dawn on the morning of 16th October. Francis knelt down next to my face and shook me awake. I lazily opened my eyes and stretched my legs.

"It is a bit early in the morning for coupling, my love," I yawned.

Francis shook his head and I could tell by the seriousness in his dark eyes that I was in for something that held far less joy.

I scrambled to sit up quickly. "What is the matter? Are the children all right?"

He patted my arm. "Yes, Catherine, the children are fine. I have something else I want you to see. Please dress warmly and remember to bring your woollen muff. It is very cold outside."

My curiosity was piqued, but I knew better than to ask questions when Francis was in a hurry. I waited until he left the room and got out of the warm comfort of my bed. I glanced out of the window and saw the web of frost in the corner. Winter would be early this year. I called for Matilda and she bustled in to help me. She brought out the warmest gown I had, black velvet and damask, and dug out my oldest hood, the one with the gable. I had not worn that hood since my days in Calais, but I knew it would keep me warm and I was fairly certain this was not going to be a social call.

Francis returned to fetch me and we met his brother, Henry, in the great hall.

"Francis?" I finally worked up the nerve to ask. "Where are we going?"

Without looking at me Francis grabbed my hand and as we walked out the door, he said, "I am taking you to see the work that is being done in your sister's name."

A crowd had gathered in the middle of the city. We had to push our way through the bundled up bodies to get a good look at what was going on. Two pyres stood next to each other, a pile of logs gathered beneath them. I frowned at Francis. What had he brought me to see?

He gazed into my eyes and mouthed the word, "Watch."

Soon, we were being jostled around to make way. Two men wearing bedraggled, filthy rags were being led to the pyres by men I assumed were the queen's guards.

Henry bent down and whispered in my ear. "That is Nicholas Ridley and Hugh Latimer."

I knew Nicholas Ridley. He had been a chaplain to old King Henry and the Bishop of London under Edward and I had seen him and heard his sermons many times. But I no longer recognised him in this form. The charismatic preacher I remembered had been replaced by a scrawny weak man. The name Hugh Latimer did not sound familiar to me, but he looked as desperate as Ridley did. They made their way slowly to the pyres, stopping for a moment so another man could tie two small bags around their necks, then the guards took their time tying them up. The men murmured prayers and the fires were lit.

Both men tried to remain stoic, biting their lips until they bled to keep from calling out, but as the flames grew higher and licked at their legs, Ridley cried out.

"Into thy hands, Oh Lord! I commend my spirit!"

But the Lord did not help him. The wood was green and wet and the fire could grow no higher than his waist. While Ridley cried out in agony, the fire grew stronger around Latimer.

When the flames began to curl their hot fingers towards his face, Latimer shouted to Ridley, his voice dry and gravelly, "Be of good comfort Master Ridley and play the man! We shall this day light such a candle by God's grace, in England, as I trust shall never be put out."

Francis's quiet amen was almost drowned out by the sharp crack of gun powder. It was then that I realised what was in the bags tied around their necks.

As Ridley screamed out, "Lord have mercy on me! I cannot burn!" I began to silently pray. Please God let his suffering be over. The smell of charred flesh was overwhelming and my stomach began to churn. I closed my eyes against the falling ash blowing in the breeze. Charred piles of it had already begun to pile up on the shoulders of Francis's cloak, but I reined in my instinct to brush it off. That pile of ash was symbolic. It represented the death of my ignorance.

Mercifully a man stepped out of the crowd and lifted a burning stick to the top of the pyre. After the bang of the gunpowder, a blanket of silence fell upon us all. We all kept our eyes to the ground and shuffled away from the scene as the guards cleaned up the mass of charred remains. I felt the bile rising in my throat as we returned in silence to Greys.

The carriage stopped abruptly, bringing my thoughts back to the present. The door banged open and Henry's face came into view.

"Lady sister, we have decided to stop for the night. The horses are weary and I think it would be best to give them a bit of a rest before we carry on. We have only arrived at Horsham so it shall be a few more days until we reach Dover." he said, anxiously awaiting my response.

I nodded. "That is fine, Henry. I will rouse the children and get them in the inn for the night. Thank you for keeping me informed."

Henry tipped his hat and closed the door. I heard him barking orders at the servants. I glanced around the carriage. Elizabeth was propped up on one side of Matilda, and Richard was lying with his head in her lap noisily sucking his thumb. All three were soundly sleeping. Little Francis was curled up on the seat beside me, snoring softly, and I could see baby Anne's little feet starting to move in the basket I had laid her down in. I chuckled softly to myself. I guess Anne was not really a baby any more. She would be two years old in a couple of months. Anne was the result of Francis's joyous return home that autumn of 1554. She came during the suffocating heat of July and the moment I looked at her deep amber eyes and rosy pink lips, I thought of my Aunt Anne. I only wished that she was alive to see her namesake.

I leaned over, kissed my son's flushed cheek and whispered, "Francis, time to wake up."

He emitted a louder snore in reply.

"Francis," I whispered a bit louder this time.

His eyes fluttered open. "Are we there, Mama?"

I tucked a sweaty curl behind his ear

"No baby, we are going to stop here for the night. Can you help Mama wake the others?"

He sat up and grinned.

Francis and I managed to get the other children and Matilda up. I wrapped Anne against my chest and we piled out of the carriage. My son, Robert, who was now six and old enough to help, was filling the trough with water for the horses. Henry dragged a trunk behind him and beckoned us to follow him into the inn.

Matilda and I settled into our room with the little ones, filled their bellies and tucked them into bed. After all was quiet, we sat down to our own dinner. The bread was stale, but the wine was delicious and it warmed me after the frosty day on the road.

Matilda was quietly picking at her food. After an interminable silence she turned to me, "Do you think things would be different if the queen had truly been pregnant?"

I considered her question. Around the time I realised I was pregnant with Anne, rumours had begun to seep out of the court that the Queen was with child as well. It was not formally announced until later in the spring, but the countryside had been abuzz with rumours that we could expect a prince come early summer. When I received a letter from the Princess Elizabeth that she had been summoned to Court for Easter festivities and the queen's lying-in, I knew the queen was indeed pregnant.

We had all waited with bated breath, but word never came that the queen had been delivered of a child. By the time the leaves began their seasonal change, the queen was out of confinement with no baby to show for it. Without even being in the queen's presence, I felt her heartbreak. The only thing Mary had ever wanted was a husband and an heir. Now, both were out of her reach. King Philip had run back to his own lands leaving his wife to take out her disappointment on the reformers. At the time, I did not know that the burnings had ramped up, but all was finally clear to me that October when I saw Ridley and Latimer.

"Truth told, Matilda, I really do not know. Maybe things would be worse because the queen would have her heir. She would need to make her kingdom safe for her child. It would do no good to have challenges to the church." I paused and then went on. "There is no way to be certain. All that we can do is trust in Francis and do what he thinks is best until it is safe for us to come back."

I saw the glint of tears in her eyes and felt a wave of compassion. Matilda was only older than me by five years, but already she had strands of grey in her chestnut hair. She had given up her life to help me in mine. What a shame it was that Matilda would probably never have children. She would be a wonderful mother. I thought about my own children, the ones who had been left behind.

As if reading my thoughts, Matilda whispered, "They will be just fine, Lady Knollys."

I tried to force a smile. "I hope so, Matilda, I miss them terribly."

Lettice was now thirteen, vivacious and full of life. I did not want her to be like me, naïve to the ways of the court, coddled by her mother until she was fifteen. So we had sent her to Hatfield. Princess Elizabeth was back in some form of favour thanks to King Philip and I figured that if any household could teach Lettice some courtly manners, it would be Elizabeth's. The princess was overjoyed to have Lettice in her care. I also knew that if anything happened to the queen and Elizabeth came to the throne, Lettice would be well-placed to find a position at Court.

Our boys William and Edward, now twelve and ten, were living under the care of Ambrose Dudley. Ambrose's ill-fated father had been executed for his part in helping Jane Grey onto the throne, but Ambrose and his brothers had been released from the Tower in the past few years and had come under the protection of King

Philip. Ambrose was given back some of his lands, but none of them were truly welcomed back at Court. Ambrose's brother, Robert, had been close friends with Francis during Edward's reign and they were one of the few families that Francis truly trusted. They were all on their best behaviour for the queen, so their household seemed the safest and I had agreed to let my boys stay there until we returned from the Low Countries.

I missed my children, but in my heart, I knew they were in the safest homes possible while the rest of us made this journey. It was for our daughter, Mary, that I mourned. Sickness had run rampant in the countryside during the spring of 1556. All of the children had caught the fever and all were spared except my Mary. We fought back with everything in our arsenal, even bringing in the doctor to bleed her, but in the end her body gave up. We buried our sweet daughter on Easter Sunday. Mere weeks after her death, Francis was on his way back to the Low Countries.

The burning of the Archbishop of Canterbury had sealed his resolve. He knew that once a man of that high position had been burned, there was no going back. The archbishop, Thomas Cranmer, had been one of King Henry's closest advisers. Not only had he secured the king's divorces, he had been instrumental in many of the changes in Henry's version of the English church. It was no secret that Queen Mary hated him for it. She believed that if it had not been for Cranmer, then her mother would have died in comfort at her bed at Court and not suffering in the cold, banished from her husband. It came as no surprise when Cranmer was locked in the Tower. When he was moved to Bocardo prison in Oxford with Ridley and Latimer, we were certain he too would be burned. But as we watched Ridley and Latimer go up in flames, Cranmer watched on from a tower overlooking the grounds.

After the burnings, Cranmer was sent to Christ Church, where he proceeded to sign his name to five recantations.

"Five! Five times he forsakes the true religion!" Francis had shouted when he found out. "He even recognised the pope as the leader of the church! This is an abomination!"

I tried to comfort him and reminded him that Cranmer was only trying to save his own life, but Francis would not hear it. He locked himself up in his study for days, furiously writing letters to other reformers in his circle.

Sadly, Cranmer's recantations could not save him. In March, he was returned to Oxford and burned in the same spot as his friends, Ridley and Latimer. Francis and Henry were there to witness his burning, but I had seen enough. I stayed home and prayed for Cranmer's soul. I still have no idea what Cranmer said that day as the flames burned out his life, but whatever it was, it lit a fire in Francis and he was more determined than ever that we flee our home in England. That spring he left us in the care of Henry and began his journey to Basel, Switzerland. He was gone for almost a year before we received instructions to join him, and now we were on our way.

Matilda rose and began to sort through the trunks looking for my night shift. We had a long journey ahead of us and we both needed our rest. She helped me out of my layers of damask and we both settled into bed, I in the big tester with my children, she in the trundle bed on the floor beside mine. In my exhaustion, sleep came quickly.

I found myself in the middle of a town square. The smoke from the fires was so thick I could barely see through it. Keeping my head down and my eyes on the ground, I felt around through the fog of smoke. The smell of roasting flesh filled the air and my ears rang with the screams of the damned. I yanked my hand back when I felt the heat of the flames. The smoke began to clear and as I looked up, I could see the woman tied to the stake, enveloped in fire. My watering eyes blurred my vision, but I could make out her distended stomach, swollen with child. She gave a great scream and a rush of blood splattered on the ground. It was then that I realised, the baby had been born. It was hanging by its cord between the woman's legs.

I lunged at the fire grasping for the child. The intense heat scorched my skin. A cluster of blisters appeared on the back of my hands, but I reached in further until I had the child. I pulled back, yanking until the cord was free. Before I could tend to the wailing baby, it was snatched from my hand by a dark figure and tossed back into the flames.

A voice boomed beside me, "This child shall share in its mother's sin!"

I looked up into the mother's face and my heart stopped when I saw my daughter, Mary, looking back at me. An unearthly scream erupted from the depths of my soul and my world went black.

"Lady Knollys!"

My body was convulsing. Was this the end?

"Lady Knollys!"

Who was calling my name?

"Catherine!"

My eyes flew open. I was not convulsing, Matilda was shaking me awake. I had soaked my night shift in sweat. My hair hung limply over my face.

Matilda brushed my hair out of my eyes and put her arm around me, helping me into a sitting position.

"Please, Lady Knollys, you will wake the children. It was only a dream. You are safe with me and your family."

I looked around, the familiarity of the room returning to me. Sure enough, the children were asleep next to me. Edward was snoring softly and Anne was sucking noisily on her thumb. I felt so foolish that it did not even offend me that Matilda had chastised me.

"Matilda," I sighed, and lay back on the bed. "It was terrible. Can you please bring me something to drink?"

Matilda walked over to the table by the fire and came back with a mug of ale. I gulped it down, the cool liquid soothing my dry throat. I handed it back to her. "Thank you."

She nodded. As she walked back towards the table, a muffled

knock sounded at the door. In the firelight I was certain I saw her grimace. She set down the mug and padded over to the door. I watched from the bed, but I could not see who was there. They exchanged low whispers and after a moment, Matilda closed the door and shuffled back to her trundle bed, eyes cast to the ground.

"Matilda, who was at the door?"

In the firelight, I could just make out the crimson flush rising in her cheeks.

"It was Master Henry," she said quietly. She busied herself with the blankets and settled down into her quilts.

I decided to give her an escape.

"He must have heard my screams and came to see if I was all right," I said, lying back against the pillow, even though I knew full well that if the children had not heard my screams, there was no way he had heard them down the hall.

"Yes, I assured him you were fine," she said, pulling her quilts up over her chest and closing her eyes.

I smiled to myself and blew out the candle on the table above her head.

We lay quietly in the dark, neither one of us sleeping, but both trying desperately for that peaceful slumber.

After an hour of restless tossing and turning, I let out an exasperated sigh.

"Lady Catherine?"

"Yes, Matilda?"

"Will you tell me what you were dreaming about?" she asked tentatively.

I hesitated. I did not want to scare Matilda, but I could not get the gruesome scenes out of my head. I knew I had to share them, get them out of my mind before I would be able to sleep peacefully tonight.

"Matilda," I started. "Do you remember when Francis, Henry and I went to town and returned covered in ash? You asked what happened, but I refused to tell you?"

Matilda rose out of her cocoon of blankets. "Yes, my lady. You went to see the burnings."

I held out my hand. "Wait, how did you know?" I had never told Matilda about the burnings. I didn't want to cause her undue worry and I couldn't bear to talk about the things that I had seen that day.

Matilda shifted uncomfortably, but after a moment she admitted, "Master Henry told me."

I knew then that my suspicions were right. Henry would never have shared such information with my maid, unless they had a closer relationship than I was aware of.

I sat up and reached for Matilda's hand. "Matilda, are you and Henry ...?" I could not even finish the sentence in my amazement.

Matilda's eyes widened. "No, my lady! No! We have done nothing of that sort. Master Henry is nothing but proper. It is just that - sometimes - he confides in me. I think that, with all of the losses you have suffered with your mother and Maude and Mary, he doesn't want to add to your suffering with worry, especially when Sir Francis is at Court. He adores you and says often that he is closer to you than his own blood sisters. But, like you, he has the scenes in his head of the horrible things he saw that day and has seen in town since. I guess it helps him to talk them through with me."

I squeezed her hand and smiled, "It is all right, Matilda. I thank you for the comfort you have given Henry. It is true that after watching two men burn to death for nothing other than their beliefs I have been filled with anxiety for our safety. What Henry does not realise is that he is not the only one keeping secrets. I too know what our queen and her ministers have been doing. I've heard the conversations between the servants and they make my stomach turn. A particularly wretched story invaded my dreams tonight. Ever since I heard it, I have been unable to banish it from my mind."

Matilda leaned forward and said quietly, "If it helps Master Henry to talk to me about it, maybe it will help you as well."

"Sweet Matilda, God bless you for having such a compassionate heart."

She smiled at me and gave my hand a small squeeze, nodding her head to urge me on.

"Francis had already left for the Low Countries and I was still under the grey cloud of Mary's passing. I was tired of being in the house so I went out to the gardens to take in the cool autumn air. The leaves were turning these beautiful shades of orange and yellow and I wanted to enjoy the flowers before everything turned brown. I sat down on the bench behind the hedge that faced the clothes line. I could hear the washer-women behind me, chatting as they worked. I was hidden behind the hedge so they did not know I could hear them. I didn't pay them any mind, I was there to enjoy the sunshine not to chastise the servants, but then I overhead them talking about a woman in Guernsey. Her name was Perotine Massey. That July she had been accused of not attending church and she and her mother and sister had been sentenced to burning at the stake. Word of her story had just reached Greys that week when the butcher's son came from town to bring us our meat.

Now, after the deaths of Ridley and Latimer, I was not surprised to hear of another burning, but I must admit I was taken aback to hear that it was a woman this time. But that is not the worst of it. No, the worst part was that Perotine was with child. The servants didn't seem to know whether the bailiff was aware of this or not, but the fact remains that a pregnant woman was burned at the stake. While she was burning she gave birth to a little boy and when a bystander reached into the fire to try to save him, the bailiff ripped the child from his arms and tossed him back into the flames, claiming that the baby shared its mother's sin."

Matilda had gone pale, but I could tell she was trying to keep her composure. She had always had such a tender heart with children. I knew that the very idea of an infant being tossed into the fire was too gut-wrenching for her to even fathom. But she had offered herself as a confidante and she appeared determined to hear my story.

"How horrible," she breathed.

I nodded. It was beyond horrible. It was unconscionable. How could the Princess Mary I knew have become so monstrous that she could allow this to happen? I grappled with this in my heart.

Matilda replied as if she had been reading my mind, "Perhaps the queen did not know that she had sentenced an infant to death. You said yourself that the bailiff did not know. Perotine may not have even been aware of her condition. Perhaps it was truly an unfortunate accident."

I shook my head, "I have told myself that over and over, Matilda, but I have borne eleven children and I knew that I was with child from the very early stages. For Perotine to have been so far along that she would have actually given birth, she had to know. She had to feel that life kicking inside of her. And what of her belly? How could she hide it? And most importantly, why would she? She had benefit of the belly. I would think that would be her first defence."

Matilda shrugged. "I cannot tell you, my lady. I too cannot imagine that she would not plead benefit of the belly, but we were not there. We did not witness it first-hand. We have only the gossip of two washer-women who did not witness it either. I think that for your own comfort you must give Queen Mary the benefit of the doubt."

I sighed inwardly and contemplated Matilda's words. I knew that she was right, but I was finding her reasoning hard to accept. I had given others the benefit of the doubt in the past and been bitterly disappointed. But in the case of Perotine, it was unlikely I would ever know the truth and I did not want to know that my half-sister was capable of being that cold.

Matilda broke the silence. "Was it of Perotine that you were dreaming of my lady?"

"In a way," I replied. "I dreamt I was there. That I pulled the baby from the fire and after the bailiff ripped it from my hands, I looked up and instead of seeing Perotine, saw my own daughter, Mary. My beautiful girl... lost to the flames." I paused. "I know Queen Mary had nothing to do with her death, but I think that because I heard Perotine's story so soon after her death and deep in my grief, I cannot help but link them together."

Matilda patted my hand. "Mary is with the angels now, free from pain."

I raised my eyebrow in surprise. "Matilda, you do not believe in Purgatory?"

She gave a lilting laugh. "Are you surprised my lady?"

I shook my head. "No, Matilda, I suppose not. You have been speaking to Henry after all. He is passionate about the Gospel. I imagine I am the only person left in our household that still questions my beliefs in the old and new religion."

Her reply resonated in my heart. "Old religion, new religion, does it truly matter? All that matters is that we have faith, the rest are merely earthly matters."

After my conscience was relieved of its burden I was able to get some sleep. Henry was pounding on the door before sunrise, anxious to be on the way. We rushed about, piling our trunks back into the carts, and continued our journey to Dover.

A fishing vessel would be waiting there for us to take us across the sea to Calais. From there we would travel by coach through France and into Germany. I was not looking forward to the channel crossing. I had almost fallen overboard the last time, but it helped to know that this time Francis would be waiting for me on the other side of this journey.

I was leading the children to our cabin below the deck when I felt a tap on my shoulder. A young sailor gave me a small bow and then held out a letter to me.

"What is this?" I asked, reaching for it.

"It arrived before your party my lady. A messenger from the queen, I believe. He did not say, but I saw her coat of arms on his riding blanket and he was wearing her colours," he replied and then turned, heading back to work.

I held the letter in my hand and felt the bile rise in my throat. This was it. We were to be burned now. My hands shook as I broke the seal.

I stopped myself from opening the letter. I needed someone to be with me when I read the terrible news. I left the children with Matilda and ran upstairs to the deck to look for Henry.

He was standing at the railing, staring out at the sea.

"Henry!" I called out.

He turned back to look at me, his face darkened with concern. "Yes, Catherine?"

I called breathless, "A letter from the queen."

His hands dropped from the rail and he ran to me. "What does it say?"

Shaking I said, "I... I do not know. I have not the courage to open it."

"You must," he urged, pushing the envelope back towards me.

I willed my hands to stop their trembling and slowly opened the fold.

I scanned the page and sighed with great relief once I realised the danger was over.

"Well?" Henry asked.

"*Mistress Knollys,*

It is with great regret that I must write this letter. It has come to my attention that you and your family fear me and for that reason, have taken it upon yourselves to flee my rule. My heart aches with sadness that someone that has known me for most of my life has such fear for me that they would abandon their home. It breaks even more that this confirms for me that you have turned from the True Religion of the Holy Catholic Church. I admit it does not surprise me much since you are the child of a Boleyn. And possibly - no, that cannot be true - I cannot bear to believe what has been whispered. I am certain my father had no reason to, but he held you in great affection and unlike the rest of the women in your family, you have always shown kindness towards me. For a child of the Boleyns, you had a sweetness I never could decipher. I must assume it came from William Carey, though he never treated me with great respect either. In any case, I know that as a wife, you must follow your husband's command even if it is incorrect - as Sir Francis certainly is - for believing you are in

*any danger. Because of your duty and because of the kindness you
have shown me in the past, I have written today to assure you of your
safety, should you return home. I assume you will, for I have been told
that your lovely Lettice is still unmarried and living with my sister
at Hatfield and that your sons are in the care of Ambrose Dudley. I
will see to it that no harm should come to them, as no child should
suffer for their parents' folly as I have. I pray that while you are in the
midst of these heretics, you learn their true nature and return to the
Catholic church, urging your husband to join you in its righteousness.*

Mary the Queen"

Henry's face burned in anger. Before he could shout, I placed
my hand on his chest.

"Henry, we leave with the queen's protection. It may not be her
blessing and she can pray all she wants for our return to her church,
but the important thing is that she will not pursue us. She has also
assured us that your niece and nephews will be safe while we are
gone. We must look upon this letter as a blessing."

He opened his mouth to protest, but closed it again after a
moment. He was still enraged at the queen's remarks regarding his
brother, but he I hoped he could see reason. He sighed and removed
my hand from his chest.

"Fine, Catherine. Please go back down to your cabin with
Matilda and the children. I need to calm down."

I could not let his command pass without a sly remark, "Would
you like me to send up Matilda?"

Henry gave me the startled look that confirmed his feelings
towards my maid. I turned on my heel, skirts swishing behind me.

When we arrived at Calais, a small contingent of coaches and
carts awaited. It appeared that those of us on the island were not the
only ones escaping to more tolerant regions. The spring rains had
arrived at last, softening the dirt roads, turning them into a bog of
mire and muck. When the day was dry, the going was just as rough
because the wheel ruts from the travellers before us were steep and

hard on the horses. By the time we reached our resting place for the night, the children had spent most of the day bouncing around the coach and found standing on solid ground difficult.

We were on the road for almost four weeks before we reached Frankfurt, but along the way I saw the most beautiful sights I had ever seen. Our journey started out as a scene of rolling green hills as far as the eye could see. Past Tournai, the hills gave way to the forested mountains of the Ardennes. We travelled under a canopy of trees, lulled by the sounds of the rushing river. One clear afternoon we stopped beside the water to take our supper. The children crept towards the river's edge while Matilda and I prepared a plate of bread and oranges for them. I kept looking over my shoulder, making sure they were not getting too close as the current was swift, and as I turned back to the plate I heard Matilda's sharp intake of breath.

I dropped the plate and spun around, ready to run for the children. When I saw what Matilda was reacting to I stopped. A black bear was sniffing through the brush, her young cub trailing behind her. The children were busily toeing the rocks on the river bank, paying no attention to the danger lurking behind them. I crept slowly down to them, trying not to make a sound. Elizabeth caught my eye and parted her lips to say something, but I put my finger to my own to hush her. She gave me a quizzical look and gathered the younger children together, shushing them as I had done her. When I reached them, I turned them all to see the sight across the river. After that day, when the road was rough and I was exhausted, I tried to think of that mother bear leading her cubs to safety and reminded myself that though the journey was treacherous, soon we would be reunited with Francis.

When we reached Cologne we turned out of the forest and followed the Rhine valley most of the way to Frankfurt. As we got closer, my exhaustion was replaced by a strange mixture of giddy apprehensiveness. My stomach was in a perpetual knot and I found myself clenching my jaw in anxiety. I was overjoyed at the prospect of seeing my love again. My heart had ached at his absence. It is

hard to imagine a feeling of loneliness when you are surrounded by
a house full of children and servants, but it was always there. That
deep ache I felt when I reached over in my sleep to the empty side
of the bed. No warmth to comfort me. The knowledge that Francis
would be waiting for me at the end of this journey was what kept
me going.

Yet this excitement was tinged with the anxiety of what could
be waiting for me in this foreign land. I thought of the Lady Anne
of Cleves, her gruff accent and strange clothing. We all grew to love
her, but it took some time to embrace her differences and many
members of the court were still not all that accepting. Would I be
accepted in this new land? Most importantly, would my children?
Were we leaving behind one kind of danger to encounter another?
I tried desperately to tamp down my emotions, but I knew they
could only be assuaged after I saw Francis. I craved his assurance.

Just less than ten miles outside of Frankfurt the rain began
to pour. Most of our train had split off throughout the journey to
places like Strasbourg, Aarau and Zurich so our party had become
small and, after so long on the road, we were eager to reach our
destination. Henry conferred with the other riders and they all
decided to carry on rather than wait out the storm. I insisted that
Robert ride in the coach. It would do no good to have a sick child in
this unfamiliar land. Robert looked disappointed to ride with the
younger children, but he took it in his stride when I reminded him
how proud his father would be that he had ridden so far.

The rain splashed on the timbered roof of the coach as it bounced
through the mud, lulling me into a daze. I was so exhausted that
I missed our entrance into the city. Before I realised it, the coach
had stopped. A loud knock on the door startled me. I sat up and
gestured to Matilda and the children to do the same. The door flew
open and a familiar face came into view.

Francis's hair was soaked and rain dripped from his nose, but
his eyes were bright and his smile wide.

"Here is my family!" he exclaimed.

"And Matilda!" piped up little Francis from his perch on her lap.

Francis chuckled and gave little Francis a wink. "Well, my son, I have known Matilda for so long that I suppose she is my family, but thank you for the gentle reminder," he teased.

I could not make out Matilda's face clearly in the dimness of the coach, but I was certain she was blushing.

"Come now, children," he said, gesturing through the doorway.

Richard and Robert were the first to jockey for the door, pushing and shoving to be the first out. Elizabeth slipped silently behind them, gripped their shoulders and guided them through the door. Matilda lifted little Francis from her lap. I grasped his sweaty hand and led him down the steps. Matilda followed behind with Anne on her hip.

The rain had finally died down, but the ground was wet and slippery. I used my free hand to lift my skirts out of the mud.

After all I had seen on our journey, I had expected a more pastoral scene, but we were in the middle of a crowded city and the house loomed above me the moment we stepped onto the street. Francis waited patiently with the children for me outside the great oak door to the house. The scent of roasting meat wafted out of the wide, opened doors. My mouth watered. Two young men strode out and headed for the carts, working quickly to unload our small cache of possessions. I met Francis at the door and he wrapped me in a tight embrace.

"I have missed you so, my love," he whispered in my ear.

Before I could respond, he pulled away and led me into the house, Matilda and the children following behind.

The warmth of the fire immediately enveloped me. The fire crackled and popped in a room lit by soft candlelight. We made our way back to the dining room and were greeted by a chorus of voices.

A man - who looked to be about twenty or so years older than me - stood and gave me a small bow. "Welcome to my home, Lady Knollys. Please, please come sit," he said, gesturing to the table. Six strapping young men of varying ages smiled back at me from around the table. A plump rosy-cheeked woman nodded in agreement.

Francis placed one arm around my lower back and gestured with the other to the family at the table. "Wife, I would like you to meet Master John Weller of London, his wife Isabell and sons, John, Jasper, Edmund, Geoffrey and Peter."

They each smiled and gave a nod at the sound of their name.

I eagerly returned their grins. "Thank you for welcoming us into your home."

Then Francis gestured toward the other end of the table. "This is Sir Thomas Knot. He was a student with me at Basel."

The young man jumped out of his seat and bowed eagerly in my direction.

Flustered, I waved him off. "Oh, that was not necessary."

"Pleasure to meet you, my lady," he said, straightening up.

Francis nodded to him and he returned to his seat.

Matilda ushered the younger children to follow behind one of the maids and Francis, Elizabeth and I took three of the remaining chairs at the table, leaving one for Henry. He joined us a few moments later and the introductions commenced again.

The maid returned and, with the other maid, began to bring out the dishes for our dinner. Two roasted chickens, a lamb pie, some salted herring and a cheese tart sat steaming before us.

The boy called Edmund grinned at me, "I have been waiting for this pie for months!"

Indeed, the meagre days of Lent were over. It was time to feast.

Frankfurt, Germany:
June 1557 – November 1559

Our new home was nothing like our manor back in Oxfordshire. Where Greys was airy and open, this place was crowded and cramped, overtaken by the smells and sounds of a house full of people. It was cosy though. Master Weller was a merchant back in England and had been made a burgher of the city so his lodgings were much more comfortable than most who shared our exile. Regardless of how well-appointed the house was, there were still twenty-one people living under one roof and such cramped quarters came with their own set of inconveniences.

The close stool was always in use, the smell of food constantly wafted out of the kitchen, and unruly shouting matches often erupted from the stress of living in such a tight space. Matilda and I quietly kept to ourselves, helping wherever we could. Elizabeth was old enough to pitch in as well and I rejoiced at her eagerness whenever she jumped at the chance to help out without being asked. Francis and I had raised our children well. They may be children of gentry, but they were the first to step in when a job needed doing and did not fear soiling their hands. My grandfather Boleyn would have been appalled, but I was pleased.

Francis spent his days at the small church our group had been granted by the city of Frankfurt, arguing with his fellow exiles over which prayer book to use and who would lead the sermons. No one could agree upon anything and with every social class living and worshipping together all the social rules had broken down. The artisan was equal to the knight, the servant's vote counted as much as the squire's. Birthright no longer guaranteed a higher status in this community. The puffed-up men of the gentry could barely tolerate this new order, but they had to in order to survive. Everyone was granted a voice.

My husband would come home weary from these battles, his head hanging low, bags beneath his eyes. I listened patiently as he recounted his day, my hand kneading the tense muscles in his shoulders, and soon he would relax enough for us to enjoy our time as husband and wife once again. Afterwards, my body curled up against his, he whispered, "Every night since I left you, I would lie awake and think of how I missed feeling you next to me. Your warm body curved into mine, the scent of rose water in your hair. And now you are here with me, half a world away from our home and I feel as though I am dreaming. That I will wake up in the morning and you will be gone. Promise you will stay with me."

I kissed the palm of his hand and whispered back, "I promise."

I should have known better than to promise such a thing, because a few short months after arriving in Frankfurt, I was with child again.

Isabell Weller and I sat in the solar sewing a pile of shirts. The boys were starting to outgrow their clothing and while we had the money to buy more, we had been discouraged from doing business with the local merchants. They were none too pleased by the influx of immigrants, many of them artisans, and were only too eager to take advantage of the English ladies who chose to remain ignorant of our host country's culture and language.

The maids were in the kitchen preparing the afternoon meal and the scent of smoked fish escaped every time they opened the door into the dining hall. I had been more exhausted than usual that week, but Francis had been coming home later and later and I refused to fall asleep before he was in. I sat dozing in the early summer sunlight, my needle threatening to fall from my relaxed hand. The overwhelming scent of herring overtook me when one of Isabell's maids propped open the door to let us know when supper would be ready. I turned my head just in time to vomit all over the newly scrubbed floor, trying frantically to remember when I had last had my courses.

Matilda jumped up from the corner where she had been playing with little Anne.

"My lady!"

I put one hand out and wiped my lips with the other.

"I am all right, I am all right. I think my lack of sleep has finally got to me. I am going to go lie down."

Matilda and Isabell exchanged a knowing glance.

"Please get this cleaned up before the men are home," Isabell gestured to her maid.

Matilda helped me out of the chair and up the stairs.

I gripped her arm. "Please do not mention any thing to Henry. Francis must be the first to know."

Matilda frowned at me. "My lady, I would never share your happy news. Your secret is safe with me."

I spent the rest of the afternoon in bed, tossing and turning, anxious about Francis's reaction. My husband had always been flushed with pleasure at every pregnancy. He wanted a large family and took pride in his ever-growing brood of children. But something told me this time would be different.

While we'd been sewing, Isabell had described life in exile and from that conversation I knew that several children had been born in the English settlements. Life had carried on much the same here as it did back home, but I did not want my baby born in exile. The child I was carrying in my belly would be the grandchild of a king of England and a niece or nephew of the reigning queen. Recognised or not, a child of Tudor blood should be born in England. More than that, I wanted to be home in the comfort of my own rooms. I wanted the maids who had nursed my other babies. I could not bear the idea of giving birth in an unfamiliar land with a midwife I did not know.

Eventually I fell asleep waiting for Francis to return home for the evening. His deep voice and the soft touch of his hand on my forehead brought me out of my dreams.

He tenderly brushed my hair from my face. "Isabell said you were feeling ill?" he ventured, his eyes full of concern.

"Just a little," I replied, scooting myself up against the headboard.

"Are you all right?"

"Yes Francis. I am fine," I said taking his hand in mine. "I am with child."

A smile broke out across his face. "An even dozen then?" he laughed.

I finally cracked a smile back. "Yes, husband, an even dozen."

"Well this is wonderful news, Catherine. Why do you look so serious?"

My stomach started to churn. How could I tell him I wanted to leave and travel home to have this child? I knew he would never permit it. He must have read it on my face when I did not respond.

"You want to go home don't you?" he asked.

"Well... Yes I do," I muttered. "I want my own midwife and for our child to be born in our own home - your home - the home you inherited from your father."

"I understand," he whispered.

I wrapped my arms around him.

"Please don't be upset with me. I could not bear it. I will do as you wish, Francis. If you wish our baby to be born here, then that is what will be."

He lifted my hand to his lips and then turned to kiss mine.

"Let me think on this, Catherine. We do not have much time to consider the options, but I want to be sure that we choose the safest one. I do not like the idea of you going back to England while Mary is queen. She burned the Archbishop of Canterbury at the stake. Who is to say that she will not take out her anger at my flight on you?"

Quietly, I murmured, "She says."

He turned abruptly to face me. "What do you mean 'she says'?"

I rose from the bed and walked over to my trunk. Inside, still tucked into my Bible where I left it all that time ago, was my letter from the queen. I don't know why I never showed it to Francis. I think it was because he had been so happy to see us and under so much pressure from everything else that I did not want to bring up the woman he despised so much. He would be angry at my deception, but I knew now was the time.

I walked back to the bed, holding the letter out to him.

"What is this?" he asked, taking it from me.

"It is from the queen."

I watched his face carefully as he read the letter, cringing as I remembered the queen's words of righteousness. He kept opening his mouth as if to say something, but the rebuke never came. He silently handed the parchment back to me.

"Put that back in your trunk. I never want to see it again."

"Francis, I ..."

He put his hand up to stop me. "You have given me much to consider. Now please, lay back down and rest. I will have Matilda bring your supper in a little while."

I nodded, blinking back the tears, and scrambled back under the covers. Francis kissed me on the forehead and quietly left the room.

The evening seemed to drag on forever. Matilda had come and gone with bread and ale and now I was all alone, listening to the incessant chatter going on below me. Dinner was a time of riotous conversation and it seemingly went on unabated without me. I stared out of the window until I heard the voices die down. When Francis still did not come back, I crept out and headed to the children's room. Matilda had them all tucked in nicely, Elizabeth in the big bed with Richard and little Francis curled into her arms, Robert sprawled across the pallet on the other side of the room, and baby Anne wrapped tightly in the wooden cradle Francis had had made for us by a local woodworker before our arrival. I was struck by the irony of the intricate bears carved into the wood. Matilda's trundle was pulled out but it was empty. I guessed she was still downstairs cleaning up from dinner.

I sat on the edge of the bed and ran my fingers through little

Francis's curls. They were so vulnerable in their sleep and the knowledge of that brought tears to my eyes. It had been a long and trying journey to get out here and we'd had Henry to guide us. There was no way I could subject them to a return trip so soon, and without a leader we trusted so much. This baby would be born in exile. It was the only option. My lips brushed against little Francis's silken forehead, then I got up and tiptoed quietly back to my room.

When I returned, Francis was sitting at his desk, hunched over a book in which he was methodically writing. His hand moved slowly and with great flourishes. Whatever it was he was recording must have been important for him to write so carefully. I stood quietly in the doorway waiting for him to address me. When he did, he was concentrating so hard on what he was writing that he did not even look up at me.

"Are the children all right?"

"Oh yes, I just missed them so I wanted to say goodnight, but they were already asleep by the time I got in there."

Francis returned the quill to its stand. He turned to me and silently nodded.

"Can I ask what you are working on?" I asked gesturing to his desk.

He smiled. "Of course. I keep no secrets from you."

Those words hit me hard. Of course Francis did not keep secrets from me, nor did I normally keep them from him. I could not excuse my lack of honesty, but I hoped he would eventually forgive me for it.

I sat down on the bed, exhaling a tired sigh.

"I am sorry I didn't tell you of the letter from the queen. I did not want to upset you. I see now that it upset you even more that I deceived you."

Francis strode over to the bed and sat down beside me.

"Catherine, I understand your desire to go home. I want to go home too. I miss my land, I miss being a trusted advisor to our monarch. I miss everything about England. But God has led us to this place for our safety, and I promise you that once our Elizabeth takes the throne, we shall return in all our glory."

The thought of my beautiful niece taking her rightful place on the throne brought tears to my eyes. Having lost children myself, I did feel for Queen Mary's pain, but I would be lying if I did not admit that it brought a certain relief when her pregnancy turned out to be a phantom. I could not stand the idea of Mary's child ascending the throne over Elizabeth.

I brushed my tears aside and took Francis's hand.

"Our child shall be born in exile, but raised to be a proud Englishman."

Francis smiled and added, "Our first child born without the taint of Catholic popery."

I wanted to laugh out loud at the serious look on his face. Catholicism did not seem like such a terrible thing to me when it was not used as a weapon to burn people alive, but to Francis it was a plague. I let him have his moment of righteousness, but stopped short of encouraging him. As long as my child was born healthy I did not care if it was in a Catholic or Protestant country.

Francis brought my hand to his lips and kissed it tenderly.

"Would you still like to see what I was working on?"

I nodded.

He got up and walked over to the desk, coming back with a book in his hand, the pages open to reveal his delicate handiwork. He sat down next to me and placed it in my hand. The leather cover was soft and supple in my hands. I closed the book for a moment to see what was written on the cover. It was a Latin dictionary and thesaurus for the letters A to E.

"I bought this when I was a student at Basel," Francis murmured.

I opened the book back to where my finger had stayed marking the page.

At the top of the page it said:

Here follows in order the names, with the times of the birth of the children of Francis Knollys & Catherine his wife that were married the 26ᵗʰ day of April anno. 1540. The year of Our Lord is counted to begin at Christmas.

Below that, he had listed the names and birth dates of all of our children, numbered one to eleven. He ended with the number twelve empty, waiting for the name of this child that was growing in my belly.

"Francis, it is beautiful." I said in awe.

"I never had a chance to start this when I was back in England. It finally occurred to me that I had better write it before we have so many children we cannot remember their birth dates," he said with a chuckle.

I leaned over and kissed his cheek, the hair from his beard tickling my lips.

"Thank you for this."

"You are welcome, my darling. Now, I am going to put it in our trunk to keep it safe until the child is born."

I went to bed feeling relieved that Francis had forgiven me. Once again, I realised just how blessed I had been in this marriage. Francis was a good man and I knew he would always do what was right for our family. I fell into an easy sleep wrapped in the comfort of his care.

Living in exile had fundamentally changed the way we lived our lives and that included my time in pregnancy. At home in Rotherfield Greys, we had servants and tutors to help me with the children. In Frankfurt I had only Matilda. Matilda was amazing and I would have been lost without her, but she was ill-equipped to take on the children by herself for three months, so going into confinement was out of the question. Even if she had been able to do so, there was no other place for Francis to sleep besides in our bed. It would be far too inconvenient to move him out for the duration of my final months of pregnancy.

In a way it was quite lovely. I looked forward to getting up and moving about every day, instead of being stuck inside a stuffy room unable to get out of bed. On the other hand, this pregnancy was difficult and I was so exhausted by the end of the day that some nights I longed for the comfort of my lying-in room back in England. Above all, I worried incessantly about my labour. Back home I had a midwife I trusted. She had been there to deliver all of my children and she knew my body as well as her own. I knew of no midwives here in Frankfurt and Isabell was past the point of childbearing so she had none to recommend.

One evening in early December I pulled Matilda aside and confided my anxiety. She promised that she would visit the homes of the other exiles in the community until she found a proper midwife. The next morning, dressed in my warmest cloak and muffler, she set off into the village. I waited anxiously all that day for her return. True to her word, as always, Matilda arrived, her nose reddened with the cold, eyes shining with hope and a stout little gnome of a woman in tow - the midwife that would deliver my baby.

I looked hesitantly from Matilda to the midwife and back again. The woman looked as though she had seen seventy winters. Her wiry grey hair stuck out from underneath a woollen cap perched on her head. She was diminutive in stature but looked sturdy and strong. Matilda caught my eye and nodded vigorously, a wide grin on her face.

"She came highly recommended."

I took a deep breath and nodded, trusting in Matilda's confident smile.

I gestured for them to follow me up to my room where the old woman could examine me. Matilda took her leave, discreetly heading to the children's room, and the woman followed behind me. She shuffled from side to side as she walked, almost as if she were in pain. I was certain that at her age her bones would wearily give out by the first landing, but she never made a sound of complaint as she followed me up the stairs.

I led her inside my room and pointed towards the bed. "Here?"

She nodded, still never making a sound. I reached behind to

loosen my stomacher and then lay down on my back. She shuffled over and placed her gnarled, swollen hands on my belly, caressing it like a crone divining a fortune. Then she bent over and laid her ear against me. Just at that moment the baby kicked and I saw it make contact with her ear. She gave a great bellow of laughter and I could see the gaping holes where her teeth had rotted out. But I was relieved to finally receive a sign of life. I allowed myself to relax as she continued her examination.

Eventually she straightened and offered her hand to help me sit up. She held up two fingers and I nodded, "Yes, about two more months."

She smiled that toothless grin again and grunted, "Good, good."

I didn't know how much English she knew but I asked, "Matilda can get you when it is time?"

"Yes, fine," she replied, nodding emphatically.

I heaved a sigh of relief. I would not know until the time came if she was as skilled as it was claimed, but something in that laugh of hers gave me hope. I had to have faith that she would take care of me.

My time came as a snow-storm raged outside our window at the end of January. True to her word, the midwife returned, shuffling into my room behind Matilda. I accepted the pain and gave myself over to her practised hands.

The wind howled through the eaves as I laboured for four days. There were moments when I thought I would die from the agony, but I pressed on. Having not eaten a scrap of food in days, I hardly had the strength to push, but I refused to give up and, finally, on the evening of the fourth night, I gave a final push and fell back in exhaustion.

The child unleashed a great yell at the indignity of it all and I knew as soon as I heard his scream that he would survive. I closed my eyes and tumbled into the darkness of sleep.

While the rest of the household celebrated Candlemas, I trudged through a dark dream-world of my own creation. I awoke only twice, soaked in the sweat of my fever. The first time was after a searing pain across my belly brought me screaming into consciousness. The second was during one of the many blood lettings that I was told later were performed on me. Before I emerged through the haze of childbed fever, I dreamt of my aunt, Anne. Her raven hair billowed behind her, her shadowy body wrapped in an ethereal glow. Her deep brown eyes alighted on mine and she whispered, "Not today, Catherine."

Much to everyone's relief the fever broke, but I was heartbroken that I had missed my son's first week and I still did not even know his name. It was the first question I asked when I finally found my raspy voice.

The midwife grinned as she placed the squirmy bundle in my arms.

"Thomas, his name is Thomas," replied my much relieved husband. He looked as haggard and exhausted as I felt.

Thomas curled his delicate hand over my finger and tried desperately to pull it into his mouth.

"For my grandfather Thomas, or my uncle Thomas?"

"Neither," he replied.

I looked up and Francis's face was twisted in emotion. He glanced at the midwife busily folding blankets in the corner and then looked back to me. "Thomas for Thomasine - the woman who saved your life."

I grew stronger each day. We didn't have a wet nurse in exile so, as with Maude, I was able to breast-feed again. I felt as though I had missed out on precious bonding time all those years I had handed over my child to the wet nurse so it was a bit of a thrill for me to ignore all those traditions of the nobles. I nursed my baby and rocked him to sleep instead of employing someone else to do those motherly duties.

Shortly after Thomas's birth we learned that Calais had fallen to the French. It was England's punishment for supporting King Philip's attack on France.

"This is what happens when the queen marries a foreign prince!" raged Francis that night.

All of England had been in uproar when Mary married the son of the Holy Roman Emperor, Prince Philip of Spain. The union had come as no surprise to me. The emperor, Charles V, was Mary's mother's nephew and the only person who truly aided Mary throughout the years of her mistreatment, first by her father then by her brother and his councillors. He even offered to spirit Mary out of the country during her brother's reign so she could be free to worship in the Catholic faith in Spain. While the people of England saw Prince Philip as a foreign invader, Mary must have seen him as her saviour. Saviour or not, now that Prince Philip was King Philip after the death of his father, all of England's treasury and military were at his disposal and he did not hesitate to put them to good use.

The people of England would never forget this loss.

In September, word reached us that the queen was deathly ill. She believed up until the spring that she was with child, but once again it was a wish that would go unfulfilled. While I mourned the inevitable passing of my half-sister, the rest of the exiles celebrated.

"Why are you so glum Catherine?" Francis asked one night during a raucous celebration in the Weller home. "The queen is deathly ill with no son to inherit the throne. King Philip will be on his way back to Spain where he belongs and Elizabeth can take her rightful place on the throne. Most importantly, we can all go back home."

"Francis," I replied. "I have known Mary since she was just a girl. The girl I knew then was nothing like the queen we know now. That Mary was graceful and regal. Her compassion knew no bounds. She practically raised Elizabeth after Anne was murdered. She doted on Edward and even in the beginning of her reign sought to dole out mercy to the likes of Northumberland and Suffolk. She did not even want to execute poor Jane Grey until the rebels made it impossible for her not to. I didn't need to see the way she was treated by our father and the neglect she suffered at his hands to read it all over her face every time I saw her at Court. Mary was not always the monster you see her as. Above all, she is still my sister. We share blood and I will mourn her as I have mourned my aunt, uncle and mother."

Francis quieted for a moment. Finally he stood, walked over to me and kissed my cheek. "I understand, my love. While I will not mourn her death, I will respect your wish to do so. You have always been so kind-hearted, seeking the good in people when others cannot see it. It is one of the many reasons I love you."

He kissed the back of my hand and took his leave. The next day preparations began for our return trip home.

Part V

Triumphant Return

The frigid winter air could not push out the muggy heat from the press of bodies that crowded the corridors at Whitehall. There was a new monarch on the throne and everyone who was anyone in England was there to swear fealty to the steely-eyed ginger beauty who only a few short years ago languished in the Tower waiting to climb the scaffold. The dirt of the Great North Road was packed down by the feet of pilgrims making their way to Court.

I kept my pomander to my nose to guard against the stale musky scent of sweaty bodies and gripped Francis's hand to avoid being trampled. As soon as we arrived at the presence chamber, I dropped his hand so I could straighten my skirt. The buttery silk had become wrinkled in the crowd and I did not want to meet our new queen looking dishevelled. A familiar voice caused my heart to stop.

"Mother!"

I jerked my head up and searched for the source. My daughter, Lettice, was pushing through the crowd towards me. The girl I had left behind nearly three years ago was now a young woman. She wore a brocade bodice and skirt in a dusky russet, and a kirtle of deep gold that set off the golden red ringlets that cascaded over her shoulders. A white lawn ruff graced her slim shoulders, a new style I was sure she had picked up from her time at Hatfield with Elizabeth. I threw my arms around her in a warm embrace, burying my face into her soft rosemary-scented hair.

"Oh how I have missed you," I whispered.

She stepped backwards and broke into a confident smile. "Are you pleased?" She asked. She held out her skirts and twirled around, the brocade billowing out around her.

I grasped her smooth hands. "You look wonderful. You have grown into a beautiful young woman."

She knelt down for my blessing, "It was a gift from the queen."

I had a feeling that Elizabeth would continue to be very generous to Lettice after she had spent so much time with her during her exile at Hatfield.

Francis leaned in to kiss her on the cheek. "I am sure you have been a fine example of the loyalty the Knollys have for their queen. She will be sure to reward you as you continue to serve her as a maid-of-honour. Your mother has already been made chief lady of the privy chamber and will serve as one of her closest intimates. Soon, I imagine we will be asking her permission to make you a match."

Lettice's cheeks flushed crimson red and she straightened up, arching her back. I heard a silky voice call out Francis's name. Robert Dudley sauntered over to us in a dark emerald satin doublet. The sleeves were slashed to show the silky fabric beneath and his dark blue hose highlighted his well-muscled calves. He too wore a stiff white ruff. So it begins, I thought to myself. Soon everyone would be sporting this new accessory to please the queen.

Seeing Robert in these fine clothes told me that he had begun to rebuild his influence. Robert and Francis were well-acquainted during Edward's reign. Robert's father, the Duke of Northumberland, had lost his head on the block after his failed attempt to place Lady Jane Grey on the throne. Robert and his brothers had spent many months in the Tower as the sons of a traitor, living in constant fear of their own lives. But when they were released, they served King Philip so well in his wars that Mary allowed them to go back to their lives and their properties. However, they had never been allowed back at Court.

"Lord Knollys! I am thrilled to see you have returned to us from the Low Countries," Robert cheered, giving Francis a hearty slap on the back.

Francis nodded. "I am thrilled to have returned. By the time we left I had had enough of the tumultuous bickering between the settlements. Do we use this prayer book or that one? Which hymn is proper? We want this preacher, not that one." He sighed heavily. "It is a wonder that we accomplished anything."

Robert grinned. "I saw your boys, William and Edward, quite frequently while you were gone. Fine young men they are. Ambrose was happy to have them and I trust they learned much during their stay with him. Elizabeth will be glad to have them at Court."

As the men talked I glanced over at Lettice. She was watching Robert intently and laughing demurely at everything he said. Her face still carried a light blush and I noticed that she was trying to force her bust out, hoping he would notice the womanly curves she was developing. She was every bit as coquettish as the maids that had come before her. I would have to rein her in before she made a fool out of herself. Robert was a married man and certainly not in the market for a new wife.

I placed my hand on Francis's arm. "I am so sorry to interrupt, my love, but I am certain the queen is waiting for us."

"I can take you," offered Robert. "I am due to see her as well. We need to discuss which palfreys would be best for her coronation."

"Master Dudley is the queen's new master of the horse," explained Lettice, a dreamy smile on her face. "He spent much time hunting with Her Grace at Hatfield and she was so impressed with his loyalty that she promoted him straight away."

Ah, so that was how Lettice was familiar with Robert. I am sure he had ingratiated himself quite well to Elizabeth when it had become obvious that the former queen was on her death bed. Francis seemed to think highly of Robert, but I would take more convincing. I had seen far too many men play the dutiful courtier when favours were freely flowing only to turn tail when it suited them better, and I would not have Lettice being taking in by one of these men only to wind up with an illegitimate child from a married man and an unsavoury reputation. I would have to keep my eye her...and him.

I put an arm around Lettice's shoulder and guided her in the direction of the presence chamber.

"The queen is waiting. Let's go."

The presence chamber was filled to bursting with eager courtiers pacing over the newly polished floors. It had been many years since I had been to Whitehall, but I noticed that in the three months since her accession the queen had made some alterations. The holes had been patched in the tapestries and new rugs had been laid down. A crackling fire flickered in a hearth that had been scrubbed to gleaming. I inhaled the scent of fresh pine and juniper and wallowed in its familiarity. The foul smells of our home in exile had become a distant memory.

It was at Whitehall where I made my entry into the court and laid my eyes upon the Princess Elizabeth for the very first time and it would be at Whitehall where that princess would begin her reign as Queen Elizabeth. It was hard not to think of Anne as I waited for her daughter to come out to greet us. She would be thrilled beyond words that Elizabeth had rightfully inherited the throne. After the pain of birthing twelve children of my own, I thought of Anne giving birth to the baby girl who would grow up to be a queen. It was terrifying enough to go through childbirth for the first time without the pressure of a king's desire for a prince. I could not begin to imagine her distress when it was revealed that her child was a girl. She must have been disappointed but, according to my mother, she had never let it show. Anne hid any terror, disappointment or fear she ever felt to the death.

The door opened and immediately we all dropped to show reverence to our new queen. I waited patiently with my head bowed for Elizabeth to raise us. When I finally lifted my eyes, I was amazed to see the young woman before me. Her hair was piled on top of her head and studded with a vast array of emeralds and rubies that sparkled in the firelight. She wore an elaborately embroidered brocade gown that matched the green of Robert's doublet over a wide farthingale. Her gold necklaces glimmered down the front of her bodice and, just as I suspected, it was topped off with an enormous ruff trimmed in gold lace and diamonds. In her long pale fingers, she carried an ornate white ostrich feathered fan.

"Lady Catherine! Mine own sweet cousin," she called out, pointing at me with the fan. "Please come tell us about your time abroad. We are overjoyed to have you back and in our service."

It was a strange feeling hearing her use the royal pronoun. I was certain I saw the same sparkle in her eyes that I often saw in our father's eyes. "I am pleased to be back, Your Grace. I have missed the rolling green hills of England and I am so grateful for my appointment to your Privy Chamber. Thank you."

Her amber eyes flashed and she lowered her eye lids as in remembrance, "That day at Westminster, before I left to go back to Hatfield...I have thought about that day several times since then. I feel as if I owe you *my* thanks. Not one person before or since has taken the time to speak to me of my mother. It meant the world to me and for that I would love to have you by my side."

I was speechless. It surprised me that she had thought of that incident so often. As if reading my mind, she fumbled at her girdle pulling a small frame out of a fold in her gown. It was the miniature I had given her all those years ago.

"I keep it with me always," she whispered. She brought the miniature to her lips and placed a delicate kiss before she tucked it back into the fold.

I wanted to reach out and hug her, but I knew that would be inappropriate. Now that she was queen, her body was holy and untouchable unless bidden by her to do so. I gave her a warm smile instead and curtsied again.

"Doctor Dee has chosen a most auspicious day for my coronation, but before we get there I have some knights to make. I am sure you are pleased that your brother Henry will be made a knight of the bath the day after tomorrow. I will also be promoting him to the peerage. He will now be known as Baron Hunsdon. Unlike my dear cousin, Lady Lennox, Henry Carey did not abandon me in my time of need, nor did he see fit to torture me with the sound of clanging pots and pans during my time at my sister's court so he will be justly rewarded. I hope you will be there for the ceremony."

"I would not miss it if my life depended upon it," I laughed and sneaked a glance over at Lady Lennox. Her face was red with fury. She yanked on her poor young son Lord Darnley's arm and dragged him out of the room. I assumed there would be no knighthood for him.

Elizabeth held out her arm and Robert hustled over to take it. She gestured to us. "Come, a feast awaits us."

That night we ate until our stomachs could hold no more and danced until our feet gave out. The next morning we processed by barge to the Tower where Elizabeth, like all the monarchs before her, would lay claim to the mighty fortress before being crowned. There Henry's ceremony was celebrated with much pomp. His wife, Anne Morgan, was dressed in her best and wore a giddy smile, no doubt thinking of the new lands that Henry would be given.

The next morning we bustled around Elizabeth, preparing her for the procession to Westminster. She looked regal in a gown of cloth-of-gold and cloth-of-silver with Tudor roses woven into the fabric, trimmed in ermine. Rubies and drop pearls were draped across her bust and emphasised the point at the bottom of her bodice. The long train trailed behind her. Her hair cascaded down her back, worn loose in the way that only virgins can wear it and worn like that of her mother at her coronation. I had giggled at this because it had been quite obvious that Anne was no longer a virgin at her coronation. She was visibly pregnant with Elizabeth at the time, but that was of no consequence to her. She was determined to be crowned like a virgin just as her predecessor, Catherine of Aragon, had been.

We stepped outside into the dazzling sunlight. A light snow had begun to fall dusting the streets, covering up the filth and grime. Robert Dudley lifted Elizabeth into her litter. He was dressed like a nobleman in a crimson velvet doublet with cloth-of-gold sleeves that contrasted well with the pure white of the queen's palfrey. It was his duty as master of the horse to lead out her personal horse.

They painted a pretty picture together riding out into the street, reminiscent of Guinevere and her knight. As we left the Tower the lions in the menagerie gave a great roar. Everyone else was startled at the thunderous growl, but it made me giddy with pleasure. I knew the roar was a message from our father, the lion-like king, a message of pride that his cub was continuing his legacy.

We were greeted by a quivering mass of people. They pushed and shoved trying to get closer to their queen. Proclamations of 'Long live the queen' and 'Long live good King Harry' were shouted from shopkeepers and street urchins alike. Children perched on the shoulders of their parents to get a better view and more than one rooftop was occupied. Through it all Elizabeth smiled benevolently, waving graciously to her admirers.

Along the way, we were treated to pageants and plays honouring Elizabeth and her family. At Fenchurch the children recited poems and songs, and at Gracechurch the past was resurrected in a series of tableaux. Three stages were erected with the figures of Henry VII and Elizabeth of York, our father Henry VIII and Anne, and the queen herself on the third. All hailed the unity of the red rose of Lancaster and the white rose of York. The roses themselves were strewn as far as the eye could see.

Festive banners and streamers were hanging from every window and the conduits ran with red and white wine. From Cheapside to Ludgate and beyond, Elizabeth was met with enthusiasm and reverence. When she stopped to make one of her many gracious speeches, she knew how to play to the crowd. She impressed them with her humility and charmed them with her wit. The frigid air set my teeth chattering, but I knew that it was not only the cold air that sent shivers down my spine. It was as though a younger feminine version of our father were walking among his people. At the mention of old King Harry, an elderly man in the crowd turned from the queen weeping. In that moment, I felt the old king's presence acutely.

We finally arrived at Whitehall where we would spend the night before the ceremony. I waited for Elizabeth to climb out of her litter so I could escort her back to her rooms. When she finally reached me, her face was flushed and she took big gulps of air as if she could not catch her breath.

Concerned I asked, "Are you all right, Your Grace?"

She nodded slowly, her hand raised to her chest.

"Yes, just a little flushed. I am really quite all right, no need for panic. We shall go to my chambers as planned so I can dress for the banquet."

She offered her cool clammy hand and I took it, leading her to the bedchamber.

It was apparent to me that Elizabeth felt quite ill, but she never let on to others that she felt anything other than wonderful. She sat on the dais under a gold-trimmed cloth of estate with a pleased look on her face while her courtiers celebrated and feasted. She sent all of the best dishes out to her favourites, but she did not partake in much of her own food. A nibble here and a sip there just so her ladies would not get suspicious, but I knew better. After the tables were cleared, Elizabeth took to the dance-floor with her prized courtier, Robert Dudley. Whatever illness she was feeling earlier seemed to be swept away while she spun around the floor with Robert. Seeing her so happy finally put me at ease and I sought out my own love, Francis, to dance the night away.

The next morning we paraded through the newly gravelled streets of Westminster on a carpet of fine azure cloth. The crowds stampeded the carpet after Elizabeth passed and began tearing off bits of the cloth for souvenirs. The Countess of Lennox, Margaret Douglas, carried Elizabeth's train and was nearly knocked over in the melee. At Westminster Hall, Elizabeth was vested with her robes of state and joined by Owen Oglethorpe, the Bishop of Carlisle. The honour of the queen's coronation should have gone to the Archbishop of Canterbury, but the current archbishop, Nicholas Heath, refused on the grounds that Elizabeth would not agree to return England to the Catholic Church. I was certain that his predecessor, Thomas Cranmer, would have been more than thrilled to crown Elizabeth, just as he had crowned her mother nearly twenty-seven years ago. But Cranmer had gone up in flames on the stake. He would not crown anyone ever again. With all of the bishops sulking over Elizabeth's refusal to pacify them, the duty of the day fell to the first bishop who accepted and that was Oglethorpe.

Our burgeoning group traipsed into the abbey heralded by trumpets. Elizabeth was enthroned on the chair of estate and the pageantry began. She made an offering of gold and accepted the oaths delivered to her by the bishop, and just as her sister, mother and father before her, she was consecrated and anointed in holy oil. She received the sword, sceptre and orb, and kissed the Pax. Elizabeth then returned to her seat to hear Oglethorpe's Mass, but the moment he raised the Host she withdrew from the service.

A murmur went through the crowd. She had done this to Oglethorpe before. During Christmas Mass he had raised the Host even though she had explicitly told him not to. She had stormed out of the chapel in protest. I pitied him. Bishops such as he had been raising the Host, depicting the corporeal change from bread into Christ's body, for centuries without incident. Now, men like my husband and William Cecil proclaimed that the bread was just bread, merely symbolic, but it would take more than just a decade of inconsistent change to convince the devout Catholics that their traditions were wrong.

Thankfully Elizabeth returned with little commotion, having changed into a mantle and surcoat of plush violet velvet trimmed in ermine fur. At the conclusion of the mass, we filed out of the abbey and returned to Whitehall.

The celebration banquet lasted well into the early morning hours and all of the excitement took its toll on Elizabeth. The next morning, the jousting tournaments had to be postponed while she was kept to her bedchamber with excruciating stomach pains. Mary Sidney and I fussed around her like worried mother hens, but by the next day she was in better spirits and able to partake in the festivities in the tiltyard. My cousin, Thomas Howard, 4th Duke of Norfolk, led the four challengers. We went to great lengths to make sure that Elizabeth was layered in her warmest clothes to keep out the chill, but I still fretted. She was still young and unmarried with no heir on the way. Her death would throw the country into the turmoil that our father had imagined before Edward was born. That whey-faced son of Lady Lennox, Darnley, was the heir presumptive until Elizabeth could give birth to her own, and I could not stand the idea of him sitting on her throne.

Francis caught my eye and I left Elizabeth's side for a moment to speak with him.

"What is she doing out here?" he whispered, alarmed.

I threw my hands up. "She is the queen now, Francis, not the little princess we knew. Look at all she went through to get here. Do you honestly believe that she would miss her own tournament?"

Francis groaned. "Make sure you keep her as warm as possible and tonight when you put her to bed, lay warming bricks under her covers and get a night cap on her head."

I raised my eyebrow. "Francis, how many children have I raised?"

"I know, I know. But I am sure I do not need to remind you of what might happen if she dies before she has an heir."

I narrowed my eyes and shook my head. "No, you do not. I remember my brother Edward quite well, thank you."

He softened and held his hand out to me. "Catherine ..."

I crossed my arms, "I have a job to do if you would please excuse me."

"Go on then."

The nerve! While he was off on the king's business and then learning the new religion across the channel, I was at Greys raising our children and tending to their sicknesses. He would not know the first thing about treating a fever, let along preventing one. I growled under my breath and then tried to shake off my irritation. I had Elizabeth to worry about, not Francis. He could spend his time concerned about the Privy Council and his duties as vice-chamberlain, I would worry about the warmth of the queen's bed and nightgown.

In the end, Elizabeth did not fall ill that evening. After my duties were done I, still buzzing from all the wine and music, headed back to our rooms to celebrate with Francis, our previous argument forgotten.

A few months after the tournament, during a beautiful sunny spring day on the bowling lawns, I vomited in front of the queen.

"My lady cousin," she laughed, leaping aside. "Was it something you ate or do you harbour yet another occupant in that fruitful womb of yours?"

I moaned in disgust and tried to straighten myself up. "I am so embarrassed, Your Grace. Please excuse me."

She wrapped her arm around Robert Dudley's and they shuffled aside. "The horrid things women must do to bring children into this world. Come, Robin, let's walk in the gardens. The lilies are beginning to bloom and I would like to gather some for my bedchamber."

Robert ushered her away from me without giving me a second look.

As Elizabeth and her favourite wandered off, Mary Sidney ran across the lawn to my rescue. She handed me her handkerchief and reached behind me to loosen my stomacher.

"No doubt my brother would love to put an occupant in *her* womb," she scoffed. "Ever since he became her precious master of the horse, he has been insufferable. And she as well. Not even a kind word for her cousin on this happy occasion."

She paused for a moment making sure I had wiped all the traces of my sick away.

"Anyway – Are you all right?"

I nodded.

"Yes, I am fine. Thank you, Lady Sidney. It was very kind of you to help me. I am just a knight's wife, I would hardly expect Her Majesty to jump at my call," I laughed nervously.

Mary frowned, "You are right, but you could expect some

compassion, especially for her kin. It is not as if she has an abundance of friends and family by her side." She glanced furtively around and then lowered her voice. "They all come running to her side now, but the moment there is an uprising that any of the nobles could stand to gain from will they still be there?"

"Mary, you don't think ..."

"I don't know what to think, Catherine. But I have seen enough around here to know that since old King Henry died, no one has been safe on the throne and I pray to God that my brother does not cause Elizabeth to lose it. Tongues are wagging in every dark corner of this castle. 'The queen and her horse master!' they laugh."

Calmly, I put my hand on her arm. "Mary, I serve the queen in her bedchamber, I can assure you that they are not lovers."

"Catherine, I believe you and I know ... well, at least I hope ... that my brother would never take it that far, but the rest of the court does not know that. The rest of the world does not know that."

I sighed. "I will mention it to Francis and maybe he can bring it up during a Privy Council meeting."

"No!" Mary exclaimed. "Please don't. I do not want the queen or my brother to know I have spoken out of turn. I think, at this point, all we can do is stand back and pray that our queen comes to her good senses before it is too late."

I nodded in agreement. "Your words are safe with me."

Mary had good cause to worry. When Elizabeth refused a wedding proposal from her former brother-in-law, King Philip of Spain, it sent out a message to the continent. England would not return to the Catholic Church. I was witness to the dreadful scene. King Philip's ambassador, de Feria, could not escape from her presence chamber fast enough. He skittered out of the room with her shouts nipping at his heels like rabid dogs.

The pope recalled the Vatican's ambassador to England in haste and issued a papal bull calling on all the faithful Catholics to depose their new ruler. Their ascent to heaven would be celebrated by the angels for their work against that heretic bastard Elizabeth.

The day she received it, we were excused from her bedchamber so she could meet with Secretary William Cecil in private. Her infuriated screams could be heard down the corridor.

Through all of the dramatics, and even though her councillors quaked with fear, Elizabeth refused to change her habits or give in to the pope's threats. She continued to ride out every day with her master of the horse by her side, hunting and hawking until nightfall. Then, when the moon was high and the quarry had settled into their beds, Elizabeth would entertain her faithful servant with cards or conversation in front of the fire in her richly appointed, candle-lit bedchamber.

Elizabeth did not fear the pope and, to show her detractors, at the end of the Lenten season, she made Robert Dudley a Knight of the Garter. To emphasise his promotion, we celebrated his election in grand style.

Elizabeth was determined to play her part as the benevolent queen during the first Easter of her reign. On Maundy Thursday the guards rounded up twenty of the poorest women and ushered them into the courtyard at Whitehall. We trailed behind Her Majesty into the bright spring sunshine with our offerings, our arms leaden with Elizabeth's cast-off gowns.

The women sat, anxiously fingering the tattered rags hanging off their scrawny bodies, on beautifully upholstered chairs that had been brought outside just for the occasion. We waited and watched in wonder as Elizabeth knelt down to each one with a bucket of warm water and a rag to clean their dirt-caked feet. When she stood up from her task, she laid a blessing upon each head and gestured for them to come to us for a gown and a silver cup.

This act of contrition was nothing new. Every queen, stretching to as far back as before I could remember, had dropped to her knees to wash the feet of the poor at one time or another. While this seemed commonplace for the ever pious Catherine of Aragon and my aunt Anne, who was ever eager to please the people, it seemed out of place for Elizabeth to be on her knees in supplication. This was the same Elizabeth who had laughed at my morning sickness, the same Elizabeth who had screamed in a dreadful tantrum when things did not go her way. This same Elizabeth looked up at those pitiable ragged women with true compassion in her eyes, scrubbing as though she were shining a gold plate instead of the filthy feet of an unfortunate. She was truly an enigma to me.

Surrey, Nonesuch Palace:
August 1559

I begged and pleaded with the queen to be allowed to go back home to Greys instead of going on progress, but she would have none of it.

"Catherine, of course I need you on this journey," she said. "It is my first progress and I need to show the people of England that I have the support of my family. As much as I despise her, I have even informed Lady Lennox that she is to accompany me as well."

I placed both of my hands on my ever-increasing belly and forced a smile. "I will do as you command, Your Grace."

After a few weeks on the road sweltering in the muggy heat of July and August, our never-ending train of coaches passing through the cheering hoards and being entertained at the finest houses in Eltham, Dartford and Cobham, we arrived at the magnificent palace of Nonesuch to stay as guests of the Earl of Arundel. The earl was desperately hoping to be considered for Elizabeth's hand in marriage and had gone to great lengths to make his intentions known. For the last couple of months he had been paying off some of the maids-of-honour, inducing them to whisper pretty words about him in Elizabeth's ear. I avoided him at all costs, but it was nearly impossible once he had taken to slinking around Elizabeth's rooms uninvited. I imagine he found her first progress the perfect opportunity to show off the purchase of this palace from her now deceased sister, Mary.

My father would have been enraged that Mary had sold his glimmering building. Always wanting to have the best of everything, he had built a castle like no one had ever seen before and christened it with the name of Nonesuch to prove it. In fact, there *was* nothing else like it. With the exception of Hampton Court, the king's other palaces looked positively ancient in comparison. He had said that he built it in celebration of the birth of his long-awaited son, Edward, but it had seemed to me to be a monument to his lost love, Queen Jane Seymour. Her death cast a pall over the king. She had not lived long enough to see his love slip away from her like Catherine or Anne and so she would be forever on a pedestal in his eyes. He poured out his grief for her into this lavish, dream-like palace.

Seeing the heavily spired octagonal towers rise up into view as we approached the palace truly was like being in a dream. The elaborate stucco panels gracing the sides of the walls and towers appeared in greater detail as we got closer. Each panel was intricately carved with a scene from mythology, telling those stories of old antiquity. The mullioned windows sparkled in the sunlight. A light breeze blew through the air, fluttering the banners that hung from the onion-shaped roofs that topped the towers. The sight took my breath away.

"No wonder he died broke," Lady Carew whispered in my ear. Elizabeth was staring at us and as soon as she turned her head to look out of the window of the carriage, I elbowed Lady Carew with a distasteful frown. Elizabeth could not stand to have anyone say unflattering things about our father in her presence. She would not hesitate to repay the unkindness to anyone who dared to voice it.

The train of coaches, horses and carts snaked its way around the palace and through the glamorous wooden gates of the outer courtyard. Once we stopped, the door to our coach flew open and in the doorway stood our host. The earl's thin lips were stretched into a smile so wide that his eyes were almost squinted shut. His bulbous nose was the colour of a cherry. At the sight of the queen, he dipped into a very low bow.

"Welcome my queen! Welcome to Nonesuch!" he preened.

Elizabeth offered her hand to him and he helped her down to the ground. "It is no small wonder that my father loved hunting here," she apprised. "I would love to take advantage of your parks while I am here. I made certain Sir Robert brought my best horses."

The earl's ears flushed a blood red. He had invited the queen here to further his suit for her hand and there was no way that he was letting his biggest rival, her master of the horse, get the pleasure of taking her hunting in his parks.

"Your Majesty, no one knows these parks as well as I do. I would be honoured to take you out tomorrow morning. First thing!"

"That sounds wonderful, Arundel." She turned to us. "Ladies, I will see you in my rooms."

We nodded in unison to their backs as they proceeded on to the inner courtyards.

A grand feast was set up on the front lawn of the castle. Tents were raised in a cluster to hold all the delicacies on display and the fountains dripped with red wine. The earl's personal musicians surrounded a stage for dancing set up on the grass. A chair of estate sat at the edge of the stage so that Elizabeth could sit and enjoy the entertainment.

Francis knew this was an excellent opportunity to mingle with the most powerful men of the court, but he was concerned about me and spent much of the night making sure I was as comfortable as possible.

"I understand why she insisted on dragging you along, but I am still not happy about it," he muttered as we sat in the shade of a large oak tree and watched the maids dance.

"She is the queen and I vowed to serve as she commanded. My life is not in any danger and it is still another two months until the child comes." I shifted in my seat to relieve the sharp pain on the back of my thigh.

Francis chuckled at the scowl on my face, "Think of Arundel's outrage if you were to give birth on his lawn and ruin all his fun."

"Ah, yes. I would not dare dream to take the attention away from him."

Francis was quiet for a moment, staring out at the stage where the queen was alternately being led out in dancing by both Arundel and Dudley, each man trying to best the other with the complexity of their steps.

Finally he said, "It is like watching a duel isn't it? Each man trying to out-do the other to win her heart. Yet, each one ignores the outrage that her choice of either one of them would cause. Still, she leads them on and, against their better judgment, they dance for her, hoping and praying that she will reveal her intentions."

"But I thought you supported Robert Dudley in his suit? And with rumours going around that his wife is sick, I am certain it is only a matter of time before he is once again an eligible bachelor."

Francis replied thoughtfully, "It seems like only yesterday that we attended his wedding to Amy, doesn't it? They had seemed so in love, marrying in spite of his father's outrage that Amy was of such low stature. Now that lovely girl wastes away, biding her time, while her husband plays the smitten courtier to the queen."

"Then why do you support him, Francis?"

"He is my friend, Catherine. All those years at Court, while my own brother was tending to our lands and watching over you, Robert Dudley was as close as a brother to me. I don't agree with the way he has treated Amy, but he is my friend and I will support him. He is certainly a much better choice than Arundel or William Pickering. Besides, I think the queen has her mother's intelligence and ambition and I do not believe she will choose any of those fools to be her consort."

"Just promise me that you will not fall to the queen's charms while I am back home at Greys having this child," I said, giggling.

Francis cupped my chin and kissed my lips. "As far as I am concerned, *you* are my queen and I fell to your charms long ago. Besides, with my brother still away in the Low Countries, it is high time I head back to our estates and I plan to ask the queen tonight if we may leave together for home instead of going back to London."

Relief flooded over me. The only birth Francis had attended was Thomas's when I had almost died of fever. The fact that he would leave the court behind to attend this one told me how much that incident had affected him. Unlike Robert Dudley's wife, I would never have to worry about Francis setting me aside. His love was not just pretty words said in moments of passion. His love was in acts of compassion and kindness. His love was sitting under an oak tree with me instead of socialising with the powerful men of the court and coming up with an excuse to leave the queen to be with me as I gave birth to his child when other men would have preferred to be in the luxurious halls of her palace. My marriage may have been arranged, but it truly was a love match.

Oxfordshire, Rotherfield Greys:
October – December 1559

True to his word, Francis went to Elizabeth that warm evening at Nonesuch to beg leave. The next morning, while she rode out with Arundel and Dudley to chase down the enormous stag that was rumoured to roam the park, Francis and I borrowed one of the earl's litters and hitched up Francis's beloved horse to take us home.

It had been months since we had seen the children. Thomas now toddled around beneath our feet and Anne had begun to learn her letters. They all looked so grown up and I felt a pang of guilt when I saw just how much I had missed. I realised then how spoiled I had been for the last decade. Unlike most of the women I knew, my presence had not been demanded at Court for many years. I had been able to stay home and watch my children grow up. Now that Elizabeth was on the throne, my days with them would be few until they were old enough to come to Court. I was determined to make the most of it while I could.

Francis and I spent the balmy evenings lying in bed talking about the future while the cool breeze through the open window ruffled the tapestries and played over our bare skin slick with the day's sweat. The leaves finally began to change and the muggy heat that had blanketed the countryside started to dissipate. We revelled in the first rain of the season, huddled together before the fire while the fat drops of water pelted the windows. The world felt so safe and warm at Greys that I found myself dreaming up excuses to stall the return to London.

In mid-October our new baby girl arrived. It was a short and easy labour and I could see the relief in Francis's eyes once it was over. He insisted that we name her Katherine.

"After all of the children you have borne me, you deserve to have a namesake. Besides, she may be the last child we have," he said, putting an end to my resistance.

"Are you calling me old?" I exclaimed. The startled look on his face caused me to dissolve into laughter. "I guess you are right, I am in my thirty-fifth year. I am sure that my baby childbearing days are coming to an end."

So I gave in. I was honoured that he felt that way, but I did feel a little silly naming my child after me, so I let him believe that Katherine was named for me, but in reality, when I looked at her honey-coloured eyes and the natural blush of her rosy cheeks, I thought of my cousin Katherine Howard. We would call her Katherine but, as I watched Francis scribble the date of her birth in the Latin dictionary he had brought with him from the Low Countries, I instructed him that her name was to be spelled with a K. I laughed when I realised later that he had spelled my own name with a K many years before when he had begun to list the names of our children. The secret would be safe with me.

Lettice and Harry both came home for Christmas and we celebrated as a family with a lovely roast, several meat pies, fig pudding and a tower of sugared subtleties. Harry and his father drank warm malmsey before the roaring the fire and caught up on the news of the court while Lettice and I did needlework in my bedchamber. Ten year-old Bess hummed a carol and practised her dance steps in the corner. It was lovely to be surrounded by my children.

Lettice stopped moving her needle for a moment and stared out of the window as if waiting for someone to appear at the end of the snow-covered lane.

"What has caught your eye, my darling daughter?"

She shook her golden red curls and furrowed her eyebrow. "I think someone is coming down our road. Are we expecting guests?"

She rose out of her seat, interest piqued, and walked to the window.

I anchored my needle in the fabric and tucked a stray hair back under my linen cap. "I will go down and let your father know."

Lettice drew a sharp breath, "It is *him*! What is he doing here? Are you planning to marry me off to him?"

"Who are you talking about, Lettice?" I questioned her back.

She stomped her dainty foot and curled her hand into a fist at her side.

"Walter Devereux," she whined. "The Viscount of Hereford."

I set down my embroidery and carefully headed down the stairs. Bess had already run to the window to stare out next to Lettice.

"Francis ..." I called out.

He rushed over to the bottom of the staircase.

"Are we expecting a visit from the Viscount of Hereford?

Francis grinned, "Ah! He took me up on my invitation. Did you see him from the window? I should go and meet him."

He started to turn around, but I reached out and grabbed the back of his doublet.

"What is going on? Why is Hereford here and why is our daughter so upset about it?"

Francis frowned. "Why should Lettice be upset? I would think Hereford would be an excellent match for her. He is a viscount and a baron, not to mention that he is descended from Anne Woodville, sister-in-law to Edward IV. He comes from a respectable line and I am certain Lettice will enjoy his manor at Chartley. He really is quite enamoured with our girl."

I shook my head. "Francis, our daughter loves being the centre of attention at Court. She will be intolerable if she is trapped in the countryside."

"Catherine, Lettice is sixteen now. The same age you were at our marriage. She is no longer a little girl. It is time she learned that she does not always get her way. Besides, once she realises that she will be able to dress in the newest fashions and take precedence after her own parents, she will thank us for making her such a good match."

"All right, I shall speak to her. I promise she will be on her best behaviour."

I climbed back up the stairs to find Lettice lying face down on the bed, sobbing into a pillow. Bess was rubbing her back and whispering to her.

I sent my younger daughter downstairs and sat down on the bed next to my eldest one.

"Lettice, why are you crying? This match is far beyond what you should expect. You will be a viscountess. Please tell me why you are so upset."

Lettice sat up and, after a few sniffles, finally confided in me. Hereford had gone out of his way to be very kind and pay her special attention, but she was desperate to stay at Court. She loved her special treatment by Elizabeth and it seemed that she had grown quite popular while her father and I had been home at Greys. Another man had been paying her attention as well, a man that she fancied far more than poor Hereford.

At first she would not reveal to me who had been showing her favour, but eventually broke down and admitted that it was Robert Dudley.

"Lettice! Have you gone mad?" I shouted. "Robert Dudley is a married man. He is not on the table for marriage negotiations. And even if he were, the queen would never allow it. You need to put him out of your mind immediately!"

Lettice pouted. "But his wife is very ill and they say she may not make it much longer."

My blood boiled at her callous remark. Being among the chattering and self-important maids at Court was turning her into a person I did not recognise.

"Lettice Knollys," I said very slowly, trying to keep my voice low. "I did not raise you to be so cold-hearted. You will put Lord Robert out of your head this instant and then you will go to your room to put on your best gown. You will come downstairs and you will entertain your future husband with a smile on your face. Then, tonight, you will get on your knees to say your prayers and you will thank the Lord that you have a father who would make you such a wonderful match and then you will pray for Sir Robert's wife, for her health and well-being. Do you understand?"

I had never needed to speak to my daughter in such a way and I could tell by the stricken look on her face that she was as startled as I was. She swallowed hard and then nodded.

"Yes Mother, I understand," she whispered. "I will have my maid help me change."

She got up without further protest and left the room. I sat for a moment composing myself, and then I marched downstairs, determined to be an excellent hostess to my future son-in-law.

Francis shot me a questioning look when I entered the hall. Hereford had already joined him and Harry in front of the fireplace. All three stood as I approached.

"Lady Knollys, it is a pleasure to see you again," Hereford said, dipping into a small bow.

I offered him my hand and he placed a light kiss on the back of it. "Welcome to our home. Lettice should be down in a few moments. Please say you will stay for supper."

"Of course, thank you for the invitation," he said graciously.

I looked him over carefully. I found him far more handsome than Robert Dudley. His soft brown eyes were earnest, even his nose was straighter than Robert's. He and Lettice would have fine children. I wanted to shake my daughter for her insolence, but then I remembered Richard and how desperate I was to marry him before I found out that I had been promised to Francis. Then I thought of her comment about pitiful Amy Dudley and I reminded myself that while I had loved someone I should not, never once did I wish ill upon anyone to fulfil my desires.

I shook the uncomfortable thoughts from my mind, smiled and took Hereford by the arm. "Come, we shall sit in the solar. The view is much nicer."

Francis and Harry followed dutifully behind me.

Lettice came down sometime later and, while she certainly had not dressed in her best, she was humble and gracious to her suitor.

She wore a simple grey gown with a high ruff, hoping that the lifeless colour would make her appear dull, but it only enhanced her alabaster skin and brightened the red hue of her hair. It was obvious from Hereford's rapt stare that she had failed miserably at making herself unappealing.

Hereford and Francis talked so long into the night that I offered the viscount a spare room for the evening. He accepted graciously and was gone in the morning before I arose.

I noticed a rolled up parchment lying on the table as I walked through the hall. I paused to read the elegant script. It was a summons from Elizabeth. She requested our return for the New Year festivities. My heart sank. Our familial respite was over. It was time to get back to the business at Court.

London, Greenwich Palace:
March – June 1560

The trip back to London seemed twice as long as it should have been. The weather was miserable and cold. I had been back in the queen's rooms for only days before I was laid low with a fever. Elizabeth sent her best doctors to my bedside and with the care of my maid, Matilda, I was on my feet again in time to take over my new duties – the care of Elizabeth's new pet monkey.

It was a dreadful thing, this New Year gift Elizabeth had received. The wild, gamey scent of it assaulted my nose and its shrieks pierced my ears. When I reached my limits in dealing with the thing, it took all of my willpower not to remind Elizabeth of her mother's distaste of the creatures so beloved by Catherine of Aragon. Instead, I bit my tongue, knowing that it would only agitate Elizabeth more.

William Cecil worked Elizabeth into a frenzy over her imminent assassination by Marie of Guise and her faction. The Regent of Scotland was enraged that Elizabeth had insinuated herself into the battle with her lords. Marie brought in French troops and was succeeding in beating back the Protestant rebels until the English Fleet arrived in January. Cecil convinced the queen that she was not safe and banned her from accepting any gifts, lest they be laced with poison.

Elizabeth feared for her life, but she refused to show any fear. Instead she showed us rage. Many nights I retired to my bedchamber with Francis, sobbing over an insult hurled at me after some small mistake I had made – handing Elizabeth the wrong ring from her jewellery box, exhaling too loudly when I bent over to roll her new silk stockings up her leg, or moving about too much during the night on the pallet I slept on at the end of her bed. My days with Elizabeth had become emotionally exhausting.

Elizabeth's burden lifted in June when Marie of Guise died in her bed and the fears of her assassination finally began to subside.

"Lady Knollys," she called out across the presence chamber, her slender hand raised, beckoning me to her chair of state.

I stopped my conversation with Lettice immediately and walked over quickly, dropping into a low curtsey before her seat.

"Please, please, get up," she gestured.

I straightened up and smoothed my skirts, keeping my gaze low.

Elizabeth stood. "My lady cousin, I realise that I have not been the easiest person to serve these last months and I apologise for any harm I may have caused. You are the last person in my service whom I would want to hurt and I love you above all others."

My eyes began to well up, but I blinked hard, willing myself to hide my emotion.

"Yes, Your Grace. I understand."

She continued, "You once gave me a trinket of my mother's and I have treasured it all this time. I carry it around with me and gaze upon it when I find myself needing a moment of courage." She gently patted a small purse tied to her skirt. "I have wondered how to repay you for that kindness, but nothing had ever seemed to convey my gratefulness. I prayed over this and the Lord sent me an answer."

She paused for a moment and I waited, holding my breath, wondering where this story was leading.

Elizabeth smiled and reached for my hand. She tucked a small object into the palm of my hand and closed my fingers over it.

"This was found during an inventory of my father's possessions. I would like you to have it. Please wait until you have returned to your room to look upon it for I am certain you will feel a flood of emotion. Just tuck it away and tonight when you settle into your rooms, bring it out. Carry it with you, as I do mine, and look upon it, not when you need courage, but when you need patience - with me. When I test your love, as I am sure to do, look upon it and remember that I still need a mother's guidance and kindness. As the one woman in my service that was closest to my own mother, I hope you will continue to guide me in the way that she would have had she been allowed to live long enough."

I was speechless. Elizabeth had never been shy of showing her emotion, but it was very rare that she would intimate such personal thoughts. I saw her as the studious, eager-to-please child once again.

"Thank you, Your Grace. I am beyond appreciative for your gift, but I am afraid that my guidance would be nothing like your mother's. Yes, your mother was kind and compassionate, but she was also ambitious and courageous and she had the heart of a lion. I merely have the heart of a lamb."

Elizabeth smiled. "Beloved cousin, you do yourself such a disservice when you fail to recognise the strength of the lamb's heart. Was Jesus not the Lamb of God? If ever there was a symbol of courage, you could find no better one than He."

I gripped Elizabeth's hands in mine and gave them a small squeeze.

"Your mother would be proud to see her daughter ascend to the throne as you have. In you, it was all worth it. The hatred of the people, the anger from the courtiers, the death on the scaffold. She would do it all again if she had known that your ascension would be the result. Remind yourself of this in times of turmoil and that will give you all the strength you need."

That night, after I removed my gown, I held out my gift from Elizabeth. It was a miniature of my mother. She looked so young and beautiful, a simpering smile playing across her lips. The miniature must have been made during her time as the king's mistress. It was the only likeness of her that I had ever seen and I knew I would treasure it always.

While William Cecil was in Scotland hammering out a new treaty with the rebellious lords, Elizabeth and her Court were on the annual summer progress. Elizabeth hunted and hawked across the countryside with her master of the horse attached at her hip. It was rare to see them separated from each other, especially since the only man who dared to come between them was across the border. The rumours of Robert Dudley's familiarity with Elizabeth reached a fever pitch when a Mother Annie Dowe of Essex was locked up for spreading a rumour that Elizabeth was carrying his child. The ladies of Elizabeth's bedchamber knew the folly of that statement as they changed the blood-stained sheets during the queen's courses that month, but the men in her service were not privy to such private matters. Rumours such as these needed to be stamped out immediately. Unfortunately, Mother Dowe's imprisonment did little to stop the slander against them and Elizabeth did herself no favours by carrying on like a love-struck princess.

By the end of August, Francis was at the end of his tether.

"Does she not realise what danger she brings with this behaviour? No one will take heed of our overtures for marriage agreements and the ambassadors laugh behind her back. How does she ever expect to get a consort who will give her an heir when she behaves like a silly girl?" he ranted as he paced the floor of our bedchamber at Windsor. "Cecil will be furious when he returns to this news."

"I agree with you, Francis, but Elizabeth has been denied much in her life. She will take affection where she can get it and Robert

Dudley is showering her with it. He is your friend, have you tried to talk sense into him?"

Francis shook his head. "He will hear none of it. He thinks that she will marry him and make him her consort." He threw his hands up. "And she might for all we know. She refuses to share her mind on the matter. But it may not be for the best. We need alliances and Dudley cannot bring us that. I love the man as though he were my brother, but he can bring nothing to the table except pretty words and strife to the council. The last thing the queen should do is isolate herself from the eligible princes of Europe."

He sat down on the edge of the bed and hung his head in frustration. I sidled up behind him and wrapped my arms around his strong chest, laying my head on his back.

"Francis, at this moment Robert Dudley is a married man and Elizabeth would never agree to bigamy. Let her have her fun and worry about this if, God please forbid it, something happens to Amy."

Francis wrapped his arms around mine and bent down, kissing my hand.

"Catherine, Amy Dudley is very sick and not likely to make it through the winter."

"I hope that when I am on my deathbed, you wait until I am cold to start looking for my replacement."

Francis turned and laid me down on the bed. "Dudley is a fool."

He leaned over me and kissed me passionately. When we finally came up for air, Francis whispered in my ear, "Promise you will never leave me, for I could never replace you."

We had been hearing for almost a year that Amy Dudley was on her deathbed, but as the months carried on with no word of her passing most of us assumed that her sickness was just a convenient rumour that was passed around any time Dudley wished to remind Elizabeth of his impending widowhood, or she wished to disentangle herself from whatever marriage negotiation was on the table that week. So when news arrived two days after Elizabeth's birthday celebration that Amy had indeed left her earthly body, the court was thrown into shock.

The morning was like any other that early autumn. Lettice and I sat near the fire in Elizabeth's privy chamber, busily embroidering a counterpane for her impending wedding. My fingers were stiff from working the W and L patterns through the heavy fabric and I had to stop momentarily to flex and straighten them. Lettice hummed quietly while she worked – a hymn I had taught her as a child.

Elizabeth laughed heartily at some joke Dudley told her. I could not hear what they were saying, but they had been speaking in hushed lovers' whispers for hours while they played cards.

A short rap at the door brought us all to attention. Elizabeth did not like to be disturbed in her private time with Robert Dudley, so we knew that whoever was waiting on the other side of the door was either brave or stupid.

Lady Jane Howard sprinted from her cushion towards the door. She propped it open slightly and spoke to the yeoman guards in hushed tones. After a moment, she nodded and stepped back to let in the visitor.

Dudley nearly fell off of his seat. "Bowes! What are you doing here?"

The man, Bowes, bobbed a low bow and kept his face to the ground. "Please forgive me, Your Grace. I do not mean to intrude, but I have word regarding Sir Robert's wife," he stuttered, ignoring Dudley and addressing Elizabeth.

She kept her seat and threw her arms out towards him. "Well? What was so important you had to disturb us?" she asked irritably.

Bowes finally raised his head and looked at Dudley. "There has been an accident. Lady Dudley sent her servants to the fayre yesterday and when they returned, they found her lying at the bottom of the stairs. Her neck was broken."

Dudley puzzled over this revelation as the colour drained from Elizabeth's face. She stood up quickly, drawing herself to her full height. "Tell us man! Is she alive or dead?" she said in a commanding voice.

Bowes' hands started to tremble. "I do not know, Your Grace. I left Abingdon as soon as we found her. By the looks of it, I do not believe she survived the fall."

Dudley found his voice. "You left her unattended?" he roared, throwing his hands in the air. He started towards Bowes, fists clenched, but thought better of it and turned away at the last moment. The man's hands were shaking so violently I worried that he would fall over from fright.

Elizabeth stepped in. "Go back to Cumnor and await further instructions. You are dismissed."

Bowes nodded and made haste for the door. A deep silence filled the room. My eyes darted around the other ladies in attendance and, like Lettice, they all stared at the floor making no sound.

The silence was broken by a guttural groan from Dudley.

"I will be the one to blame for this! My reputation will be destroyed," he cried.

Elizabeth looked at him with steely eyes, as if she were witnessing his vanity and self-centredness for the first time. His only thought upon hearing of his wife's demise was of self-preservation.

"Robin, you must write to your cousin, Thomas Blount, at once. As your chief officer, he will need to take charge. Luckily he is already on his way there. You are dismissed to your home at Kew to arrange your affairs. Do not return to Court until I summon you."

Dudley stared at her, his mouth agape at his dismissal. When she turned away, he clenched his jaw shut, made an overly exaggerated bow and backed out of the room.

"Lettice," Elizabeth called over her shoulder. "Get me Cecil. Now."

The ladies who served Elizabeth in her bedchamber took turns spending the night on a small pallet beside her bed. As much as we loved her, we all looked upon our nights in her bedchamber as an exhausting duty. If she did not sleep, neither did we. And it was many a night that she had far too much on her mind to find any rest. I was certain tonight would be no exception.

It was to be Lady Carew's night on the pallet, but Elizabeth chose Kat Ashley for the job. I was not surprised by this. Mistress Ashley had been a confidante of Elizabeth's during her childhood at Hatfield and, more than once, had risked her life to come to her aid when her Elizabeth had overstepped her bounds during Edward's short reign. The two had been inseparable for most of Elizabeth's life and, inwardly, I felt relieved that Kat would be there to comfort Elizabeth. I was taken aback, then, when she turned her eyes to me and said, "No ... Catherine will serve me tonight instead."

Kat, Blanche Perry and I helped Elizabeth out of the layers of damask and linen she wore. Then Kat stood behind her and plaited her long golden red locks into a braid as Elizabeth stared off into space. Once the evening ritual was over and Kat and Blanche had been excused, she bid me goodnight and crawled silently into her bed, drawing the black silk hangings shut. I wriggled down into my quilt and waited. Sure enough, an hour later the silken curtains began to sway back and forth with her agitated tossing and turning. Finally, they burst open and Elizabeth launched herself out of bed, already chewing her fingernail.

I scrambled to get up, but she held out her palm, "No, please not get up on my account, my lady. I will be all right in a moment."

I let her pace until she tired herself out, throwing herself back onto the bed, her long, delicate fingers a ragged, bloody mess.

I sat up and pulled my knees to my chest. "Please, Your Grace, is there anything I can do for you?"

She waved her hand dismissively and drew herself up to a sitting position. She gazed at me sadly. After a moment she said, "Yes, actually. Tell me what to do."

I made light of her request. "Your Grace, I could never presume to give you advice. You are God's anointed - what could I possibly have to offer you?"

She shifted. "What would you tell your children? What would you tell Lettice if she were in love with a man like Dudley? If she were in love with a man that could tear her world apart?"

Her question was too close to the truth. Lettice *was* in love with a man like Dudley. In fact, she was in love with Dudley. Should he choose her over Elizabeth, Lettice's world would crumble. She would be banished from Court, her prospects dried up. My only words of advice to Lettice had been to stay away. I couldn't very well tell Elizabeth to stay away from her favourite courtier and master of the horse. It would be impossible for her to do. I had to tread lightly in my answer.

"The world is full of men who are vain, egotistical and scheming. But those same men can be quite endearing, full of love and tenderness. Your father was that way. He had no hesitation or reservation about setting Catherine aside, banishing her to the most remote fortresses the crown owned. But ... he did it out of his deep and sincere love for your mother. Does his heartlessness towards one woman negate the devotion he had to the other? No. Is he dangerous? Possibly ... your father adored your mother above all others. He tore apart his *own* way of life to satisfy her. He broke with the church, put his close councillors to death and angered most of Christendom in his pursuit of her. But in the end, she too lost it all ... on the scaffold."

I paused, checking Elizabeth's reaction. She was still, her face passive, but listening.

"If your mother was here, right now, and we asked her if she would do it all over again. If she knew that the outcome was her death, would she still have aspired to be the king's wife? I know her answer would be yes, because seeing you on the throne would have been worth it. The fact that you now rule England has made every sacrifice worth her blood. You can have Robert Dudley, but is it worth the possible sacrifice of your crown?"

Her eyes were bright, but she blinked the tears back hard, refusing to shed even one.

"Why must it be one or the other? Why can I not choose whom I marry? My father chose five of his wives. My sister chose that insufferable Philip."

I sighed. "You are right, but they both suffered the consequences. You must find a new way if you want to have Dudley and secure your throne."

I paused while she considered this. Then I had a bolt of inspiration.

"If there is one lesson you could learn from your mother, that lesson would be to never expose your true mind. You do not have to make your intentions known, now or ever. Have Dudley. Keep him close as your favourite, but do not ever let him know where he stands. You are the queen. You do not have to justify your intentions to anyone. This may be the only way you can have both."

Elizabeth's face finally relaxed. She even ventured a very small smile. "My mother would do that wouldn't she?"

"Your mother had her fair share of emotional displays, but I don't think any of us ever truly knew her intentions. She knew the power of mystery and played it well."

She nodded, her face drawn into a frown. "I wish she were here to guide me. I would give anything to know what she was like or even just to remember the sound of her voice. After seeing my father execute two of his wives and almost arrest a third and watching Philip abandon my sister, I do not know that I shall ever marry. Marriage does not seem to be an enviable state."

I thought of Francis and my heart longed for him. "Oh but it can be, Your Grace. It can be wonderful."

The next morning, I stumbled back to my own rooms and fell exhausted into bed while Elizabeth headed out into the park-lands with a small retinue to hunt. Chasing down that stag was a way for her to chase down her fears and conquer them. I was certain that Elizabeth would arise victorious. In the afternoon her lord secretary, William Cecil, admitted the Spanish ambassador, de Quadra, into the presence chamber to see her as she settled in from her morning hunt.

She told the ambassador that Lady Dudley was either dead or imminently so from her fall down the stairs, but swore him to secrecy because she had not released that information to the court. He narrowed his beady eyes and pledged his discretion, but I could tell from the way he eagerly licked his lips that he was eager to dash off a missive back to Spain.

After their conversation, Cecil led the dismissed ambassador out of the presence chamber. It was not long before word got out that Cecil had told the ambassador of the rumours going around that Dudley had planned to poison his wife so that he could marry Elizabeth. Cecil vehemently denied it, of course, but the damage had been done. Even if Elizabeth wanted to marry Robert Dudley, there was no way she could now. I saw the pleasure on Cecil's rosy cheeks now that his closest competitor for Elizabeth's confidence had been brought low. An opportunity had presented itself and Cecil, like any other nobleman, had spun it to his advantage.

Within days Elizabeth dispatched an inquest to Cumnor Place, where Lady Dudley had been living, to investigate her death. For nearly a week we waited for answers, closeted with Elizabeth pacing her rooms, anxious and pale.

On 15th September, Dudley was exonerated, the inquest deeming Lady Dudley's death an accident. I still had my doubts. It was far too suspicious that Amy's servants had left her unattended. That was unheard of for a woman of her status. And the reports coming back to Court implied that her maid Mrs. Picto indicated her suspicion that Amy had committed suicide – a mortal sin. The pieces did not add up for me. It may be that Robert Dudley did not have a direct hand in her death, but if she was desperate enough to imperil her mortal soul and take her own life, then he had certainly driven her to it.

Fortunately for Dudley, my own personal thoughts on the

matter did not count for anything. Soon enough he was back at Windsor in high favour partaking of the entertainment in Elizabeth's rooms. For decency's sake, we all wore our mourning black for a month. I was more determined than ever to get Lettice out of Court and away from Robert Dudley. It was time to get the marriage preparations underway.

It was nearly impossible to convince Elizabeth to let us go home for Christmas celebrations at Rotherfield Greys, but finally she relented, for it is not every day that my eldest daughter is married to a viscount.

Lettice had poor Lord Hereford so enamoured with her charms that he was more than happy to accommodate her wishes to be married in our family chapel rather than at his manor in Chartley, so we made merry in the weeks leading up to New Year and welcomed our new son-in-law to the family in the comfort of our home.

After our celebrations, Hereford returned to Chartley to prepare his home for the arrival of its new mistress and Lettice returned to Court with Francis, Henry and I.

London, Greenwich Palace:
June – November 1561

The storm raged outside my window. Rivulets of rain traced down the leaded glass and the sky thundered overhead. A bolt of lightning flashed across the sky, bathing my bedchamber in an eerie glow. I snuggled closer to Francis, scared by the raw power of it all. I closed my eyes and thought of Calais. The sound of the thunder reminded me of the cannon crash of the ocean against the steep cliffs. As the sounds lulled me to sleep, I found myself drifting into the dream of the apple orchards at Hever once again.

Barefoot and muddy, I tore through the trees and burst into a clearing. But this time, there was no scaffold. There was no sword. I heard only the sounds of laughter.

"Come play with us, Catherine," two faint voices called out.

Out of the shadows ran two little girls. One was as dark as a raven, the other was as fair as honey. I could not see their faces as they ran away from me hand-in-hand. I couldn't be sure, but something told me it was a portent of death.

The rain was still pouring down when we awoke and the gardens outside my windows had become a quagmire. We barely had time to settle into our day before Queen Elizabeth received word that the spire of St. Paul's Cathedral had been struck by lightning during the storm. The fire was so hot that it had melted the leaden bells, pouring them over the roof like lava from a volcano. I was not surprised to later hear a Catholic servant remark that God was punishing Elizabeth for not reuniting with Rome and for flaunting her licentious lifestyle.

Robert Dudley had been restored to his previous eminence. The events of last autumn were not yet forgotten, but he was soon returned to Elizabeth's good graces. It was a particular matter of discord with Secretary Cecil when Dudley was given the rooms next to Elizabeth at Greenwich.

Under the simmering tension at Court, the thunderstorms of June gave way to the suffocating heat of July. Elizabeth's annual progress got underway and we moved to the cooler air of the countryside. The queen enjoyed herself at great expense to her people. The wealthiest nobles hosted our enormous party at every stop. Great feasts filled the tables and every night held music and dancing. The revelries continued until our arrival at Ipswich.

The trouble with the Grey ladies started shortly before Christmas. Ladies Katherine and Mary Grey, cousins to Elizabeth and sisters to that poor soul and reluctant queen, Jane Grey, were downgraded from ladies of the bedchamber to ladies of the Privy Chamber. Katherine took it as a great insult and made her irritation quite plain. While there had been talk for months about Katherine marrying the Earl of Arran and creating an alliance with the Scots, Katherine was plotting with the Spanish ambassador in the hope of marrying King Philip's son. Elizabeth was, of course, outraged that Katherine was undermining her and sought to put her in her place.

However, it all turned out to be a very elaborate distraction. Katherine truly had no intention of marrying either. She had her own plans. Katherine had been secretly meeting with the Earl of Hertford, Edward Seymour. Seymour was the son of the Duke of Somerset, the man who lost his head by order of our departed child-king, Edward. Not one of us ladies had even been aware that anything was amiss. None of us except Seymour's sister, Jane. We found out later that she supposedly witnessed the marriage, but by the time the truth came out, poor Jane had been dead for some time.

Katherine hid this wedding and, somehow, her pregnancy for months. She had seemed to me a bit rounder in the face, but I had assumed that with all of the feasting and celebrations this year she had gained some weight. I know I was certainly feeling more bloated than usual.

Then, one night in Ipswich while Elizabeth slept in the adjoining room, Katherine slipped in to Lord Robert's room and spilled out all of her secrets, begging him on her knees to speak in her favour with the queen after having been refused and soundly rebuked by Bess St Loe for her indiscretions. Those of us waiting on Elizabeth the next morning were privy to all of those secrets as she unleashed her rage.

Elizabeth demanded obedience from her subjects and if anyone of royal blood should marry without her permission, the consequences would be severe. She fought a delicate balance to keep her throne secure and she had learned many lessons during the years that men fought in uprisings in her name against her sister. She would not tolerate such open rebellion during her reign. To make matters worse, John Hales had only recently written a book supporting Katherine's claim to the throne as great-granddaughter of Henry VII. The very idea that Katherine could be pregnant with a son must have made Elizabeth's blood run cold with fear. There were still many in England who considered Elizabeth to be a bastard and a heretic. A male heir born to a Catholic sympathiser with a claim to the throne would make the perfect focal point for rebellion.

Immediately upon our return to Whitehall, the guards dragged the eight months pregnant Katherine Grey off to the Tower to await the birth of her child. Seymour was abroad, gallivanting across the continent with the son of William Cecil, so his incarceration would be delayed. But I had no doubts that he too would find himself a resident of that dark fortress.

The day after Elizabeth's birthday in September, the court moved on to St. James's Palace. The crowds had gathered prior to our arrival making it nearly impossible to reach the main gate. As my tawny palfrey pranced around the children running underfoot, I glanced up in awe at the imposing red brick façade of the palace built by my father during his courtship with Anne. I wondered if Elizabeth would think of her mother as she lay in the enormous state bed that Anne had certainly slept in. Anne had been no stranger to fear and had endured her fair share of betrayal. A few years on the throne had shown her fair daughter that her journey would be marked with trials as well. But Elizabeth had an advantage – she was the daughter of Henry – and not above imprisoning her own flesh and blood when they acted to deceive her.

The court relaxed for a week at St. James's and then the procession wended its way back to Whitehall, where we all took part in lavish celebrations and gorged on all the food and wine that the palace had to offer as Elizabeth tried to put the fact that her cousin, Katherine Grey, had recently given birth to a boy out of her mind. Elizabeth was going to make sure that no vain, little slip of a girl languishing in the Tower was going to upstage her celebration. By the time the frigid autumn winds of November arrived, my body had begun a mutiny against the extravagance of my diet and I found myself fighting against a general feeling of malaise and an overwhelming urge to sleep at all hours of the day. Even the most innocuous of comments would send me into a slump of depression and it seemed that I was always crying for no good reason. When I realised my dresses were in need of being let out, I knew the time for all this extravagance was over.

I groaned against the bright sunlight streaming in through my windows.

"Matilda, is it already time to greet the day? Can you please come back in a couple of hours?"

Matilda snorted, "My lady, the queen has specifically requested your attendance today and I am sure you do not want to keep her waiting. Now, if you'll please excuse me, I have to fetch your gown."

I stretched my arms out. I had already flung the counterpane off in my fitful sleep. It seemed like I woke up in a flush of heat every night now. I called out, "Something light please! I do not think I could bear wool or brocade today."

Matilda stuck her head through the door. "My lady, winter is in the air and snow is already upon the ground, but if you insist upon something cooler ..." she trailed off.

"Now how difficult was that?" I asked as she shuffled into the room with a pale blue linen kirtle and a dark grey velvet skirt.

I got out of bed and took my time washing with the basin of warm water. I felt relief from the heat as the water cooled against my skin. It felt even better when I used my fan – a gift from Elizabeth – to move the air around my face. When I was satisfied, I stepped into the skirt that Matilda was holding out. To my dismay it no longer fit.

Matilda stepped back and eyed my stomach critically. "My lady? I thought you would have told me if you were with child."

I shook my head. "Matilda, you change my sheets, you know that my courses have not stopped. I am certain that all of the meat pies and marchpane have just left a lasting impression and a need to let out my skirts."

She nodded warily. "I am sure you are right. I will see if I can find something more suitable for you to wear."

It was true that my courses had continued, but they seemed to come rather haphazardly in the last few months and while I was certainly as exhausted as I had ever been with my other pregnancies, I did not find myself with the familiar sickness I had come to know so well, only this general feeling of unease that I attributed to poor habits.

Perhaps I had reached the end of my childbearing days? I was

now in my thirty-seventh year and had given birth to thirteen
beautiful babies, yet I was overwhelmed with sadness the instant
that I realised that I would probably have no more.

Elizabeth was visibly irritated that I was so late getting into
her chamber. It would do no good for me to try to explain my
melancholy to someone who had never carried a child in her womb,
so I did what she liked best and threw myself on her mercy.

"Oh, get up! Get up!" She gestured and raised me up from my
knees. "I have a plan for today, but we need to get moving. Send
your lady for your cloak and muff."

I sent Lettice after Matilda and turned back to help Elizabeth
into her riding cloak. I was puzzled to see that her maid was not
holding a cloak. She was holding a simple wool gown of muddy
brown that looked far too ordinary to grace a queen's body.

I didn't bother to ask why she would wear such garments.
Elizabeth hated to be questioned and I knew she would share
her intentions soon enough. Once we had her trussed up like
a common serving girl, we covered her radiantly golden red hair
with a brunette wig and topped it off with a wide-brimmed hat to
cover her face. She was transformed from the queen of England to a
young maid in mere seconds, and I bit the inside of my cheek at the
look of surprise on Lettice's face when she entered the room with
my cloak and muff.

Elizabeth scanned each of our faces for a reaction and then
burst into peals of laughter.

"Today, my good ladies, we serve my dear cousin Katherine
Howard, Lady Berkeley while she spends the afternoon at Windsor
playing at the butts."

I stared at her in disbelief.

My befuddled face only made her laugh even louder and in a
giddy voice she chided, "Do not stare at me as though I have lost
my mind, Lady Knollys! This shall all be in good fun and I cannot
wait to hear what my courtiers have to say about me when they
think they are safe from my presence. For a few hours, I am nothing

more than a maid servant, so please treat me as such. Now, some one fetch Lady Berkeley, she will need to ready her barge."

Much to Lady Berkeley's credit, she displayed no show of emotion on her face when presented to Elizabeth in her disguise. She only sent word to her servants to prepare the barge to take us to Windsor for the morning to practise our archery skills. Elizabeth had been cunning to single out Lady Berkeley for this game, because it was well known around Court how much she loved field sports. The fact that she was at the butts on the grounds of Windsor while the rest of the ladies of the court were at Whitehall would never draw suspicion.

We traipsed out of the palace down to the quayside on the banks of the Thames and I finally saw with my own eyes the reason why the maids-of-honour giggled behind their hands whenever Lady Berkeley walked by. Down near the bottom of her gown was a large splotch of white bird dung. I heard that she kept her merlins mewed in her chambers, but now I saw the proof flouncing against her backside as she skipped excitedly towards the river. If her grandfather, the stodgy old haughty Duke of Norfolk, were not already dead, he would have died of embarrassment at the state of her dress. The irony tickled me with pleasure.

The morning frost had not quite melted by the time we reached the fields outside Windsor, but the sun was climbing higher in the sky and it wouldn't be long before the ground warmed enough to ease the chill out of our feet. I found myself wishing that I had listened to Matilda's advice as I pulled my cloak tighter around me, but who would have expected that Elizabeth would plan such an adventure? I didn't know if it was love or obsession that caused her to behave like such a silly girl, but I worried that important people would find her antics very unbecoming. Elizabeth would fight the stain of bastardy for the rest of her life and, as a reigning queen, her sex put her at a disadvantage. She need not bolster her critics.

Lettice, and I stood around gawking at the other courtiers engaged in friendly competition, the men jeered and cheered their compatriots at turns and horsed around like young men, while the queen scanned the field and Lady Berkeley happily drew her longbow. She hit her mark at almost every attempt. When she tired of that, she convinced Lettice to give it a try and they took turns while Elizabeth zeroed in on her own target a few hundred yards away.

Robert Dudley was so bedecked in jewels that he faintly glistened in the sunlight. It was hard to miss him on the field as he preened about. We heard him barking orders at his servants while the men in his group took turns showing off their prowess. I was terribly bored with this show of masculinity, but Elizabeth stood enthralled. She could not keep her eyes off the man. She smiled broadly when he hit his mark and muttered encouraging words to him under her breath when his arrow sailed off in the wrong direction. It was as if all others had faded from her sight. It confirmed that while Elizabeth's mind had taken marriage to Robert Dudley off the table, her heart had not.

Elizabeth's whispered words must have carried on the breeze to Dudley's group because it wasn't long before he noticed our small coterie and took his leave of the gathered band of men. As he strutted across the grass, Elizabeth scrambled behind me. She tried desperately to stay out of direct contact lest he saw right through her disguise.

"Good morrow, my ladies!" he called out. "How wonderful it is to see you out enjoying the sun and fresh air on this chilly day."

Lady Berkeley dropped her bow to her side and ambled over to greet our visitor.

"Yes, we could not ask for better weather!" she exclaimed, her cheeks flushed with the cold. "How are you shooting today? It looks as though you have some stiff competition." She gestured towards the rainbow of doublets that had just now noticed Dudley's departure and had turned in our direction with curiosity.

The two exchanged idle chitchat, but once Dudley realised that Lettice was Lady Berkeley's shooting partner he could hardly keep eye contact with her and excused himself at his earliest chance and made a beeline for my daughter.

"Mistress Knollys! Your beauty is by far your much stronger suit than your archery skills. Please, dear girl, let me help you with your stance."

I did not need to turn around to feel the heat from the look Elizabeth was giving the pair as she watched Dudley snake his arm around Lettice's, pressing his body close into her backside.

I immediately marched over and quickly pulled the bow out of their hands.

"Actually, my lord, she is no longer Mistress Knollys. It would be far more appropriate for you to refer to her as Lady Hereford as she has been married to that lovely young viscount, Walter Devereux, for a year this Christmas. Of course, you are so busy in service to the queen that I cannot blame you for not being aware of every marriage that goes on in England, so I am certain you can be forgiven this once. But please do not forget, for Lettice now outranks even her mother and we do her much disrespect to forget her title." I gave him a patronising smile. "Come along Lady Hereford, I am certain the queen has risen for the day and will be calling for us shortly." Lettice shot me a horrified look, but I grabbed her wrist with my free hand and dragged her off, calling out over my shoulder, "Please enjoy the rest of your day Sir Robert. I will tell the queen that you send your regards!"

The tension in the air on the ride back to Whitehall was nearly unbearable. Even Lady Berkeley, who had chattered incessantly on the way to Windsor, sat in stony silence. My stomach lurched in disgust at the spectacle we had just subjected Lady Berkeley to. Unlike our similarly named cousin, this Katherine Howard did not thrive on drama, and it would not surprise me in the least if the experience caused her to stay away from Court even more frequently than she did now.

Lettice sat quietly, but with a thinly veiled sense of satisfaction that when the veneer of royalty had been removed from Elizabeth, it was she who Robert Dudley had chosen. I knew this would only encourage her pursuit of him even more.

I had little time to worry about Lettice's future before it was decided for me. That afternoon in Elizabeth's bedchamber, as she ripped the wig off of her head and threw it against the wall, she shouted, "She leaves tomorrow for Chartley!"

It was time for my daughter to make her home at her husband's estates and start producing heirs. She could not be trusted around the queen's horse master at Court. I hoped that she would someday make her way back into Elizabeth's good graces.

London, Whitehall:
March 1562

Under the stress of my guilt and anxiety from the incident at Windsor, I finally succumbed to my dwindling spirits and took to my bed. Initially Elizabeth was livid. She thought I was withdrawing from her service to punish her for her exile of Lettice, but when she finally visited my rooms and saw my sorry state, she summoned her personal physician to care for me and remained by my bedside.

Mister Richard Master performed a perfunctory exam and confirmed Matilda's suspicion. I was with child. How could I have not known? After thirteen pregnancies the signs should not have escaped me, but I had been oblivious. The fact that my courses had continued greatly concerned him and he immediately ordered the leeches for my bleeding.

Fear for my unborn child crept over me like a dark shadow. I prayed fervently for the child that grew in my womb and held on to the hope that he or she would be safely delivered. But my instincts prepared me for the worst.

The doctor kept me abed until we knew that the bleeding had been successful and when no courses came towards the end of December, I was released from my chamber in time for the Yule celebrations.

Though I was still feeling terribly exhausted and weary, seeing Francis for the first time in months set me ablaze. How I longed for his calming presence and his assurances that all would be all right. He had been travelling on the business of the queen and had taken a few weeks on his return journey to Court to rest at our home at Rotherfield Greys and prepare our estates for the coming months when his brother, Henry, would be leaving on a diplomatic mission to the Low Countries. I begged Elizabeth to allow me to meet him at home, but she demurred, insisting that she needed me at Court, and in any case, I was ill and certainly not disposed to be travelling. I was sorely disappointed, but there was little I could do.

Robert Dudley went to visit my husband immediately after the incident at Windsor to complain about my rude outburst, so a few days after his arrival at Court Francis gave me the required lecture. But I knew by his poorly suppressed grin that he was not angry with me. In fact, he thought it quite amusing that Dudley had behaved so terribly, completely unaware that Elizabeth was witnessing the whole interaction.

"If that did not put her off of him, nothing will," he sighed. He still harboured concerns over her reluctance to declare her intentions for a consort.

However, the fact remained that I had offended a great favourite of the queen and we would have to make amends when an opportunity presented itself, he reminded me. I resolved to take no notice if I happened to see such an instance, but Francis could apologise all he liked.

My brother-in-law, Henry, bound for the continent, came to Court for the holidays and, as an apology for exiling my eldest daughter, Elizabeth invited the rest of my children to the palace to partake in the festivities.

I could hardly believe my eyes when I saw how much William and Edward had grown. Now, so close to adulthood, it wouldn't be long before they were regulars at Court. It was likely that Francis had planned their future roles during his time back home. Bess was as lovely as ever. It dawned on me that she would be fourteen next year and would likely serve as one of Elizabeth's maids-of-honour. She would most assuredly beckon the attentions of all the young men at Court. I hoped that she would be more circumspect in whom she paid her favours to than her elder sister had been.

Robert, Richard, little Francis and Anne visited as well, but Thomas and Katherine were deemed too young to journey in the weather. I missed seeing them so much, but I looked forward to my lying-in when I would be home and could hold them in my arms again.

Harry had just been recommended for provostship at Eton by Bishop Grindal and was unable to attend the celebrations. I was filled with admiration at the accomplishments of our children and took great pride in showing them off during their visit.

Elizabeth showered them with sticky sweets and they delighted in the miniature wooden toys she gave them. In return, Bess helped me finish the carpet I had embroidered for Elizabeth's New Year present. It was made of a deep indigo silk and fringed in gold. We sewed a small purse with the leftover fabric and trimming and Francis filled it with gold sovereigns to use as his offering to Elizabeth.

My gift from the queen was a most unexpected gesture. In addition to the gold plate that was her customary New Year offering to her favourites, I was surprised with a small spaniel.

A knock at the door after our morning prayers led us to a hinged wooden box in the corridor outside of our rooms. The box trembled and then a high pitched whine came from a hole cut in the top.

Francis cautiously opened the lid and a golden ball of fur lunged into his arms. We agonised over a name for her, but decided upon Ginger when we caught her creeping behind Anne as she dropped crumbs from her chunk of gingerbread on the floor, gobbling them up as fast as she could.

After the holidays, the children went back to Greys and I resumed my duties, but this time I had a small companion who followed me everywhere I went.

The March torrents turned the knot garden where I liked to take my exercise into a muddy bog so I was spending the afternoon walking the long gallery at Windsor, as I tried desperately to dislodge the baby's foot from under my rib. My brother's wife, Anne, Lady Hunsdon, walked with me. She was normally very quiet, not prone to sharing confidences with the other women, but she opened up to me and we spoke of the children that had left us far too soon. She had lost three sons shortly after their birth and their deaths were still as raw as they had been on those sad days so many years past.

I enjoyed her company and it was healing to commiserate with someone who had suffered the same losses as I, so I was somewhat disappointed when my brother appeared to disturb our chat, grinning from ear to ear.

"Anne ... Catherine ... It is finished! Come, have a look!"

Anne and I exchanged a knowing glance as she hid her amusement behind her hand. Henry was having his portrait painted and he was so excited by it he would burden the ear of anyone who would listen. The work was being done by a Dutch artist who had arrived at Court with John Dymock bearing a portrait of King Erik of Sweden. King Erik was desperately wooing Elizabeth with very little success, but Painter Steffen, as he was called, had been fielding requests for portraits from the court elite for months. Little was known about this newcomer from the Low Countries, no one was even quite sure of his last name. Sometimes he went by Van der Meulen and sometimes Van Herwijck, depending upon who had commissioned him. But no one seemed to care for he had plenty of work to occupy him and even Francis was thinking of hiring him to commemorate his first years as the queen's vice-chamberlain.

Henry strutted ahead of us as we made our way to their rooms. He led us to the sparse chamber that he had been painted in. Only a tall table that Henry leaned against as he posed and an easel displaying the work stood in the room.

It was a fine portrait and my brother looked every inch the serious courtier in it. I was reminded of our great-uncle, the third Duke of Norfolk. It seemed, however, a bit maudlin for my taste. It was almost monochromatic in its use of the colour black. The detail was impressive though, and I could tell by my brother's beaming face that he was beside himself with pride.

"It is perfect, Henry. He captured your essence very well."

"I'm glad you think so, sister," he replied. "For Francis has commissioned a work from Painter Steffen as well."

Francis had, in fact, commissioned a painting from Painter Steffen. Only it was not to be of him. It was to be of me.

"Catherine, I wanted to do something in commemoration of your birthday and to capture the sight of you in full bloom of child since this will most likely be our last. You have been so beautiful in your pregnancies and your fertility is the crown of your womanhood."

I groaned in disgust. I certainly didn't feel beautiful. I felt wretched and bloated. This pregnancy had been the hardest I had ever been through and, in a way, I was beginning to look forward to the end of my child-bearing days.

"That's just it, Francis. I am in no condition to be standing for hours at a time while some stranger stares at me, capturing me in my bloated, sweaty monstrosity for all eternity."

My face crumpled and the tears began to stream down my face. The idea of standing on my aching swollen feet for weeks on end in a stuffy room overwhelmed me. I sat on the edge of the bed and held my face in my hands.

Francis stood silently for a moment and then he sat down next to me and wrapped his arms around me. I buried my face in his neck, breathing in the fresh citrusy scent of the marjoram I freshened our cupboards with. The scent and his musky warmth, mixed with my emotions, caused a stirring in my groin.

He tilted my face towards his and joined my lips to his own. My pulse quickened at the softness of his lips and the tenderness of his touch. I felt a rush of sweet agony when he pulled away. "I am so sorry," he whispered breathlessly.

"No, I should be the one to apologise," I argued earnestly. I tenderly rubbed my chin against the burn from his stubble. He saw and placed a gentle kiss on my tender skin.

"You were only trying to show your appreciation for me and

I, very unappreciatively, got upset for no reason. This pregnancy seems to be wreaking such terrible havoc on my body. Now that we are in Elizabeth's Court, you are so busy that I hardly ever see you. I long to be with you."

The tears had returned in my revelation of emotion, leaving salty tracks on my hot cheeks.

Francis wrapped me tighter in his embrace and trailed soft kisses down the back on my neck.

I looked into his eyes. "I love the queen dearly. She is my sister and my sovereign, but she is so demanding and moody. She is at turns manic with joy, then worked into a rage over some slight that she thinks has been paid to her. Half of the time, the councillors have no sense of her desires so they seek us out for answers. Though we are with Elizabeth during her most intimate hours, we have no more knowledge of her than they do. It is exhausting to serve such a demanding mistress."

Francis carefully removed the stiff lawn ruff from my collar, smoothed down my bodice and brushed away my tears.

"I didn't realise you were so unhappy, Catherine. I too wish that we could return to our quiet life at Greys, but that is not yet to be. We've accepted security in the service of the crown. We have been able to live our comfortable life because of our loyalty. Our children will never face the uncertain future that you and your mother knew. Even if we could retire at this time, you know that the queen would never allow you too far out of her sight. You are of the blood royal and it is far safer to keep you near."

"Francis, I would never ..."

"Catherine, any fool can see that you are the most devoted servant Elizabeth has. But, like you have said before, she was so often the focus for rebellion during Mary's time. Her throne will not be safe until she marries and has an heir. Until that time, everyone is suspect."

"She probably does not even know," I started to argue.

Francis kissed my forehead and then held my gaze. "Wife, the mere colour of your hair is more than enough to cause suspicion.

The fact that you look so much like the old king and almost nothing like your brother raises doubt. She may never know for certain, but I am certain that she, like everyone at Court, has suspected for some time. I sympathise with your unhappiness and I understand your pain, but our lives will never be easy. Many years will pass before we are allowed to retire to our estates. You must find some way to make peace with the queen and your life here at Court. Soon Bess will arrive to help occupy your time and it will not be long before Lettice gives us some grandchildren for you to chase about. Have faith, my love."

The painting went ahead as planned and as miserable as I was, standing for hours with sweat pouring off of me from the interminable layers of clothing I had chosen, I was enamoured with the result.

Elizabeth's court often seemed a dour place in perpetual mourning due to her preference that her ladies be attired in muted shades of black and grey. Elizabeth's desire was to stand out like a brilliant flower among her people. If I was going to wear such dull shades memorialised on canvas for all of eternity, I refused to look as bland and colourless as my brother.

I selected my best brocade gown, crisp white and trimmed in the finest cloth of silver. Over it I wore a black cloak with close fitting sleeves slashed through to show the downy rabbit fur underneath. It had been a wedding gift from Francis, cut loose so that I could wear it through my expected pregnancies, but it had been so fine that I only brought it out on very special occasions. Golden rope worked into intricate leaves stood out brightly against the dark velvet. I chose my best girdle, a thick rope chain with an enormous medallion. I regretted my arrogance after the third day of struggling under its enormous weight.

As old as I felt, I was pleasantly surprised to find that I looked quite young and graceful in the finished piece. My stiff ruff hid the full chin that plagued me and while a bit of grey hair peeked out from under my coif, I had nary a wrinkle to be seen. My skin appeared supple and unlined, a small smile playing across my lips, so similar to the miniature of my mother that I gazed at so often.

I marvelled at Painter Steffen's handiwork. He had been a pleasure to sit for and it was his idea to include my spaniel, Ginger. His humorous nature was an excellent distraction during those long, uncomfortable days. I was sad to see him go, but I was relieved that I would be returning to Greys to give birth.

Oxfordshire, Rotherfield Greys:
May - August 1562

On Saturday afternoon, 9th May, I was delivered of a healthy baby boy. Francis was beside himself with excitement and, much to my dismay, determined that the naming of our son would be the perfect opportunity to pay tribute to Elizabeth's perpetual favourite.

"I refuse to name our son Dudley!" I cried as I flailed my arms, desperately attempting to right myself against the headboard.

"Catherine," he started calmly. "Robert Dudley is my close friend and confidante. I know he would be immensely pleased and it would erase any ill feelings that may linger from ..."

"You will never let me forget that will you?" I interrupted him.

I was annoyed, but I had to appreciate his logic. I had a healthy baby boy with strong lungs, bright eyes and a perfect, upturned nose. Though I feigned irritation, I was so thrilled with the warm bundle of blankets in my arms that I couldn't have cared less what name my husband chose.

Dudley grew and flourished in those first few weeks. He ate hungrily at his nurse's breast and reminded us constantly of his existence with his lusty screams of indignation when his needs were not immediately met.

But one chilly June morning, his cries were absent. I woke up early, eagerly anticipating his arrival in my bedchamber, as I was still abed recovering. The absence of his cries was not the only thing that worried me. A deadly silence permeated our home. All the hustle of daily activity in our home had ground to a halt. My anxiety increased every hour that passed with no appearance from the nurse.

When Dudley's nurse finally entered my room with tears streaked across her face, I lost my sense of sanity. I leapt out of my bed and grabbed the first thing within my reach. She ran out of the room slamming the door as the vase shattered against it, sparkles of glass raining onto the floor.

I wanted to scream, I wanted to cry out, I wanted to do anything to release the pain, but nothing would relieve me. I allowed the feeling of numbness to overtake my mind. Dudley's death had no explanation. The nurse went in to see to his morning feed and found him cold and still. The light of his spirit had gone out like a whisper in the night. I searched desperately for someone to blame, but there was no one, save God, and how can you blame God for carrying out His plan? I had already railed at God enough to no avail.

Francis went back to Court a few days after Dudley's birth. When he left me, I had no inkling that the next time I would see him would be to bury our son. He tried his best to comfort me, but I could not give in to his care and I was terrified to share any intimacies. I could not risk pregnancy again. The pain was too raw.

Elizabeth allowed us to mourn in peace for a month's time, but as the civil war in France came to a head and negotiations to meet with Mary Stuart, Queen of Scots, broke down, our presence was commanded. In the damp stifling heat of August, we began the journey back to London and the opulent Hampton Court Palace.

Elizabeth's face looked pale and drawn. She complained of a headache one night, but in the morning she seemed to have recovered, merely pleading that she was quite exhausted. I spent the night on the pallet next to her bed and could attest to the tossing and turning plaguing her rest. It was quite unusual for Elizabeth to be so quiet and docile so only Lady Mary Sidney, and I attended on her, dispatching the unnecessary maids and only allowing in those councillors deemed important enough to disturb her rest.

She sat before the blazing fire wrapped head to toe in a woollen quilt, dozing off now and again, sometimes in the middle of a sentence. Mary Sidney and I entertained ourselves with our embroidery. Lettice had written that she was with child and I was determined to complete the buttery yellow silk blanket I was working on before the baby came. As the outside light faded into night, the tiny rabbit I was working to create out of needle and thread was turning into an unrecognisable blob so I gave up for the night. I set my work aside and rose to check on Elizabeth.

Her face was aflame and her skin burned to the touch. I called Mary to help me remove the quilt. As we yanked it off her, she sat up and made an unusual request.

"I think to have a bath. Please call the maid."

Mary and I exchanged a fearful glance. A bath was the last thing she needed. Being submerged in the water could worsen her symptoms.

Mary bravely countered, "Are you certain Your Grace? A bath may not be such a good idea right now."

Elizabeth's glassy eyes flashed. "Are you questioning me, Lady Sidney? I may feel unwell, but I have not lost all my faculties."

"Not at all, Your Grace, I will call on Nan to draw you a bath."

Against our better judgment, Mary and I eased Elizabeth into the scalding water. I pinned her hair up carefully and prayed that it did not come loose and get wet and then set to work pouring the water over her shoulders and back, trying to keep them warm as she soaked in the basin.

We dried her as thoroughly as possible and guided her into her warmest woollen night shift. After organising the bath, we had directed the maid, Nan, to warm bricks in the fire to put at the bottom of Elizabeth's great tester bed to ward off any chill she might take from the bath.

That night, we both slept on the pallet next to Elizabeth's bed.

She was worse in the morning. Her guttural moans were enough to send a chill down my spine. We sent for her physician, but we found no remedy even after the application of all the poultices and leeches he prescribed. Smallpox was the dreaded diagnosis, but it seemed that nothing could be done until the angry red spots erupted on her body. Within days, Elizabeth lost the power of speech and we feared that all hope had been lost.

The councillors panicked. Francis described the chaos, "This councillor emphasises the right of Lady Katherine Grey to succeed, while that councillor argues that it is the Earl of Huntingdon's crown to take. Some of us want to refer it to the judiciary, while others argue that the question is the council's to decide. Each man believes his opinion to be the correct one and the only thing that many can agree on is that they do not want Mary Stuart taking power. Her claim is by far the greatest."

My brother Henry was the only councillor who dared come to Elizabeth's bedchamber. He paced nervously outside the Privy Chamber, demanding updates on her health. Unsatisfied with the court physician's diagnosis of impending death, he went in search of any other doctor who would take a look.

Henry Carey was not a man prone to violence so it deeply

unsettled me to see him drag in the German doctor by knife-point, but he gave us the results we were looking for. Mister Burcot carefully wrapped Elizabeth in a flannel quilt and the four of us carefully lifted her out of bed and placed her on the pallet bed that had been moved over to the fireplace. After nearly two hours in blazing heat, Elizabeth finally found her voice. Henry called in the council to hear her directive. None of them was pleased with her request.

In her delirium, Elizabeth breathlessly addressed the rumours that had run rampant about her intimate relations with Robert Dudley, decrying any notion that they had ever acted inappropriately or that anything but words had passed between them. She requested that for her love of him, should she succumb to death, he was to be appointed Protector of the Realm and she dictated his pension for such a position.

The council stood dumbfounded before her. They had been expecting such a command, but what could they do? Their sovereign had spoken. They plied her with empty promises and filed out of the room in great distress.

A crimson rash finally broke out on Elizabeth's skin. Francis demanded my dismissal until she had fully recovered. Smallpox was highly contagious and I was still healing from my pregnancy and birth. Mary refused to leave Elizabeth and she stayed on, never leaving her bedside.

Fortunately Elizabeth recovered fairly quickly and the council never had to make the distasteful decision to promote Robert Dudley to Protector. Unfortunately for Lady Sidney, her devotion to Elizabeth was rewarded with her own contraction of the dreaded pox, which had sped its way through London and laid waste to the rich and poor alike. Elizabeth emerged from her sickbed almost completely unscathed. Poor Mary, on the other hand, was horribly disfigured with scars and begged permission to return home. I lamented her absence from the bedchamber.

Now that Lady Sidney was gone, Elizabeth demanded my presence more than ever. I begged leave to attend Lettice's childbirth at Chartley in December, but I was rebuffed at the mere suggestion of my departure. I attempted to enjoy the holiday festivities at Whitehall, but my mind was on my daughter. I was thrilled when a letter arrived at the end of January describing an easy birth that culminated in the arrival of my first grandchild, Penelope Devereux.

London, Whitehall Palace:
February – September 1563

I ducked just in time to avoid being hit by the flying dish. It bounced off a unicorn tapestry that hung on the wall and landed on the polished floor, shattering to pieces.

"How *dare* that little harlot have another bastard? And right under my nose! Why is no one on guard outside their cells? Answer me!"

Elizabeth sat red-faced and rigid with rage. A messenger from the Tower had come to tell her that Lady Katherine Grey had given birth to yet another son. It was impossible that such a thing had happened. Katherine and Edward Seymour had been imprisoned since the truth of their marriage came to light during Elizabeth's first progress. They were in separate cells and not allowed visits since Elizabeth considered their marriage to be invalid. However, the Lieutenant of the Tower had taken great pity on them and arranged a secret rendezvous that resulted in Lady Katherine's second pregnancy. To make things worse for himself, he had kept her pregnancy a secret until it could be hidden no longer.

"Get out!" Elizabeth spat at the messenger.

She burst into tears at the slamming of the heavy door. I rushed over with a silk handkerchief.

"Now I shall never hear the end of this marriage business. All I hear from my council is that I need to marry and have an heir, that my throne will never be safe until I do. And now my cousin, the whore, has had herself another son just waiting to take my place. I will not stand for this treason."

"Your Grace," I said carefully. "Katherine may have two sons, but with no witnesses to her marriage, they are illegitimate and no threat to you. She is just a young girl whose head was turned with pretty words. If she were plotting against you, her methods were weak and ill-thought out. Show the people you are not afraid of her. Be the gracious queen your mother was. To show fear only increases her perceived power. Let them see that she is beneath your worry."

Elizabeth wiped her nose and then pulled off her glove. She chewed her fingernail thoughtfully, carefully considering my advice.

She pursed her lips. "I suppose your words have merit. She *is* beneath me, yet I am still concerned. However, I too was accused of many traitorous plots against my sister when I had nothing to do with them. I shall take your good counsel under advisement, Lady Knollys."

I didn't realise I had been holding my breath in anticipation of her response to my audacity in questioning her until I released it. I didn't know if my words had made any difference, but for the moment she was calm.

Soon Secretary Cecil was knocking at the door and Elizabeth's composure was restored as if nary a tear had been shed. Her emotions were wiped away and hardened determination came back into her face.

"Cecil, you will release the Lieutenant of the Tower from his duties today. Sir Edward Warner will serve us there no more."

Cecil bowed low and began to retreat from the room.

"Wait ..." she called out. "Lady Katherine is to be released into the care of her uncle, Sir John Grey at Havering. She will be separated from her children and for now their wardship will be in my care."

I sympathised with Elizabeth's rage. Those nine days when Katherine's sister, Jane, reigned on the throne instead of Mary a mere decade ago made the Grey sisters a threat to Elizabeth. Did they have a better claim? Possibly. Their grandmother had been sister to King Henry VIII, but before he died the king laid out the stipulations for his succession, naming Elizabeth after Edward and Mary, and his word was law. However, Katherine was young and beautiful and, most importantly, fertile. She had already demonstrated that she could give birth to boys. To Katherine's supporters, Elizabeth was a barren spinster. The more fear Elizabeth showed of the Grey sisters, the more power behind their cause. In any case, Sir John Grey was loyal to the crown and it would be far safer to have Katherine under his thumb.

"Harry, look at how you have grown!" I exclaimed wrapping my arms around my eldest son. I stepped back and admired the dashing figure he cut in his grey velvet doublet and cloth of silver trimmed ruff. He let his burnished brown hair grow longer and a fine beard graced his chin. His cheeks retained their boyish colour, but he looked every inch the courtier. I could not believe that the baby I had held in my arms was now in his twenty-second year. He was recently elected to Parliament and Elizabeth had invited him to Court to take part in the St George's Day celebrations.

"I am pleased to see you as well, Mother." He said, bending down to place a light kiss on my forehead. "The other children send their love. Bess can talk of nothing but debuting at Court next year, but I have reminded her that in addition to music and dancing, she needs to increase her lessons on the Scripture and learn to behave in a virtuous and Godly manner ... Unlike our sister, Lettice."

"Harry," I said, placing my hand on his offered arm. "Lettice is virtuous and Godly. She is just easily distracted by worldly things. How kind of you to guide your younger siblings. However, it is also wise to remember that not everyone's holy zeal can match yours."

"Well, we would all be better for it if they did, but I will try to keep it in mind."

I laughed at my son's obstinacy as we strolled down the corridor.

"We must arrange your marriage, my dear boy. You need some children of your own to raise."

On St George's Day, the newest Knights of the Garter were elected during a ceremony at Windsor. That night they were feted with a lavish dinner in Elizabeth's private quarters. It was a great honour not only to be elected to the Order of the Garter but also to be invited to take part in the ceremonies. A few short years ago, my brother was knighted during this very celebration and now my son would bear Elizabeth's train during the march to the chapel. Elizabeth had done much to promote her Boleyn relatives. I wondered if my grandfather, Thomas, would have finally been proud of us.

London, St. James Palace:
August - September 1564

During the most oppressive heat of the summer, Elizabeth's retinue set out on the annual progress. We would be spending time in Cambridge at the university during our journey. On 5th August, we meandered through Haslingfield and Grantchester. At Newham, the Lord Mayor of Cambridge met our enormous party and waited patiently while the queen conferred with Robert Dudley over which horse she preferred. We rode into the town, met with trumpet blasts and jubilant calls of "Long live the queen!"

The entertainment was never ending with a grand assortment of banquets and masques, dances and plays. Elizabeth enjoyed the attention and extravagance so immensely, it was decided that we would stay for a day longer than planned. We followed Elizabeth on horseback as she toured the colleges. I sat in boredom through the Greek oration at Christ's College. The highlight for me came at the end of the visit when both Francis and my brother, Henry, were created honorary Masters of Arts.

After Cambridge, we moved on to Hinchingbrooke. In the morning, a performance by the youngest students ridiculing the Catholic Mass so angered Elizabeth that she left in the middle of the masque and took the torchbearers with her. She left the astonished students behind to stare after her swishing skirts in the dark. The students were not the only ones puzzled by her hasty departure.

"Why does the queen insist on playing us for fools?" Francis raged as he paced the small cottage we were lodged in. "She refuses to participate in the Mass, yet she chastises anyone who dare question it. Are we to return to Rome now? What madness is this?"

I sat on the corner of the bed, amused by his indignation. On more than one occasion, Elizabeth had made it quite plain that England would not be returning to the Catholic fold, but for the staunchest reformers in her council that was not enough. They wanted her to decry their foul ways and condemn the pope and all he stood for. They wanted proof that she aligned herself with their cause.

The councillors would never be satisfied. Elizabeth was a pragmatist and she would never allow one side to trump the other. She had not survived the faction wars of her father's and sister's reigns without learning a few things about the hearts of men and how they were corrupted with power. With every changing decision and every ambiguous directive, Elizabeth reminded her council that the power lay solely with her. In regards to religion, in regards to her marriage, in regards to foreign relations, she would change her mind at a moment's notice the instant her council felt secure. It was the only way she knew to guarantee her security. Allow no man to directly influence her decisions.

When we arrived at St James's Palace near the end of September, Elizabeth had tired of irritating her councils in regard to her preference on religion. Instead she would remind her favourite that he too was never secure in her affections.

While Robert Dudley had been brought low by the scandal of his wife's death, his status at Court had never been higher. It was evident to me that Elizabeth would never take him as her consort, but it appeared that neither her council nor Dudley, himself were convinced that marriage to him was officially out of the question. I could hardly blame them for their assumptions. Elizabeth continued to lead them on a merry dance, never confirming nor denying her true intentions, and the moment that Dudley sensed her within his reach, she laid waste to his ego with the suggestion that he marry her cousin, the Queen of Scots.

Dudley worked hard to keep his composure as he stood before Elizabeth in the Privy Chamber, but his eyes gave him away.

"Are you certain, Your Grace, that you wish me to move to Scotland to marry your cousin?" he asked in an incredulous voice. "How can you even propose such a thing?"

"My lord, you would be king. And if it would be easier, I could invite you both to reside with at my court. This is an excellent match. I shall send Ambassador Randolph to inform Mary that should she agree to marry an Englishman of my choosing, I shall make her my heir," Elizabeth explained, a smirk dancing across her lips. Dudley had taken far too much license with the power she bestowed upon him. It was time that, like one of the horses he was master of, she reined him in. She knew he would never agree to the arrangement and Mary would never accept it so what did she have to lose? It would certainly quiet the rumours that were going around that she intended to take Dudley as her consort and, perhaps, she could thwart Mary's plans for a strong match with a Spanish or French suitor.

A crimson flush crept up behind Dudley's ears. "But, but I had hoped ..." He stuttered, nervously adjusting the elaborate white ruff at his neck. He cleared his throat.

"You hoped for what, Lord Robert? You hoped to be my consort? I have told you and my councillors already that I am not of a mind to take a consort at this time, but I assure you that I will apprise you all of my intention when I am ready." She swatted the air as if the very idea of her marriage was an annoying bug.

Dudley's eyes narrowed and his jaw clenched when he realised the futility of his argument.

"I am yours to command as you wish, Your Majesty."

He dipped a very low bow as he retreated towards the door. At the last second he turned and marched out in a huff, his black cape swishing behind him. Elizabeth's pink lips curled into a satisfied smile. For a fleeting moment, I was certain she winked in my direction. I shook my head, certain I imagined it. I thought back to that wretched night in her chambers after the death of Amy Dudley and the advice I gave her. Perhaps she had been taking it to heart all this time. Why she would ever listen to mere knight's wife

when she was God's anointed was beyond my comprehension, but
I must admit I felt flattered that she deemed my thoughts worthy.

In a great show of generosity, Elizabeth elevated Robert Dudley
to the Earldom of Leicester and Barony of Denbigh. Officially it
was done to raise him high enough that the Scottish queen would
not be wholly offended that such a lowly bridegroom was offered.
Dudley was still Elizabeth's Master of the Horse after all. Mary
Stuart would believe some outrageous joke had been played on her.
Unofficially, Elizabeth was placating Dudley's damaged ego. If, in
fact, Mary Stuart called her bluff and married him, Dudley would
still be at Court and it would not serve Elizabeth well to have him
sulking around.

Ever the tease, while Dudley was on his knees before Elizabeth
during his investiture, she tickled the back of his neck as she fastened
his mantle right in front of the French and Scottish ambassadors. I
bit my lip to keep from exploding into peals of laughter. It was no
wonder the council was in an uproar. As soon as they were certain
that Elizabeth had made up her mind, she destroyed their security
with one subtle gesture. A twitch of the finger and her intentions
were exposed. The Scottish ambassador scurried off the instant the
ceremony was over, a sneer of disgust on his face.

Ultimately, the elevation of Dudley did nothing to endear him
to Elizabeth's royal cousin and marriage negotiations ground to
a halt. If Elizabeth hoped Dudley's new title would increase her
council's respect for him, she was sorely mistaken. It only served
to inflame their animosity. Dudley's inclusion in the nobility
particularly enraged my brother.

The title of Earl of Wiltshire had reverted back to the crown
upon the death of my grandfather. After the execution of Anne
Boleyn and the exile of my mother to Calais, Thomas Boleyn had
lived out the rest of his life as a disgraced man. The reversion of his
title upon death was expected, but since Uncle George was dead
and our mother was the first born, Henry felt the title should be

his by right since we had been restored to favour. Instead, King Edward had bestowed the title upon William Paulet, and he had held the title for the last fifteen years.

Henry seemed to accept the slight, but I knew that he felt that he deserved promotion, not only as a cousin to the queen, but for his loyal service. Even when Mary was on the throne, Henry had never abandoned Elizabeth. Now that she saw fit to bequeath an earldom on the son of a convicted traitor, the old wound was once again inflamed.

Part VI

A Woman Most

Beloved of the Queen

London, Durham House on the Strand and Whitehall Palace: July 1565

"Lettice! Look at that gorgeous pregnant belly! Why did you not write of your condition?"

I stood clear amazed to see my eldest daughter full with child striding confidently into our rooms at Durham House.

"Mother, did you announce every one of our conceptions with such fanfare? I would think that would get ever so tiring after a while. Particularly since you and Father certainly did not know when to stop," she said, brushing my hand away from her protruding womb.

Hurt by her callous remark, I gazed at this cold woman my daughter had become. She had always been high-spirited and quick with a cutting remark, but her utter condescension was foreign to me.

"Such disdain you have for your parents, Lettice. Whatever could we have done to deserve such treatment?"

After brushing me aside, Lettice went to the window to stare out at the sunlit Thames and the spires of Westminster in the distance beyond. At my prodding, she whirled around and glared at me.

"What have you done?" she scoffed. "You allowed me to be banished to that horrid manor at Chartley. I was abandoned in the country with nothing to do but lie on my back while that bore of a man turned me into a brood mare. How could you let her send me away? And all because she knows the truth, the truth that when her crown and her power are stripped away, her precious Robin prefers me."

I stared at Lettice in horror. Her lip was curled in a sneer, her fists clenched at her side. She may as well have hit me with them for all the pain that her words wrought.

I swallowed hard, took a deep breath and willed my voice to be level, "Lettice Devereux, you brought your exile upon yourself. I warned you that Robert Dudley would bring you trouble. You are a married woman and it is your duty to bear your husband's children. You should consider yourself lucky that your father took such great care to match you to a man who loves you as much as Hereford does. Though to be honest, I am beginning to wonder why when you subject him to such horrible treatment."

Her eyes widened, enraged at my rebuke.

"You will never again call me Lettice Devereux," she spat. "I am Lady Hereford."

She took a moment to allow her to words sink in and then ran from the room without a second look back. I collapsed on my bed in tears. I had woken up that morning thrilled to have my family reunited for Harry's wedding celebrations and had never anticipated Lettice's outburst. She ran out of the room before I had the chance to tell her that Elizabeth had invited her back to Court.

My maid, Matilda, wandered in a few seconds later with my gown for the festivities and found me in a sorry state "My lady, what is wrong? Are you ill?" She threw my dress on a chair and ran over to the bed.

I sat up quickly. "I am fine Matilda, truly. Only a bit overwhelmed." I rubbed my eyes and dragged my fingers through my hair, trying desperately to straighten myself. "Can you please bring me a washcloth and a basin so I may wash my face?"

Matilda nodded and scurried off to her task.

I gazed at my red-rimmed puffy eyes and swollen lips in the mirror.

"You will not ruin your son's wedding." I told the tired and drawn-looking woman staring back at me. "Lettice does not dictate your happiness."

Harry looked upon the young and elegant Margaret Cave with much the same admiration his father had looked upon me on the day of our own wedding. The pale blush hue of her wedding gown enhanced the golden cascade of her hair. With her pale skin and almond eyes that matched the deep blue of the sea, it was little wonder that Harry, despite his severe nature, had fallen for her charms.

I had had my reservations when Sir Ambrose had approached Francis regarding marriage negotiations, but Margaret had shown herself to be as sweet-natured as she was described and I was pleased to welcome her into our family. I hoped that her bonny disposition would bolster Harry's humour.

While I watched my son and his new wife glide effortlessly across the dance-floor, I longed for the days of my own youth. Francis sensed my melancholy. I felt his arm snake around my waist and his warm breath tickled my ear.

"There's my lovely wife. Can I tempt you with a dance?" he whispered and tenderly nuzzled my neck.

I turned around and felt so overcome by my love for him that my knees quaked. "Of course, Sir Francis, I would never deny you."

Elizabeth and her court returned to Whitehall after the happy celebration of Harry's nuptials in time to find a very ill Kat Ashley. Two days later, she was dead.

Elizabeth was inconsolable. She had been virtually raised by Kat and her death threw Elizabeth into a spiral of despair. I was immediately promoted to her place as chief lady of the bedchamber and spent the next weeks comforting her in her grief.

My new position required constant companionship to Elizabeth and seeing her distress over Kat's death ignited my maternal instincts. I was starting to see her as one of my own children. She was the ruler of England and head of the church, but she still had a heart that felt love and pain. It broke just as easily as mine. Just as I still loved Lettice when she hurled such hurtful words, I would still love Elizabeth when showed me the same.

Coventry and Kenilworth:
August 1565

Despite her mourning, Elizabeth determined that her annual progress go on as planned. Robert Dudley, eager to show off his newly acquired castle at Kenilworth, invited the court for a grand party. Our arrival at Coventry in mid-August was greeted by the mayor, Humphrey Brownell, and the recorder, John Throgmorton. Under the shelter of a thicket of trees shading us from the scorching summer sun, the mayor knelt before Elizabeth's palfrey with the great mace of the city in his raised hand. As he did, a great plume of dust was raised by his voluminous crimson gown and Elizabeth tried unsuccessfully to stifle a cough. Mr Throgmorton humbly offered the mace to the queen in 'her most regal power and merciful authority.' The mayor touched his pale chapped lips to the mace and then placed it in her hands with a purse containing twenty marks.

Elizabeth turned to those of us behind her on horseback and benevolently smiled. "It is a good gift. I have but few such gifts."

"If it pleases Your Grace, there is a great deal more in it," piped up the mayor, the lower portion of his gown now covered in a fine dust.

Elizabeth turned back to the city leaders and pulled on the reins to steady her high-spirited horse.

"And what is that?" she queried.

The mayor again bowed low in reverence. I noticed the sheen of sweat across the back of his neck. "It is the hearts of all your loving subjects."

A wide grin broke out across Elizabeth's face. "We thank you, Mr. Mayor. That is a great deal more indeed."

After Elizabeth bestowed upon the mayor a humble nod of

appreciation, Mr Throgmorton launched into an extensive speech welcoming Her Majesty to Coventry, flattering her vanity with a list of all her virtues. "She has no comparison," he praised. We all shifted uncomfortably upon our horses in the thinning shade until his long-winded oration came to an end. Elizabeth, delighted by his remarks, praised him highly and returned the mace to the mayor, who once again knelt beside the recorder.

From my perch on the tawny mare I rode, I saw a wave of relief flood across the mayor's face as Elizabeth gestured to him to rise and mount his horse. He led us first to Bishop's Gate where Elizabeth bequeathed a gift of money to the library, then on to White Friars where we lodged for the next two days.

The Monday following, we arrived at Kenilworth. Dudley appeared at the gates in a resplendent costume. A black leather doublet covered a silky satin shirt, white as snow. His lawn ruff was embroidered with silver trim. He wore a bright jewel on each finger and his perfectly white hose emphasised the fine cut of his legs. He topped off each shoe with a brilliant ruby, red as blood.

"Good morrow, my queen!" He exclaimed with an elegant bow. "Welcome to Kenilworth."

Dudley made certain that Elizabeth's first visit to Kenilworth, now it was in his keeping, was a memorable one. The night of our arrival she surveyed her small retinue from a dais in the great hall with her favourite seated on her right-hand side as his servants brought in one silver dish after another piled high with the best cuts of meat, a whole pig and a roasted swan redressed with its feathers. An enormous stag, killed in one of the many hunting parks that surrounded the castle, served as a centrepiece to the elaborate feast.

Among all this luxury I found myself relieved that it was necessary for Lettice to stay behind at Whitehall due to her advanced pregnancy. Her home at Chartley could never compare to Dudley's glorious castle. Such opulence would serve only to inflame her lust for him even more.

After several days of entertaining masques and hunting parties, we began the slow return to Whitehall.

London, Whitehall:
August – December 1565

A grim report awaited Elizabeth upon our arrival at Whitehall. Lord Darnley, the son of Lady Lennox, had managed to complete his intended marriage to the Queen of Scots.

"This is your fault, Cecil!" Elizabeth exclaimed at her exasperated secretary. "I demanded his return and instead, they made him a duke, and now he is a king! He should never have been allowed to go to Scotland in the first place."

William Cecil nervously stroked his beard. "Your Majesty, I have already heard from the Earl of Bedford that Lord Darnley's violent and drunken behaviour is driving Mary Stuart's supporters from her court. He makes enemies as we speak and it is only a matter of time before the matter resolves itself. Be patient, my queen. Darnley will be his own undoing."

Elizabeth jabbed one long bejewelled finger into the centre of his richly embroidered indigo brocade doublet. "You had better hope so."

Lettice was now into her seventh month of pregnancy, but she did not allow it to stop her from using every skill she had to draw the attentions of Robert Dudley. Their flirtatious behaviour quickly inflamed court gossip. Francis shared few words of comfort during my nightly lamentations on the subject.

"Lettice already resents what little we interfere in her life as it is. Displeased as I am with her behaviour, there is little we can do without alienating her further," he counselled.

I was relieved when Dudley excused himself from Court to visit his sister, Lady Sidney, who had once again taken ill. I still thought of her fondly and felt terrible guilt for the scars she suffered from her care for Elizabeth during her smallpox outbreak. I prayed for her speedy recovery.

With the target of her affections gone and a quickly expanding womb, Lettice departed for Chartley at the end of September to await the birth of her child.

My daughter was not the only one disappointed in Dudley's exit from Court. Elizabeth was in a vindictive mood after her favourite dared to leave her side and began to transfer her favours onto one Thomas Heneage, a new Gentleman of the Privy Chamber.

Her flirtation with Heneage ended as quickly as it began upon Lord Robert's swift return, but her hasty remarks to my brother, Henry, were to have lasting repercussions.

The gardens at Whitehall were shedding the last of their full summer blooms and the leaves had begun the metamorphosis into their vibrant autumn colours, prompting my brother's wife and I to take our exercise out on the garden path rather than in the stuffy long gallery. The faint breeze was cool enough that we did not need our cloaks, yet we were both glad that we had worn velvet gowns against the chill.

Anne was her usual quiet self, but several times it seemed that just as she had a mind to say something, she stopped herself and we continued walking on in silence. After several of these hesitations, I reached out to cup her elbow and stopped her by a bare rose bush.

"Anne, what is it? It appears as though you have something on your mind, but not quite the courage to speak it. You know you can trust my confidences. Is something vexing you?"

Anne's rich dark eyes sought mine and I read the anxiety in them.

"Oh, I am certain it is nothing, merely a friendly jest by the queen. Henry will come around to her true meaning. He takes her careless remarks far too literally. I am being silly." She broke eye contact and waved me away, headed back down the path.

I quickened my pace to catch up to her. "What do you mean 'a friendly jest'? Has Henry angered the queen? She didn't mention such an incident to me in her bedchamber last night."

"Well, of course she wouldn't," Anne said stopping abruptly. "She wouldn't because she didn't mean what she said. She was only angry with Robert Dudley and spoke rashly, but Henry is already upset that Dudley was raised to earl and now ... Well ... he has had enough and is plotting with your cousin Norfolk to overthrow his reign as her favourite."

Henry was plotting against Dudley? Francis had never mentioned such acrimony between them, but he had been distracted with Elizabeth's affairs and had little time as of late to be involved in petty disagreements.

I continued to push for answers. "Will you at least tell me what the queen said to Henry?"

Anne sighed, obviously irritated with my questions. "She told him that he should be her master of the horse."

I burst into a fit of laughter. I saw the crimson flush creeping into Anne's cheeks and my hands flew to my mouth, desperate to muffle the sound.

"Anne ..." I chided. "Tell me that Henry did not really believe that she would appoint him to Dudley's position."

"Yes! Yes, he did!" she exclaimed. "And when Dudley returned from visiting his sister and wormed his way back into her affections, Henry was livid. There was nothing I could say to calm him. He's joined the Lords Norfolk and Sussex in their quarrel and now there is no stopping them."

Surprised by her own outburst, she whipped her head around, looking from side-to-side to make sure that no one was listening. Then in a conspiratorial whisper she added, "They have even decided that they will all begin wearing yellow to show unity."

I groaned. "What shall we do with them, Anne?"

She put her face in her hands and shook her head in frustration.

"I wish the queen would just decide on a husband. How can she ever expect to control the men in her court without a man on the throne to guide them?"

I stared out at the garden and spied a rose bush with a lone bloom still vibrantly red among the browning dead branches. I immediately thought of Elizabeth's mother. Her daughter had no need of a man to control her courtiers. She was already doing a fine job of it on her own. My sister-in-law just didn't know her well enough to see it.

Sure enough, I knew that a full-blown battle had begun between my brother and Elizabeth's favourite when the trio of conspirators paraded through court in their yellow hose and doublets. By the time of Ambrose Dudley's wedding in November, his brother's supporters had their own uniform - the recognised hue of royalty – purple.

Anne nervously fiddled with her girdle as we watched the men warily eye each other during the tournament held on the tiltyard at Westminster to honour the Earl of Warwick's marriage to the Earl of Bedford's daughter, but I paid little attention. I was far too excited for my son, Harry. He had won the initial joust.

After the celebrations, Francis and I received a letter from Lettice that she had been delivered of a son. Somewhat recklessly, she had decided to name him Robert.

The Christmas season came to Court as a great blizzard settled a thick blanket of perfect white snow on London. We attended a quiet Christmas service and then followed Elizabeth to her Presence Chamber where she dined in state with her closest companions. When the last of her company drifted off to their beds, Robert Dudley begged her for a private audience. The other maids and I hung back as Elizabeth and her favourite moved on to the Privy Chamber. After a few moments of awkward silence, Blanche Parry and I took our leave to prepare the bedchamber.

Elizabeth stared intently into the mirror while I combed her long locks. Shimmering strands of grey hair had begun to invade her golden red tresses, reminding me that thirty-two years had passed since her birth. I plaited her hair quickly and placed a cap on her hair to keep out the chill.

"Mistress Parry had the maid put a warming brick in your bed. It should be ready for you now," I said gently, helping Elizabeth to her feet.

"Oh thank you, Lady Knollys," she offered distractedly as she glided across the room to her enormous tester bed.

I walked around the room blowing out the candles as the light from the fire crackling in the hearth was bright enough to keep us from tripping in the night. I made sure the steward loaded it with fire-wood before he left for the evening.

Elizabeth sat quietly on the rich purple velvet quilts, and waited patiently for me to finish my duties. When I was done, she gestured for me to sit beside her. I perched gingerly on the edge of the bed, not wanting to wrinkle the bedding.

"Tell me, how does our cousin Lettice fare after the birth of her child? A boy named Robert, I believe? Does it not seem strange that her first son was not named for his father Walter?"

I hesitated, not sure how to respond. I agreed with her assessment, but Lettice was my daughter and I did not want to add to any irritation that Elizabeth already felt for her.

She could see my discomfort and placed her hand on my shoulder. "Have no fear, Catherine. You have no control over your daughter's impetuousness. Of course she would attempt to charm Lord Robert, he is rather handsome after all. I just feel pity for poor Hereford with his ungrateful wife."

I breathed a sigh of relief. "Yes, Your Grace. I know not what to do with her and her single-minded ambitions."

Elizabeth nodded. "Yes, well it will be some time before we invite her back to Court. It will be good for her to be home with her family."

Tears pricked at the back of my eyes. It had been nearly a year since I last saw my children. As much as I loved Elizabeth, serving her never filled the empty void I felt at the separation from them. I blinked hard, willing the emotion to pass and swallowed the lump in my throat.

"Yes, Your Grace. She should consider herself very fortunate."

Elizabeth removed her hand from my shoulder and indicated that I should take my place on the pallet next to her bed. Once she lay down, I closed the silk curtains around her bed and crawled under my own quilts.

The room was silent except for the popping coming from the hearth. As I was drifting off to sleep, Elizabeth's voice roused me.

"Lord Robert asked me to marry him this evening."

I bolted upright and stared into the blackness of her bed, hidden behind the curtains.

"What did you say?" I asked. And then, remembering my manners, apologised for my impertinence.

Elizabeth peeked out from behind the curtain. "It's quite all right, dear cousin," she laughed. "I was just as surprised at his gumption."

I relaxed and allowed a giggle to escape. "Well?"

She made a sour face at me. "Of course I gave no answer. Would you ever expect anything different?"

"Never," I responded as I lay back down on the pallet.

The curtains fell back into place and Elizabeth snuggled back into her bed.

"Oh, one more thing," she called out before falling asleep. "I think it is time for you to be with your family as well. Tomorrow I will advise Sir Francis that he may return with you to Greys. That is our New Year gift to you. And bring Bess back with you upon your return. I am in need of a new maid."

An enormous smile broke out across my face and excitement filled my heart. "Thank you, Your Grace, I am so appreciative ..."

Before I could finish, I was met with Elizabeth's snores.

I wondered how I could fall asleep after such wonderful news.

London, Whitehall:
April 1566

I had not realised how much I needed the respite until our horses trotted through the gates of Rotherfield Greys. I was overjoyed to see how well my children were getting on and marvelled at how much they had grown since we last saw them.

I immediately sent for a seamstress to begin work on Bess's new court wardrobe. She was thrilled to return to London with us and we delighted at the fabrics we chose for her new gowns. Rich velvets and damasks all in the subdued shades of grey and black Elizabeth preferred were purchased, along with new linen and silk for her undergarments. Our family was wealthier than most, but not so wealthy that we could afford to lavishly dress all of our children, so Bess's new costuming was certainly a treat.

Robert and Richard had learned well from their uncle Henry and were tending to our properties during Henry's travels to the continent. They both were gifted caretakers and I knew they would make excellent husbands one day.

The friendly competition that little Francis and Anne had built up provided never-ending entertainment for their father and me during the duration of our visit. Anne was determined that Francis would never best her at anything simply because he was a boy. She rode her palfrey as hard and as fast as he did his and even their tutor served as a target, each jockeying to win his approval. It seemed that Anne had taken after her namesake in more than just appearance. She would do well at Court.

Thomas and little Katherine were still small enough for cuddles and I spent many evenings with them sitting before the fire delighting them with tales from our time in London.

It was bittersweet to think of all the life that my other three children were denied. Mary, Maude and Dudley haunted my thoughts and, at night, I found myself dreaming of the adults they would have grown to be.

We returned to London in March with revived spirits, but much had happened during our absence. Having received no response to his marriage proposal and suffering great offence at Elizabeth's flirtation with the Earl of Ormonde, Robert Dudley retreated to his estates in the country. The Duke of Norfolk also took his leave, hardly bearing the wound inflicted upon him by Her Majesty for preferring Ormonde. Elizabeth told me later that she had tired of the constant bickering between Norfolk and Dudley and chose to shower Ormonde with such affections that both would flee for their vanity and give her some peace.

The dramatics at our court, however, paled in comparison to the dastardly deeds going on in Scotland. Shortly after our arrival, Cecil burst in to Elizabeth's bedchamber as we dressed her to deliver the news. While a heavily pregnant Mary Stuart dined with her secretary Rizzio, our treacherous cousin, Lord Darnley, ambushed them with the Scottish lords and stabbed the secretary to death right before Mary's eyes. How the trauma did not cause early labour, I would never understand. I admired Mary's strength, but I was also astonished by her lack of judgment in marrying a man like Darnley. A man like him would always undermine her rule.

As the howling winter winds died down and the flowers began to wake from their long slumber, the spring rains washed away all traces of Dudley's irritation and he returned to Court. Now that the weather had calmed enough for longer travel, Elizabeth had a mission for Francis.

"Just when I get used to the comfort of having you with me, the Queen sends you off on another errand," I whined, snuggling deeper under the covers and closer to the warm comfort of my husband.

He dragged his fingers through the hair at the back of my head, anchoring it in his hand, and kissed me passionately. "It is only for a month or two at most. I shall be home in time to go on progress at least." he said after our lips separated.

I groaned. "I know, but Ireland is so far away. Why is she making you go? I thought Henry Sidney was Lord Deputy of Ireland now. Does this not fall under his duties?"

Francis leaned back on his elbow, playfully narrowed his eyes at me and turned up his nose. "Do you dare question our queen?" he said in mock surprise.

I giggled at his impertinence and pulled him back on to the bed. I curled my fingers through the dark forest of hair on his chest. "You know I would never. I only worry for your safety," I said quietly.

Francis stilled my hand with his own, rolling over to face me again. "You have nothing to fear. I will only be in Ireland long enough to assure the queen that Sidney is doing the right thing in restoring the O'Donnells. The skirmish between the Irish clans and the Scots is ravaging the country and the queen needs to be sure that she is supporting the right man. I will return before you've even missed me."

I wrapped my arms around Francis and buried my face in his chest. "That is not true, I miss you already and you have not even left."

Francis informed me that he needed to return to Greys for some unfinished business before journeying to Ireland for two months. Much to my dismay, Elizabeth insisted that I stay behind at Court, and it was just as well as I wanted to pack Francis's trunk during his absence.

I accomplished much in my husband's short absence, but there was still one more item to complete before he returned from Greys, my anniversary gift to him. It had been twenty-six years since we wed and I wanted to give him something special to thank him for the wonderful life he had given us. He told me a story on our wedding night about how his family came to own Rotherfield Greys. His father, Robert, served my grandfather, Henry VII, and was appointed to wait on Prince Arthur. As a reward for his loyal service to the crown, my father, Henry VIII, granted him Greys in 1514 for the rent of one red rose at mid-summer. In honour of this family tale and our home at Greys, I was embroidering red roses on a silk undershirt. I wanted to present it to him before he left for Ireland, so I worked through the night to finish it in his absence.

The night before his return I sat hunched before the candlelight and tried desperately to coax the silken roses into bloom as my eye-sight failed in the near-darkness. A rap at the door surprised me and I pricked my finger with the sharp needle. Hot red blood seeped into the white silk, colouring in the empty spaces of the rose.

"God's blood!" I cursed, involuntarily sticking my wounded finger into my mouth.

I looked down at the ruined cloth in frustration. It was a metaphor for my whole life. My blood seemed to ruin all of my plans. I breathed a deep sigh and laid the shirt aside to see who had so rudely interrupted me. My annoyance was further compounded when I saw who awaited me on the other side of the door.

Robert Dudley leaned nonchalantly against the frame and gave me a simpering smile.

"Lady Knollys, I am so sorry to have disturbed you. I was hoping that I could speak to you for a moment."

I briefly racked my brain wondering what he could possibly want and faked my most gracious smile.

"Of course, Lord Robert, please come in. May I offer you some wine?"

He nodded, so I called for Matilda and asked her to bring a tray of refreshments in. We made small talk until my dutiful maid returned with the wine and a plate of bread and cheese. I waited for Dudley to sit and then I perched on the edge of a cushioned stool.

He took a sip of wine and cleared his throat.

"Lady Knollys – Catherine ... May I call you Catherine?"

The queen's favourite could call me anything he wanted, so I nodded meekly.

He continued, "Catherine, I have known your husband for many years. He has been a friend to the Dudleys for as long as I can remember. I treasure his friendship and know that I can always count on his loyalty."

He paused and searched my eyes for any display of emotion. I kept my face blank, but relaxed.

"He speaks very highly of you and your brother, Ambrose," I offered.

Dudley shifted uncomfortably in his seat and nodded. After an awkward moment, the reason for his visit became more apparent.

"But what of you, Catherine? Do you speak highly of me as well? It seems that I may have offended you in some way and so I have come to offer my apologies in hopes that our friendship may be mended."

Somehow I avoided choking on the sip of wine I had just taken. Robert Dudley was apologising to me? I was confounded by this turn of events. I frantically searched my mind for an appropriate response.

"My lord, you have no reason to apologise to me. I take no exception to my husband's friendship with you. It seems I am the one who should apologise for any affront I have caused you. My sincerest apologies are offered," I said scrambling to my feet.

Dudley gestured back to my stool. "Please sit, Catherine. There is no need for formalities. I simply want to know what I can do to mend this awkward situation that has arisen between us."

My hands trembled, but I managed to lower myself back down to the stool in a dignified manner.

I replied before I lost my courage. "Well, if we are eschewing the formalities, Lord Robert, I will be honest. I hear you declare your perfect love for my cousin the queen one moment, and in the next you beguile my daughter with your charms. You pressure the queen into a marriage that you know, quite well, would make her more vulnerable than she has ever been. I want to believe for her sake that you have the best of intentions, but I have a difficult time judging such by your actions. Elizabeth has survived much to take her place on the throne and I distrust anyone who should covet it from her."

I felt the heat radiating from my cheeks. I was astounded by my temerity in speaking so frankly. I waited nervously for the rebuke I deserved.

Dudley stared at me for a moment and then broke into a great laugh.

"My lady! I would never seek to covet your cousin's throne. That is hers by birthright."

Was he mocking me? My body started to shake in anger. I stared at the empty hearth, took a deep breath and tried to control my emotions. After a tense moment of silence, I felt Dudley lean towards me. His hand was surprisingly warm against my own. Startled, I turned to look at him and found myself seeing a kindness in his eyes that I had never noticed.

"Lady Knollys, you are a true and loyal servant to your cousin, the queen, and I beg forgiveness for reacting poorly to your well-founded fears. The love I bear Elizabeth is true, just as the love I bear your beautiful Lettice. Do you believe it is possible to love two people at once? I never did until I met your daughter."

He had found my weakness. Yes, I did believe it was possible. I suffered the same fate. I never was relieved of the love I felt for Richard, so I understood the effects of such emotions.

"Yes, my lord, I do believe it is possible and I can see by your earnestness that you speak from the heart. I apologise for treating you with such suspicion, but you must understand that I only did so out of fear for the women I love most," I offered meekly.

Dudley smiled kindly and righted himself, taking his hand from mine. "I do understand, Catherine, and that is why I sought you out this evening. I care for Francis as a brother and I would like to end any enmity between us. I have enough discord with your brother Henry. I would like to keep my enemies few," he added with a light chuckle.

"Ah, yes. My brother - that is a battle you will have to fight on your own I am afraid, my lord," I replied with a relieved smile.

"Well, he should be happy," he began, rising up from his chair and smoothing the tails of his doublet. "I am certain now that the queen will never marry me and so, for now, I have ended my pursuit. As for Lettice, should she ever find herself in need of a husband, I shall be the first to offer my hand."

I led him towards the door, my stomach finally relieved of the tense knot it had worked itself into through the conversation. As I opened the door, I said, "I hope one day you find a companion that makes you as happy as Francis has made me."

He kissed my hand in farewell and replied, "I hope so as well, Catherine. And the secret of your second love will always be safe with me."

I spared him an appreciative nod, but I knew that I would never need to be grateful of his discretion, for I had no secrets from Francis. My heart would remain his forever.

On Progress, then London, Whitehall and Westminster: August 1566 – January 1567

Just as he promised, Francis returned from Ireland at the end of July in time for the annual summer progress. We left Greenwich in early August and set out to visit the Grey Friary in Stamford. Cecil was eager for us to visit his home, but understood Elizabeth's avoidance due to his daughter's illness with smallpox. She had never fully recovered from the fear she felt during her own bout with the disease and looked upon re-infection with dread. From the friary we moved on to the palace at Woodstock, the home that served as her prison during her sister's reign.

While in Oxford we were treated to tours of both Oxford University and St John's College and entertained with public debates, sermons, lectures and plays. During an afternoon performance of a play by Richard Edwards, we looked on in horror as the stage collapsed during the production. Three bloodied bodies were dragged from the rubble. Elizabeth's merry mood was undeterred. She sent for her surgeons and ordered an encore performance for the next day. During the festivities Francis, along with several other courtiers, was once again honoured as Masters of the Arts.

Initially Elizabeth had demurred on her intention to visit Robert Dudley's newly renovated home at Kenilworth when gossip ran rampant that the court anticipated an engagement announcement. But, as I expected he would, Dudley convinced her to come anyway.

We found Kenilworth to be far grander than our last visit.

Dudley had even begun to make improvements on the vast garden that dominated the property. I thoroughly enjoyed evening walks with Elizabeth among the last roses of the season. I breathed in their heady scent and marked the memory for the wintry days ahead.

We returned to London in September and lodged at Westminster so Elizabeth could call her Parliament.

Elizabeth's efforts to drum up much-needed funds backfired on her. Francis informed me that the Commons refused to approve the award of any funds until she settled the question of her succession. Parliament's patience with her refusal to either marry or name a successor had run out.

In October, the Lords joined the Commons in their ultimatum. Elizabeth was furious. In a fit of anger, she banned Dudley from the presence chamber, fed up with the pressure he put on her to give in.

The Spanish ambassador, de Silva, was a constant fixture in Elizabeth's rooms during Dudley's exile while she railed against Parliament. Whenever she wavered in her obstinacy, he was there to bolster her resolve and encouraged her to avoid compromise.

"With the birth of the Scots queen's son, it is more important than ever that the Queen name her successor. De Silva knows that and is using her pride to lead her around to his master's benefit." Francis snarled as he threw a muddy boot across the floor. He sat at the edge of our bed and dragged his hands through his wind-tangled hair.

I climbed up behind him on my knees and wrapped my arms around him. I embraced him tightly and then moved my hands up to his shoulders and kneaded the tension from them.

"Will you do as she asks? Will you address Parliament with her demands?" I asked quietly.

Francis leaned his head back and nuzzled my cheek.

"Of course I will. I would serve the queen in any way she demanded of me and I am honoured that she would deem me worthy of addressing her Parliament. That being said, I think she is making a grave miscalculation."

I moved off the bed and wandered over to the cupboard to retrieve my night cap. "You have to understand Elizabeth's point of view," I called over my shoulder. "When her sister was on the throne, she was the heir apparent and rumoured to be the instigator of every treasonous plot. When Mary was on her deathbed, her courtiers abandoned her and beat a path to Hatfield to ingratiate themselves with their new queen. Elizabeth will never let that happen."

I glanced at Francis's reflection in the mirror. He was nodding thoughtfully. I dabbed a bit of rosewater around my neck and made my way back to the bed. Francis pulled me down next to him and pressed his lips to the tip of my nose. "That is my wife, beautiful and intelligent," he sighed contentedly as he lay back on the bed and drifted off to sleep.

Francis's plea for Parliament to cease their demands and trust in the queen to name a successor in her own time fell upon deaf ears and, ultimately, Elizabeth was forced to capitulate. She finally compromised, telling the members that in exchange for one third of her demanded sums, they could hold an open discussion on the question of the succession. In their jubilance at Elizabeth's assent, they granted her the funds without further discussion. For the time-being, her desire had won out.

Elizabeth stared longingly out the window of her bedchamber at Whitehall at the birds as they flew across the frozen Thames. The early morning sunlight glinted off the emerald brooch that she fingered absentmindedly at her neck.

"I envy them," she murmured.

"The birds, Your Grace?" I asked as I smoothed out the heavy brocade skirt that we would dress her in for the day.

She turned from her perch before the window and pursed her lips in thought. Then she rose and strode purposefully towards me. She tweaked my nose and broke into a broad smile.

"Yes, my dear cousin, the birds," she said throwing her arms in the air. "They are free to do as they please. They can mate when and with whom they choose. They have no need for trifles such as gold and silver. They need only to spread their wings and take to the skies when it suits their fancy, no need of a train of litters to follow them across the country. How is it that the lowly bird has more freedom than a king?"

I didn't have an answer for her. I remembered wishing for the same thing long ago, but in exchange for giving up those things that I believed I wanted, I was blessed with a loving husband, beautiful children and a security I never realised I needed. Elizabeth had none of these things.

As if reading my mind, Elizabeth stopped my hands, knocking the skirt out of my grasp, and gripped them in her own. "At least I have you. Francis never agrees with my policies, but I know that neither of you will ever forsake me. Everyone else serves me out of some ambitious desire, but I have never believed it of you, Catherine. I can never thank you enough for your sincere kindness over the years."

I tried unsuccessfully to swallow the lump in my throat. "Your Grace, you are my – I mean – we are family. I could never have treated you any other way." I blinked away the tears threatening to spill over my flushed cheeks.

Part VII

Release

London, Whitehall: April – June 1568

I woke up drenched in sweat, my heart pounding. It had been years since the last time I dreamt of the orchards at Hever and never had the dream been so vivid. This time, I was no longer a child. I ran barefoot through the apple trees searching desperately for Francis. I still felt the stab of the sharp twigs on my tender feet and I still smelled the sweet, putrid stench of rotten apples. I saw my husband in the distance, but the closer I got to him, the further away he appeared to be. I called out to him, but he never turned around. He was always just out of reach.

A wave of relief washed over me as I rolled over to find his solid, comforting presence snoring softly beside me. I eased myself out of bed, careful to avoid waking him, and tiptoed to the wooden table that held my wash basin. Matilda had already filled it this morning while Francis and I slept. I glanced in the mirror and, horrified by my reflection, immediately regretted it. My braid had come undone in the night and my sweat soaked hair was plastered against my cheek. I quickly ran a comb through the tangles and re-plaited the braid. A cool splash of water wiped the traces of slumber from my eyes.

"Won't you come back to bed my love? I am not yet ready to greet the day," Francis called from his warm cocoon under the covers.

It would be one of the last leisurely mornings we spent in each other's arms.

"Tell Moray that I would like to purchase the Queen of Scot's pearls." Elizabeth called out to Secretary Cecil as he shuffled out the door, anxious to complete his correspondence with the Earl of Moray, the newly appointed regent of Scotland for Mary's son, King James.

Mary had abdicated her throne the previous July after a spring of utter turmoil. In February, the Earl of Bothwell had very conveniently rid Mary of her petulant husband, Lord Darnley. She had never fully reconciled with Darnley after his part in the cold-blooded murder of her secretary and it was whispered that she had instigated Bothwell, her new favourite, to the challenge. Darnley was dispatched in an explosion at his house at Kirk O'Field. In April, Mary was kidnapped by Bothwell and by May, after her pregnancy from his purported rape of her was confirmed, they were wed at Holyrood.

Infuriated, the lords confronted both Mary and the earl as it had begun to appear that the kidnapping and rape may not have been wholly unwilling on Mary's part. After an unsuccessful skirmish at Carberry Hill, the earl fled to Denmark leaving Mary to be captured by her lords. Shortly after her incarceration at Lochleven, Mary miscarried twins. Weakened and exhausted, Mary finally relinquished her throne.

Elizabeth fumed over this turn of events. She railed about the audacity of the Scottish lords in deposing their anointed queen. I had sat by, many months previously, in a tense Presence Chamber while she berated Cecil for his support of the Earl of Moray. She screamed that she would go to war with the Scots to avenge her cousin's treatment. But the dramatics were all for naught. Elizabeth soon realised that there was nothing she could do to improve Mary Stuart's situation.

By autumn she had become more circumspect about the upheaval in Scotland and decided that action against Scotland would do more to harm Mary than help her, and she was not willing to risk her own throne in support of her Catholic cousin.

Since then, tensions had cooled between Elizabeth and Moray

and she was turning Mary's imprisonment to her own advantage. I felt certain that the Scots queen's pearls would not be the last piece of jewellery that Elizabeth would purchase from her confiscated coffers.

I stared at Elizabeth in bewilderment at the detached way in which she instructed Cecil to purchase the pearls. It never ceased to amaze me how quickly she could change her allegiances.

Shortly after the arrival of the Scots queen's pearls, we learned that the queen herself had daringly escaped from Lochleven and engaged the Scottish lords at Landside. After she was defeated, she fled Scotland only to be picked up by Elizabeth's agents in Workington and hauled to Carlisle castle.

"Father, have you any news of the Baron De la Warre's response to my proposed marriage?" Anne asked hopefully as we bid our goodbyes to Francis. Elizabeth had chosen him to welcome the Scots queen to Carlisle, but we all knew that there was much more to it than that. She wanted information on Mary. Francis and his companion, Lord Scrope, were to serve as her spies.

Francis bent down and touched his nose to hers. "You will be the first to know of it," he replied lightly and kissed her cheek.

Anne flashed a brilliant smile and ran back towards the castle doors. My second youngest daughter had arrived at Court a few short months ago and found herself enamoured with life in London. The competition with her brother prepared her well for service among the queen's maids.

I glanced towards the sky and noticed that it had darkened to a slate grey.

I frowned at Francis. "Do you think it will rain?"

Francis laughed. "If it does, I promise I shall ride in the carriage."

He shook his head and sauntered over to me. He wrapped his arms around my waist and held my gaze. "Would you cease your endless worrying? Everything will be fine."

I wrinkled my nose. "Francis, you know that as long as I am

breathing I am worrying. I have sixteen people to worry about. It takes up a lot of my time."

"Sixteen!" Francis exclaimed in mock surprise.

"Yes," I giggled. "I added in the queen. I worry about her the most."

"As do I, my love ... As do I." Francis murmured into my ear.

We reluctantly pulled out of our embrace, each of us not ready to let the other one go. But the sky had darkened and it was time for Francis to get on the road.

"I will write soon," he promised as he climbed upon his tawny horse and waved goodbye.

I watched Francis and Lord Scrope as they trotted away, their horses were followed by a carriage loaded with supplies for the Scottish queen.

London, Greenwich:
July – August 1568

"Are you all right, Lady Knollys?" The Queen called out of the window embrasure. She was deep in conversation with Cecil about the upcoming summer progress, but for some reason I seemed to have caught her attention.

"Oh, yes, Your Grace. I am fine," I replied in a frail voice I barely recognised as my own.

My head was throbbing and I was finding it difficult to concentrate on the needlework in my hand, but Elizabeth was determined to leave in a week and I didn't want to ruin her plans with an illness. She would not be pleased to leave me behind.

"You look very pale," she noted, a tone of concern creeping into her voice. She looked around for my daughters. "Bess, Anne ... Will you please help your mother to her room?"

The girls exchanged worried glances and hurried over to help me off of my cushion.

"Really - I am all right," I stammered as I scrambled to my feet.

Bess put her arm around me just in time to catch me as the room went black.

The steady rocking of the chair beside my bed led me from the darkness of my slumber and into the soft candlelight of my bedchamber. The occupant of the chair, my dear Bess, sat quietly reading with a quilt draped across her lap.

"How long have I been asleep?" I croaked. My throat was dry and parched.

Bess jumped at the sound of my voice. She dropped the book to the floor and leapt out of the chair, calling for Matilda.

Matilda bustled in with a mug of foul-smelling liquid and promptly made me drink it. It burned as it slid down my throat and I fought back the tears at the pain. Bess took the mug from me and placed her small hand lightly on my forehead. Before I could enjoy the cool sensation of her touch, she recoiled in horror.

"Mother - you are burning up. We need to get the doctor."

"No ... No," I whimpered. "Please just tell me how long I have been asleep."

"You have been in this bed for three days. And now your skin is on fire. We must get the doctor in here," Bess demanded with panic in her eyes.

"Three days ..." I groaned weakly. "The queen's progress ..."

Bess looked helplessly to Matilda for guidance.

"My lady, you will not be leaving in this condition. I will not call for the doctor, but you must let us treat you. We cannot allow the fever to take hold."

Matilda's face blurred and then faded from my sight.

I have only vague recollections of poultices and cool rags during my feverish haze, but whatever Matilda and Bess did in their desperation worked. I awoke to a letter from my beloved.

My Dearest Catherine,

I have just received a letter from Lord Robert Dudley informing me of your sudden and most unfortunate illness. I am very sorry to hear that you have fallen into a fever. I would to God that I was so dispatched hence that I might only attend and care for your good recovery. I write to the queen daily that there is little reason for me to wait upon this bereft lady, but she refuses to recall me home and, instead, sends me with my charge to Bolton Castle.

The Scottish queen was much aggrieved by the queen's meagre offerings when I presented her with the gowns that the queen had sent for her use. In my embarrassment I pleaded the error of a servant, but I knew full well that the queen had chosen the garments specifically.

I spend much of my days trying to calm her in her tantrums and settle her distress. By the time I close my eyes at night all I can think of is your soothing nature. I hold you in my dreams and it prepares me for the exhausting duties that I must take up again in the morning.

Please take care. I pray for your speedy recovery.
Your loving husband,
Francis

Elizabeth and most of the court had already left on progress by the time I was recovered enough to leave my bedchamber. Against my better judgment, I joined her retinue at Grafton in mid-August.

"Lady Knollys, what possessed you to leave London?" Robert Dudley spit through his clenched jaw when he caught sight of me in the corridor upon my arrival covered in sweat with my skirts rumpled from my journey. He dragged me into an empty room and proceeded to lecture me on the dangers of travelling so soon after my illness.

I had no explanation to offer him for my recklessness other than my loyalty to Elizabeth. By the time we arrived back in London at the end of the month after stopping in Newbury and Reading, I had already received another letter from Francis expressing his frustration with me.

London, Hampton Court Palace: December 1568 – to 15th January 1569

A conference was held at York in the autumn to determine the Scottish queen's culpability in the murder of her husband Lord Darnley. A casket of letters and poems was unearthed among the abandoned belongings of the Earl of Bothwell and the content of them seemed to prove that Mary had been urging the earl on in his violent plan.

Elizabeth learned of these letters soon after Mary's abdication, but it was at the conference with the Duke of Norfolk in York that the Earl of Moray finally produced them. After much debate over their authenticity, it was decided that nothing could be proved until they were compared with Elizabeth's personal letters from Mary at Westminster.

The Earl of Moray arrived at Westminster the first week of December to present the letters to the Privy Council. The court had, by this time, moved to Hampton Court Palace for the Christmas festivities.

I hoped that Francis would be allowed to return home for the celebrations. Until the Scottish queen's guilt in his husband's death was settled, there was no real reason that Francis could not leave. He had completed his task in welcoming Mary and transferring her to Bolton. His report on her character was already received by Secretary Cecil. The only thing keeping him from a speedy return to London was Elizabeth.

"Catherine, I need Francis at Bolton. He is the only man I trust to serve me in regards to that woman," Elizabeth insisted.

She had her hands raised in the air waiting for me to drop her linen night shirt over her head. I tugged gently on the fabric, trying hard to avoid catching her hair. She still retained her slim youthful figure and I eyed with envy the way that the fabric laid across her narrow hips.

I stayed behind her and spoke as I plaited her hair. I knew better than to make eye contact when challenging Elizabeth. I would inevitably lose my nerve.

"Surely Lord Scrope is capable enough," I replied lightly. I did not want Elizabeth to think I was directly questioning her authority. "It would be wonderful to have Francis home for Christmas."

Elizabeth turned around. Her face was calm and her voice was steady. "Catherine, I cannot risk it. Mary is known for her abilities to charm men to doing their bidding. I cannot depend on Lord Scrope to avoid her seductions. Your husband is incorruptible. He has the most integrity of any courtier that has ever served me and, most importantly, he loves you. He would never allow Mary to compromise his faithfulness."

I understood her position and I realised then that convincing her to change her mind would be fruitless. I nodded that I understood and reached out to pull the curtains open on her tester bed. As she crawled under the covers she muttered, "You really should take it as a compliment."

I participated as little as possible in the festivities leading up to Christmas. I felt melancholy at Francis's absence and I missed my children. Lettice had still not forgiven me and Elizabeth was not ready to allow her back to court. Harry was spending Christmas at Bolton with his father. Bess and Anne would be here, but the rest of my children were to stay home at Greys.

On Christmas Eve, I invited my maid to take dinner with me in my bedchamber.

"My lady, this is far too much for me to eat. You will have to roll me out of your room on a cart!" Matilda exclaimed. Her eyes shone with excitement in the candlelight at the bounty on the table before her. Tiny silver plates of fig custard and marchpane garnished the savoury meat pie in the centre.

"Please, Matilda," I laughed. "Eat as much as you like. Thank you for spending your Christmas with me."

Matilda smiled at me and then she furrowed her brow. "Where are your beautiful daughters? I am certain I saw Lady Anne leaving your room earlier today."

I leaned across the table for the wine and poured Matilda a generous cup.

"Matilda, you know very well that this is the most important time for the beautiful young girls of the court to be out in their finest gowns, making merry and dancing with every handsome young man that asks. I could not deny them that." I gave her a sly wink. "They did offer, but I insisted that they partake in the banquet and masque."

We ate until our bellies were full and then slipped leftover scraps to my little spaniel, Ginger. Afterwards, we relaxed in my cushioned chairs before the fire and lost ourselves in the stories of our youth. We roared with delight at silly escapades from our childhood and cried tenderly over the people who were no longer with us.

After Matilda told a particularly moving story about my mother's generosity and compassion, I was moved to demonstrate my own.

"Matilda?" I asked after a quiet moment. "Are you still in love with Henry Knollys?"

The firelight danced across her wine-coloured cheeks and a look of longing came over her face.

"I never told you this, but when he returned from his mission in Germany a few years ago he proposed marriage. I denied him of course. Who was I to marry him? His sister-in-law is the daughter of a king and one of the queen's closest companions. I was nothing but a maid. Besides, I could not leave you, especially after Dudley's death. And I was afraid. I was afraid that you and Francis would be angry with me for my presumption."

"Matilda, I could never be angry with you!" I cried. Inspired to action by her honesty, I leapt from my chair and ran to my dress cupboard. I threw open the doors and rummaged around for the pale blue brocade gown that I wore to Edward's coronation. When I felt the familiar fabric brush my fingers, I giggled with glee.

I thrust the gown at Matilda. She stared at me, mouth agape.

"Matilda, I release you from my service."

Her eyes widened. "I spoke out of turn – please don't be angry with ..."

I stopped her. "Take this dress and go back to Greys. Henry will not be able to resist you. You go with my blessing."

Matilda's eyes shimmered with tears as she threw her arms around me.

"Go," I whispered.

I felt my spirits rise at the sight of her scampering out the door.

The next morning I awoke to the same throbbing pain in my head that had plagued me in the summer. I blamed the wine from the evening before, but in the back of my mind a cold fear came creeping in. The bright winter sun streaming in through the windows intensified the pain and try as I might to urge myself out of bed I had no desire to emerge from the covers.

Bess and Anne came to visit. They regaled me with every detail of their wonderful evening. Anne tittered excitedly about Thomas West asking her to dance. She could hardly contain her glee when Bess reminded her that if the marriage negotiations were successful, one day she would be his baroness.

Though they worried about me, I pleaded my overconsumption of wine and shooed them off to enjoy the celebrations. I spent the rest of the evening in bed dozing off to the sounds of a crackling fire in the heart and to the comfort of my spaniel curled against back.

When I did not emerge from my chamber by 1ˢᵗ January, the queen paid me a visit. She fretted over my condition and sent her doctor to care for me. He prescribed bleeding and an awful concoction of herbs. The fever did not burn nearly as hot as before and abated after a few days under his care.

Elizabeth refused to leave me alone while I recovered and spent many evenings by my bed reading from the Gospels or reminiscing about her days at Hatfield. My guilt over Lettice's betrayal with Robert Dudley was worsened when she told me how much she had enjoyed having my daughter with her while we hid away in the Low Countries and how she had hoped that one day Lettice would be her closest companion.

I wanted to rail against Dudley for causing such a breach between cousins, but I didn't have the heart. He would be as miserable as they were, for neither was at liberty to freely give their love to him.

I received a moving letter from my own love just as I had begun to feel well enough to get out of bed.

My Dearest Catherine,

I have received word from Secretary Cecil that you are again ill with fever. I wrote back to him expressing my desire to return home, but once again I was refused. I shudder in anger at this mistreatment. I have performed every task that the queen has given me and yet she adamantly refuses to grant my small request.

I have decided that when I am finally allowed to return, I shall resign my post and return with you to our home at Greys where we can live a quiet life in the country. We may fall to poverty, but I do not care. I only want to be by your side.

I pray daily for your recovery and beg the Lord to spare you from your pain. I will think of you until you are in my arms again.

All of my love,

Francis

I fell asleep with Francis's words clutched tightly to my breast. As I dreamt of my quiet life in the country with Francis, the fever returned to ravage my body. Elizabeth's doctor ordered another bleeding, but the fever would not abate this time.

Elizabeth's face was bathed in the pale moonlight. Her eyes were sunken in and hollow. She brightened at my stirring and immediately reached for my hand.

"Elizabeth," I whispered.

"Yes, Catherine?"

The effort it took to speak pained me, but I swallowed hard and continued. "Please take care of my family. When Lettice does something that angers you, remember the love that I have for you and forgive her. Find places in your court for my sons, as they will have families to feed. Help Francis to find good men for our daughters."

Elizabeth's hand trembled in mine, but she put on a brave smile. "Don't say such things, Catherine. You will recover from this fever just as you did before. I will always care for your family, but you will be here to make sure of it."

I closed my eyes and took a deep breath to remember the scents of life. The juniper in the rushes, the linen on my bed, the rosewater in Elizabeth's hair. I took it all in one last time.

"Tell Francis that I will always love him and that I will be waiting for him," I murmured faintly.

I felt Elizabeth's lips on my cheek and heard her voice. "Yes, Catherine. You must wait for him."

The orchards of Hever were in full bloom and the faces of the two little girls from my dream were finally clear to me. It was my mother and Anne, and they were calling my name.

THE END

Catherine Knollys' Memorial

Catherine Carey Knollys died on 15 January 1569 (new style dating) in her rooms at Hampton Court, where the court had retired to celebrate the holiday season. Elizabeth was inconsolable upon her death and, for a time, she worried her councillors with her refusal to even stomach food in her grief. The queen graciously funded a lavish funeral for her departed chief lady of the bedchamber and had her laid to rest in St. Edmund's Chapel at Westminster Abbey.

There is a commemorative plaque in the Abbey that reads:

"The Right Honourable Lady Catherine Knollys, *chief Lady of the Queen's Majesty's Bedchamber, and Wife to Sir* Francis Knollys, *Knight, Treasurer of Her Highnesses Household, departed this Life the Fifteenth of January, 1568, at* Hampton-Court, *and was honourably buried in the Floor of this Chapel.*

This Lady Knollys, *and the Lord* Hunsdon *her Brother, were the Children of* William Caree, *Esq; and of the Lady* Mary *his Wife, one of the Daughters and Heirs to* Thomas Bulleyne, *Earl of* Wiltshire *and* Ormonde; *which Lady* Mary *was Sister to* Anne Queen *of* England, *Wife to K.* Henry *the Eighth, Father and Mother to* Elizabeth Queen *of* England."

Underneath is a Latin inscription which, when translated, reads:

"O, Francis, she who was thy wife, behold, Catherine Knolle lies dead under the chilly marble. I know well that she will never depart from thy soul, though dead. Whilst alive she was always loved by thee: living, she bore thee, her husband, sixteen children and was equally female and male (that is, both gentle and valiant). Would that she had lived many years with thee and thy wife was now an old lady.

But God desired it not. But he willed that thou, O Catherine, should await thy husband in Heaven."*

Catherine's husband Francis never remarried after her death. Though he would have been a very eligible bachelor in the Elizabethan court, he preferred to live out his final twenty-seven years as a widower.

An elaborate monument was erected at Rotherfield Greys by their son, William Knollys, with the effigies of seven sons, six daughters, and William's wife. It still stands in the church today.

*Taken from the website of Westminster Abbey http://www.westminster-abbey.org

Author's Note

I have always felt that it is the duty of a historical author to finish with a word to his/her readers regarding the authenticity of the history he/she portrays. While artistic license can make for very vivid imagery and often assist the reader in connecting with the protagonist, we must always remember that the people in our stories were real historical figures and deserve an honest assessment. Too often historical fiction writers have slandered the reputations of these long deceased people, no longer around to defend themselves. While I have taken license with certain events in my story, I have made every effort to keep the characterisations of these amazing people intact, and every change I have made has been in the realm of possibility, meaning that while there is no record of the event ever happening, it is not impossible for it to have occurred.

First and foremost, I would like to state that very little record of conversations between the people of the times exists, therefore most of the dialogue has come from my imagination. The same can be said for the letters from Elizabeth, Mary and Francis. I have referenced some of the wording in the *Cor Rotto* letter from Elizabeth, but it is not entirely incorporated. We do know that Francis almost always ended his letters with "Yours Assured", but those have been almost exclusively dispatches to the queen's council members and I have taken a far more personal tone in his letters to Catherine. The only pieces of dialogue that are purely authentic are the words spoken by Ridley and Latimer as they suffered at the stake.

The characters of Richard, Susannah and Matilda are creations of my imagination. I have found no record naming Catherine's maids and it is possible that more than one served her at various points in her life, but, for simplicity's sake, I have only included Matilda. Since Susannah is a fictional character, her ties to Kat Ashley are also fictional.

Throughout the story, Catherine attempts to come to terms with her parentage. I have chosen to portray her as the illegitimate daughter of Henry VIII, however not every historian would agree with that assessment. Whether or not Henry VIII fathered Catherine is still a contentious debate. While we have an exact birth date for her brother, Henry, we don't actually have a birth date for Catherine. The best estimates put her date of birth in the spring of 1524. It has been estimated that Mary Boleyn's affair with the king commenced in 1522 and continued, based on land grants made to William Carey, through to 1525. However, we must remember that Carey was a trusted courtier and it is possible that the land grants were given after the cessation of the affair. Catherine's birth definitely falls within the timeline needed for the king to father her. However, Mary was, indeed, married during the time of this affair so Catherine's lineage is not quite so cut and dry. We also do not know exactly how the affair started and the king only formally acknowledged the relationship with Mary once. Anything I have described regarding Mary's relationship with him is pure conjecture.

Unless DNA testing is done, we will probably never know the truth, but in my own personal opinion, I have always believed that Henry VIII fathered Catherine. When Catherine's portrait is compared to Elizabeth I's, the similarities are striking and, when accompanied by the circumstantial evidence, I think a strong case can be made. However, it is not unknown for cousins to appear more alike than siblings and, certainly, Catherine and her family would have been heavily promoted by Elizabeth whether they were sisters or not. For further reading regarding Catherine's parentage, I highly recommend any work by Anne Boleyn's esteemed biographer Eric Ives.

In 1534, Mary was banished from the court for her marriage to William Stafford and resulting pregnancy. Anne was, by that time, queen and it was felt that Mary had brought dishonour to the Boleyn name by marrying a man of such low standing without royal permission. There is very little in the historical record regarding Mary and William Stafford until the death of Thomas Boleyn in 1539, when Mary came into her inheritance of Rochford Hall. There is absolutely no record of the child she was carrying in 1534. I have assumed that Mary returned to Calais with Stafford after her banishment, as it seems unlikely that she would be welcomed back to the family's home at Hever. We know that Stafford was in Calais in 1539 because he is listed as someone who accompanied Anne of Cleves on her departure from Calais to England. It is possible that Catherine stayed at Hever until she was called to Court to wait on the new queen, but I have placed her with her mother and Stafford in Calais. Since there is no record of Mary and Stafford's child, I have assumed that he or she was either miscarried or died at a very early age. For further reading on Mary Boleyn, I suggest Alison Weir's biography.

I have tried to portray Lady Rochford in a far more sympathetic light than she is usually treated by historical fiction writers. Though she has been slandered for centuries for testifying against her brother and sister-in-law, we really don't have any evidence of what she said in her testimony and anything that that has reported otherwise has come from very unreliable secondary sources. Her reasons for any testimony at all could be for a number of reasons, but it is unlikely that she would seek the destruction of the man who supported her. It is very likely, however, that she was under extreme psychological distress when interrogated by Thomas Cromwell. Her miscarriage is a complete work of fiction, serving only to make her more sympathetic. While regarded as fiction in this novel, it is safe to say that a pregnancy would certainly be possible. George and Jane Rochford were a co-habitating couple and there is absolutely no evidence of any distress or scandal in the marriage and while George was certainly a court flirt, there is no evidence that he was homosexual or that he engaged in extra-marital affairs. For more information on George and Jane Rochford, I suggest Clare Cherry and Claire Ridgway's excellent biography *George Boleyn: Tudor Poet, Courtier & Diplomat*.

We do not have an exact timeline of the Knollys' journey to the continent during Mary I's reign, but we do have snippets of information regarding specific events. We have a letter from Calvin dated 20th November 1553 describing his visit from Francis and Henry Knollys (the son) and praising Henry's "holy zeal". There is no mention of Catherine or any other children and Catherine had only given birth in August so it is unlikely that Francis would have dragged her on such a long journey. Francis and his son would have joined either John á Lasco's congregation, who sailed from Gravesend on 15th September 1553, or the Glastonbury Weavers, who left from Dover the next day. He resurfaces in June 1555, fulfilling his duties as Constable of Wallingford Castle. It is possible that he was conducting his affairs from across the Channel, but he must have returned at least by October 1554 as Catherine was pregnant with their daughter Anne by that month.

The next time the Knollys resurface on the continent is in Germany in June 1557 when Catherine and five of their children are recorded as living with a John Weller of London in Frankfurt. It is most likely that the children included would have been the five youngest, leaving the whereabouts of Henry, Mary, Lettice, William, Edward and Maude unknown. It can be safely assumed that Henry was continuing his education at Magdalen College, but the whereabouts of the rest can only be guessed. I have placed Lettice in the household of Elizabeth at Hatfield (some historians have posited this same theory), and William and Edward in the home of Ambrose Dudley as we do know that the Dudleys were very close friends of Francis. Ambrose's home seems a likely place for them to stay during their parents' exile. There is no adult record of Maude or Mary and no recorded marriages for either of them so, in my story, they died young. Their lifespans are still debated based on the monument constructed at the Knollys' tomb.

While we have a record of Catherine being in the household of John Weller, I could find no record of Weller's family other than the fact that he had five sons, so the names of his wife and children are entirely from my imagination. We do know that a man by the name of Thomas Knot was an acquaintance of Francis's from his time at the University of Basel in 1556, so I have included him in the household. We also have a record of Henry Knollys (Francis's brother) at Frankfurt and know that he stayed on after Francis and Catherine returned to England, until 1559.

There are several theories for why, exactly, Francis fled England during Mary's reign, but I tend to believe, based on the evidence, that the original reason for his self-imposed exile was at the urging of William Cecil. There is evidence that Cecil sent Francis to scout out locations for English refugees and sought to strike a deal with the Protestant leaders across the Channel. If they would harbour these refugees, the refugees would, in turn, attend their new religious schools and become educated in the new religion. As the burnings ramped up during Mary's reign, Francis's reasons became more personal and he found it necessary to call his wife and children to these newly established settlements in Germany. Once Elizabeth came to the throne, they returned rather quickly. For more information regarding the migration of the exiles and their life on the continent, I recommend *Marian Exiles A Study in the Origins of Elizabethan Puritanism* by Christina Hallowell Garrett. It includes the most comprehensive records regarding this event.

The death of Amy Robsart Dudley is probably one of the most debated subjects in Elizabethan history and to this day, no historian has rendered a conclusive, provable verdict. For this reason I have kept the circumstances of her death muddled. However, I have kept the timeline of events leading up to and after her death intact. There is a wealth of references available on this subject and I suggest reading several of them for varying viewpoints.

The death of Perotine Massey has been recreated according to the evidence we have for it. There was indeed a woman of that name who was burned at the stake during her pregnancy. She did give birth to a son and the baby was tossed back into the fire by the bailiff. It is unclear whether either the woman or the queen's agents were aware of her pregnancy.

The miniatures of Anne and Mary that I have described in the novel are not based on any in existence. The collection of these miniature portraits by the nobility is well-recorded and so it is more than likely that both Anne and Mary would have had these portraits made during their time at Court. There may actually be one or two of them in a museum or private collection, but we don't have enough evidence to conclusively point to the identity of the sitters.

During Elizabeth's bout with smallpox, the only woman recorded as serving her is Mary Sidney. The inclusion of Catherine during her illness is entirely fiction.

Fairly recently a debate has cropped up as to the identity of the painters Stephen van der Meulen and Stephen van Harwijk. I find this debate quite fascinating and have included it in my narrative. However, it is by no means settled and there is not enough evidence to determine if they are, in fact, the same person.

Henry Carey's irritation over Elizabeth's failure to name him as the Earl of Wiltshire comes much later than I have illustrated in my novel. It is said that when Elizabeth attempted to bestow the title upon him at his death, he refused stating that as she never found him worthy of the title in life, he would not be worthy of the title in his death. It is likely, though, that Henry harboured ill-will over the promotion of Robert Dudley as demonstrated by his plotting against him with other members of the nobility. And I am certain that his desire for the title of earl had long been simmering before his death in 1596 and could account for some of his aggrieved behaviour towards Elizabeth's favourites.

The final point I leave you with regards the Knollys children. Anywhere from twelve to sixteen children have been attributed to the couple, but I have based my narrative on the Latin dictionary that was discovered in the private collection of a Knollys descendent. The inner cover reads exactly as I have described it in the text, only the spellings have been modernised. I have kept the dates of birth intact and because there is no mention of a child name Cecilia, I have not included her, though several other lists have included her. As to the naming of their children, it seems that most of them may have been named for family members and so I have included this in the text. Thomas was most likely named for a family member or friend (possibly Thomas Knot as he was linked with Francis during Catherine's pregnancy, Francis's grandfather Thomas Peniston, or Thomas Boleyn), but I have named him after a midwife that did not exist. There is also no record of Catherine suffering from childbed fever. We do not even know if Thomas was born abroad, but it seems unlikely that Catherine would have travelled alone back to England during her pregnancy.

Acknowledgements

It is not only the writer that deserves credit for the labour of love that is novel writing. For, had it not been for the wonderful supporting players in my life, this book may not ever have come to fruition.

First and foremost, I must thank my family: my husband Kyle and my son Logan. They have very graciously allowed those rascally Tudors to become like members of our own family for nearly a decade. Logan, only five, has never known life without the shadow of the hulking King Henry and his bevy of wives. I'd like to thank them for allowing me to be consumed with the lives and events of five hundred years ago, and for their support and encouragement along the way. They are my heart and soul.

I would like to thank my mother Judy and my sister Michelle for serving as the inspiration for Mary and Lettice. And a special thank you to my mother, father Neil, and stepmother Angela for encouraging my love of books. It built the foundation of my ability to be a storyteller and taught me that there is a whole world outside of my own that I couldn't even begin to imagine. Just like Catherine, I too have the most amazing and wonderful in-laws, Teri and Steve. Thanks to all of these very special people for all of their support and kindness.

It is not only my blood family that has encouraged and supported my aspirations along the way. A special thank you goes out to Derek Gilbert. How many people out there can call their boss their friend? I am lucky enough to be one of those few. Thanks to Derek for the precious gift of time and for always making sure to annoy me with positive comments when I really didn't *want* to hear them, but definitely *needed* to hear them.

I would like to thank Elena Kuhnhenn for her bravery in taking on the task of being the first non-family member to read my work in the early stages of our friendship. Thanks to Elena, not only for taking the time to read my work, but also for not being afraid to give me an honest assessment and to listen patiently to my constant worries during the publishing process. In the words of Harry Potter, "You're Brilliant!"

Words cannot express my gratitude to the dynamic duo of Tim and Claire Ridgway. Heartfelt thanks to Tim for all of his work in bringing Cor Rotto through the publishing process. He has done an amazing job fine-tuning my story and crafting it into the beautiful work that you, the reader, now hold in your hands. Tim demonstrated much patience, guidance and, above all, faith in me to produce a work worthy of MadeGlobal's publication. Thanks to Claire for all of her encouragement and support over the years, for bringing Anne Boleyn's true story to light and for not thinking I was completely mad after reading my first email. She is a true blessing and a fabulous role model.

Thank you to Susan Bordo for giving the world the first inkling of my work by publishing a snippet on the Creation of Anne Boleyn website, and to Susan Higginbotham and Sarah Butterfield for all of their encouragement and support.

Finally, thank you, dear reader, for choosing to read my book. I hope that you have enjoyed reading it as much as I enjoyed writing it.

If I have forgotten anyone, I deeply apologize. So many friends and family members have offered nothing but the kindest of words. Their excitement over my work has served as inspiration during the most trying times. Thank you.

This book is dedicated to my guardian angels: MMC, AJS, MAR and AB.

ADRIENNE

The Family of Catherine Carey

I used Sally Varlow's work "Sir Francis Knollys' Latin Dictionary: New Evidence for Katherine Carey" to determine when Catherine and Francis's children were born. It was a list found in Sir Knollys' personal dictionary and is held by a descendant of the family in a private collection.

The Parents

Catherine Knollys: April 1524
Francis Knollys: 1511

The Children

Henry "Harry" Knollys: April 6, 1541
Mary Knollys: October 28, 1542
Lettice Knollys: November 8, 1543
William Knollys: March 23, 1545
Edward Knollys: October 12, 1546
Maude Knollys: March 19, 1548
Elizabeth Knollys: June 15, 1549
Robert Knollys: November 5, 1550*
Richard Knollys: May 15, 1552*
Francis Knollys: August 14, 1553
Anne Knollys: July 19, 1555
Thomas Knollys: January 28, 1558
Katheryn Knollys: October 21, 1559
Dudley Knollys: May 9, 1562

Adrienne Dillard

Adrienne Dillard, author of *"Cor Rotto: A Novel of Catherine Carey"* is a graduate with a Bachelor of Arts in Liberal Studies with emphasis in History from Montana State University-Northern.

Adrienne has been an eager student of history for most of her life and has completed in-depth research on the American Revolutionary War time period in American History and the history and sinking of the Titanic. Her senior university capstone paper was on the discrepancies in passenger lists on the ill-fated liner and Adrienne was able to work with Philip Hind of Encyclopedia Titanica for much of her research on that subject.

MadeGlobal Publishing

Non-Fiction History

- The Fall of Anne Boleyn - **Claire Ridgway**
- George Boleyn: Tudor Poet, Courtier & Diplomat
  - **Claire Ridgway**
- The Anne Boleyn Collection - **Claire Ridgway**
- The Anne Boleyn Collection II **- Claire Ridgway**
- On This Day in Tudor History - **Claire Ridgway**
- Katherine Howard: A New History - **Conor Byrne**
- Two Gentleman Poets at the Court of Henry VIII
  - **Edmond Bapst**
- A Mountain Road - **Douglas Weddell Thompson**

Historical Fiction

- The Truth of the Line - **Melanie V. Taylor**
- Cor Rotto: A Novel of Catherine Carey - **Adrienne Dillard**
- The Merry Wives of Henry VIII - **Ann Nonny**

Other Books

- Easy Alternate Day Fasting - **Beth Christian**
- 100 Under 500 Calorie Meals - **Beth Christian**
- 100 Under 200 Calorie Desserts - **Beth Christian**
- 100 Under 500 Calorie Vegetarian Meals
  - **Beth Christian**
- Interviews with Indie Authors - **Claire Ridgway**
- Popular - **Gareth Russell**
- The Immaculate Deception - **Gareth Russell**
- The Walls of Truth - **Melanie V. Taylor**
- Talia's Adventures (English|Spanish)- **Verity Ridgway**

Please Leave a Review

If you enjoyed this book, *please* leave a review at the book seller where you purchased it. There is no better way to thank the author and it really does make a huge difference! *Thank you in advance.*